PASSAGEWAY TO DEATH

I got out of bed, lit my lamp and began to feel along the wall. At about shoulder height the segment of wall between the molding and the armoire slid aside. I peered into the opening. A narrow flight of stairs ran downward and at the bottom I could just make out a small lever. I knew at once that it would release the secret-panel entrance into Jay Caldwell's room.

A slow shiver ran through my body. If a person could enter Jay's room from the secret passageway, they could also enter mine! Terrified, I tried to think of a plan.

Tomorrow I would ask one of the footmen to bring up my trunk. I would fill it with heavy objects and place it in front of the panel. It might not stop an intruder, but it would certainly create a warning noise.

One thing I would no longer consider, no matter what: I would not leave Soundcliff. I wouldn't run because I was afraid. For good or for ill, my life had become inextricably entwined with this strange house—and the mysterious lives of those who lived in it . . .

SOMETHING FOR EVERYONE—
BEST SELLERS FROM ZEBRA!

FRIENDS (645, $2.25)
by Elieba Levine
Edith and Sarah had been friends for thirty years, sharing all their secrets and fantasies. No one ever thought that a bond as close as theirs could be broken . . . but now underneath the friendship and love is jealousy, anger, and hate.

EPIDEMIC! (644, $2.50)
by Larry R. Leichter, M.D.
From coast to coast, beach to beach, the killer virus spread. Diagnosed as a strain of meningitis, it did not respond to treatment—and no one could stop it from becoming the world's most terrifying epidemic!

ALL THE WAY (571, $2.25)
by Felice Buckvar
After over twenty years of devotion to another man, Phyllis finds herself helplessly in love, once again, with that same tall, handsome high school sweetheart who had loved her . . . ALL THE WAY.

RHINELANDER PAVILLION (572, $2.50)
by Barbara Harrison
Rhinelander Pavillion was a big city hospital pulsating with the constant struggles of life and death. Its dedicated staff of overworked professionals were caught up in the unsteady charts of their own passions and desires—yet they all needed medicine to survive.

Available wherever paperbacks are sold, or order direct from the Publisher. Send cover price plus 50¢ per copy for mailing and handling to Zebra Books, 21 East 40th Street, New York, N.Y. 10016. DO NOT SEND CASH!

The Mistress of Soundcliff Manor

By Deborah Wood

ZEBRA BOOKS
KENSINGTON PUBLISHING CORP.

ZEBRA BOOKS

are published by

KENSINGTON PUBLISHING CORP.
21 East 40th Street
New York, N.Y. 10016

Copyright ©1980 by Deborah Wood

All rights reserved. No part of this book may be reproduced in any form or by any means without the prior written consent of the Publisher, excepting quotes used in reviews.

Printed in the United States of America

For Ed, Louie, Bimbo, and Max

ONE

Surely I was not the only frightened passenger on the deck of the *Star of Britain* that April morning in 1898—can it have been only two years ago? But a huge cheer had gone up from the other steerage passengers as we glided up New York Harbor and spied the Statue of Liberty slipping by the port rail. What a vision she was. I appreciate her now in memory as I could not then, her dramatic stance, torch thrust skyward, gilded by the morning sun, the shimmering shield of harbor waters at her feet. Joy had seemed to banish, at least for the moment, the terror of my fellow immigrants, and I believed that I, Lillie Lorimer, was the only wholly miserable person among that agitated throng.

The shores of New Jersey, Staten Island, and Brooklyn girdled the harbor at a middle distance, and unsure of the geography of my new home, I wondered, "Where is New York?" Where was that rough, raw city I had read of and feared? The harbor shores seemed almost bucolic beyond the tugs and barges and steamers and sailing ships that crowded the waters. The area of human habitation was enormous, yet peaceful. This could not be New York, I thought—not Manhattan Island, the center of wealth and poverty, of commerce and culture, the adolescent giant grown from the infant settlements of nearly three hundred years ago.

The lower tip of Manhattan had appeared over the bow of the *Star of Britain*, but we were almost upon it before I saw and recognized it through the mass of passengers. The steerage decks had been jammed with people ever since our embarkation at Liverpool six days before. The cramped quarters below the water line were stifling, and the human cargo—for so we had begun to feel ourselves—inhabited the decks day and night. We almost forgot the existence of the first and second class passengers on the upper decks. Nor did any of us seem to resent the inequitable system that would allow those with the means to have bought first or second class passage to debark in Manhattan as easily as wealthy travelers anywhere in the world, while we who were forced by poverty to travel in steerage would be unloaded onto barges and taken to the immigration station for examination. In America, as everywhere, wealth equalled worth.

Yet, the impoverished were not debarred. In spite of the indignity of the immigration process, and although some were denied entry for cause, most were admitted. For this, our fears aside, we were terribly grateful.

I am not a tall woman, and the crowd on deck, which had stood so joyfully erect as we passed Liberty Island, now began, as if at a signal, to bend and stoop. Bundles were being gathered and identity papers and money examined and counted for the hundredth time. And suddenly I could see the tip of Manhattan looming rapidly over the bow, then vanishing behind the superstructure as we moved by its western edge.

If I had been frightened, now I was terrified. I plunged my hand into my reticule for the third time in half an hour. It was not my passport I sought, nor the few pounds that stood between me and destitution—I had guarded these carefully and knew they were safe. What I looked for now was a letter and along with it a photograph, a photograph of such poor quality to begin with and now so worn and cracked from frequent examination that I could discern the face only because I had gazed at it so often I had memorized it.

Because I had looked at his photograph so often and because he looked so much like my father, although we had never met I suppose I knew my Uncle Frank Lorimer's face better than any face on earth. And yet I was terrified that I would not be able to find him or recognize him among the crowds at the immigration station. I was equally afraid that he would not recognize me, for it had seemed to me, when I contemplated the photograph I had had taken to send him in return, that I looked very much like any rather pale, plain young woman in England.

I unfolded the letter I had received from Uncle Frank, folded and unfolded so often it had fallen into two pieces at the crease. "Dear Lillie," I read. "Mrs. Fein is writting this for me as you will see the writting is too fine to be me own. I am sory little bro. Martin is ded and hope you come to New York and I will look out for you even thow I do'nt have much I will try. Let me no when and wher and I will meet you. Love, Unkle Frank Lorimer."

Upon receiving his letter, I had booked passage and written to Uncle Frank the name of the ship and the day of its arrival. I didn't know exactly where or how he would meet me, for I was unsure of the debarkation process for immigrants. The new immigration station at Ellis Island had burned to the ground a few months earlier, I had been told, and we would be processed at the old Barge Office at the Battery. They might as well have told me we would be processed in Timbuktu for all I knew of the location of these places. I hoped that Uncle Frank knew or would be able to find out how to find me, but I even worried that he might not have received my letter.

Perhaps a braver person would simply have rested assured that everything would work out, but although I was well educated and outwardly poised, I was really very shy and sheltered. My father had seen to that. I was his little china doll, as he had told me so often. My feet would never touch bare earth, he vowed, not while he was alive. He had counted, of course, on his staying alive, and so had I. Why had neither of us ever imagined that he might die—not that he might die, but that he would die, and very probably years before his little china doll? Why did neither of us think of preparing me to get on alone in the world? Or does anyone ever prepare for the unthinkable?

Daddy could not have helped fussing over me and taking care of things for me. It was his way. If Mother had lived, I imagine he would have doted on her instead, and I might have grown freer and stronger. I used to stare and stare at their wedding portrait. So young, so sweet. Daddy was eighteen and Mother only seventeen. Most people look stiff and solemn in photographs, but Mother and Daddy were simply beaming, the love just dancing in their eyes. Mother was looking directly outward—she must have been smiling right into the camera lens—and Daddy was looking at her. They were holding hands.

I have never seen a photograph like it. I believe that many would find it in poor taste to display love so openly, especially before a camera. But the portrait is very dear to me. I hoped, yet did not dare to hope, that I could one day find someone to love as dearly as Mother had loved Daddy, a man who would look at me as he had looked at her.

I once asked Daddy why he and Mother had struck such an informal and openly emotional pose for their wedding photograph. "I don't know," he had said. "I just remember that I wanted to look at Elizabeth forever." One year later I was born, and when I was two, Mother died. She was only twenty and had caught a cold which became pneumonia. I suppose I was too young to really miss her. Besides, Daddy became both mother and father to me. A neighbor once told me that after my mother died, my father carried me almost incessantly, so much so that I forgot how to walk for awhile.

Daddy owned a small shop—china and household things. I didn't know how much the shop earned us. Whatever I wanted, Daddy got for me. Luckily, I was not a greedy child, for as it turned out, our income was modest. Yet he bought me lovely clothes and sent me to the best schools. I studied geography, history, and current affairs. I had tutors in French and literature and painting. I learned to sew beautiful decorative stitchery. I learned dancing and deportment. I learned to play the organ.

In a way, Daddy had placed me in an impossible position. I became too upper-class in manner and education to appeal to a man of the lower classes, but I was too lower-class in family background to be accepted by the upper classes. I had been educated and prepared to be a lady of means, the wife of the sort of man who, in England, would never marry a shopkeeper's daughter.

I understand this only now. At the time, I was blissfully unaware of my predicament. I would have been happy to fall in love and marry, and I was as susceptible to romantic daydreams as any young woman. But Daddy took such good care of me and made my life so pleasant, so free of care, that I was perfectly content and almost unaware that friends' and neighbors' tongues had begun to cluck over my being unmarried at the advanced age of twenty-four.

And then Daddy died quite suddenly. He had never been sick a day in his life. The doctor said his heart had simply stopped. I could scarcely believe it, and I was overwhelmed with terror as well as grief. I had no idea how to run the shop. In any case, I quickly learned that Daddy had incurred debts in his efforts to provide for me so lavishly, and that the debts could be met only by selling the shop. The proceeds of the sale, which friends of Daddy's arranged for me, allowed me to satisfy Daddy's creditors and restore his good name, but the amount of money that remained was very small indeed.

Another woman in my position would have sought employment at once, perhaps as a tutor or as a companion to an older lady. But I had been taken care of like a child all my life, and instead of looking for work, which I had no idea how to do, I looked for someone else to take care of me. There was only one person in the world I could think to turn to, and that was my only living relative, Uncle Frank Lorimer.

I knew only the sketchiest details of Uncle Frank's life. He had worked in a cotton-spinning factory from his very early years to help support the family. But when the American Civil War had broken out, the blockade of the southern states by the Union navy had prevented most shipments of cotton to England. In 1863, out of work at the age of fourteen, Uncle Frank had decided to go to sea. He lied about his age and signed aboard a ship destined for the Port of New York. But he had been violently seasick during the whole voyage and abandoned the idea of being a sailor and even of returning to England and had simply remained in New York.

In the ensuing years, Frank had exchanged perhaps half a dozen letters with my father, enough for Frank to learn that his younger brother Martin had married Elizabeth Sands and had a daughter Lillie and that Elizabeth had died. I suppose Daddy had learned something of what Uncle Frank was doing in New York, but it all meant very little to me as I had, of course, never seen Frank. Daddy had not saved his letters, but I did find Uncle Frank's address in Daddy's desk. I wrote to tell him of his brother's death, and in desperation begged him to allow me to come to New York as I was now all alone in the world. In reply, I received the letter I have described, the one I had worn in two, the one bearing Uncle Frank's photograph and his kind invitation.

I will not pretend that Uncle Frank's letter wasn't a shock. I didn't know who Mrs. Fein was, but if Frank had had her write the letter because her "writting" was better than his, then it was apparent that Frank was illiterate, or nearly so.

That Uncle Frank might be an uneducated man had not occurred to me. I suppose I had assumed he would be like Daddy. Daddy had finished school and, although he spoke in working class accents, he could certainly read and write; indeed, he enjoyed reading novels, writing a bit of romantic poetry, and escorting me to an occasional concert. He was far from uncultured. I don't know why I had not realized that Frank, who had run off to sea at the age of fourteen and who had worked even earlier, would hardly have acquired much schooling.

What in the world had he been doing in New York all these years? For the life of me, I could not recall Daddy ever mentioning any detail of Frank's life or circumstances in America, and Frank's letter to me, via Mrs. Fein, offered no clue. I had always imagined him living in a little house or apartment with a wife and children and pursuing some respectable trade. His letter left me wondering if I had been mistaken about all of these imagined details. If he had a family, for instance, would he not have had his wife or a son or daughter write for him? If he pursued a respectable trade, would he not be able to write a letter himself?

Nevertheless, his letter was welcoming, his photograph looked like Daddy, and I was so helpless that I hesitated not one day after Uncle Frank's letter arrived in asking Daddy's friends to help me book passage to New York. Whatever Uncle Frank was like, he was all I had.

Now, the *Star of Britain* was moving close to the pier with its huge, corrugated iron shed. I wanted to push my way to the rail to begin searching the faces below. But so, it seemed, did everyone else, and I just stood where I was and prayed, "Let me find him, please. Let him find me." The wait seemed interminable, but at last I saw the crowd beginning to move and an immigration official standing near a portion of railing which had been moved aside to reveal a gangplank now affixed to the ship's side.

Like some thick, stubborn syrup, the steerage passengers poured through the opening and down the plank, but as I came to the top, I saw that my eagerness had been premature. All the passengers, including the first and second class ones descending planks from the upper decks farther along toward the bow, were vanishing through wide openings in the side of the enormous shed that covered the pier. No one but dock hands could be seen on the narrow strip of pier between shed and ship.

Like all the other steerage passengers, I moved along with some effort, hauling a rather large bag and hoping that I would be able to find my trunk at the baggage area of the immigration station as we had been told we would.

As I came through the opening into the shed, blinking into the dimness, I could see a crowd gathered outside ropes strung from one end to the other. The first and second class passengers were waving and calling to friends and relatives as they moved rather quickly past tables of customs officials. Already, a number who had completed the ritual of customs were through the ropes, embracing those who waited, and walking off with them toward a far opening. I could not see but could imagine the press of horses, carriages, and cabs on the pavement beyond.

There were no customs tables and no waiting friends and relatives for the steerage passengers.

Instead, those who had debarked ahead of me were being ushered quickly along a roped aisle to another opening at the opposite end of the shed where the barge that would take us to the immigration station was docked. I was still looking anxiously about, wondering if Frank might have come straight here, but I saw no one who looked like him, and the woman behind me said kindly, "Don't worry, dear. They meet us at the Battery, I hear."

When we were all aboard, the big barge swung away from the pier and south again. It was a brief trip, for the Battery, I learned, was the name given to the southern tip of Manhattan which had once held a fort and a battery of cannon. But we had to wait nearly an hour before being let off the barge, for the *Star of Britain* had not been the only bearer of immigrants to reach New York that day. Far from it. We were one link in an endless chain of ships that stretched out behind us over the harbor and the Narrows and the great ocean to Europe. On some days, they said, strings of ships were held at anchor in the harbor, one behind the other, as the masses of immigrants debarked and were funneled through the immigration process. At times, immigrants stepping off the barges at Ellis Island had not even been able to enter the crowded building but formed a long, slow-moving line from dock to doorway. Since fire had temporarily forced the use of the old Barge Office at the Battery while Ellis Island was being rebuilt, the situation was even worse.

When I had begun to think I would die of

frustration and anxiety, we docked at last and were permitted to debark and enter the enormous Barge Office. I was dazed. I had never seen so many people in one place in my life. Here were not just one but several shiploads of people moving past tables of immigration and Coast Guard officials, in and out of crudely partitioned cubicles for medical and intelligence tests. And here, also, were swarms of men recruiting immigrants for work crews for the New York waterfront, the mines of Pennsylvania, the western railroads. I was told that the recruiting activity was forbidden and could be prevented at isolated Ellis Island but had become an uncontrolled pestilence at the Barge Office. In the frantic, noisy throng, my hopes of finding Uncle Frank were vanishing fast.

Through it all, our line wound on and on like an enormous caterpillar. At the far end of the room, the cacophony seemed to reach an even higher pitch. There, I learned, was where a small percentage were being denied immediate entry for reasons ranging from inadequate identity papers to suspected disease. Many would be admitted later after laying their cases before panels of hearing officers. Some of the sick would be sent to hospitals on a place called Ward's Island to be admitted when they were well. Some were simply sent back to their countries of origin.

When someone told me that some of those detained were waiting for relatives or sponsors who had failed to meet them as expected, my heart sank. The immigration officials might decide that I could make my way in America without Uncle

Frank, but I knew I could not.

At last I saw an official coming along the line and heard him calling my name. "Miss Lillie Lorimer? Miss Lillie Lorimer?" Uncle Frank had paid the man to locate me with the message that he was in the waiting area, and I gave him a few coins to go back and tell Uncle Frank I had received his message. After that, the process seemed to proceed swiftly and easily. I presented my papers, faced a line-up of doctors and nurses, and answered innumerable questions. Then I was through and there waiting, unmistakably, was Uncle Frank.

Dear Uncle Frank. He did look like Daddy, although older and shabbier. But Frank was a man who, despite poverty and hard work, remained cheerful with always a smile or a grin and a kind word. I felt safe the moment I saw him, and I loved him at once.

"Listen, Lillie me girl," said Uncle Frank after our first tearful embrace, as he held my hands in his two huge, rough ones. "I'm a poor man and a bachelor. I board in with a family name o' Fein up on Orchard Street. Ye'll have to do the same till yer set up, anyhow. They're expectin' ye, so don't worry. Now come along."

I was too stunned with relief to absorb his words. He picked up my bag and led me to a booth where I converted my English pounds to dollars. Then he located my trunk in the baggage area and swung it up onto his shoulder, carrying my bag in his other hand, and we emerged from the building.

Before us, across Battery Park, rose the city—my city now, I thought, my country. My immigration papers, placed firmly in my reticule, were the key to the golden door. In the proper time, five years hence, I would become an American citizen. England was behind me now, forever.

"I bet ye've had nought to eat," Frank said. "Ye must be proper starvin'." I was, and I nodded my head in reply. A vendor was selling steaming meat pies from a wagon, and Uncle Frank bought two of them. We carried them to a park bench, and as we began to eat the savory pies, Uncle Frank kept up a line of cheerful chatter, telling me about himself, but not asking me much about Daddy and Mother, subjects he seemed to know would have sent me into a flood of tears.

Frank, it turned out, was a street worker. "When I come to America, I thought the streets was paved with gold," he cracked. "But as I have since been helpin' to pave 'em, I can testify as there ain't a ounce o' gold in 'em." It was poor work and hard work, yet I didn't pity him. His enjoyment of life was deep and pervasive, and his difficult form of employment had not dampened his spirits. "At least it's outdoor work," he exclaimed. "It's a sight better'n bein' cooped up in some factory!"

"Is it steady work?" I asked.

"Ah, yes, 'tis. I seldom want for work, even though it's day labor. The city's growin' so fast, and they're always rippin' up the streets that's already paved. It's dead funny. New Yorkers can't never seem to leave good enough rest. Why, the best time as I ever had for steady work was back in '91 to '93 when they was layin' the cable road down Broadway. We dug up a ditch fifteen feet wide and three or four feet deep right down the middle o' the street a few miles long so people had to cross it on wooden bridges. Somebody got quoted in the papers sayin' 'The next man as tears up Broadway oughter be lynched.'" Frank enjoyed a deep, rich chuckle.

"That must have been quite a job," I said.

"Well, it wasn't layin' the cable as was so hard, it was workin' around all them gas an' water mains an' telegraph an' 'lectric wires. It's a right shock to see what all is under the streets, it is. An' I hear now as they're thinkin' o' rippin' up all that cable we laid and puttin' in a 'lectric trolley line."

"It's hard to imagine that New York was just a little Dutch settlement and some tribes of Indians three hundred years ago," I put in, drawing from my history studies.

"Ye'll be amazed, I guarantee it," said Frank. "Even if ye been to London. London is a cow pasture compared to New York, just in traffic alone. An' the crowds! Shoulder to shoulder in the business districts an' even places like Orchard Street where the poor people crowd together to save on the rent. It's a proper circus."

I shuddered. I had never been to London. Liverpool, where I had boarded the *Star of Britain*, was the biggest town I had ever seen. New York terrified me. I put my hand through Frank's arm for courage.

"Have no care," he laughed. "It's a great place! I tell ye, workin' in the streets o' New York is like goin' to a carnival. There's always some barmy thing goin' on. Why, one time, I rescued a millionaire's daughter."

"You did really?"

"Indeed I did," he grinned. "It was about two, three years back. I was fixin' a curb on Liberty Street when this fancy rig pulls up and out steps a man in one o' them coats with a fur collar. He starts into a place o' business there, an' the driver steps down to tie up the horse. I can see this little red-head girl in the carriage, maybe twelve years old. The driver is just reachin' up for the bridle when the horse bolts an' starts to run. I drops me tools an' takes off after the horse. About mid block there's a pie wagon that's startin' to turn onto Broadway, an' it's sideways across the street an' the horse is comin' right at it, draggin' the carriage an' the little girl behind. The horse rears up an' he kicks over the pie wagon. Well, that gives me time to catch up an' grab hold o' the horse.

"The rich man comes runnin' up behind me. Now, if I hadn't of caught the horse, the next man would of—it was really the pie wagon what saved the girl—but the man starts to thank me, an' believe it or not, a rich man like that, he's got tears on his face. He lifts his daughter down an' holds her like she could break, as I guess she might have done if the carriage turned over."

"The girl must have been terrified," I commented.

"Didn't seem to be. Seemed to think she'd had a big adventure. She says, 'Oh, Daddy, it's all right. It was thrilling!'"

Frank mimicked the high voice and well-bred accents of a little rich girl so well that I laughed.

"Well, that was quite an exciting event," I said.

"Oh, that ain't all," said Frank. "The man shakes me hand an' slips me a hundred dollar bill! An' he gives the same to the fellow with the pie wagon an' gives him his card an' tells him to send him the bill for the pies and fixin' the wagon, an' he gives me his card, too, an' says never hesitate to call on him if I need anything."

"Who was the man?" I asked.

"Well, I still have the card," Frank said. He reached into his inner breast pocket, drew out the calling card, now somewhat dogeared, and handed it to me.

I read the name and gasped. Even in England, he was well-known as one of the wealthiest and most powerful men in America. "Jay Caldwell," I breathed, fingering the card wonderingly.

Quickly, I handed it back to Frank, fearing the responsibility of holding the fragile card. Frank laughed and studied it for a moment. "Ye know about Jay Caldwell over in England?"

"Everyone knows about Jay Caldwell," I said simply.

"An example, he is. Or rather his grandfather is, old Eli Caldwell. A poor immigrant lad, an' today they own railroads an'— an'— I don't know what all."

"How did he do it, old Eli?" I wondered aloud. It was beyond and yet fascinating to me. All I had known and all I expected ever to know were men like Daddy and Uncle Frank, men who worked hard to earn little and never rose above their station, whether in England or America.

"Well," said Frank, "I can't say as I know. Financin'—some kind o' financin'." It was as great a mystery to him as it was to me.

Frank slid the card back into his inner pocket. "I don't believe Jay Caldwell killed his wife like they say he done," he said soberly. "Would a man what can cry over his little daughter kill his wife?"

I could remember only vaguely the newspaper accounts of ten or so years before about the mysterious death of Jay Caldwell's wife—I had been only a young girl. There were no murder charges, I recalled, only rumors. And I thought he had remarried not long afterwards.

But there was no more time to discuss the affairs of the rich. We had finished our lunch, and we rose. Frank took up my bag and trunk once more, and we made our way across the park to the cable car stop.

Battery Park was one of the loveliest spots I had ever seen, the greenery set off by the shining harbor and the Statue of Liberty behind, the towering buildings ahead. People were everywhere, hurrying this way and that, and a newspaper vendor was calling out the headlines of the day: "President McKinley Asks Congress for Authority to Intervene in Cuba," I recall. I had read about the American battleship *Maine*. It had gone to Cuba on a goodwill tour, then blown up in Havana Harbor in February. Hundreds of men had been lost, and relationships between America and Spain, Cuba's owner, had been badly strained.

"Will there be war?" I asked Uncle Frank, shuddering.

"Probably," he answered cheerfully. "It's time we had a good foreign war. Pull us all together."

I recalled that Uncle Frank had come to America in the midst of the conflict between the northern and southern states, so I could understand his viewpoint if not share it. After all, no one knew whether the Spanish had blown up the *Maine*, or if it had been a tragic accident. And while there was a movement among Cubans to be free of Spain, was it America's duty to help them?

Then I recalled that I was now, as of today, an American, if not yet officially, at least in my heart. I must stand behind my new country, not regard it as a foreigner.

"Ye read about them things?" Uncle Frank laughed. "That's a rare thing for a little girl. Some might call it unladylike!"

I felt myself blushing. Uncle Frank was right, of course. Because of the unusually broad education and the freedom from household cares my father had afforded me, I had developed an interest in the broader affairs of the world, the world of men, and rather less skill in domestic matters than I should have had. I confided as much to Frank, and his reply sent a cold chill down my spine.

"Well, ye won't be havin' much time for world affairs or domestic chores either. Ye'll be havin' to earn wages now."

How? I wondered, but I was too frightened to utter the question, and I dared not confide that until this moment, I had thought that Uncle Frank would provide for me.

"Here comes our car," Frank broke into my

thoughts. We had walked partway across the park, and now I saw a cable car rumbling around the curve, rolling to a halt, and disgorging passengers. Frank hoisted my trunk to his shoulder once more and took my bag in the opposite hand. "Come on, Miss Lillie Lorimer," he called. "I'll show ye Broadway, or part o' it anyhow. We'll be gettin' off at Grand Street."

We stepped onto the rear platform of the car, and I held tight to a pole as the car started up, swung around the circle, and headed up the fabulous avenue called Broadway. Frank dug some coins from his pocket to pay the uniformed conductor who had made his way through the crowd to the rear of the car, although I would have sworn that there was not space enough to pass among the tightly packed bodies. It was amazing to contemplate that the conductor must fight his way from one end of the car to the other, over and over, all day long.

But now Frank had begun calling my attention to the sights along the way. He had told me to expect crowds, but never could I have imagined such crowds as these, each person hurrying along on his own errand or piece of business, seemingly unaware of every other person, each pushing and dodging on a zig-zag course through the throng. Where were they all going? What were they doing?

"Business," Uncle Frank said. "This is the business district."

The street traffic moved in the same chaotic manner as the people, and our cable car nosed brutally through the carts and wagons and carriages and pedestrians crossing in mid block like a slow-moving but unstoppable rhinocerous among a herd of gazelles.

"There's Wall Street," Uncle Frank called out. "That's where the wall was across the north end o' the old Dutch colony. We've grown a bit since then, eh?"

"Indeed," I replied breathlessly, hanging on for dear life to my pole.

"There's Liberty Street," Uncle Frank pointed out a bit later. "Right down there, on that corner, that's where I caught Jay Caldwell's horse." I gazed in wonder and then, just above Liberty Street, I pointed to the large statue of a man with a wooden leg perched in an arched window embrasure below a handsome sign reading "Stuyvesant Insurance Company."

"Peter Stuyvesant," Uncle Frank informed me. "Old Peg Leg Peter, Governor of the Dutch colony."

On we rolled past hundreds of places of business, each with its own sign across a building facade or hanging out over the street—"Louis L. Schwartz & Co., Tailors," "The Brig Camera Company, Photographic Outfits," "Home Made Lunch"—then a massive columned building Frank pointed out as the Post Office.

I was struck by the many American flags billowing out over the street, not only before the Post Office building but extending from the fronts of business offices and raised on poles mounted on rooftops. I had heard that Americans were extraordinarily patriotic, and here was the confirmation.

We passed Fulton Street, and I began to observe the faces of the New Yorkers more closely. They seemed to me to be uniformly pale and pinched, and I could read in them the terrible tension and effort of working, of surviving, in this maelstrom of a city. They almost looked to be suffering from some universal fever or disease, and I mentioned the notion to Frank.

"It is a disease," he laughed. "It's called money-makin'."

Soon we passed the magnificent, glistening white City Hall and its lovely park, and there was a large stand selling copies of a newspaper called the *New York Journal*. "The main office is right over there on 'Newspaper Row' by the park," Uncle Frank indicated. "It's Hearst's paper. Ye heard o' him? He seems to have a big interest in stirrin' up this war idea. Sells papers, I guess." And indeed there was a large crowd gathered about the stand.

City Hall vanished behind us, and still we rode block after block, and still we seemed to be in the very heart of the city. Where were its limits? Or did it have limits? This great city must stretch out over a vast territory the extent of which I could only imagine. And if New York was this big and yet a mere dot on the maps of America I had studied, how enormous must the nation be? It made me dizzy, and the British Isles shrank in my mind to toy-size. How limited had been my horizons, both geographic and mental, until now. How this new city and new land expanded one's ideas of life's possibilities! That an immigrant boy like Eli Caldwell could amass a fortune and his grandson stand at the pinnacle of American society no longer seemed so strange.

I gazed at the passing street signs as if enchanted—Chambers Street, Pearl Street, Leonard Street, Canal Street, Grand Street. With a start, I realized that this was where Frank had said we would get off, and he was already lifting my trunk as the car ground to a stop. He stepped agilely to the ground, set down my case, and reached up his free hand to help me down. I watched the cable car move off up Broadway which seemed to stretch on endlessly to the north.

"We've a few blocks to walk now," Frank told me. "Are ye up to it?"

"Oh, yes," I said, and we started off down Grand Street. The crowds began to change as we moved away from Broadway and deeper into the tenement neighborhoods to the east. There were fewer men in derbies and more in caps. Suitcoats became rarer and shirtsleeves more common. And the ladies were not so elegantly dressed in hats and suits of rich, dark fabrics, but went hatless along the streets in cotton dresses or skirts and shirtwaists and even with aprons tied on and shawls thrown about their shoulders. Most carried market baskets over their arms and were purchasing goods and produce from carts, wagons, and stalls along the streets.

The press of humanity was as great as in the business districts, and as we turned at last into Orchard Street, I realized that many of the street's occupants were not going anywhere in particular. They had made the pavement an extension of their crowded living quarters. Neighbors stood talking and arguing together. Hordes of children played on the stoops and in the streets. Occasionally, a mother leaned from an upper story window to summon a child or call to a peddler or a neighbor. If the buildings were as crowded within as without, I wondered suddenly where an extra person like myself could be fitted.

I had been caught up in Frank's warmth and the excitement of seeing New York. Now I felt terribly lonely and more attached than ever to my uncle. Frank had said that Mrs. Fein expected me, but once again I took his arm, realizing that without him, I would have no place at all.

In mid block we stopped, and Frank lowered my trunk to the bottom step of a flight leading to the narrow stoop of a dingy tenement building. He drew out a handkerchief to wipe his brow.

"This is it, Lillie," he smiled. "Never ye mind. We'll get ye set up soon enough," he added, observing what must have been a very frightened look in my eyes.

It was drawing on toward evening now, and I noticed that a number of the men and women in the street seemed to be returning home from work. Several carried large bundles of fabric cut to various shapes—piecework, I was to learn, brought home from garment-sewing workshops to eke out meager daytime earnings—and two young men and a girl carrying these fabrics turned up the steps where we stood.

"Is this her?" said one of the young men.

"Yes, 'tis," said Frank and introduced me to three of Mrs. Fein's children.

We entered the building, and I was at once nearly overcome by the darkness, the closeness, and the odors of the hallway. It was as if I had entered one of the circles of the Inferno. Panicky sensations of claustrophobia gripped me, and it was only the fear of losing sight and touch of Uncle Frank that propelled me up the five flights of steps he was rapidly mounting behind the young Feins.

If the dark and odorous hallway was a horror, the flat was almost equally frightful. It consisted of two rooms inhabited, I learned, by nine human souls, the widow Mrs. Fein, her four youngest children—five others having married and established their own homes—and four boarders, including Uncle Frank and myself. Frank was paying my share until I could find work and pay my own way.

The boarders' beds were afforded a small degree of privacy by sheets suspended from the ceiling. I gathered that providing a separate cot for me was a sacrifice and a large favor to Frank. I believe that Frank had purchased the cot, but giving up the space for it cramped the others even more severely than usual. The two other lady boarders shared a bed, Mrs. Fein shared a bed with her daughter, the two older sons shared a mattress on the floor, and the youngest child slept on cushions placed across two rude straight-backed chairs with the rungs tied together.

The grimness and unhealthfulness of the rooms can be imagined. This was no fault of Mrs. Fein who tried to keep things clean, but of the age and disrepair of the building and the crowdedness. Great patches of plaster had fallen from some of the walls, exposing the laths underneath. The front room had been papered in some past era, but the paper had yellowed and dried and was curling away from the walls. In the back room, the same fate had befallen the paint which was chipping from the walls and lying in the corners like permanent snowflakes.

A rusting stove jutted from one wall of the front room, and two or three cookpots rested on it. There was a sink that disgorged cold, rusty water from a pipe, but the building's occupants had to go down to the small yard behind the building to make use of the common "outhouse." The beds, cots, a few straight-backed chairs, and a plain table were the only furnishings except for an ancient sewing machine in one corner. Those who had brought home piecework sat about the table or at the machine, working by the yellowish illumination of a kerosene lamp. The youngest child curled feathers for hats by pulling a knife across the barbs.

Mrs. Fein was a careworn woman. Her dark hair was severely bunned and liberally threaded with white. Cracked shoes protruded beneath her brownish cotton dress and stained apron. Her hands were rough, the nails thick and ridged. Every line of her face bespoke exhaustion. She welcomed us kindly, however, and showed me a corner where I could put my trunk and bag and two pegs on which I could hang my clothing. Then, after pointing out the cot with its worn and yellowed bedding which would be mine, she ladled out two bowls of cabbage, broth, and meat for Frank and me. The meat, I conjectured, was a special treat in honor of my arrival.

There was neither space nor time for everyone to sit down to a meal together, and so the bowls were taken by several at a time as they entered, and each person rinsed his own dish and spoon before settling down to the evening's occupations. I was embarrassed because I had not thought of washing my bowl until I saw Frank washing it for me. Before the supper process was over, some were working at the table so that workers sat across from eaters, and I wondered how, or if, the food was always kept from spattering the fabric and feathers.

All of the household members were friendly enough, and they asked politely about me, my life in England, and my voyage to America, listening to my tale as they worked as if to an entertainment. At last, someone asked the question I dreaded.

"What will you do?"

"I don't know," I replied. "But I'm willing to do anything," I quickly added. I looked from one to another as if someone would give me an idea, but no one replied. I was not even sure that I had told the truth, for it was to avoid the necessity of supporting myself that I had flown to America and Uncle Frank, and I was no more confident than before of my ability to work for a living. I watched them all sewing at the rough garments and thought of the delicate embroidery stitches I had learned. I had never sewn a garment in my life.

And if I could not sew, what would I do to earn my way? I could only hope that Uncle Frank would find something for me, something suited to my meager talents.

Then one of the boarders went to the sink and filled a wash basin, and various members of the household began to retire behind the hanging sheets to wash and change into nightclothes. Suddenly, I realized that I had not made any proper speech of thanks, so I gathered my courage and strength of voice to speak to the entire group.

"Please," I said, "I just want to thank Mrs. Fein and all of you so much for welcoming me, and especially I want to say thank you to Uncle Frank. Without him and you, I simply have no idea what would become of me."

"That's right. Single ladies have an awful time," piped up Mrs. Fein's daughter. "One of the needle girls at the dress factory didn't show up the other day and they found her dead in this little room she had in a cellar on Hester Street. Starved to death, she did."

"Anna!" Mrs. Fein spoke sharply. But the girl had spoken the truth, and it stung me to the quick. A single woman, even with a skill, could die in this enormous, anonymous city. I had no such skill, only Uncle Frank.

Young Anna helped me to fill the washbowl for myself and gave me a square of flannel and a bit of soap. Shyly, I stepped behind the sheet that shielded my cot and nervously disrobed and sponged myself. I put on the nightdress I had taken from my bag, and then I heard Uncle Frank's voice from the other side of the sheet.

"Hand me the bowl, Lillie, and I'll empty it for ye." He had realized that I was too timid to step out into the room in my nightdress as the others did to empty their washbowls. I handed the bowl to Frank, then quickly grabbed his sleeve and poked my head out to kiss him on the cheek.

"Good night, Uncle Frank. I love you," I said.

"Good night, Lillie dear, and have no fear," he smiled.

All through the night I tossed and turned on my cot, then fell into a fretful slumber just before dawn. When I awoke, it was late. Frank and the others had gone off to work and the youngest child to school. I arose hastily and found Mrs. Fein, market basket on her arm, about to go out."

"You'll find tea on the stove," she said. "Help yourself, and I'll be back soon." Then the flat was empty. I dressed and poured my tea. But I had no sooner sat down at the table than I heard a terrific pounding at the door.

"Mrs. Fein!" a man was shouting. I hesitated only a moment before opening the door. The man who had sounded so distraught stood in the hallway in rough workclothes, a cap in his hands.

"Mrs. Fein isn't in," I said.

"Oh, dear, Miss. Then I hate to bother you, but someone has to take the body."

"What body?" I asked, the words ringing out strangely as behind the man I could see two others carrying a form up the stairs.

"It's Frank Lorimer," he said. "A horse kicked him in the head. He's dead."

TWO

My throat knotted. Fear, grief, disbelief, and a wash of nausea clamored for possession of my mind and body. Fortunately, the men asked no response of me, for I could not have spoken had the future of the universe depended on it.

They pushed past me into the flat, carrying Uncle Frank's body roughly, exhausted as they must have been by the flights of stairs and by their own fear and horror. I suppose they thought I was Mrs. Fein's daughter or just another boarder, for all they said was "Dreadful sorry, Miss," and "It was terrible," and "We got to get back. Mrs. Fein will take care of him," and "Don't worry."

Don't worry! *Worried* described the state of my mind as adequately as *damp* would describe the state of a person who has encountered a tidal wave. The earth had been washed from under my feet, and I did not know how to swim.

My first coherent thought was for Frank. I had known him less than twenty-four hours, and yet I loved him dearly. He should have lived to be very old, and I would have taken care of him like the devoted daughter he had deserved. I went to the bed where they had laid him. I sat by it and held his hand and felt it cooling in mine. Oh, Frank, Frank. You tried to help me when I needed help, and I never had the chance to repay you.

Tears came then, and abysmal fear. What was I to do now, without Frank? I would have to find work, but what? I had no skills, I could not sew clothes, I had no experience as a teacher or governess. And I could hardly stay here with Mrs. Fein, eating at her table at her expense and taking free the place another boarder could pay for, meanwhile waiting to stumble upon some form of employment the nature of which I could not even imagine.

Mrs. Fein came home, and I told her what had happened to Frank. She was very kind, although upset about Frank of whom she was very fond, and she embraced me and assured me I could stay on until I "found something." But in her eyes I read my own concerns. "What can she do? How long will it be before she finds work?" I could frame the questions but not the answers.

Old habits of thought die hard. I had always been cared for. When Daddy died, I had turned to Uncle Frank, and I could not seem to deal with the fact that I was now alone, utterly alone, in a country and city I knew little about, with almost no resources. Like a bee that flies madly about a room, bumping into the same walls and corners again and again and failing to find the open window, my mind darted to and fro, seeking another benefactor, another person to take care of me. "Who?" I asked myself again and again. I should have been asking "What?" What could I do to help myself?

There was to be a very simple, even wretched, interment for Frank. He had followed no religion, but at my request a minister was prevailed upon to say a few words over his body before it was taken to a public burial ground that same afternoon.

The minister was to come to Mrs. Fein's flat, and I did not want to see Frank all dirty and unkempt in his work clothes, nor did I want Frank buried that way. On a hanger on a peg in a corner, I found the suit Frank had worn the day before. Mrs. Fein helped me to wash and prepare Frank's body and to comb his hair, and then I took down the suit. As I held the fabric in my hands and opened the jacket and saw the lining, I realized with a sad shock that the suit was new. He had bought it for the occasion of meeting me. I paused. Surely someone in the neighborhood would appreciate having the suit. It seemed a dreadful waste, in a poor community such as this, to bury the suit with the man. When the minister came, I could give the suit to him to add to the missionary barrel, I thought. Frank had a set of clean work clothes that would do just as well, and perhaps he would rest more comfortably in clothes he was accustomed to.

Still, I couldn't give up the idea of putting the

suit on Frank, to honor him in the only way I could.

My long hesitation must have given away my thoughts, for Mrs. Fein said suddenly, "Listen. Don't you think about giving that suit away. He was a nice man, and we all loved him. He should be buried in his best." We dressed Frank in his new suit, and I wept openly, for of course he looked like my father as well as my uncle, and I had lost them both.

Bless Mrs. Fein. If she had not spoken I might have given away the suit, and if I had, what would have become of me? I simply cannot imagine, but certainly my destiny would have been utterly different. On such delicate shifts of fortune do our lives often turn.

The minister had come and gone and the trip to the burial ground was about to start when Mrs. Fein motioned me to one side. "You'd better go through his pockets," she said. "He might have had some money or a watch or something, and if so you should have it."

"I don't want to do that," I replied. "It seems— indecent."

"No, it isn't," she said. "You know very well he'd want you to have anything of his, and no one else should do it."

She was right, I felt, and with great misgivings and silent apologies to Frank, wherever his spirit was by now, I gingerly slipped my hand in and out of the pockets of his suit while Mrs. Fein watched.

"There's nothing," I said.

"Inside pocket," she directed. "You forgot that one."

I slid my hand into the inner breast pocket, and as I did I had a sharp mental image of the last time I had seen Frank's hand going into the same pocket, so that I knew before I touched it what I would find there. My fingers closed on the small oblong of cardboard, and I drew it out into the light.

"What is it?" Mrs. Fein asked.

"A calling card," I said. "It's a souvenir." I realized that Frank must have placed it in the pocket of his new suit for the express purpose of showing it to me and telling me about it, his proudest possession, his most exciting memory.

"Well, it's yours now. It's a small thing, but it'll be something to remember him by," she said.

I put the card into my reticule without reading it, but my fingers traced the raised letters, and I remembered very well the name it contained.

The burial of the city's indigent is carried out with the same dispatch and the same intent as is the disposal of the city's refuse. So it was not very late in the evening when Mrs. Fein and I returned from Frank's poor grave. I fell exhausted into my cot and slept a hard and deep sleep.

In the morning, I said very little to the others, accepting their sympathetic remarks with the best grace I could muster. But my mind seethed and my heart pounded under the glaze of adopted composure, and as soon as everyone had gone to work and Mrs. Fein to her marketing, I pinned my blonde hair into a neat bun and put on a plain dark suit and hat. Then I wrote a note, placed it on the table, and went out.

I walked up to Grand Street, then directed my steps west toward Broadway. When Frank and I had got off the Broadway cable car, I had noted how that thoroughfare sliced on northward through the city. Now, I slipped the small card from my reticule and read the name and numbers they bore—"Jay Caldwell . . . 577 Fifth Avenue."

I had studied a map of New York before my departure from England, and while I did not remember much about it, I did think that Fifth Avenue was farther north than Grand Street, and I believed that the Broadway cable car might take me there. I waited on the corner of Broadway and Grand until one of the frighteningly large and swift cars stopped, and I saw the conductor standing on the rear platform.

"Excuse, me," I called out, hurrying toward him. "Would this car take me to Fifth Avenue?"

"We cross her at Madison Square," said the conductor. I hastened up the steps, and the conductor helped me to select the fare from among the American coins which were still strange to me.

"Will you tell me when we reach Madison Square?" I asked, and he assured me that he would.

Under different circumstances, I would have enjoyed the scenes of the great city unfolding before me. Even in my anxiety, I noticed that it became more beautiful, more spacious, and less crowded as we moved north.

At Tenth Street, there was an elegant shop with

deep awnings and trellises behind which patrons sat at outdoor tables sipping coffee and eating pastries. It was the Vienna Model Bakery, and a fellow passenger who had appointed herself my guide told me that free bread was given out to the poor at midnight each night, the long breadline partaking of the generosity of the owner, Mr. Fleischmann. Next to the Vienna Bakery stood a beautiful church. It was Grace Church, the church attended by so many of New York's wealthy, my guide informed me, even though "society" had now moved much farther north, and attendance at Grace Church was preceded by a long carriage ride. It illustrated, I thought, the city's cruel juxtaposition of poverty and wealth, the breadline forming each night in the shadow of the society church.

Four blocks farther on, we swung round a curve into a large square dominated by the statue of a military hero on horseback. The park encompassed a beautiful fountain and well-kept beds of flowers, and many persons were seated on the park benches enjoying the spring sun dappled by the thin shade of tender early leaves. Across the street were a row of theaters, many closed, and the woman told me that the theater district had moved north to Herald Square. But many shops were thriving about the square, including a large book shop called Brentano's I thought I would enjoy visiting one day. This was Union Square, she said, and Madison Square would be coming along nine blocks hence. There Broadway angled across Fifth Avenue, and that was my destination.

On we rode, past Arnold Constable and Company, a large emporium with many shoppers entering and exiting its doors, until shortly we stopped alongside another large park, and both the kind lady and the conductor informed me that this was Madison Square.

As I departed the cable car and thanked my two friends, I was quite overwhelmed by the park's beauty. Madison Square seemed to have been made the special preserve of the nursemaids of New York, and hundreds of white wicker perambulators with dainty parasols shading the occupants' tiny faces rolled along the walkways, an occasional go-cart or new-style black baby carriage dotting the parade.

A smartly dressed lady and gentleman crossed Twenty-third Street. The gentleman hailed one of the hansom cabs that lined the curb, and they drove off up another broad street which was, the corner sign told me, Fifth Avenue.

I looked up and down it and, like Broadway, it appeared to be a very long street. I don't know why I had assumed that my journey would be at an end once I had found Fifth Avenue. Obviously, I could be very far from the address engraved on Jay Caldwell's card. I started north on Fifth Avenue, and the progression of numbers told me that I was going the right way, but that I did, indeed, have a very long way to go.

I noticed that horse-drawn public coaches traversed the avenue, less modern but also less terrifying than the behemoth Broadway cable cars. I might have boarded one of them, but I didn't know how far I had to go, and I was very much aware of how limited my funds were. At any rate, I was soon lost in awe at the long march of magnificent mansions that ascended the great avenue, most in brownstone, some in white and gray limestone, and for the time being I was content to walk along and gaze at them. Block after block ran the phalanx of ostentatious facades. Here and there a landau or brougham stood at the curb. One door opened as I approached, and a gentleman emerged accompanied by a servant in gray uniform. The two of them stepped into the very first automobile I had ever seen. The servant, acting as driver, took hold of the steering device and off they drove up the avenue, looking for all the world as if they would topple from their unsteady perch at the first bump.

The relative emptiness and quiet of Fifth Avenue, compared with the teeming crowds and noise of Orchard Street and Grand Street, underscored the fact that what the rich do not have, or have to put up with, is as much a part of their world as the things they do have.

What were my plans as I walked the long blocks? What did I propose to do or to say upon reaching the Caldwell mansion? What did I think Jay Caldwell could do for me? Did I believe that he would wish to honor a promise of help he had given so long ago to a stranger when the recipient of the aid was to be a substitute? And did I really believe Jay Caldwell to be the kind of man who would pity a destitute woman, the wealthy and powerful Jay Caldwell, a man accustomed to controlling people rather than helping them—a man who was said to have murdered his first wife?

I do not know. I seemed to feel myself in the hands of Providence, with no practical or specific plan whatever—an indication, I suppose, of the extremity of my distress and also, I must admit, the result of my lifelong helplessness and dependency. I walked and walked, as if in a trance, taking in the sights of Fifth Avenue as a tourist might, with no conscious thought other than of the distractions of the moment, ignoring the dull ache of hurt and dread.

As the blocks passed, I seemed to fall deeper and deeper into the trance so that I might almost have forgotten the address I was seeking and passed the house by. What aroused me? Perhaps it was the fact that the Caldwell mansion was several degrees more imposing than most of the homes I had passed, and more beautiful as well. The dazzling white limestone was extensively and gracefully carved. And the facade was much broader than the others on the avenue, broad enough to front one of the few ballrooms in a private home in New York.

I had just passed the Windsor Hotel at Forty-seventh Street when, as if by instinct, I stopped before the Caldwell mansion. A wide flight of stone steps led to an enormous carved oak double door. Both wood and brass fittings were polished to a high shine. I raised my eyes to the number 577 carved into the stone archway above the impressive entrance.

I stared, not quite able to realize that I had reached my destination. And then, before I could collect my thoughts or form a plan of approach, the double doors sprang open and out came a parade of workmen carrying barrels, boxes, and trunks toward a large, heavy wagon standing at the curb.

I was aghast. Was it possible that I had come all this way only to learn that the person I sought was in the very act of moving?

I stood watching the procession of household goods for some minutes before I noticed that an ample woman with gray hair, a pearl gray dress, and a crisp white apron had come to the doorway and was eyeing me.

"Miss," she called. "Are you looking for the Caldwell house?" I nodded. She reached out her arm to stop a workman who was about to carry a large trunk out the door. "Just a minute," she said sharply. "Can't you see there's a lady coming?" and she motioned me up the steps.

"Come in, won't you?" the woman said, and I walked through the door into an enormous entrance hall dominated by a magnificent brass and crystal chandelier and a grand curved, carved marble staircase. The workman stepped back to let me pass.

The entire experience of the last several weeks had been so unreal, so unlike any part of my existence until Daddy's death, that the incredible fact of being invited cordially into the Caldwell mansion as if I were expected surprised me only mildly. My life had taken on the quality of a dream.

The woman directed me to an open doorway on

my right, and I entered a sitting room that dazzled the eye with its brocades and velvets, its carved panelings and moldings, its tapestries, its deep carpets, its rich ornaments, and its heavy lamps—all electric, I noted.

"I am Mrs. Morgan," the woman said. "May I give Madam your name?"

"My name?" I said slowly. "Why, my name is Miss Lorimer. Miss Lillie Lorimer."

"Oh, what a pretty accent you have," Mrs. Morgan smiled. "English, are you?"

"Yes," I replied. "But I plan to take American citizenship as soon as I can."

"That's lovely," she said kindly. "I'll be back as soon as Madam can see you. Please take a chair." And out she went.

Now my mind started to recover from its benumbment, and I began to realize how very strange and awkward was the situation in which I found myself. Mrs. Morgan had seemed to expect me, or to expect someone, but had not expected to know that someone's name. It seemed to be understood that the expected someone would speak with "Madam." Who Madam was I did not know, but she was undoubtedly Jay Caldwell's mother, wife, or another lady of importance in the Caldwell household.

I was suddenly horrified that I had allowed Mrs. Morgan to usher me into the house and to take my name and go off to announce me without telling her why I was here and that I had hoped to see Mr. Caldwell. The reason I had not done so, of course, was that I really had no rational explanation of my presence nor of my business with Jay Caldwell. I could not have explained it to myself, let alone to Mrs. Morgan.

But if explaining myself to Mrs. Morgan would have been difficult, explaining myself to Madam, whoever she was, would be impossible. I got to my feet and started for the entrance hall, hoping to find Mrs. Morgan and to set things straight before the charade had gone too far.

The workmen seemed to have departed with their load. A stack of barrels and boxes in the hall told me they would return, but for the moment there was no sign of Mrs. Morgan nor of anyone else. Or so I thought until I raised my eyes to the doorway just across the entrance hall. A little girl of about three stood in the exact center of the doorway, watching me.

If ever there was an appealing child, it was she. Her pale gold hair had been drawn back from her face and caught with a large blue bow at the back of her head, but soft ringlets had escaped all about her face. She wore a short blue dress and a starched white pinafore with an appliqued blue duckling on its bib. White stockings and little white kid boots peeped from under the dress. Her cheeks were delicately flushed, and her dark-lashed eyes were like enormous violet pansies.

"Did you see my cat?" she said in a clear, high voice.

"No, I haven't," I smiled. "Is he lost?" I crossed the great hall, forgetting for the moment the predicament I was in. There was temporarily nothing to be done about it, and this sweet baby had captured my attention.

"She's a girl," the child said, nodding her head up and down to signify that the cat was, in fact, lost.

"What's her name?" I asked.

"Ginger," she said.

I held out my hand and she placed her small one in mine. "Let's look for her," I said. "We'll call to her and tell her you miss her. What's your name?"

"Bonnie."

"Well, Bonnie, I'm Miss Lorimer," I said. "Now where did you see Ginger last?"

"In here," she said, and she led me into a sitting room that had been furnished in an ornate oriental decor.

"Here, Ginger," I called.

"Here, Ginger," Bonnie echoed.

"Bonnie misses you, Ginger," I called.

"I misses you, Ginger," Bonnie chimed.

We toured the room, peeking under draped couches and behind richly carved and elaborately lacquered Chinese screens. There were several windows which, behind their heavy draperies, looked out onto Fifth Avenue and one door at the far end of the room. All were tightly closed.

"She must be here," I said. "There's no way out except the way we came in."

As we stepped past one especially large screen, a tiny ball of orange, gray, and white calico-patched fur sprang out, fastened its small teeth on Bonnie's shoe buttons, and rolled playfully onto its back, kicking at her foot.

"Oh, Ginger," she squealed and happily stooped

to gather the kitten up in her arms. "You hided from me!"

At that moment, a uniformed footman appeared in the doorway from the entrance hall.

"Miss Bonnie," he said, "I'll be taking the cat now."

"No, Geoffrey," Bonnie protested, squeezing the kitten tightly.

"You know your mother doesn't want to travel with the cat," said Geoffrey, "so give it here."

"No! She's mine!" Bonnie said, squeezing harder. For a moment I feared for poor Ginger's life and breath, but Geoffrey, a big, crude-looking man, had crossed the room and easily wrested the kitten from Bonnie's arms. Little Ginger almost vanished within his heavy hands. With no further word, Geoffrey and Ginger departed.

A wrenching sob rose from Bonnie's chest and set her small shoulders to heaving. She poked her fists into her eyes and great, fat tears streamed over her scarlet cheeks. Her nose ran, and she lowered one fist to wipe at it.

For a moment, I was at a loss as to how to comfort her, for I didn't know where Ginger had been taken and when or whether she was to be reunited with Bonnie. I don't believe Bonnie knew, either. I could cheerfully have kicked the brutish Geoffrey, but my mind was occupied with the immediate need of soothing Bonnie.

Luckily, small children are easily distracted. Looking about the room, I spied a carafe of water and some tumblers on a tray. I led Bonnie to the couch by the table on which the tray rested and lifted her onto my lap. I poured a glass of water and handed it to her. Her two fists came away from her face and grasped the glass, and she took a big swallow. The face-rubbing and the sobs had been interrupted by the familiar and comforting act of drinking water. I took out my handkerchief and wiped her nose.

"Let's look out the window," I said. "Let's see what the world is doing out there, all right?" She nodded, the hiccoughs and sobs still too near the surface to permit speech.

We walked to one of the windows, and I drew back the dark draperies. The spring sunlight flooded the room. There was a deep window seat, and I lifted Bonnie up and let her kneel on it, facing the street, while I sat beside her. One small dimpled arm wound about my neck. I held her waist and stroked the distress-dampened curls about her face and neck with my other hand, drying them between my fingers.

"Look at the carriage," I said. "Where do you think it's going?"

"Uptown," she said.

"Why are the people going uptown?"

"To visit."

"There's a man walking."

"He's going downtown."

Bonnie was all right, now. She still felt hurt, but she had become absorbed in the street scene, and I rubbed her back in slow circles while we made up stories about the people and things outside the window.

I don't know what caused me to turn and look

back over Bonnie's shoulder. I believe I sensed his presence. As Bonnie's baby voice droned on, I found myself gazing at a man who was standing in the doorway that had been closed when I entered the room.

His gaze met mine evenly, and his expressionless face did not change. He was a tall man in his middle thirties. Because of his broad frame, he was probably even taller than he looked. He was coatless. He wore a dark vest and trousers and a white shirt with no collar. A shock of dark, almost black straight hair fell across his forehead, and his eyes were a deep, clear gray. They were large and deep-set with thick black lashes and very dark, straight brows. Bonnie's brows were fine and fair, and her eyes were violet-blue, but their shape and depth and the dark lashes were his.

Before I could collect my wits sufficiently to stand up and speak, the man turned and closed the door behind him. Bonnie had not seen him and was still talking. How long had he been watching us? I had to calculate it. I had had my back to that door since Bonnie had begun crying and I had led her to the water tray. Had her crying attracted his attention? Had he opened the door then? Had he been watching her—and me—all this time?

I wondered who he thought I was. I knew who he was. Despite his informal attire, he had radiated such power and self-possession that he could only have been the master of this house. I was certain that the man who had stared at me, then turned away, was Jay Caldwell.

I shivered. I had felt his power, but was it power

for good or for evil? There had been no warmth in his eyes, only cold appraisal. What sort of man was he? I had been wondering. And now I had seen him, but I knew no more than before. He had been grateful to Frank for saving his daughter—an older daughter than Bonnie, no doubt. This had led me to hope that he was a man capable of kindness in spite of the dreadful rumors about him. But here was a man who could watch his little girl sobbing and not step into the room to help comfort her, a man who could see a strange lady in his parlor and not offer a greeting, could even turn away and close the door upon her.

I knew that I had missed my opportunity, that I should have seized that moment to present myself to Jay Caldwell, to remind him of Uncle Frank, to show him the card, to ask him to help me. I also knew that I could not have done or said any of those things to the cold, impassive man I had just seen. At that moment, I felt just as Bonnie had felt when Ginger was snatched from her arms. I could have sobbed like a little child. Jay Caldwell was obviously not the kindly man my desperation had led me to imagine. My hopes were dashed.

I had to get out of that house, to make my way back to Orchard Street as quickly as possible and face whatever fate had in store for me. I shuddered as I thought of the working girl Mrs. Fein's daughter had described, found dead in her poor room. I was certain that my ability to care for myself was even less than that young woman's had been; yet I had no choice. I stood and was about to tell Bonnie good-bye when Mrs. Morgan appeared in the hallway door.

"Oh, there you are, Miss Lorimer. I see you've found Miss Bonnie. Isn't she a darling? She would be one of your charges, of course, along with Miss Marta and Master Leo. They can all use some good schooling."

A governess—I realized with a start. The Caldwells had advertised for a governess, and Mrs. Morgan had assumed that I was here in answer to the advertisement. I glanced behind me out the window just in time to see a handsome, well-dressed woman descending the steps of the Caldwell house and turning up Fifth Avenue. She had obviously been interviewed just before me, and if she was not the perfect woman for the job she certainly looked it.

I opened my mouth to tell Mrs. Morgan that a mistake had been made, to say that I had changed my mind, to make any hasty excuse, and to talk my way out the door. Instead, my eyes met Bonnie's. A vision of mean Geoffrey and then of cold Jay Caldwell, a desire to know if sweet Bonnie would get her Ginger back, a desire to see her well cared-for, and the desperate knowledge that I really had no alternatives—all these passed through my mind in a flash, and I was flabbergasted to hear myself saying, "Very well. I'm ready," and to find myself following Mrs. Morgan's starched apron bow across the great hallway and up the marble staircase.

I knew, of course, that I had no real chance at the position. Any number of qualified women must have applied for the job, and while I had been very well educated at my father's expense and indulgence, I had had absolutely no experience as a teacher. Nevertheless, I followed Mrs. Morgan down a carpeted second floor corridor and heard a woman's voice answer "Come in" to her discreet knock. We entered a sitting room done entirely, it seemed to me, in ice-blue satin and rosewood.

"This is Miss Lillie Lorimer, ma'am," said Mrs. Morgan. "Miss Lorimer, this is Mrs. Caldwell."

By her age, I surmised that Mrs. Caldwell was Jay Caldwell's second wife. She sat at a small writing table and made no gesture of welcome, nor did she indicate that I was to be seated, so I simply remained standing where I was in the center of the carpet before her.

Her dark hair was piled atop her head in a mass of tiny curls. She appeared to be a tall woman. Certainly she was attractive, even beautiful. Yet she seemed to be angry—I hoped not at me—and her ill temper had distorted her features unpleasantly.

"Well, Miss Lorimer," she said, "What are your qualifications?"

"My education has been extensive, I do love children, and—I'm certain I could serve you and your children well," I stammered.

It sounded lame, even in my own ears, so that I was very much surprised when Mrs. Caldwell did not immediately thank me for coming and send me on my way. Instead, she said, "I understand you have met Bonnie already. Mrs. Morgan," she turned to the housekeeper, "please ask Marta and Leo to come in."

Mrs. Morgan stepped out of the room, and a few moments of awkward silence passed while I wondered how Mrs. Caldwell could know that I had already met Bonnie. But my musings were cut short when Mrs. Morgan reentered with a girl of perhaps fourteen—the daughter Uncle Frank had saved, I thought—followed by a boy of about eight. The girl looked sullen, but as sullenness is common in adolescents, I gave it little thought. She was a pretty child with long auburn hair and green eyes. The boy was a small Jay Caldwell, coloring and all, but sweet shyness seemed his nature rather than his father's coldness.

"Marta and Leo," said Mrs. Caldwell, "meet Miss Lorimer, your new governess."

I'm sure I did not hide my astonishment as I accepted Marta's curtsy and Leo's bow and their handshakes. I don't know what I said to them—something kind, I hope. Then Mrs. Caldwell spoke again.

"Well, as you know, we are leaving for Soundcliff tomorrow, our home on Long Island. Mrs. Morgan will explain the travel arrangements and see that your luggage is picked up and sent out. When we arrive, I shall expect you to outline for me your plan of instruction for each child, including Bonnie."

I was dismissed with a curt nod, and Mrs. Morgan led me out of the room.

"Won't you come downstairs with me," she said, "and I will explain our travel plans."

"Of course," I breathed, giddy with joy. A job, a wonderful job, teaching three beautiful children and living in a marvelous home. I could not believe my good fortune.

As we started toward the staircase, however, another door along the corridor opened, and an elderly gentleman emerged. He walked with a cane, slightly dragging one foot. It was apparent that he suffered a partial paralysis, perhaps from a stroke. As we came to where he stood, he put out a hand as if to stop me.

"You the new governess?" he asked.

"Yes, sir," I replied not at all certain of who he was or how he could know already of my employment. Information seemed to travel strangely through the very walls of this household.

"Well, that's good for the children." The old gentleman spoke slowly, painfully. "But if I were you, I'd run for my life."

THREE

"Would you like a cup of tea?" Mrs. Morgan asked me.

Suddenly, I realized that I had taken nothing since the few sips of tea at Mrs. Fein's table the morning before. I was so hungry I was nearly faint, but I managed to say merely, "Yes, thank you, that would be very nice," and to sound, I thought, as if I had finished a hearty breakfast just a few hours earlier. As I would learn, however, it was difficult to pull the wool over Nellie Morgan's eyes. She was shrewd as well as kindly, and no doubt that was why she had survived forty-three years of service with the Caldwells.

Mrs. Morgan ushered me back to the ground floor and then through a short corridor under the staircase, on through a large, well-equipped butler's pantry off the dining room, and into the kitchen. There she introduced me to Ada Wirth, the cook, a plump blonde woman in her late forties who cheerfully set out tea for me. The two women insisted that I eat a roast beef sandwich almost too thick to bite into and a large slice of berry pie along with two cups of strong tea with milk and sugar. I had seen daintier teas, but none had ever been so refreshing.

As I ate, Mrs. Morgan told me something of her own history.

"I'm the only one left from the old household," she began. "I was one of the first old Mrs. Caldwell hired—that was Mr. Eli's wife—back in '55 when they built Soundcliff out there on Long Island. I was only seventeen, a local Long Island girl. I started as a kitchen maid, and a pretty poor one," she laughed, "but here I still am." As housekeeper, I would learn, Mrs. Morgan now headed the entire staff of house servants.

"That was Mr. Eli who spoke to you in the hall upstairs," she went on. After his strange remark to me, she had introduced him as "Mr. Caldwell," and I had already guessed that a Mr. Caldwell his age was probably Eli Caldwell, Jay Caldwell's grandfather, the "immigrant lad" who made good, as Uncle Frank had described him.

"Does Mr. Jay Caldwell's father live here as well?" I inquired.

"Mr. Jay's father? Oh, no. Mr. Harry died—well, let me see now, almost nineteen years ago."

"Mr. Harry and his wife was boatin' out on the Long Island Sound, and a storm come up, and they was drowned," put in Ada, who herself had been a young kitchen maid at the time of the tragic accident. "After that, old Mr. Eli just doted on young Mr. Jay."

"Mr. Eli *always* doted on Mr. Jay," Mrs. Morgan said, then hastily arose as if sorry she had been speaking so freely. She had not lasted so long and served so well in the Caldwell household by gossiping about the family to strangers. "Would you care to stay here tonight?" she changed the subject. "I think it would be best. We'll be leaving very early tomorrow. If you'll give me your address, I'll send someone to fetch your things or take you there to pack them and return if you'd rather."

I decided to accept Mrs. Morgan's suggestion, and within the half hour a driver had been dispatched to Orchard Street bearing a note of explanation and gratitude to Mrs. Fein. There was no need of my going back myself, I thought. I had never really unpacked my things, and the driver could pick up my bag and my trunk just as they were. Besides, I was just too tired. I had found a safe haven, I felt, and I was suddenly as limp as a rag doll.

"Good. That's settled," Mrs. Morgan said as the driver set off on his errand. "Now let me show you your room."

Gratefully, I followed her up a flight of stairs that spiraled from the kitchen to the third floor, then into an airy gable room with yellow sprigged paper on the walls. The wooden bedstead, dresser, and washstand were painted in soft tones of gray and green with clusters of pink and yellow roses. A yellow quilt lay upon the bed. Rag rugs covered polished floors. White curtains fluttered at a dormer window that opened outward. Beyond the window spread a picturesque jumble of tarpaper rooftops, water towers, and chimney pipes. I thought the view romantic and the room the prettiest I had ever seen.

"I'll send you up some night clothes. And I expect you might want your supper on a tray. There'll be plenty of time tomorrow to meet the rest of the staff, the ones going to Soundcliff."

I sat down on the bed and sighed. I thought I was in heaven. Only the unnerving memory of old Eli Caldwell's words marred my mood—"If I was you, I'd run for my life." But their chill had begun to melt under the warmth of Ada and Mrs. Morgan's kindness. These two pleasant, down-to-earth women had been with the Caldwells for so many years. Surely, I thought, there could be no very great danger in this household.

"Is old Mr. Caldwell ill?" I asked Mrs. Morgan, hoping she might put the strange encounter into perspective. Perhaps, I hoped, she would tell me that he was senile and not responsible for his disturbing remark.

"Oh, yes," she said. "He had a very bad stroke quite a number of years ago—I guess it's been 25 years now. He hasn't been very well in all these years. Didn't affect his mind, though. He's just as bright and sharp as he ever was." I must have worn a look of distress, for she seemed suddenly to grasp the reason for my query and added, "I wouldn't pay any mind to what he told you, though. He does have his own ideas about some things." For the second time that afternoon, I had prompted Mrs. Morgan to discuss the Caldwells a bit more than she felt was proper, and she quickly took her leave.

Shortly after, a young maid who introduced herself as Susan Sayre brought me a nightdress and informed me that towels and soap had been left for me in the bath across the hall. I stepped across to enjoy a sponge bath with steaming tap water and lavender-scented soap, then returned to my room, put on the nightdress, and slept. I awoke to a discreet rap at my door, and Susan brought supper in on a tray. I ate, then slept again and didn't waken until Mrs. Morgan knocked. The tray was gone. It was dawn.

I found to my amazement and pleasure that my dress had been brushed, my shoes had been shined, and my underthings had been freshly laundered, ironed, and returned to my room. I dressed hastily and went down to the kitchen for breakfast.

It was not an enormous kitchen, but large enough to accommodate easily the big black six-burner range, a capacious sink, cutting and mixing counters, and a long table at which the staff took meals, usually in two or three shifts. The work space extended into a large back pantry that contained two big ice boxes and shelves for staple goods and the butler's pantry between kitchen and dining room that contained a copper sink and was lined on three sides with glass-fronted cupboards. This was the pantry used for washing up, for polishing and storing silver and glassware, and as a staging area for the serving of meals.

The staff members who were already seated at the kitchen table when I came down were those who were to go to Soundcliff, those most valued or needed by the Caldwells and who were always with the family, whether in New York or at the Long Island Estate. Some even traveled with the family to Europe every second or third summer. A few, such as Ada, Mrs. Morgan, and Hans Arnold the butler, had been with the Caldwell family for many years. Others, such as Susan Sayre, the young maid who had brought my supper, Nancy Vance, who was Mrs. Caldwell's lady's maid, and Geoffrey Hand, the head footman who had made off with little Bonnie's cat Ginger, were more recent employees. Nancy and Geoffrey seemed to be an "item." They sat together and talked to each other throughout breakfast, to the exclusion of everyone else, bestowing adoring looks across the small space that separated their chairs.

The others made a pleasant to-do over me, fetching me plates of eggs, toast with jam, bacon, creamed beef, steaming cereal, and fried mush with syrup. It was a great deal more than I could even attempt to eat, and they made many kind and joking remarks of the "We'll have to fatten her up" variety. I knew that I would have to practice restraint, for I realized that one could indeed "fatten up" at Ada Wirth's table.

There were other members of the staff not present who would be staying behind at the Fifth Avenue mansion. Besides caring for the house, they would serve Jay Caldwell whose business affairs, I was told, would keep him in New York for a large portion of the April-to-October season which Mrs. Caldwell and the children planned to spend at Soundcliff.

I felt a twinge of disappointment at this news. I had unconsciously looked forward to seeing and learning more about the legendary millionaire in spite of the instinctive fear I had felt of him the day before. Fear mixed with fascination, I admitted to myself. And then I put the thought aside and fixed my mind upon the day's journey and my new responsibilities. It was true that I had come here to seek Jay Caldwell because of his promise to my uncle, but it was to his wife that I owed my job and to her and the children that I now owed my best efforts and my loyalty. But I remembered my own father and could not help thinking that it was a shame the children would not see more of Jay Caldwell. It was hard for me to imagine a childhood spent without a father's closeness and love.

Breakfast done, Ada commended her kitchen to the care of the second cook, and we all went out through a side door and down a short alleyway to Fifth Avenue where a line-up of carriages was waiting for us. With relief, I spied my own trunk and bag among a wagonload of last-minute luggage and boxes. Ada, Mrs. Morgan, Susan Sayre, and I were helped into a very large and very old but well-cared-for C-spring barouche. Mrs. Morgan told me that it had been Eli Caldwell's pride and joy when she first joined the family, and it was kept and maintained to please the old gentleman. Our driver's name was Bob Harrigan, and he kindly told me that he had delivered my note to Mrs. Fein himself and that she sent her best wishes.

Then, off we rolled down Fifth Avenue to Thirty-fourth Street and thence along Thirty-fourth to the East River ferry slip. As Bob helped us down from the high carriage step, I saw that a large ferry boat was docked and waiting for us.

"This is Mr. Jay's weak link," Ada chuckled.

"What do you mean?"

"See them letters?" She pointed to the big, white block letters printed on the side of the boat: LIH&MRR.

"What do they stand for?"

"Long Island, Hudson, and Mohawk Railroad. The road Mr. Eli built. It runs from Montauk Point out on the end of Long Island through New York all the way to Schenectady up on the Mohawk River above Albany. Now, between New York and Albany it crosses the Hudson River on a trestle bridge. But there's never been a bridge built here across the East River between New York and Long Island—not for the LIH&M, anyhow. So the passengers from Schenectady have to get off at the Grand Central Station up on Forty-second Street and then take carriages down here and take the ferry across to Long Island City and then get back on the train to Montauk Point—and vice versa from Long Island to Schenectady. It's the weak link."

"Indeed," I agreed.

"Mr. Jay always talks about building a tunnel

65

under the river so people can ride the LIH&M straight through from Schenectady to Montauk Point without getting off the train. It gives me the shivers. I don't think I'd have the nerve to go down under the river on a train like that, would you?"

"I don't see why not," I said. "It seems a marvelous idea to me. Why doesn't he build it?"

"Oh, I don't know. It's got something to do with this war Mr. Eli and Jay've been carryin' on with Mr. August Flammon." Her casual mention of another famous American railroad tycoon startled me. "But I don't know what it's all about except it's been goin' on for years."

I was enormously curious to know more about the "war" between the Caldwells and August Flammon and how it affected the dreamed-of tunnel under the East River, but I was sure that Ada had told me all she knew of it. Some day, I hoped, I would learn more about how America's daring millionaires operated. From my lowly vantage point, it seemed to be a game—on a grand scale and with huge stakes, but a game nevertheless—and I wanted to know how it was played.

We had boarded the ferry now, and had taken seats in the passenger cabin. The staff had begun to chatter with greater and lesser degrees of excitement about the summer ahead at Soundcliff. Young Susan, for example, declared that she looked forward to the country air, the riding, and the boating that the family, and to a more restricted extent, the servants would enjoy.

"And there's going to be a big Fourth of July party," she declared, her eyes sparkling.

"It's a tradition," Ada said. "There's been a Fourth of July partly at Soundcliff every year the family's been there since Mr. Eli built it, hasn't there, Nellie?"

"Yes, but July's a long way off," said Mrs. Morgan.

"But there will be one this year, won't there?" Susan persisted. "I thought maybe with Mr. Jay and Miss Eleanor not getting on so well and Mr. Jay staying in the city—"

"Don't worry," said Nancy Vance. "Miss Eleanor is already talking about it. She'll have it, with or without her wandering husband."

Nellie Morgan scowled at the two younger women, and Susan blushed while Nancy scowled back.

"Well," Nancy said defiantly, "it's the truth. Everyone knows it about Mr. Jay and Miss Eleanor."

"The younger generation," said Hans Arnold softly but sternly, "has no sense of discretion. Let's close this topic."

But the hints Susan and Nancy had dropped about Jay Caldwell and his wife were humming in my mind. So her name was Eleanor, I thought. An elegant name perfectly suited to her dark, aristocratic beauty. And I had certainly found Jay Caldwell to be a striking-looking man. Good looks, wealth, social position, adorable children—what more could a man and wife want or need? What could be wrong between them? Yet I did not doubt that Susan and Nancy had spoken the truth of the matter. The demeanor of both man and wife—Jay Caldwell's cold and aloof, Eleanor Caldwell's angry and harsh—bespoke the unhappiness that had been described by the two young servants. For the first time, I felt a true foreboding about the family I had been hired to serve.

The East River crossing was short, and soon we felt the shudder of reversing engines and the bump of the ferry against pilings. We had arrived at Long Island City, and we quickly debarked and walked through the cavernous ferry shed and out into the sunlight. Across a platform stood a short train of cars bearing the LIH&MRR insignia. They looked to be far more polished than the average railroad car and this, I discovered, was because it was the Caldwell family's private train.

We boarded the forward car, and I found that it was appointed much like an ordinary railroad car except that it was handsomer than the ordinary. The aisles were thickly carpeted, the seats upholstered in the finest red plush with spotless starched white linen antimacassars over the backs. The wood paneling was oiled to a fine patina and a shaded lamp was affixed to the paneling between each pair of seats. Frescos adorned the long ceiling, and brass chandeliers hung over the aisle. I thought that the car would be very inviting indeed at night with the lamps and the chandeliers lit, but now the morning sun beaming through the south windows lent its own golden glow to the rich interior.

Ada told me that the family's own cars at the rear of the train were far more elaborately furnished as bed-sitting rooms and had, on occasion, taken Jay

Caldwell all the way to Chicago. The private cars had been carried across the East River on barges to the Manhattan yards, attached to an engine, pulled to Schenectady, then transferred from the LIH&M to the Empire State Railroad, the great eastern line that connected New York State with Chicago and such great western lines as the Chicago and Northwestern, the Santa Fe, and the Chicago, Rock Island, and Pacific. Later today, the private family cars would serve the more ordinary function of transporting Eleanor Caldwell, Eli Caldwell, the three children, and the nursemaid Margaret Dobbs to Soundcliff. The space of time between our arrival and theirs would allow Mrs. Morgan and Hans Arnold to see that all was ready in the house as a whole while Nancy and Susan prepared Mrs. Caldwell's rooms to her liking.

On board the train, I found myself seated facing Geoffrey Hand and Nancy Vance who was still smarting from the dressing-down she had received from Nellie Morgan and Hans Arnold. She settled her long frame sullenly against the red plush and removed a straw hat from her dark hair which she wore much like Eleanor Caldwell's in a high pile of small curls.

"It's all the truth," Nancy declared once again to Geoffrey and me. "Miss Eleanor is miserable. Mr. Jay is hardly ever home. I know it's the common thing for men to have flings, but it doesn't make the wife any happier, does it? Especially after she stuck by him when Miss Charlotte died—that was his first wife, you know?" she added confidentially for my benefit. "The authorities said it was suicide, but then they never arrest a man in Jay Caldwell's position, do they?"

Even Geoffrey was taken aback by this pronouncement. "Nancy," he warned, "Miss Lorimer is new here."

I thought it a strange reprimand. Was his concern for the reputation of the Caldwell family, for my sensibilities, or for the possibility that I would report this loose and slanderous talk to one of the Caldwells? I chose to appear to accept the second alternative. "I really don't care to hear such private conjectures about Mr. and Mrs. Caldwell," I said firmly.

"Well," said Nancy. "I'm not saying he killed his first wife. It's just the talk you hear. But I do know Miss Eleanor stuck up for him when everybody thought he did it, so I think he owes her something, doesn't he? Not that she's any joy to get on with," she added rather bitterly, "and not that she's any angel herself."

"Excuse me," I said, overcome with embarrassment, and I got up and went to join Nellie Morgan and Ada Wirth. I wanted very much to ask them why such an unpleasant, indiscreet, and disloyal person as Nancy Vance continued to be employed as Mrs. Caldwell's personal maid, but I knew that this was not my business either.

Instead, I tried to learn something about my new position. I certainly did not want to disclose to anyone that I had stumbled into it by error, so I tried a roundabout approach.

"It's too bad that a new governess had to be hired

so close to moving to Soundcliff."

"Oh, it's not quite a coincidence," Ada said cheerfully. "The one before you thought we was going to Europe this year. I guess we all did till last week when Mr. Jay announced he couldn't get away this summer and Miss Eleanor and the children would go to Soundcliff. In some ways, Soundcliff ain't the cheeriest house in the world. In fact, it's a little spooky if you ain't used to it. The last governess spent last summer there and only stayed on after because she thought she'd get a trip to Europe out of it this year. When she heard it was Soundcliff again, she give notice. So Miss Eleanor had to look quick to find someone. She don't like Long Island girls,"—here Nellie Morgan, herself a "Long Island girl," winced slightly—"and a lot of New Yorkers don't like to leave the city, so it ain't that easy."

"What do you mean when you say that Soundcliff is spooky?" Incredibly, until now I had given no thought to what the Long Island house would be like.

"Oh, it's not spooky," said Mrs. Morgan. "It has a lot of old passageways because it used to be a stop on the Underground Railroad."

"Something to do with escaped slaves?" I asked, rummaging among my memories about American history.

"Yes. You see, Mr. Eli was an abolitionist. That means he favored abolition of slavery. A lot of folks up North here who felt as he did helped slaves escape. Their homes were called stops on the 'underground railroad,' the escape route, you see.

Only Mr. Eli was wealthy enough to do it in a grand way. He used to bring them over on the ferry and out to Soundcliff on the train. That's why he had the house built with false rooms and panels and passageways behind the walls. There were all kinds of places to hide, and if the slave hunters should find one passageway, there'd always be another way to get out. Mr. Eli was the only one who seemed to know all those passageways quite by heart. He planned them all with his architect, and I think he got a kick out of thinking it all up like a big maze or a puzzle. Personally, I've come to know the passageways, too, because after all they have to be cleaned once in awhile, and Mr. Eli always wanted me to do it. The fewer people that knew about them the better, he said, even after President Lincoln emancipated the slaves and there wasn't any real use for the passageways any more. But at that time, after the Civil War, all the children started to play in there, Mr. Jay and the children he played with. So I think the ones that were children then knew the passageways best of all."

"That doesn't sound so spooky to me," I said. "I don't think anything is very spooky once it's been explained, not even secret passageways in an old house."

"Well, there's been a kind of a sad air about the place, I think, since Miss Charlotte died there," said Ada. That line of conversation was halted abruptly by a sharp look from Nellie Morgan. But in spite of Mrs. Morgan's vigilance and protective attitude about the Caldwells, I knew I was bound to learn more about them, for so many of the others seemed to share the natural human love of gossip, even if not of the vindictive variety Nancy Vance favored.

And in spite of Eli Caldwell's warning, in spite of the bad feelings that seemed to prevail between Jay and Eleanor Caldwell, in spite of the hints about Charlotte Caldwell's mysterious death that might have been murder, and in spite of the supposed "spookiness" of Soundcliff, I could not suppress my eagerness. A summer at a large estate on the shores of Long Island Sound seemed perfectly wonderful. There surely could be no threat to me personally, whatever the problems within the family. And more than anything I wanted to protect the three beautiful Caldwell children from the unhappiness around them, to create an island of peace and contentment, of accomplishment and security. Despite my inexperience, I felt certain of success, for although I was afraid of so many things in the world, I had never been afraid of children. I felt a thrill of happy anticipation.

The train followed the main LIH&M track straight down the center of Long Island for some miles, then switched off onto a private spur toward the North Shore, the rocky coast of Long Island Sound, crowned with the jewel-like estates of the rich, side by side, separated from one another by vast private acreages. Ada told me that the North Shore of Long Island was nicknamed by some "The Gold Coast," and no wonder.

At last we reached the Caldwell land, the train

pulled to a halt, and we stepped down onto a platform beside a station house that was about three-quarters the size of a regular passenger station and picturesque enough to belong to a toy train set. There was a snow-white limestone gravel strip alongside the single track, bordered by a neat low hedgerow behind which stretched a perfectly manicured greensward. A flagstone walk extended from a break in the hedge to the door of the white frame station house with its gingerbread trim and sparkling windowpanes. Along the walk and around the station house, flower beds were alive with early crocuses and daffodils.

Inside the little station, a small pot-bellied stove, blacked and polished, was giving off just enough warmth to erase the April morning chill. Spotless terra-cotta tile floors set off gleaming oak benches lined with forest-green velvet cushions. As we trooped through, I spotted a small kitchen off the waiting room where a station agent's office might ordinarily be, and Ada told me that tea or other refreshments were often served to parties of guests waiting here for carriage rides to the house or for the train back to New York.

But carriages and drivers were already waiting for us on the gravel drive beyond the station house, and within moments we were rolling along a private roadway that ran through a large virgin pine and oak woodland from the station to the main grounds. The length of the ride was the first clue to the size of the estate—275 acres, Ada told me. The staff required at Soundcliff, she added, included twenty house servants and 128 grounds keepers, grooms, boat-keepers, and others.

The road emerged from the woods by a little white gazebo and then wound past an array of buildings and facilities identified for me by Ada, Mrs. Morgan, and Hans Arnold as the stables, the barns, the hennery, the piggery, the peacock houses, the greenhouses, the tennis courts, the nine-hole golf course, the bowling alley, the party pavilion, and two guest "cottages," each of which was commensurate with my previous idea of a mansion. Not to be seen, beyond the main house and at the base of the cliff on which it sat, were a boathouse and yacht slips.

Frequently, Ada told me, Jay Caldwell commuted to Soundcliff from Manhattan aboard his yacht *North Star*—it had been named by Eli in honor of the old slave escape route—rather than taking the more cumbersome ferry-cum-private train. A small silence followed this observation as we all, I am sure, pondered the unspoken question: would Jay Caldwell be coming to Soundcliff this summer? And, I wondered, would all the boating and gaming facilities throb with the life and gaiety they were obviously intended to, given the strained atmosphere of the unhappy household? How gay, for example, could the Fourth of July party be under the circumstances?

Even the extensiveness of the grounds and outlying buildings did not prepare me for the mansion itself, a vast edifice of gray granite perfectly designed in a mixture of Jacobean and Gothic revival styles. It was a complex construction of peaked windows and pinnacled roofs, turreted walls and vine-hung trellises, and a tall central tower that must offer an impressive view of the Sound and the surrounding countryside. Every bit as awesome as any baronial castle in England, it had also something of the grave and somber aura of a medieval monastery.

We drew up under a wide porte-cochere, mounted broad, shallow steps, and were inside the immense entrance hall with its vaulted Gothic ceiling.

"Well, now, you must see the Sound, first off," said Mrs. Morgan, and she led me through the main living room, which must have been forty feet long and forty feet wide, I thought in amazement. There was a fine pipe organ console, its pipes just visible behind carved open-work fruitwood panels, but there was no time to examine it as Mrs. Morgan was already disappearing through the wide French doors. I hurried after her and found myself standing on a deep flagstone piazza, its under-roof painted robins-egg blue, its low stone walls permitting an unrestricted view of the Sound.

The view took my breath away, for Soundcliff was situated on a promontory, giving the impression, from this vantage point, that the house was surrounded by the brilliant blue waters. Of course I had observed as we approached the house that wide lawns spread out to the west and south of the mansion, the south lawn accommodating the great circular drive and the west lawn leading away to the stables and other outbuildings. But the eastern and northern facades, the piazza-side and the rear of the mansion, extended almost to the edge of the promontory. From the north end of the piazza, there was room for only a narrow path to extend along the rear wing, and partway along its length there was a notch in the cliff that looked almost as if someone had snipped out a piece with a giant pair of scissors. Within the notch, the cliff dropped straight downward from the foundation of the mansion. A small bridge with sturdy rails had been built over the notch and the narrow path extended from its two ends.

A few feet beyond the piazza wall, a network of wooden steps and rails led down over the sheer, sharp rocks of the cliff face that curved off to the east, and at the bottom was a pleasant, sandy beach. There, I could now see the boathouse and the docks.

From the kitchen door at the rear of the mansion, Mrs. Morgan told me, a narrow driveway just wide enough to accommodate a single wagon permitted deliveries and connected with the wider service drives to the west and south of the mansion. Thus, I had now attained a mental image of the four sides of Soundcliff.

"Low tide," Mrs. Morgan was saying, pointing out over the water to what appeared to be a very small, rocky island topped by a lighthouse. "You can see the Execution Rock. At high tide, it disappears and you can only see the lighthouse." She led me back inside then and inquired, "Shall I show you your domain?"

"Please."

The schoolroom, she told me, was on the third

floor, and I expected that we would climb the stairs, but instead Mrs. Morgan approached a small elevator beside the great oak staircase. "We don't often use the elevator when the family is here," she explained. "It has to be free for their use. But it's all right now."

"This is quite unusual, isn't it, in a private house?" I inquired as the elevator bore us slowly upward.

"Yes. It was installed for Mr. Eli. He has such difficulty walking since his stroke, you see."

The elevator stopped with a soft bounce, and Mrs. Morgan opened frosted glass doors, then a pair of wrought iron gates, and we stepped into the third floor hallway.

"This is more or less the children's floor," she explained as we walked along toward the rear of the house. "This is Marta's room, and here is Leo's." She indicated two doors on our left. "The next one here is the nursery. Bonnie sleeps there, and so does Miss Dobbs." She pointed out what appeared to be a suite of rooms, and I imagined a playroom as well as a bath and sleeping quarters.

Mrs. Morgan stopped at a door opposite the nursery suite and opened it. "Here is the schoolroom," she said. My heart leaped. The schoolroom. My schoolroom! We went in.

It was enchanting. A large blackboard filled most of one wall. Intriguing cupboards lined others, and I caught sight of a large varnished globe on a table. There were a wide polished desk and a chair on a low platform at one end of the room—for me—and eight students' desks with seats attached. The tops of the desks could be lifted on hinges to reveal space inside for books and paper. Each desk had an inkwell, and a small iron container at the side of each desk contained pen-wipers and blotting paper. The desks were varied in size.

"There have been different numbers of children here at different times," Mrs. Morgan explained, "and sometimes guests' or neighbors' children join the lessons. When Mr. Jay was small—he was an only child, you know—Mr. Harry didn't want him to be lonely, so the Archer children used to take their lessons here with him. The Archer estate is next door, you see. Miss Eleanor was one of them. So was Miss Charlotte."

"Miss Charlotte?" I asked. "She was Miss Eleanor's sister?"

"Cousin," Mrs. Morgan replied shortly and started for the door. "You'd like to see your own room, I expect."

But I was sorry to leave the little schoolroom so quickly, and privately I vowed to come back that afternoon to explore the cupboards and to open the windows that gave so invitingly on the eastward cliffs to let in the salt air.

I found my trunk and bag already deposited in my room which was just behind the schoolroom. It was at the very rear of the "family wing," separated by a door at the end of the corridor from the plainer servants' wing at the back of the house over the kitchen and service areas. Mrs. Morgan's room was just across the corridor from mine, also within the family domain in deference, I imagined, to the length of her service. If I wanted anything during the night, I was merely to knock at her door, she said.

My room at Soundcliff was far more elaborate and even more delightful than my room at the Fifth Avenue mansion had been. Six slender mullioned windows bordered with strips of ruby glass opened from a recessed bay, the bay set off by a pointed arch and tied-back flowered draperies. A small lacquered table with a vase of fresh flowers was placed within the bay. Above it, a multicolored stained glass lunette was brilliantly illumined by the morning sun.

The carved four-poster bed had a valance and spread of the same fabric as the window draperies. A leather-topped writing table and chair with tapestry cushion faced the wall opposite the bed. A large mahogany armoire stood near the bed. A pale gold faille chaise and a tapestry armchair rested upon a worn but beautiful oriental rug in rich jewel tones of dark blue, red, and gold. Crowning the ecru walls was a rib-vaulted ceiling painted a soft gray-blue. Lamps were placed about the room, an especially pretty pink-shaded one resting upon a mirrored dressing table, and I imagined that, come evening, the lamplight would glow invitingly.

There was a private bath, and just as I thought of the joy of a long soak in the deep porcelain tub, Susan knocked at my door and asked if she could take any of my dresses down to be pressed. I took a wine-colored cotton from my trunk and gave it to Susan. By the time I had finished my bath, the pressed frock was laid out on my bed, and I put it on and combed and pinned up my hair. Much refreshed, I went down to the first floor by the main staircase, and as I did so I caught a brief glimpse of the second floor corridor off which the adult Caldwells' suites must lie.

Anxious for another look at the Sound, I stepped into the great living room Mrs. Morgan had first shown me. I was headed for the piazza when the organ caught and held my attention. A few days earlier, I would have thought the organ lessons my father had paid for to be the least useful aspect of my education. Now, I was suddenly taken with the idea of teaching Marta and Leo and one day even little Bonnie to play.

I looked about. No one was nearby. The organ would disturb no one if I played softly, and I was overcome with fascination for the magnificent instrument. I climbed the steps to the bench, sat down, and began to touch the pedals, keys, and stops. I found an electrical switch that activated the bellows, pushed it, and heard a whoosh of air from the bowels of the organ. I pedaled back the swells to soften the tone and began to play a Bach fugue.

I was thoroughly absorbed in my private concert when, without warning, a panel next to the organ slid open, and a tall, fair, elegantly dressed man stepped out of the wall. I gasped, and my hands flew to my face.

"Oh, do play on," he said.

FOUR

"I'm terribly sorry," I stammered.

"Indeed you should be," said the tall, fair man in blazer and flannels who now placed an elbow casually on the organ console and smiled into my eyes. "A lady seated at an organ must always apologize to a gentleman emerging from a wall. It's in all the etiquette books."

"Oh, I am sorry," I said again and blushed.

"You must stop saying that." He threw back his head and laughed with enjoyment. "Here," he said, still chuckling as he held out a hand to me. "Let me help you down from there."

I took his hand and allowed him to help me off the bench and down the little set of carpeted steps. Then, releasing my hand, he bowed. "Pemberton Archer. I don't believe we've met."

"I'm Lillie Lorimer," I said. "I'm the governess."

"A new one! That's luck! Last year's was a pickle. And did not play the organ so far as I know."

"Well you see, Mr. Archer, I thought I might teach the children to play—" Then I began to laugh, for the twinkle in his eye was infectious. "You certainly did give me a start."

"I dare say. I have a dreadful habit of taking shortcuts around here. I'm forever startling someone that way. Actually, I only meant to stop by and say hello to Eleanor."

"Oh, well, Mrs. Caldwell isn't expected until late this afternoon. The staff came this morning," I explained.

"Good. It gives me time to get acquainted with you." There was sincerity as well as humor in his voice. I thought he was the most likable person I had ever met.

"Here," he said. "Let me remove a bit of the mystery. Do you see this?" He pointed to a rosette carved into the paneling beside the organ. "Push on it."

Hesitantly, I touched the rosette, then gave it a firm push. The panel slid aside, revealing a dark, narrow stairway that disappeared downward behind the wall to the left. Another touch of the rosette and the panel slid shut.

"There's a corresponding lever on the other side, should you ever want to open or close it from inside. However, I don't advise exploring in there.

It's extremely easy to get lost if you don't know the passages."

"So I should imagine," I said. "In any case, I have no desire to attempt it. I shudder at the very thought."

"Well, if you ever become curious, just give me a shout, and I'll take you on an expedition. I'm quite serious about your not trying it alone."

"I won't," I said firmly. "What I had really meant to do when I came in here was to go out on the piazza and have another look at the Sound."

"I'll go along, if I may."

We stepped onto the piazza, and Pemberton Archer led the way to a grouping of deeply cushioned wicker chairs.

"We can chat here and also have a perfect view. It's a delicious spot," he said.

I gazed out over the water, and then I exclaimed, "Oh, look! The tide is rising."

"It is," he said, "but how did you know it?"

"The Execution Rock is almost out of sight," I said. I was very pleased with my observation.

"Oh, yes, so I see. Who told you about that?"

"Mrs. Morgan," I replied. "A grisly name, Execution Rock. What does it mean?"

"I'm not sure," he said. "Some say it's just that boats used to wreck on it when it was hidden by the high tide before the lighthouse was built. Others say they used to tie criminals to the Rock at low tide and let them slowly drown as the tide rose. That was our favorite version when we were children. We used to play at tying each other up down on the shoreline rocks below Soundcliff. We'd pretend it was Execution Rock, and the person being tied up was supposed to be the criminal we were leaving to drown in slow agony. Rather a frightful game, wasn't it?"

"It certainly was," I agreed. But nothing looked very frightening in the sun-drenched blue world beyond the piazza, not even Execution Rock. Whatever its history, it was now no more than an interesting sight.

We chatted easily, and in minutes, it seemed, we were friends. He asked me how I had come to take the job as governess, and to my amazement, I found myself telling the truth. "I'd rather you didn't say anything to anyone," I added. "One day, when the opportunity arises, I shall confess it myself. But—"

"But you want a chance to prove you can do the job first. Of course you can count on me," he said, and I knew I could.

"Well, you've told me about you. I suppose I owe you a return of the favor," he said at last. "My story isn't nearly as exciting as yours, though. I'm Eleanor's cousin and was Charlotte's cousin, too. She was Jay's first wife, as you may have heard. Our fathers were the three Archer brothers. They were rather famous out here for owning one big estate with three houses on it, one for each of our families. We three cousins grew up very close, in age as well as residence. The Caldwells were our neighbors, and we had our lessons over here with Jay—upstairs in the schoolroom. Have you seen it?" I nodded. "Jay and I and Charlotte and Eleanor were the only children for miles around, so we had to depend on one another. We were the four little ghouls who loved to play 'Execution

Rock' together," he smiled.

A pleasant hour passed as Pemberton Archer and I talked about Long Island, compared England and America, and explored a mutual interest in music. And then, before I knew it, the afternoon had gone by, the shadows had lengthened, and two carriages were rolling up the drive bearing Eleanor Caldwell, Eli Caldwell, the nursemaid Margaret Dobbs, and the children, Marta, Leo, and Bonnie. My true life at Soundcliff had begun.

I devoted that evening to writing the outline of the children's studies that Eleanor Caldwell had requested, and the following morning, dressed for a day of teaching in my plainest gray dress, I knocked at the door of the library and entered at her bidding.

It was a long, narrow room with deep arm chairs placed about a central rectory table. Small oriental rugs lay upon a diamond-patterned parquet floor, and two great brass chandeliers were suspended from the paneled ceiling. Glass-fronted bookcases lined the walls, interrupted by a black marble fireplace centered on one long wall. A great stained glass window divided into three panels took up most of one end of the room, and the sun shining through it cast golden lights over all.

Eleanor Caldwell was seated on a small settee by the window, a ledger book open on her lap, apparently going over some household accounts. She wore a brown and gold plaid silk morning dress, and its close-fitting bodice, puffed sleeves, and full skirt set off her slender figure to perfection. The dark curls that crowned her sleekly upswept hair softened the high forehead and the intense, luminous brown eyes. Once again, I was struck by her aristocratic beauty. Never had my own small stature, blonde hair, and blue eyes seemed to me to constitute a more pallid and less imposing presence. I felt like a small white moth on display under a bell jar beside a monarch butterfly.

"I've brought the study outline you requested, Mrs. Caldwell," I began. "I do hope you approve. I'm very eager to begin working with the children."

She extended one graceful hand, heavily ornamented with rings, and without comment took the small sheaf of papers from me. Once again, as she had done during our interview in New York, she left me to stand awkwardly before her in the center of the rug, and she began to read what I had written, turning the pages slowly, one by one. Then she lowered them to her lap. With the thumb and index finger of one hand she pinched the bridge of her nose and she closed her thick-lashed eyes as if gathering strength for an unpleasant task. I began to tremble, but when she spoke, it was not of my plan but of the children.

"Bonnie is a baby, of course," she said, "but she is already spoiled and over-indulged. She won't learn much but needs structure and discipline." She looked at me sharply, and I nodded the acquiescence she seemed to be waiting for—although, I thought privately, a three-year-old must surely need love quite as much as discipline.

"Leo is too timid. I doubt you can do much about that. Unfortunately, a man's influence is lacking in his upbringing." I was startled by this naked reference to Jay Caldwell's absence, but I said, "I shall do my best, of course."

"Marta is very nearly beyond hope," she sighed. "Stubborn and rebellious and ill-mannered. Her interest in books is, at present, overshadowed by her interest in various young men. She is rather too precocious in that respect. She needs to be curbed."

"She is a very beautiful child," I offered, feeling some need to intercede for Marta.

"Beauty is skin deep," Eleanor Caldwell said flatly and with evident displeasure at my impertinence. "I'd like to see some character developed there."

I must not have hidden my distress, for she added, "Please don't think I'm 'down' on Marta because she is not my own daughter. It just so happens that she is a difficult child. You'll see."

I was surprised, and I berated myself for not having put the facts together myself. I had known that Jay Caldwell's first wife had died about ten years earlier. Marta being fourteen would, of course, be Charlotte's child, while Leo and Bonnie were Eleanor's.

Abruptly, Eleanor Caldwell handed me back my outline. "This plan will do as well as any other, I suppose. I leave it to you. I have nothing to do with it anyway."

With this incomprehensible remark, I was dismissed. I had come downstairs full of eager anticipation. I left the library depressed and uncertain. What did she expect of me? She seemed to have no confidence in either the children or me. And I simply could not fathom the statement that she had "nothing to do with it anyway." She had hired me, hadn't she? It was like a Chinese puzzle that one cannot solve no matter how one turns it over.

I decided to have some tea before going up to the schoolroom where I had asked Margaret Dobbs to bring the children at ten o'clock. We would start at nine thereafter, but I had anticipated a longer conversation with their mother this morning.

Ada left me to my own thoughts over my tea, being busy with her own tasks. The tea did steady my nerves and helped to put the unpleasant library scene into perspective. Mrs. Caldwell had warned me not to think that she was down on Marta because Marta was not her own child. There was some truth in that, I thought, because her remarks about Bonnie and Leo had seemed almost equally unloving. I got up from the table having concluded that Eleanor Caldwell's unhappy relationship with and separation from her husband were responsible for her sour mood and harsh words, and I renewed my resolve to create an island of peace and happiness for the children.

In the hallway I noticed the little elevator, and prompted by a mood of mild defiance as well as by my refreshed eagerness to be at my job, I decided to take a quick ride to the third floor. I stepped in, but to my surprise, the elevator began to ascend before I could touch the lever, and it stopped at the second floor. As the doors opened, I was highly embarrassed to find myself face to face with old Eli Caldwell, obviously on his way down to breakfast.

"Oh, Mr. Caldwell," I exclaimed. "I'm sorry to have borrowed your elevator. I shall walk on up." I took a step toward the door, but Mr. Caldwell stopped me with a gesture. He got in beside me and moved the lever to the third floor position.

"Not often I get to escort a pretty lady any more." He spoke with some difficulty, but his eyes danced, and I couldn't help smiling. He held open the door for me at the third floor. "I want to talk to you some day," he said as the doors closed between us. I watched the elevator sink past the iron gates. Then I turned away toward the schoolroom.

I was seated at my desk at ten o'clock when Margaret Dobbs threw open the door. "Here they are!" she announced briskly. "Wide awake and ready to learn!" And she left us.

Leo and Marta hung back shyly, but Bonnie ran to me, beaming. I didn't see what she was carrying until she plunked the little ball of tri-colored fur into my lap. "Look at Ginger. 'Member? You helped me find her."

Ginger purred as I scratched around her ears. Then she stretched and flipped up her tail as I stroked her back. "Hello, Ginger," I said. "What a treat to see you again. I wondered what was to become of you."

"Geoffrey sended her with the bags," said Bonnie, leaning both elbows on my knees and staring into Ginger's green eyes. Then she looked up at me. "Can she stay? Marta said you'd say no."

I looked at Marta and Leo, wanting to include

them in the momentous decision. "What do you think? Shall we have Ginger as our schoolroom mascot?"

"Yes, Ma'am," said Leo enthusiastically.

I turned to Marta who had not spoken. "Marta?" I said. "What is your vote?"

"Yes," she said softly, then, moving toward me, "Bonnie can play with her. She's too little to do lessons all day."

"Ah, that's an excellent reason," I smiled. "I vote for Ginger, too. I'm sure she can behave herself here."

"Maybe she'll learn to read," said Leo. It was my first glimpse of his gentle and endearing sense of humor.

Bless Ginger. She was our ice-breaker. We wasted some minutes making arrangements for her. Bonnie and I fixed a cushion for her on a windowsill. Leo fashioned a cardboard mouse and suspended it from a bit of yarn for her to play with. And Marta asked permission to leave the room, returning shortly with a piece of an old rug that we fastened to a corner of my desk for Ginger to pluck at. We laughed when she tried out each of our devices in turn, taking a few swats at the mouse, sharpening her claws on the rug, then leaping onto the sill and curling up on the cushion. She looked at us as if to say, "There. Are you satisfied?" And after giving her forepaws a few brisk licks, she promptly fell asleep.

By this time the children and I were on the best of terms. I started Bonnie with some alphabet blocks and Leo with a storybook passage to prepare to read aloud while Marta and I discussed how far she had progressed in various subjects with previous governesses and tutors. She glowed when I asked if she would like to learn to play the organ.

I don't know if heaven meant me to be a teacher. I can only say that it was pure joy from the first moment, and day after day I found myself amazed at the progress each child made.

Bonnie was indeed a baby, but it was the only observation Eleanor Caldwell had made that struck me as true. After all, at three one is supposed to be a baby, and Bonnie was simply charming, never undisciplined or demanding. Through the games I set for her she quickly learned her colors, numbers, and letters, and when she sat in my lap while I read her her daily story, her eyes followed the lines of print so exactly that I was certain she was on the verge of reading.

Leo was not timid in the classroom. He was so bright and quick I was hard pressed to keep him busy and challenged, and I had no difficulty imagining him one day managing the Caldwell fortune and businesses. And he could always make me laugh.

Marta was almost as facile at her studies as Leo. She obediently completed each assignment neatly, carefully, and correctly. But she seemed distracted and rather sad. I often heard her sighing softly. She seemed relatively happy only when, with her mother's permission, I began to teach her to play the organ for which she had a natural talent.

The weeks flew by, and I became so absorbed in

Marta, Leo, and Bonnie, the happy schoolroom hours, and the beauty of my surroundings that I nearly forgot my curiosity about the adult Caldwells. But one May Saturday when the children were taking their sailing lesson and Eleanor Caldwell was away from the house—as she so often was—I decided to write some letters. As I climbed the stairs from the entrance hall to my room, I paused on the second floor landing, and I was seized with the sudden notion of looking about the family quarters—just the corridors, of course, with perhaps a quick glance through any door that might have been left ajar.

I left the landing and took several tentative steps down the corridor to a corner where another hallway led off to the west wing. As I had hoped, one of the doors along the hall was open. I hesitated, then walked quickly to the open doorway and looked in, expecting to find an elegant boudoir or sitting room.

Instead, I was shocked to find a room almost entirely taken up with an electrified model railroad, the complex of miniature tracks and facilities laid out on custom-made platforms about thirty inches high. Old Mr. Caldwell sat on a stool in the midst of the maze. Before him was a small bank of levers and buttons that controlled the passage of three tiny trains over bridges and through tunnels and past fairy tale towns and stations. At the crossings, little gates went down and up with a flashing of red lights and a clanging of bells whenever a train passed by.

"Come and see my railroad," he said without

looking up, and I jumped, for I did not know that he had seen me, and I had been on the verge of slipping silently away. Instead, I entered the room.

"Good afternoon, Mr. Caldwell. I— I'm sorry to intrude."

"Not at all," he responded. "I don't get a chance to show this off very often. Watch the roundhouse." He pointed to the middle of an intricate rail yard and began to manipulate a set of switches. A tiny engine uncoupled from its train, chugged into the roundhouse, rotated on the little turntable, chugged back out, and recoupled to the other end of the train. "Not as much fun as the stock market, but I've turned all that over to Jay, and this has its own fascination. Although I like putting it together more than running it." He laughed. "My life story."

His speech was only slightly slurred that afternoon, and I soon found that it was worth the modicum of patience required to listen to him. His impediment no more prevented him from saying exactly what he wished to say than any other obstacle had ever impeded him from accomplishing what he set out to accomplish.

"So you are a model railroad enthusiast," I remarked, not knowing how to react to the unusual sight of one of the most powerful financiers of the nineteenth century playing with an elaborate child's toy.

"It passes the time. And it reminds me," he said.

"Of the railroads you built?"

"Bought, mostly," he corrected me. He threw a master switch that brought all three trains back into the central yard, then turned off the power and nodded me toward a comfortable chair by the open windows. I sat down, and he took a chair opposite me.

"I didn't start with railroads," he said. "I started in a store. Just worked there, clerking. Man that owned it ran it into the ground. I had some savings, bought it for beans, built it up. I was nineteen years old. Then I started lending some money here and there, and in those days that's how some people got to be bankers. I was sharper and tougher than most, and I got rich. Started buying railroads."

He leaned back, becoming absorbed in his story. I said nothing. I wanted to hear it.

"I could see where the railroads ought to go, where the land needed opening up and would prosper and pump money back into the railroads. I made a bundle in the rate wars. I could always hold out lower and longer than the others—I stayed liquid enough for that—and when they'd go under, I'd buy 'em up. They used to accuse me of stock manipulation." He chuckled as if unable to suppress his enjoyment of a wicked past. "Well, I won't deny pumping up a few issues. I won't deny selling short a time or two."

"Do you know," I said, leaning forward, "I always imagined that making money was a sort of enormous game to powerful men like you, and I believe I was right!" I stopped short. What an audacious thing to say! I was taken aback at my own temerity.

But old Mr. Caldwell was not in the least

offended. He seemed flattered, rather. "Best game there ever was." He slapped the arm of his chair for emphasis. "And I was one of the great players!"

He smiled broadly and closed his eyes briefly as if reminiscing. This time I kept still, and before long he went on. "I wasn't really a railroader, though, not me. I liked buying 'em and selling 'em. Never cared for running 'em, but I hired good managers. Only railroad I ever built myself was the LIH&M, and I had a purpose for that."

"To help the slaves escape," I said.

"You know about that, eh? Nellie Morgan been telling you the family history?"

"A bit."

"Nobody ought to own anybody else. You agree with that?"

"Absolutely," I replied.

"Good. That's what I believed. Especially after that book *Uncle Tom's Cabin* come out. You ever read that?"

"No, but I've heard of it."

"Well, I was against slavery before, but after I read that book—well, I had to help those poor people. So I built a railroad to transport 'em out to Long Island, and I built a house to hide 'em in. And we'd put 'em on boats at night and sail 'em out through the Sound and up to Canada. Never lost a one. We only really came close a few times, especially right after that dratted Dred Scott case."

"Dred Scott?"

"He was a slave that escaped into free territory, and the Supreme Court ruled that that didn't make him free. He was still a piece of property in the eyes of the law. Well after that, some of these slave owners got a lot more radical about hunting their escaped 'property.' The bounty hunters'd turn up with a warrant and search the place. Pretty soon it got to be known that Soundcliff had all these passages behind the walls, so I'd smile and let 'em into the passages and then, after they got good and lost in there, I'd have to go in and lead 'em out again."

"And they didn't find anyone?"

"Nope. Half the time we didn't have any slaves here when they came anyhow. And if we did, we hid 'em well in secret rooms they couldn't find even if they passed 'em right by. But we did have one close call once."

Eli Caldwell began to tell me about a slave couple named Joe and Effie—they had refused to reveal their surname which, being the name of their former owner, they wished to abandon in their new life—and their children Mary, who was about fourteen, and Zeb, a little boy. Zeb had contracted a fever during the journey to the North and would cry out in his delirium. Eli himself, one night, led the family along the lower passageways toward the rocks and the dock where a boat had been made ready for them. At a certain moment, however, the boat boy ran into the passage from the rocks and met the small party, halting them with wild gestures and gasping words. Bounty hunters had arrived at the dock and were probably following him into the passageway.

"We were in luck, though," Eli related. "We were standing just next to one of the secret rooms, the only one that's in that lower passage down by the rocks. I pulled the lever and the four of 'em slipped inside. I slid the panel shut—I had to leave 'em in there with no light—and the panel had no sooner closed behind 'em than a small troop of bounty hunters came thundering up the passageway. I met 'em and denied having any escaped slaves on the premises, of course. One of 'em handed me a broadside describing a list of slaves escaped from various plantations down on the Maryland shore. Joe and Effie and Mary and Zeb were among 'em, and to this day, though I know the name of their owner from reading it on that list, I won't say the name to anyone. Might be bad luck some way.

"Well, those fellows went up and down through the passageways all night, but they never found that room. I had to keep rescuing one or another of 'em from the cul de sacs. I think they lost interest in the slaves after a while and were just like children, fascinated with the passageways. Along toward dawn while they were all out by the stable end of the passageways, I sent Nellie Morgan down there with some food for the little family. She was just a young 'un then, a kitchen maid. But I always liked her and trusted her. I'd taught her the passageways and assigned her to keeping 'em clean, which she still does to this day.

"So Nellie brought food down to 'em—scared 'em half to death when she opened the panel, I guess. She said they'd been sitting there in the dark all night listening to the footsteps outside and expecting to be found any minute. And poor Effie had been sitting there all night holding little Zeb with her hand over his mouth to keep him from crying out in his fever. Thank God the fever had broken and he was awake and could eat some of the food Nellie brought 'em.

"Well, we kept 'em there another week after the bounty hunters had left, just to be on the safe side. There was a nice little set of furniture in there, a big bed and a chest and a chair and so on, and of course we gave 'em candles and blankets and food and it wasn't so bad except for the waiting, I suppose. And then we took 'em out to the boat one night and got 'em safe away."

"How wonderful," I said admiringly.

"Well, I won't pretend all my reasons for building Soundcliff and the LIH&M were so noble," Eli smiled. "I wanted a house out here and a railroad to get me to it. So I just killed the two birds with one stone, so to speak. Used to like going out to Montauk Point at the end of the island. Used to go out on boats with the fishermen. So I ran the railroad all the way out there, too. Picked up some revenue from the Long Island farmers shipping their produce to New York. I figured as the population grew, the LIH&M would be there to capitalize on it, and so it's turned out. Well—so what? If I can do some good and suit myself and turn a profit all at the same time, why not?"

"And did the railroad always extend up to Albany?" I asked, eager to learn more.

"Schenectady. That's a mite north of Albany. And no, not at first, it didn't. At first there was just the Long Island part and the ferry to New York City. It was just the LI&NY then. After the war was over, though, a lot of little lines upstate started merging with one another, and I could see that pretty soon there'd be a big railroad running west to Ohio or farther, and I'd be well off to hook up with it. So I floated some bonds and bought up some right-of-way and ran my line up the Hudson and over to the Mohawk River at Schenectady. And that's where I ran smack into Gus Flammon."

"*August* Flammon?"

"The same. Where he came from I didn't know. One day I'd never heard of him. The next day, he'd bought up all those little western New York lines and formed the Empire State Railroad—biggest goldurned railroad in America at that time. He ran it all the way to Chicago before you could say Jack Robinson. But his eastern terminus was at Albany, and to get his goods to New York City he had to transship 'em down the Hudson on barges. Naturally, he wanted to buy the LIH&M to complete the line. I wouldn't let 'im. Heck! I wanted to buy *his* railroad!" He laughed. "He was younger than me, but he was my equal, Gus was. I went around him. Bought western roads, southern roads. Never could get my hands on his Empire State."

"Then you admire him," I remarked.

His eyes turned cold. "I did once, I guess."

"Someone said it's because of Mr. Flammon that there's no tunnel for the LIH&M between here and New York," I pressed.

"That's the least of what Gus Flammon did to me. But the story of the tunnel is that I didn't want to build one till we linked up with a line to the West. Otherwise, such a small operation wouldn't have warranted the capital outlay. When I ran into Flammon up at Albany and Schenectady, I was stopped. Then after Flammon got his grip on my LIH&M, he wouldn't let the tunnel be built. He used to say, 'What for? To give Eli and Harry a nice ride to Soundcliff?'"

"Mr. Flammon owns the LIH&M? I thought it belonged to Jay—to the Caldwells."

"He doesn't own it, but he has enough shares and enough cronies on the board to block anything he wants to." He gave me a sharp look. "Are you sure you're interested in all this?"

"Oh, yes," I replied.

"Well," he said, "what happened was that we were at a standoff. I couldn't buy into the Empire State, but I wouldn't let Gus buy into the LIH&M either. Then in '73 I got sick—had my first stroke—and on top of that came the big financial panic. Everybody was in trouble. Railroads folded left and right. Only a few held up and continued to make a profit. The Pennsylvania was one. The Empire State was another.

"I was in a hospital bed, and my son Harry wouldn't tell me anything. So I finally got hold of Jay. He was only about eleven then, but he was the only one I could talk to. And I said, 'If you don't tell me what's going on I'll have another stroke.' So Jay told me. The LIH&M was going under. The stock was about half value or less, and guess who was buying it up?"

"August Flammon."

"You guessed it. He was ready to pick over my carcass, but I wasn't quite dead yet. I used Jay to carry my orders out of the hospital to my boys, and I liquidated this and that and bought up all the outstanding LIH&M stock I could get my hands on. The price went up and Flammon couldn't raise enough to finish me off. He had a majority of the common stock, but I held onto a majority of the preferred. I was still chairman, and Flammon couldn't swing enough votes to throw me out."

"So you won."

"Only temporarily. I was really too sick to make a big comeback. It takes strength to outmaneuver a hyena like Gus Flammon, and I didn't have it. I just held on—stood still—kept the chairmanship. But the LIH&M was going downhill. I could see it. The management was poor, and I couldn't stay on top of it. I put Harry in charge for awhile, but he was worse. Harry just wasn't a good businessman.

"Then in '79 I had another stroke—the big one. This time I lost my speech almost entirely, and my legs were gone. It took years to recover as much as I have. At that time, the only thing I had the presence of mind to do was to resign and to get Harry voted into my seat on the board, and I still had enough power to get him elected chairman, too. I guess they felt they owed me that much. Well, inside of one year, poor Harry had made a botch of it. Flammon was gaining strength on the board, and he could have dumped us out pretty easy in a short time. Now, I would have understood that—I'd done it myself to others. But then Flammon did an unforgivable thing—" His voice trailed off.

"What did Mr. Flammon do?" I prompted gently.

"He insulted us publicly," Eli Caldwell said as if from the distance of years. "I didn't mind for myself. I've been called worse. But poor Harry. He was—crushed. Like a puppy. You see, one day at the Union Club, Harry comes into a room where Flammon is sitting with a big group. Flammon looks up and sees Harry and laughs. 'Well,' he says, 'if it isn't Harry Caldwell the railroad tycoon' —sarcastically, see. And Harry says, 'Well, you can laugh, Gus, but I'm still chairman of the LIH&M,' and Flammon says, 'Not for long, because you're a boob and your father is decrepit, and I'm going to take the LIH&M from the two of you.'

"Right there in the Union Club he called Harry a boob. Poor Harry never knew how to come back at something like that. He came home and sat down and got very depressed, because he could see the handwriting on the wall. He knew that Flammon would take the railroad and then he'd be *proved* a boob and he'd never live down the insult or the defeat. Pretty soon, Harry got himself and his wife drowned out here on the Sound."

"How dreadful," I said softly.

"Harry was a sweet fellow. I should never have put him in that position. I think he would have lived if I'd let him go his own way, just be an idle rich boy like so many others of his generation. He would have been all right like that." Eli Caldwell sighed heavily, a sigh sadder than tears. "So then I looked around, and there was only one person left to lean on, and that was Jay, my grandson, and he was only eighteen."

He smiled slowly. "I should have known Jay would have it. Jay and I were close from the time he was a baby. He's like me. Well, not exactly like me. Jay has different dreams. But he has my ability to turn a dollar, my love of the game." He gave me a nod. "I should have remembered what a job he did at age eleven helping me hang onto the LIH&M during the panic. He'd been just a messenger boy for me then, but a darned smart one. When Harry died, even though Jay was just eighteen, I had to hand all my business over to him, and he stepped right in and took over like a grownup. Jay actually talked the board into electing me again to Harry's place on the board, although Flammon got one of his henchmen voted in as chairman. I sat there for three years with Jay doing all the work for me, and when Jay turned twenty-one, I resigned and Jay was elected, and in about six months he was able to swing a couple of votes, throw out Flammon's man, and get himself elected chairman. It's true, the LIH&M is small potatoes as railroads go, but he was the youngest railroad chairman in America.

"Meanwhile, I decided I was going to live a long time, and I was crazy to make Jay wait till I died to be the head of the Caldwell family. I signed everything over to him, lock, stock, and barrel, and it's the smartest thing I ever did. He took off like a firecracker—not only built the fortune back to where it was before I got sick but doubled it.

"But there's one thing Jay hasn't done yet that

I'm waiting for."

"What's that?"

"Shove Gus Flammon out of our railroad altogether. The LIH&M is just a small corner of Jay's enterprises, but it would satisfy me to see him buy up every share of the LIH&M that Gus Flammon still has. To avenge his father if not me."

"Perhaps he will, one day."

"Maybe. If he puts his mind to it. You know, Jay could go far beyond me. He's got something I never had. I was a manipulator. Jay is a builder. But there's one thing Jay needs, and until he has it, he won't fulfill his destiny." He paused, then gave me a look I couldn't decipher. "He needs a woman, a wife, a helpmate."

I blushed deeply. "But surely—" I protested.

"I know, I know. He's married. Been married twice. Not necessarily the same thing, is it?"

"But sometimes these difficulties can be worked out," I offered. "Perhaps Mr. and Mrs. Caldwell will reconcile."

"Huh!" snapped Eli Caldwell. "I'd rather see Jay reconcile with a rattlesnake."

FIVE

A warm ray of morning sun slid across my face and woke me early. In nightdress and bare feet, I padded to the windows and swung them outward. The May sweetness rushed in to meet me.

I dressed hastily, took a roll and coffee in the kitchen, and then it was out onto the grounds for a stroll among the flower beds. The lawn rolled away like green plush toward the woods. Beyond the cliff stretched the sparkling waters, jade green among the rocks, turquoise and silver beyond. The sky was a cloudless blue ether.

I made a game of selecting a favorite among the varieties of early blooms. Having chosen the peonies with their huge, nodding double-petaled heads of pure white, tender pink, and dusky rose, I looked out over the cliff and saw a small sloop gliding in toward the Caldwell dock.

At that moment, Marta appeared on the piazza and waved toward the dock and the boat, now hidden from my view below the lip of the cliff. She hurried from the piazza to the cliff's edge where a young man, having climbed the wooden steps from the dock, soon appeared. As he came level with Marta, she stepped back bashfully. The young man had been carrying a jacket which he now shrugged on over a spotless white shirt and sharply creased flannels. Then he took Marta's elbow with more than a hint of possessiveness and walked her back to the piazza. But even from the distance of the peony hedge, I could see that their faces were rather more serious than one might expect the faces of two young people to be on a fine May morning.

I was immediately aware that Marta should not be left unchaperoned with a stranger—a stranger to me, at least. I crossed the grass to the piazza, and as I came up the steps, Marta turned toward me with a startled and worried expression that dissolved into a radiant smile when she saw that it was I. In her first look, I had recognized the nervous expression that was habitually hers when her stepmother was present.

"Oh, Miss Lorimer," she beamed. "I'd like you to meet our neighbor Jack Van Dyne. Jack, this is Miss Lorimer, the children's governess."

I believe I successfully hid my amusement at Marta's small subterfuge in separating herself from "the children" who still needed a governess. I wondered if Jack Van Dyne, a man of at least twenty, knew that Marta was only fourteen. For the first time, I realized that her figure was quite womanly; and she looked so fresh and pretty in a tiny-waisted white lawn dress, its eyelet bodice threaded with pale green ribbons and a ribbon of the same shade catching her fine, long auburn hair back from her face, that my mood turned swiftly from amusement to mild alarm. Never mind Marta's youth: the shy, happy, furtively fond glances they bestowed on one another proclaimed romance.

"I've come to invite Marta to the party my parents are giving for me on Saturday," Jack explained.

Marta flushed. "I hope Mother will say yes. You see," she told me earnestly, "it's a farewell party. Jack's off to the army next week."

"The cavalry. I'm joining Lieutenant Colonel Roosevelt's Rough Riders He's been a close friend of my father's for years. In fact, I may have a time remembering to call him 'sir' instead of 'Uncle Ted,'" he laughed charmingly.

"Oh, Jack, don't joke," Marta protested. "You'll be going to Cuba soon, I'm sure of it."

"Right-oh. I hope so," Jack declared. "And we'll mop 'em up in short order and be right back home again!"

Marta moaned and inclined her head in the direction of Jack's shoulder but straightened with a snap as Eleanor Caldwell stepped onto the piazza.

"Mother—" Marta began but got no further. Eleanor's voice sliced through the warm morning air like cold steel.

"Jack, I have told Marta and I will now tell you, you are not to see one another at all, ever. I must ask you to leave at once." Shock waves seemed to radiate across the piazza.

"But, Mother," Marta's voice was tight with anguish. Her face had gone scarlet. "Jack came especially to ask you—"

"I have eyes. I can see why he's here. Now march yourself inside, young lady, or I'll march you in on the end of a switch."

Marta gasped. Tears of humiliation filled her eyes, and she whirled and ran into the house. Eleanor then crossed her arms and pursed her lips at Jack Van Dyne. "There are laws against what you're trying to do, young man. Marta is a minor. Now get out."

Jack maintained a certain cool dignity that I admired under the circumstances.

"I would never try to harm Marta, Mrs. Caldwell." He turned to me. "I'm glad to have met you, Miss Lorimer. Please tell Marta I'm sorry I caused her trouble." He turned, strode from the piazza, and vanished down the cliffside steps.

"I'm sorry," I said to Eleanor Caldwell. "I thought he was a friend of the family. Nothing happened—"

"Please," she interrupted. "Marta is your charge, and I warned you about her forwardness with young men. I hold you responsible. Keep her on a tight leash, and never permit Jack Van Dyne to get near her again. He's six years older than she is."

"I don't think you need worry about that," I said with an edge to my voice that I immediately regretted. "He's going into the army next week."

She glared at me. "Keep a civil tongue, Miss Lorimer." And she stalked into the house.

The joyful morning lay shattered at my feet. I went inside and for once did not hesitate to take the elevator. I wanted to catch up with Marta as quickly as possible. It would not to do to have her feel abandoned at a time like this.

As I expected, I could hear her sobs as I stepped into the third floor corridor. Leo and Bonnie were standing outside Marta's door, their eyes enormous with anxiety.

"Marta's crying," Leo informed me.

"She won't let us in," said Bonnie.

"Don't worry, darlings." I stooped to give them each a hug. "Marta is a bit upset, but I'm sure she'll be feeling better soon. Suppose we see if she'll let me come in."

I tapped at the door. "It's Miss Lorimer, Marta. May I come in?"

The sobs stopped and the lock scraped open. I turned the knob and went in, closing the door carefully behind me. Marta sat on her bed, her face tear-stained, her hair ribbon bedraggled. She was holding Ginger in her lap and had evidently been crying into the cat's soft fur. The womanly impression she had given on the piazza was gone. She was just a very unhappy little girl. I sat down next to her and took her hand.

"Oh, Miss Lorimer. What must Jack think? He'll never want to see me again, even if he comes home safe."

"He thinks very highly of you, I can tell you," I

said. "He gave me a message for you. He said to say he was sorry he had caused you trouble, and he told your mother he would never try to harm you."

"Oh! That Eleanor! I could *kill* her. She's not my real mother, you know. She makes me call her Mother, but she hates me, and I hate her." The coldness of her voice told me that her feelings were real, but I tried to put a different light on the matter.

"I think perhaps your feelings are normal, Marta. I lost my mother when I was only two, and I never had a stepmother, but I've an idea it's very natural for girls to feel angry at their mothers when they are growing up and longing to try their wings, and their mothers are trying to protect them."

"It's not like that with her and me," said Marta. "I truly hate her. I always have. I think my mother did, too."

"But you were awfully small when your mother was living, weren't you? Can you be sure how she felt? I should think they would have been very close. Didn't they grow up as cousins together?"

"I don't know. I was only four, but I remember my real mother. No one believes I can remember, but I do."

"Well, darling, that was a very long time ago, and hasn't your stepmother been taking care of you now, all these years?"

Marta gave me a look of pure disgust, the kind of look that says, "What can you possibly know about it?" And I decided to take a different approach.

"In any case, she does have a point. Jack seems an awfully nice young man, but he is quite a bit older than you. After all, he is nearly old enough to be married, while you are—well—much too young to think in that way."

"I'll be fifteen in January. That's not so young. And I'd be a lot happier with Jack than with *her!*"

"But, Marta, you wouldn't want to miss your whole girlhood and the parties and dances and the fine times to take on the responsibilities of being a wife and perhaps a mother. I'm sure marriage is a great joy, but it is also a set of very serious, adult obligations—for life. Surely you don't feel ready for that. Would you take such an enormous step just to get away from home?"

"I don't know. It wouldn't be so bad if Daddy were still around. He won't let Eleanor be mean to me. But now he's gone away and left us with her, so I guess he doesn't love us any more." She started to cry again.

"He didn't go away, Marta. He's at your home in New York. He didn't go anywhere. And I'm sure he loves you and doesn't really want to be separated from you."

"Then why did he send us out here with her? Why can't we stay with him?"

"Because children always have to be with their mothers. Fathers can't stay home all day. They have business to attend to."

"She's not home all day. She's hardly ever here. She's always going off somewhere." I just shook my head, for what Marta said was true. Eleanor Caldwell's mysterious and frequent absences from

Soundcliff were the mealtime topic of gossip among the staff. Everyone wondered, but no one knew, where she went, for she would often have Geoffrey drive her out for several hours—Geoffrey who was a footman, not a driver—and Geoffrey would only laugh if asked where he took her.

"And anyway," Marta was going on, "we wouldn't mind Daddy being away during the day. He's always home whenever he can be, and meantime we'd have you and Miss Dobbs and Mrs. Morgan and all the others to take care of us."

"Well, apparently it's not to be just now. But shall we just make the best of it for the time being? And will you come and talk to me when you're feeling bad?"

Marta reached over and hugged me. "Oh, Miss Lorimer. I wish *you* were my mother." So do I, I thought as I hugged her back.

I told Marta that Leo and Bonnie were worried about her, and she gave me permission to let them in. When I left, they were all three seated on the rug at the foot of Marta's bed playing with Ginger.

Yes, Marta looked like a little girl again, but I warned myself not to be fooled. She was growing up, and the depth of her feelings could lead to grave difficulties. I had liked Jack Van Dyne, but I was quite glad that he would be gone for a time.

Suddenly, I was furious, not only with Eleanor Caldwell but with Jay Caldwell as well. A young girl needed her father. How, indeed, could he abandon her? And poor little Bonnie and Leo. What were these people thinking of? Had wealth and its trappings blinded them to the basic values of family life, to the very needs of their children?

I was distressed at the unhappy turn the morning had taken, but I could not know that the day that had come wrapped so deceptively in spring sunlight and color was only beginning its metamorphosis into nightmare.

The children were to have a riding lesson, and so I had the rest of the morning to myself. I had no further appetite for the outdoors, and I thought I would go to my room. I longed for a book to distract my mind from unpleasant thoughts, but the only books I had there were the children's schoolbooks from which I had been preparing lessons.

I walked down the main staircase to the first floor, thinking to find a book in the library; but another door stood open—left ajar by a careless maid, I suppose—and I glimpsed a room, an office whose principal furnishings were bookshelves full of books and an enormous pigeonhole desk upon which rested the first telephone I had ever seen in a private home. It was also the first telephone I had ever seen that was not attached to a wall. It was all of cast bronze, and it stood on its own little pedestal with a round bell on top to talk into and an ear piece resting on a cradle attached to the side. I wandered in to look at the telephone, then began to browse among the books.

There were law books, business texts, history books, books of biography, all handsomely bound in leather and, surprisingly, all looking as if someone had read them rather than merely lined the shelves with them. It had to be Jay Caldwell's personal library. Taken with the desire to know more about the master of Soundcliff and his world, I selected a history of American railroads. I hoped he wouldn't mind if he knew, yet I was worried enough about my unauthorized borrowing to move the remaining books together so the removal wouldn't be noticed and to memorize the spot so I would be able to return the book to its exact place.

I was starting back into the entrance hall when I saw Hans Arnold passing by on his way to the front door. He opened it and admitted a man in his middle fifties, a tall, heavy man with straight, iron-gray hair and thick black eyebrows meeting across the prominent bridge of his nose.

"Good morning, Mr. Flammon," Hans said in a surprised tone.

"Caldwell here?" His voice was nasal, rasping.

"No, sir. Mr. Caldwell is in New York, I believe."

"Oh yeah? Well, he called me over at Foxfield and told me to meet him here."

"He did?" It was Eleanor Caldwell's voice from the stairway, and I shrank back into the office. "That's all right, Hans. I'll entertain Mr. Flammon until Mr. Caldwell arrives."

Hans retired, leaving the front of the house to Eleanor Caldwell, August Flammon, and—unbeknownst to them—me.

"Jay called you? He said he was coming out today?"

"He did. Didn't you know?"

"Do I ever know what Jay is doing?" she said bitterly.

There ensued a silence so long that at last,

thinking they must have gone into the living room and that I could safely flee up the stairs, I poked my head around the doorway. Not ten feet away, partly hidden in the corridor by the stairway, Eleanor Caldwell and August Flammon were holding each other in a passionate embrace. His back was to me, and fortunately for me, her eyes were closed. I was so frightened that I not only stepped back into the office, I retreated all the way back into an alcove between two bookshelves, my arms crossed defensively over the book I had taken.

Now, once again, I heard voices in the entrance hall, but they were unintelligible, muffled by the office walls and bookshelves; so it was several moments before I realized that there were now two male voices rather than a male and a female. One voice was still August Flammon's. The other—a deep, resonant voice—was one I had never heard before, and I realized with a start that the strange voice must belong to Jay Caldwell. I had thought and learned so much about him that it came as a shock to me to realize that I had never heard him speak until now.

The voices drew near, and it was apparent that the two men were coming into the very office in which I stood, ridiculously pressed into an alcove like the guilty servant in a French farce.

I should, of course, have stepped forward, offered a simple explanation and apology, and gone my way, leaving August Flammon to think what he would about what I might have heard or seen. Instead, my fear of the two famous and powerful men and my feeling of foolishness prompted me to press back even more sharply into the alcove. With a soft creak, a panel gave way, and I stumbled backward. Unwittingly, I had stepped into one of Soundcliff's secret passages.

The two men were entering the office. Impossible to explain what I was doing inside the walls. In a panic, I felt along the inner wall where Pemberton Archer had said there would be a lever. I found it, pushed hard, and the panel slid shut. I was plunged into darkness.

Soon, however, my eyes became accustomed enough to the darkness to see light coming through two or three fine cracks in the paneling. I pushed my face close to one of these, and I could just see Jay Caldwell and August Flammon passing in and out of my narrow view as they paced and circled one another in the office beyond. I decided to wait it out. I could feel the lever when I stretched out my hand, and I would just stay put until they had gone and I could spring the latch on the dark prison I had created for myself.

Their voices were as plain as if I had been standing in the room with them:

"Well, why am I here, Caldwell?"

"Not because I crave your company. I have an offer for you."

"Don't waste my time. Get to the point."

"All right. You've been trying to buy up the Springfield and St. Louis—Don't shake your head, Gus. I know it's you. And I know you've run into a stumbling block. Someone else has been buying up shares, and you don't know who it is."

"Won't take me long to find out."

"No need. It's me."

"Hah! I might have known."

"Now, here's the thing, Gus: I have enough to control it, except for one last block of shares, and they'll be mine this afternoon if I pick up that phone. You won't have time to get back to Foxfield before I've done it."

"All right, Caldwell. It's yours. So what?"

"I know you want the S&SL to link up your northern and southern roads. You'd break my neck right now to get it if you thought you could get away with it."

"So far, Caldwell, I'd have spent this morning more profitably looking at a horse I'm thinking of buying. Big red hunter. Gorgeous animal. You'd better say what's on your mind, or I'm on my way right now."

"I'm going to let you have the S&SL. I'll tell you who's willing to sell those controlling shares, and you can call from here if you want them. Or I'll sell you whatever you need of my stock at a very reasonable price, and I'll dispose of the rest carefully so as not to depress it."

"This isn't my birthday, Caldwell, and I know you haven't lost your mind yet, so what's the catch?"

"I want you to sell me your part of the LIH&M. I'll pay twenty per cent above market value and sign a binding agreement of unlimited access and use for Empire State trains. No loss to you or the Empire State, a twenty per cent profit, and the S&SL thrown in."

"How come?"

"Let's just say I think it's time you got your paws off the Caldwell family railroad."

August Flammon broke into a harsh, wheezing laugh. It went on for several moments. He seemed to be genuinely amused.

"Good lord, Caldwell," he rasped. "What are you doing? Nursing old grudges? The LIH&M is just a flyspeck on the wall of the Caldwell empire. It's not worth a fraction of what you're offering."

"Let my reasons be mine. It took me a long time to corner something I knew you wanted. When I heard you were going after the S&SL, I figured that would be as good a bargaining piece as anything I might find. So now, if you want the S&SL, you'll sell out the LIH&M to me."

"No," said August Flammon rather quietly.

"No?" Jay Caldwell said with amazement. "You're saying no, you won't sell your LIH&M stock, not even for the deal I'm offering?"

"That's right."

A pause. "Then that's that," he said evenly. "But just for the record, would you like to tell me why?"

I had a last glimpse of August Flammon heading for the door, followed by Jay Caldwell, and I just caught Flammon's reply.

"Because I don't feel like it."

A moment of silence was interrupted by a small click that I soon realized was the sound of Jay Caldwell picking up the telephone receiver.

"Give me New York 7419." Then, "Robert, Jay Caldwell. . . . Buy it." Another click, then silence. A very long silence.

Had he gone out? I couldn't tell. But after what seemed to me to have been about a quarter of an hour, I could stand it no longer. I felt I was suffocating in a tomb, and I had heard not a creak, a sigh, nor a shuffle from the office. With my blood pounding at my temples, I reached for the lever and pressed it. The panel slid back, and I blinked as I stepped out into the sunlit room.

"Great Scott!" boomed Jay Caldwell; my vision cleared, and I saw him seated at the pigeonhole desk. "What are you doing here?"

Panic had been coiled inside me like a spring, and the sheer fright of Jay Caldwell's stern voice unleashed it. I screamed, which frightened me further, and then irrational words poured out.

"And what prompted you to turn up here today, Mr. Caldwell? A business deal? Is that all that stirs you? trains and—and money? Your children need you. Your daughter Marta is miserable and may even do something rash. And what are you doing? Making deals! And money! They *have* money, Mr. Caldwell. They *need* their father!"

I burst into tears and ran—out the door, across the enormous hallway, and up two flights of stairs to my room. I slammed and locked my door and threw myself on my bed while thoughts and feelings tumbled like a kaleidoscope in my head. Desperately, I tried to justify what I had just done. Too much had happened to me in too short a time, I told myself—my father dead, my uncle dead, on my own for the first time in my life, plunged into this unhappy household where children were bruised and neglected by self-centered adults concerned only with money, power, and illicit romance. Anyone's composure might have snapped under the circumstances.

Yet, how could I have acted that way to Jay Caldwell? I needed this job, and I wanted it. How could I bear to be separated from Bonnie, Leo, and Marta? They needed me, and I needed them. Oh, I had ruined it, ruined it. My very first personal encounter with the master of the house, and I had flung wild accusations and abuse at him. I had actually screamed and cried. What a ninny I was after all, what a stupid, incompetent ninny. I had begun—just begun—to think that I could take care of myself. But I had failed.

It was surely only a matter of moments before I would be summoned and fired by Jay Caldwell, or perhaps by Eleanor Caldwell who, after all, had hired me. She was angry with me anyway—never mind how I felt about her after my shocking discovery of her embrace with August Flammon. Now, perhaps, Jay Caldwell would tell her about my outburst and she would send for me and order me to leave.

I waited for the inevitable, and meanwhile I cried and cried, unaware that I still held Jay Caldwell's book pressed to my breast.

SIX

My sobs subsided and I sat up. I began to feel more silly than afraid. Time had passed and no one had sent for me. What on earth had I been crying about? Here I was, years Marta's senior and crying harder and for less cause than she had.

I put Jay Caldwell's book on my bedside table and went into my private bath to wash my face. I had begun to feel better, if still too ashamed to face anyone.

At my dressing table, I unpinned my hair, brushed it, and took my time piling it on top of my head and repinning it neatly. Then I took the book and moved the upholstered chair nearer the open windows where a mild salt breeze now freshened the air, and I began to read. Before long, I was absorbed in the intricate history of American railroads and the men who had built them.

Numerous references to Eli Caldwell and, later, to Harry Caldwell and August Flammon riveted my attention to page after page of detail that might, to another reader, have seemed dry and boring.

The afternoon passed quickly, and I was surprised when a chill in the air caused me to look up and note that evening was drawing on. I pressed the stem of my pendant watch and the cover opened to reveal that it was suppertime. I was ravenous, I realized. I had completely forgotten lunch in the chaos of the day.

I glanced into the mirror. All signs of my weeping had disappeared, and I looked calm and presentable. I unlocked my door and descended the back stairs to the kitchen.

I was quiet and distracted during Ada's excellent supper, for I still felt unsettled. But the others paid no attention to me. They were all abuzz about Jay Caldwell's return to Soundcliff.

"Is he going to stay?" Susan Sayre asked.

"Mrs. Caldwell says he's going to be making the arrangements for the Fourth of July party, so it sounds like he's going to be around, doesn't it?" Nancy declared.

"But didn't he go back to 577 this morning?" Ada asked.

"He went back to get his things, and Mrs. Caldwell says he'll come back to Soundcliff tonight."

"Did they make up, then? Are they really back together?" Susan asked.

"I wouldn't go so far as to say that," Nancy smirked. "Why do you think Nellie had the girls making up the red room for Mr. Caldwell?"

"That doesn't mean anything. Maybe Mr. Caldwell just likes privacy," Susan said. Geoffrey Hand guffawed and the others laughed, too. "Well, the red room is right behind her room, and there's a door between, isn't there?" Susan demanded, flushing.

"With the lock on *his* side," Nancy snickered.

"That will be enough of that kind of talk now," snapped Nellie Morgan.

I said nothing, but a vivid image of the location of the red room had fixed itself in my mind. From Susan's description, Jay Caldwell's bedroom was directly below mine. I could not have said why I found the idea so unnerving.

After supper, I noticed that the piazza was unoccupied, and I walked out onto it and gazed out over the Sound. The evening sky was silvering, lights glimmered from estates ringing the shoreline, the Execution Rock light blinked round and round, and a single bright star glittered off the point of a fingernail moon. The soft, clear purity of a perfect spring evening came close to restoring the happiness I had felt at the day's start, and with a long sigh, I stepped back into the house, feeling once again at peace.

But as I crossed the entrance hall toward the staircase, I was startled to hear an angry female voice coming from Jay Caldwell's office: "Get out of here, you nasty little beast!" A flash of bawling fur issued from the office. It was Ginger, ears laid back, tail fluffed and rigid as a cactus. Close behind came Eleanor Caldwell, swatting at her with a sheaf of papers.

"You!" she cried, catching sight of me. "Catch that wretched creature and get her away from me. I detest cats!"

There was no need to catch Ginger: she had caught me, in a manner of speaking. Having leaped from the floor onto my shoulder, she dug her sharp little claws into my flesh through the fabric of my dress. I put one hand softly over Ginger's back and stroked her head with the other, talking to her as sweetly as I could while carrying her up the stairs. Eventually, she retracted her claws, and I was able to lift her off my shoulder and nestle her in my arms.

My scratched shoulder bothered me not a bit. I was thrilled, for Eleanor Caldwell had merely ordered me to take Ginger; she had not ordered me to pack my things and leave Soundcliff. I was so pleased, in fact, that I failed to wonder what she had been doing in her husband's office.

It was difficult to get the children to concentrate on their lessons the next morning. They knew their father was at Soundcliff, but they had not yet seen him, for he had returned from New York very late the night before.

At about ten o'clock, the schoolroom door opened, and there he was. Bonnie squealed and flew across the room to throw her arms about him. He laid his hand—a broad, strong hand—gently upon her head and with his thumb he smoothed the tendrils of hair at her forehead.

Leo came to him more shyly as if, being older, he

intended to be more dignified. But his sweet little face was alight. His father held out his free arm and circled Leo in a fierce hug. Then he stooped down and kissed each of them.

Marta watched her father intently but did not go to him. Her hurt at the long separation was written on her face. Then, her father's eyes met Marta's over the heads of the little ones, and a ray of purest love burned through the air between them.

"Oh, Daddy." Her voice broke, and he came to her and folded her into his arms and kissed her hair. "Sweetheart, sweetheart. Have you had a bad time?" She nodded her head dumbly against his shoulder. "Never mind. Never mind. We'll fix it all up."

He pulled a white handkerchief from his pocket and wiped away Marta's tears, and then he said briskly, "Well, I didn't mean to make such an entrance." He looked at me. "As you see, I decided to follow your advice, Miss Lorimer."

The rest of the morning passed swiftly. One by one, the children showed him their books and papers, and he reviewed with them in detail what they had been learning. Nearly two hours had passed when he got up and said, "I'm pleased with your progress—all of you. Now, I am lunching with your mother today. And Miss Lorimer," he turned to me, "at about one o'clock I would like to meet you here for a private discussion. Perhaps the children can have a holiday this afternoon."

"Of course, Mr. Caldwell." I had been relaxed, believing that he was indeed pleased with the children's work. His request for a private conference threw me into a state of panic again. Perhaps he had told the children that he was pleased but really was not. Perhaps he had been truly angry with me yesterday and would now ask me to go.

I was far too nervous to eat lunch and spent the hour in my room; but this time, at least, I did not disgrace myself by crying. It was not my habit to change my clothing in midday, but now I bathed and put on my nicest embroidered-eyelet camisole and petticoat and a crisp lilac-and-white-striped chambray dress I had been saving for a special occasion. I took particular pains with my hair. At one o'clock, I went into the schoolroom and was surprised to find Jay Caldwell already there.

With the children no longer in the room, I saw him suddenly not as a father but as a man. He was casually dressed in light linen trousers belted snugly across a flat waist, and a dark blue shirt with rolled-up sleeves and open collar revealed strong, tanned arms and a vee of masculine throat and chest. I have to admit that my heart fluttered from more than fear. Jay Caldwell was an excitingly handsome man. Perhaps, I thought fleetingly, Eleanor Caldwell's jealousy might be warranted.

I had so steeled myself for an unpleasant confrontation that I was surprised when he began very simply to talk about the children's school work. He was happy with Bonnie's quickness. Did I agree that she was precocious? I could not reveal that I had never taught before and had no way to compare Bonnie with other children her age.

Anyway, I did think she was exceptionally bright, and I told him so.

Leo's mathematical skills were impressive. He would need them if he were to take over the family businesses one day. He seemed also to read very well. But was he, perhaps, a bit weak in American history, government, and geography? I resolved to overcome my own weakness in these areas in order to teach Leo better.

Marta had always been a good student, he told me. He was delighted that I had perceived her musical talent, and he looked forward to hearing her play the organ. "I'm partial to Marta," he said. "She lost her mother very young. Also, she is a bit special to me because she was nearly killed a few years ago when a horse ran away with her carriage." I all but clapped my hand over my mouth to keep from saying, "I know." I was far from ready to confess how I had come to the Caldwells.

Suddenly, Jay Caldwell got up, walked to the windows, and absently fingered Ginger's window cushion. "Now I have something very serious to say." My heart faltered until he added, "It's not to go beyond these walls," and happiness restored my heartbeat. Whatever he was about to say, he would not be warning me to keep it quiet if he were going to dismiss me. What an idiot he would have thought me if he could have detected the plunging and leaping of my spirits at his every innocent word. I was so shaken that I almost missed what he had started to say.

"You probably know that Mrs. Caldwell and I

have been estranged recently. I felt the children should be with their mother, but I hated being separated from them. Contrary to what you seem to think, nothing means more to me than they do."

He turned to me, and he was so much taller than I that I had to tilt up my face to meet his clear gray eyes. "I don't know why, but I wanted you to know how I feel about my children," he said. "Anyway, you brought me to my senses yesterday. I hadn't realized that Marta, especially, was so unhappy. I'm going to stay here at Soundcliff for now, although I'll be commuting to New York a good deal. I hope that my wife and I can work things out. I for one am going to try very hard. But no matter what happens, I can promise you that Marta will have her father's love, care, and protection from now on. Leo and Bonnie too, of course."

I was too astonished to speak. Jay Caldwell turned back to the window and pointed out over the Sound toward a far promontory.

"See that spit of land over there?"

"Yes."

"Foxfield. Gus Flammon's place. He's there all summer. I knew if I wanted to see Gus, I'd have to come out here. I imagine you overheard my clumsy attempt to get the LIH&M back from him."

"I—oh—" I sputtered.

"No. Don't explain. I can guess that we trapped you in the office and that you slipped into the old passageway."

I nodded.

"Well, old Gus is just as rotten as he ever was. He wouldn't give me the LIH&M, but he may have given me back my daughter." He saw my puzzled look and explained. "If I hadn't had to come out to Long Island to see him, I wouldn't have had that encounter with you." He gave a salute in the direction of Foxfield. "Thanks, Gus—for once." Then he turned back to me. "But I'm being facetious." He held out his hand, and I gave him mine. He pressed it. "Thank *you*, Miss Lorimer," he said gravely. At that moment, the door swung open and in came Nancy Vance. He released my hand.

"Sorry, sir, but Mrs. Caldwell is looking for you," said Nancy. She gave me a smile that made my skin crawl.

"Tell Mrs. Caldwell I'll be right down," he said. Then, as Nancy turned to go, "And Nancy—"

"Yes, Mr. Caldwell?" She turned back.

"When I'm in residence, you must knock before entering a room."

"Yes, sir. Sorry, sir." And she was gone.

Jay Caldwell excused himself, and I sat alone in the schoolroom for some time, feeling both exhilarated and dismayed. Nancy's interruption had upset me. I knew only too well how she might interpret the handclasp she had seen. But I wasted few thoughts on Nancy. It was Jay Caldwell I pondered most.

In my first two encounters with him—that day in New York when I had so miraculously been hired and yesterday in his office—I had marked him as cold and aloof, and his long absence from the children had reinforced that impression. But here in the schoolroom, I had seen a different Jay Caldwell, kinder, almost tender. At any rate, his love for the children seemed sincere, *was* sincere, no reason to doubt it for the scene between them had been so touching. Yes, that loving father was a side of him I had not expected to see. I had not expected to be so affected by him. I felt confused in a not altogether unpleasant way.

Over the next weeks, Jay and Eleanor Caldwell were seen only in each other's company. He was the devoted, solicitous husband, holding her chair at meals, getting to his feet to fetch her a lemonade on the piazza, holding her elbow as they walked about the grounds. They were together constantly except when he boarded the *North Star* for a commute into New York City. I witnessed his first departure from an unusual vantage point.

Soundcliff was crowned by a high, square granite tower. One morning, I came upon Mrs. Morgan directing one of the maids in dusting down a narrow flight of stairs that lay behind a third-floor hallway door that I had always supposed concealed a closet.

"Oh, no," Mrs. Morgan told me. "These are the stairs to the tower. You must go on up. There is a wonderful view."

I was enchanted by my new find. The tower consisted of a square wooden floor about fifteen feet across. The walls were of plain plaster. Rafters stretched overhead. It was an ordinary attic room except that an unbroken row of windows opened from all four walls, offering a panoramic view of water, woods, and Soundcliff grounds. As I looked out from the north window, I caught sight of Jay Caldwell stepping into a small launch. I watched it bear him out to the *North Star* which lay at anchor in deeper water. He climbed aboard, the crew pulled up anchor, and I watched as the *North Star* glided into open water, then moved off under steam power, westward toward New York. A smaller sailboat was simultaneously coming in toward the dock, and I recognized Pemberton Archer waving as he passed the *North Star,* then pulling in and tying up.

I made a tour of the other windows, noting the cool green beauty of the woods to the west and the busy movements of the grounds-keepers to the south. As I approached the east windows I spotted the family victoria just rounding a curve in the drive and circling in under the porte-cochere. I stepped back to the south windows, but the carriage was hidden by the porte-cochere roof. A few moments later it rolled out again bearing Eleanor Caldwell, and I watched her out of sight as the carriage moved into the private road through the woods.

"I wonder where she's going," I mused. It occurred to me that when she and her husband had been separated, she had gone out almost every day. But she had gone nowhere alone, so far as I knew, since the reconciliation. For a moment I had the bizarre impression that she had been imprisoned at Soundcliff since her husband's return and was now taking swift advantage of his first absence to slip away on some clandestine errand. I quickly discarded the notion. It was natural, after all, for a wife to attend to errands while her husband was gone, errands that she had no time for when he was at home. I wondered briefly if Soundcliff was beginning to affect my senses, causing me to read sinister meanings into everyday events.

I came downstairs to find Pemberton Archer sprawled languidly in a piazza chair. He sprang to his feet, pulling off a floppy white sailing hat, and beamed at me.

"I was hoping you'd be here. I got here just in time to miss Jay and Eleanor."

"Yes, I know. I was in the tower. You can see everything for miles about from up there."

"Oh, yes. We used to love playing up there. Say! Will you go for a sail with me?"

"I'd love to, but I have lessons with the children in just a few minutes."

"On a gorgeous day like this? Don't they get a holiday?"

"Yes, we're only having half days now with the warmer weather. We'll be done at noon."

"Then I'll wait. Will you spend the afternoon with me?"

"That would be lovely."

"Good! I'll have Ada pack us a picnic."

The morning passed slowly, and for once I was as anxious to be out of the schoolroom as the children were. Pemberton Archer was a pleasant and attractive man, and I was looking forward to our outing. After lessons I changed into a light walking skirt, striped shirtwaist, and a straw boater with long, navy-blue ribbons which Susan Sayre had lent me. Then I went down to meet him.

We sailed along the shoreline, and he pointed out the homes of the wealthy and famous, some topping the bluffs, others with great lawns rolling down to the beaches. I was particularly fascinated by a glimpse of an ornate pink Italian Renaissance mansion that turned out to be August Flammon's Foxfield. We turned back toward Soundcliff, then slipped into a small cove ringed by tall trees. He helped me onto a narrow strip of clean sand, and we spread our picnic.

"This is delightful, Mr. Archer," I said. "Quite the loveliest afternoon I've spent here on Long Island."

He stopped fussing with the picnic cloth and looked into my eyes. "Won't you call me Bertie? All my friends do."

"Oh, I—but I'm just an employee—"

"Nonsense. You're not *my* employee. I'd like you to be my friend. I'd like to call you Lillie, and I can't do that unless you agree to call me Bertie."

I must have looked doubtful, so he continued.

"Look. I find almost everyone on my so-called social level unutterably boring. I suppose you haven't been here long enough to know what stuffy snobs New York and Long Island 'society' consists of. There are exceptions, of course. Jay, for one. But Jay is—Jay. His way is to knock down the system and rebuild it to suit himself. Mine is to thumb my nose at it. I can easily do it. I have enough money to live as I please and let society go hang. I find my own friends—artists, musicians—

even politicians. I get a huge kick out of politics, which is supposed to be a very lower-class pastime."

"But this Lieutenant Colonel Roosevelt," I interposed. "Isn't he from a wealthy family? And wasn't he a member of your State Assembly? I thought I read it in the papers."

"Yes. And his family heartily disapproved when Teddy started hanging about the political clubs, I can tell you."

"Have *you* thought of running for public office?"

"Not me. I'm far too lazy. I like it better behind the scenes, giving money, pulling an occasional string that my money gives me the power to pull. But it's really only a hobby with me, part of whatever it is in me that makes me want to do what I want to do and know whom I want to know. And I do want to know you. So please, don't let that employee-employer, upper class-lower class stupidity spoil it for us. I think we could get on famously, don't you—Lillie?"

"All right—"

"'All right, Bertie.' Say it, Lillie. Say my name."

"All right, Bertie," I laughed.

"Yahoo!" he yelped and sprang up into a wild Indian war dance. Then he sank down beside me. "See how easy it is to make me happy?" he grinned.

"Alarmingly easy."

"Ah, Lillie, I'm going to enjoy knowing you," he said. We unpacked the cold chicken, salad, and tea and began to eat.

He was right. We did get on famously. He was lively and witty and well-read. I found everything he had to say fascinating, and he seemed to find my ideas equally absorbing. We had more in common than I should have thought possible for two people of such different backgrounds. Before the afternoon was half gone, we were genuine friends and equals, and that's why it seemed as natural as earlier it would have struck me unseemly when I asked him about his childhood with Jay Caldwell and with his cousins Charlotte and Eleanor Archer.

He leaned his head back and closed his eyes. "That's an easy question," he said. "There was just one central fact of our growing up, and that was Eleanor's passion for Jay. Everything revolved around that. They were the same age. I was a year older, Charlotte two years younger. Jay was a natural leader, and Eleanor always insisted on following him around, worshiping whatever he did. There was plenty to worship. He was good at everything. There wasn't much left for Charlotte and me to do but to tag along. Jay and Eleanor were the axis that Charlotte and I revolved around.

"We always assumed that Jay would marry Eleanor when we grew up. It was dynastic destiny. The Caldwell and Archer families had always been close. The alliance was expected. We hadn't noticed that it was a one-sided attachment. When Jay proposed to Charlotte, we were all simply flabbergasted. Eleanor was devastated."

"Why do you think he chose Charlotte?"

"I don't know, really. She was gentler than

Eleanor, very quiet and shy. I suppose she appealed to him more in that way. Perhaps he just couldn't cope with Eleanor's white-hot devotion.

"The sad part is that the marriage to Charlotte wasn't happy. She was very childlike—a pale, sweet little elf. She did love Jay, I'm sure, but he had always terrified her, too—his exuberance could seem threatening to a timid person like Charlotte. When we were children and played follow-the-leader, Jay was always the leader. Eleanor would follow him to the bitter end. I would drop out when I got tired or bored. Poor little Charlotte never got past the first stunt. When he'd come whooping and yelling into a room, pretending to be a pirate raiding a ship and carrying off the beautiful women, Eleanor would laugh and throw her arms around him. Charlotte would scream and hide in a closet. Eleanor was cold-blooded. Execution Rock was her favorite game; it simply terrified Charlotte.

"Unfortunately, I think she was almost as terrified of him in marriage. I believe Charlotte's idea of love was hugs and chaste kisses. She wasn't ready for Jay's robust nature. You could see that he tried to be gentle with her. When he came into a room where she was, he would soften his voice and scale down his gestures. But she was always nervous, edgy.

"Marta was born two years after they were married. It was a difficult birth, and I believe after that it was a marriage in form only. She became despondent. Then she died."

"Do you know how?" I asked. "Was there not

some mystery about her death?"

"Yes. Unsolved. And unsolvable, I think. One day she was found dead in her room by one of the servants. Jay had been away from Soundcliff all day. No one else had been seen in the house except the servants. None of them had any reason to kill her."

"She must have committed suicide, then."

"That's what Jay said."

"But?"

"But how do you commit suicide by giving yourself a violent blow on the temple? I suppose it's possible, but—"

"But not probable."

"No. There was a bronze bookend near the chair where we found her. And that's all we know about it. No investigation was made, no charges brought. But the rumor mill had it that Jay had come back to the house—there are dozens of ways to get in and out unseen, as you know—and killed her. Jay just kept saying it must have been suicide."

"What do you think?"

Bertie sighed deeply. "I'm not sure." He shook his head. "But there was one person who never doubted Jay for a moment. Eleanor, of course. She stood by him through it all. He needed her absolute faith then."

"And so they were married?"

"Yes. Just about a year after Charlotte's death. A year after that, Leo was born. Five years later, Bonnie." He smiled. "And then came Lillie Lorimer, a ray of light in the darkness."

"A very small ray of light, if I am one."

"Maybe it's not that the light is so small but that the darkness is so great. The marriage is a disaster, of course, not least for those sweet children."

"Why is it, as you say, a disaster?"

"I suppose Eleanor must have known from the first that Jay didn't—couldn't—love her as much as she loved him. I believe he married her because she had been so loyal to him, but gratitude isn't love, and that can't be hidden. She began to press him. 'Do you love me? Do you love me?' She constantly demanded reassurance. She would do it in front of me and others, so it must have been worse in private. Jay began to spend time at his club, his downtown office, anywhere but home. I have never heard the slightest rumor of infidelity. I don't believe he would do that to her. But Eleanor believed he was seeing other women. She would explode if he paid the smallest attention to any woman at a social gathering. Over a period of time, the situation became unbearable. They separated for a few weeks, but I hear he's living at Soundcliff again. That's why I came by this morning, to see him. How do they seem? How do they act toward one another at meals?"

"I don't really know. I've seen them together about the grounds, but of course I don't see them at mealtimes."

"What do you mean, 'of course'? Haven't they invited you to take meals with the family? The previous governess always ate with them."

This bit of intelligence flustered me considerably. No one had ever mentioned to me that the previous governess had been invited to eat with the Caldwells and, knowing nothing of what was customary in wealthy households, I had not wondered about it. "No," I said simply, trying to cover my embarrassment, "they have not invited me."

Bertie gave me a strange look. "It's Eleanor," he said. "I might have anticipated it. You're too pretty and too young. She won't want Jay making comparisons at every meal. If she feels that way, you'd better watch your step."

I couldn't understand it. Why would she be jealous of me, a woman so regally beautiful of a plain, unworldly person like me? It made no sense. But surely, as she and her husband worked out their reconciliation, her distrust of me would vanish.

"I do hope they can work things out," I said to Bertie. "The children do need—" I stopped myself from saying "their father" and finished, "both their parents."

We packed up our picnic basket and sailed back to Soundcliff. Neither Jay nor Eleanor Caldwell had returned, and Bertie shrugged. "I'll be back. To see them if I can—to see you, certainly." He gallantly kissed my hand, then squeezed it affectionately. "Bye for now, Lillie. Take care." And he was gone.

I went up to my room where I sat by the window for a long time, basking in the pleasure of my new friendship with Bertie, yet troubled by the revelations he had made. My eyes swept the water as I mused on what I had learned—until suddenly I realized that I was watching, and watching intently, for the return of the *North Star*.

SEVEN

The Fourth of July party was just two weeks off. It was to be an elaborate all-day, all-evening affair—*the* North Shore summer party—and the entire household was in a state of anticipation stoked higher and higher by the frenzied planning and preparations already under way. The excitement seeped into the schoolroom as well and, with the catalyst of early summer weather, destroyed whatever was left of our desire for serious study. We were supposed to continue half-day sessions until the end of June, but I realized that I would either have to throw up my hands and stop lessons at once or find some creative alternative activities to tide us through the month.

At the end of one unbearably hot and squirmy morning, I proposed that we make the next day's "lesson" a nature walk in the woods. The children whooped with delight.

The suggestion was no sooner out of my mouth than I realized its foolishness from an educational standpoint. I could have conducted a very nice study in the fields near my village in England, but of course I knew nothing at all about the woodlands of eastern America. I appealed to the children for suggestions. Had they any guidebooks to local flora and fauna? Or was there some member of the household staff who might qualify to accompany and teach us all?

"Oh, Miss Lorimer," Marta exclaimed, "Daddy should come with us. Nobody knows more about the Soundcliff woods than he does."

"He knows all the birds and the wildflowers and the trees," Leo chimed in enthusiastically. "He could teach us better than anybody. Can we ask him?"

"Oh, I don't think so. Don't you suppose your father has more important things to do? Business affairs and so on? Besides, he's been so busy working on the party arrangements. I doubt if he would have the time to spare." I spoke sternly, but I'm sure my eyes were glowing.

"Oh, let's ask him," Marta pleaded. *"I'll* ask him. I know he'd love it."

"Well, you may ask. But don't press him," I warned. "And don't be disappointed if he can't do it. We can improvise something, I'm sure."

Early in the afternoon, I wandered by the vegetable patch and lingered to watch the gardener make some late plantings. The garden was in a remote center of the grounds, yet Jay Caldwell seemed to have no trouble finding me. I heard a tattoo of hoofbeats on the hard dirt path, and I looked up to see him cantering toward me astride a big chestnut gelding.

He drew up easily beside me. In polished high boots, jodphurs, and short-sleeved, open-necked white shirt he looked like the dark, handsome overseer of an exotic plantation. My eyes were at about the level of his knees, and I had to throw back my head and hold my big straw sunshade hat on with one hand to talk to him.

"I hear you have a nature walk on for tomorrow," he said. "Marta says I'm invited."

"Oh, yes," I flushed. "I warned them not to wheedle you into coming if you haven't the time or inclination but I'm afraid I wouldn't be much good at it myself. I did all my nature-walking in England. I don't know how much of my knowledge would apply in your woods here."

"Meet me on the piazza at nine o'clock tomorrow. Leave everything to me." He flashed me a dazzling grin, nudged the big chestnut with his knees, and galloped off, leaving a flurry of dust in his wake. I watched his straight back and the proud angle of his head with fascination. Then I walked off down the path. It was a few moments before I noticed that I was humming.

I was on the piazza before nine the following morning and found the children already there. They were pushing and chasing one another about, as exuberant as puppies. At nine sharp, their father appeared, grinning boyishly and radiating energy.

"Troops, fall in," he called. The children lined up eagerly in front of him. He was carrying a canvas knapsack loosely over one shoulder and now he shrugged it off and plopped it onto the piazza floor. Out of it he pulled a pair of binoculars which he slung about his neck. Then he held open the pack.

"Ada has provided us with a light lunch of sandwiches and punch, leaving plenty of room in the pack. Did everyone bring what I asked you to?" A chorus of yesses and the children produced an assortment of items for the walk. Marta had brought sketch pads and pencils. Leo had a guidebook with drawings and photographs of birds, plants, flowers, and trees. Bonnie held out a neatly folded blue-and-white-checked picnic cloth I had seen Nellie Morgan retrieving from the linen cupboard for her. Each item went into the pack which Jay Caldwell then slipped on over the back of his collarless chalk-striped shirt.

"I'm afraid I have nothing to contribute," I said.

"Oh, I don't think I would agree with that," he returned with a smile that weakened my knees.

"Here we go," he announced, and we started off at a brisk pace. I was glad I had worn my short walking skirt. I worried a bit about the immodesty of exposed ankles, but I could not have kept up with him otherwise.

He loved the woods and had studied them, and his enthusiasm was contagious. As we walked along, he had each child take a turn at identifying a bird, a tree, or a flower. Using the binoculars and the guidebook, Marta quickly spotted a jewel-bright redstart dipping and diving among the high branches as swiftly and gracefully as a butterfly. With some help from his father, Leo selected a tree with smooth light-gray bark and oval, sharply-pointed, deeply-veined leaves. Comparing it with drawings and descriptions in the guidebook, he successfully identified it as a beech tree. For little Bonnie, her father chose a colored picture of wild columbine, which he knew she could easily find among the outcroppings of rock throughout the woods, and she was thrilled to locate a thick patch of the deep-red and creamy-white drooping, bell-shaped blooms almost at once.

The walk was not all study. He interspersed his lecture on the names and remarkable features of the woodland animals and plants with riotously funny or spellbinding stories of his childhood adventures. Here, for example, was the vine-tangled grove where he had once ambushed Uncle Bertie and tied him to a tree. And here was the creek where he had been swimming later that same day when Uncle Bertie had stolen his clothes. "And then," he laughed, "Bertie sent . . . two girls to look for me. He told them I was 'missing.'"

"Did they find you, Daddy?" Leo giggled, all pink at the idea.

"Almost. But I hid and sneaked home after dark."

The two girls, of course, had been Eleanor and Charlotte. His oblique way of referring to them made me realize how awkward it was for him to speak of them to the children. Which one, for example, did he call "your mother" when the three children were together?

Eventually, we found a lovely sun-dappled glade with a big fallen log at its center, and he suggested that we make it our picnic spot. He put down the knapsack, and I spread the blue-and-white cloth by the log and set out the sandwiches and punch. As we ate, he used the log for another lesson. He explained how it had grown from a seedling, fed by nutrients in the soil, rainwater, and sunlight, reached maturity, then old age, and had finally fallen in this spot. Now it was rotting, and in rotting was forming new soil to nourish new plants. He had each child take a handful of the rotting wood and feel how like soil it already was.

"This is life," he said. "It's a cycle, the new being born from the old, over and over again."

He asked the children to name creatures that might have lived in the tree while it was standing. "Birds," said Bonnie. "Squirrels," from Leo. "Maybe a chipmunk in a hole by the roots," Marta added.

"Do you think anything is living in it now?"

"Snakes and worms," Leo said.

"Maybe," laughed his father. "But take a closer look." He drew a magnifying glass from a pocket of the knapsack and set the children to examining the log for grubs and insects. He placed the sketch pads and pencils nearby and suggested that each child try to draw one of the creatures that now made the log their home. He was a wonderful teacher. I was as enthralled as the children.

After we had eaten and carefully packed up all our debris, and after the children had tired of sketching the log and its inhabitants, they asked if they could play in the woods.

"I don't know," he said. "This is a school morning. We're supposed to be studying. I'll tell you what. Play for awhile, but when you come back, you must each bring a plant specimen that we can identify when we get home. Then I'll show you how to press and dry them to keep as souvenirs."

The children vanished among the trees like woodsprites, and we were alone.

He sighed and leaned back against a tree trunk. I sat beside him on a smooth, mossy rock, tucking my skirt about my ankles as modestly as I could.

"This is wonderful," he said, closing his eyes. "I haven't come into the woods like this, on foot, for years. What memories it brings. At this moment, I wish I could go back and be a boy again. No responsibilities, only hopes and dreams."

"I understand," I said, thinking of the weight of responsibility he bore for the management of the family fortune and affairs, the marriage that, instead of lightening the burden, seemed to add its own weight.

He opened his eyes and looked into mine. "I believe you do understand," he said. "There's something in your face and your voice. You're very perceptive, sensitive. No wonder the children love you. They do, you know.

"You must promise me to stay with us, Miss

Lorimer. Don't think of leaving. If you are ever disturbed over anything—the salary, the surroundings, relationships with family or staff, anything at all—please come to me, and I will see that the problem is corrected."

"I wouldn't think of leaving," I said, perhaps more fervently than necessary.

"I hope you'll go on feeling that way." He leaned forward, holding me with a gaze so appealing, so intense that I could not move. "They have had so many disruptions. Marta lost her mother when she was four and does not get on with her stepmother, as I'm sure you've noticed. There has been a change of nursemaids and governesses at least every year. I'm not sure why. Perhaps my wife is a bit—stern—with the staff. And then, of course, our disagreements and our separation has had its effect on them.

"So you see, they need you. They need your love and your understanding. Especially Marta. She's at an age when feelings are very strong, both love and anger. And even a father can see when his daughter is growing up. I know she's been seeing Jack Van Dyne. He's in the army now, but he'll be back, and on this point I agree completely with my wife. Marta is too young for a serious attachment, no matter how nice a fellow Jack is. I'm afraid that if she becomes too unhappy at home, she might do something rash like running off with Jack. I hope she won't do that if she has you to steady her."

"And you," I said.

"And me, of course. But there are things a woman can give a girl that even the most adoring papa can't."

"I promise I won't leave them," I said. "And you know, Mr. Caldwell, I'm very glad if what I said to you that day in your office had the effect of bringing you home to be with your children. But I must apologize for the way I behaved. It's been bothering me terribly. I had no right to act that way."

Suddenly his face crinkled into a grin. "It took me by surprise, I'll say that!" He threw his head back and laughed, making me blush deeply. "Imagine the effect. I'm alone, brooding, thinking deep thoughts." He put on a mock-solemn face. "Then, the wall opens and out steps a beautiful young woman, scaring me out of a year's growth." He arched his eyebrows gleefully. "I ask her the expected question—'What are you doing here?'—and she screams, then gives me a lecture full of home truths such as I haven't heard since Nellie Morgan used to bawl me out when I was nine years old. Then she bursts into tears and runs away!" He laughed so hard he held his arms over his ribs and rocked back and forth. "I tell you, I was a shambles!"

By now, I was laughing too. "Well, I'm sorry. I'm not usually such a hysteric."

"I'm sure you aren't," he said, shaking his head. "But it was refreshing, all the same. Hardly anyone tells me the truth any more. When you have money and power, people are afraid. No one wants to call down your wrath. I can seldom persuade anyone that I appreciate hearing the truth. The only people I know who don't mince words with me these days are my grandfather and Gus Flammon, neither of whom gives a good toot for my money and power: Grandfather had it first, and Gus has more than I do."

"I'm sorry I eavesdropped on your conversation with him," I said.

"That's all right. You noticed what an ornery old bird he is, didn't you?" There was an edge of anger in his voice.

"Yes. Why do you suppose he wouldn't sell his LIH&M shares?" I asked, emboldened by our closeness and his easy good humor to ask an impertinent question. What right had I, after all, to know anything about Jay Caldwell's business affairs? But he answered without hesitation.

"My theory is that when he came up from nowhere—Gus is a self-made man, you know—my grandfather was already a wealthy and powerful financier. I think Gus saw him as the man to beat, the man to outdo. He had a kind of respect for Grandfather, but I think he saw my father and me as inheritors. We didn't build the fortune; we had it given to us. It galls him. Over the years, he built up a hatred and contempt for us. He holds onto his half of the LIH&M to spite me.

"True, the LIH&M has strategic importance as his link from the West into the port of New York, but I offered him a binding access-and-use agreement, so that wasn't his reason for turning me down. The funny thing is that the LIH&M is a very small line. Monetarily, it's not very important either to him or to me. If it vanished tomorrow, it would hardly make a ripple in his fortunes or in mine. Its importance is mostly sentimental, emotional. I want it because Grandfather built it, and because Gus Flammon once humiliated my father over it. I blame my father's death on that particular humiliation, so I'd like to pry the LIH&M loose from Flammon's grip. Not only does my grandfather want me to do it, but I can't help the feeling that my father's spirit is alive somewhere in the universe and that it would give him happiness. Flammon holds onto it for the same reasons in reverse, if you see what I mean. But I will say that I didn't know how strongly he felt about it until he turned down the Springfield and St. Louis for it. He must hate us even more than I had imagined."

"Since he's turned down your offer, what will you do?"

"What makes you think I'll do anything?"

"Because I think you're at least as stubborn as he is, and why should you let him get away with it?"

"And what do you think I should do?"

"Well—" I hesitated a moment, thinking. "You've given him a fair, aboveboard offer. It was more than he deserved, but you approached him in a gentlemanly way. Since he turned you down, I believe you are now free to get it from him in a—less open way."

"You mean I should outmaneuver him in some way—get it from him without his knowing I'm doing it?"

"And then rub his nose in it," I said firmly.

Jay Caldwell smiled broadly. "Why, Lillie Lorimer. You're a woman after my own heart. That's exactly what I intend to do."

"You do?" I said eagerly. "How?"

He searched my face as if looking for confirmation that I could be trusted. Then he spoke. "Do you know what the Empire State Railroad is?"

"Yes. It's August Flammon's, the biggest railroad east of Chicago. Its assets, rolling stock and so on, are worth about ten times the assets of the LIH&M and about ten percent more than the Pennsylvania Railroad which is the second biggest eastern road."

He looked at me in blank astonishment. "That's exactly right! How on earth do you know that?"

I told him about the book I had borrowed from his library and read cover to cover. "That's incredible," he said. "I didn't know a woman could take an interest in things like this. You realize, then, that it's the keystone of Flammon's empire."

"Yes," I said.

"Well, here's what I'm going to do." He leaned toward me, looking about as if imagining that someone might be standing among the trees listening. Then, in a low voice, so low I had to lean close to his face to hear him, he told me of his most astounding plan.

"First, I'm going to let Flammon gain total control of the LIH&M."

"What! Why?"

"You'll see. I'm going to let the word get out that I'm in financial trouble and that the LIH&M shares can be had. He'll buy them and bounce me off the board, of course. It will look as if Jay Caldwell has lost the family railroad to Gus

Flammon. He'll absorb it into the Empire State which will now run from New York to Chicago, a tremendous triumph for Flammon. Caldwell will be a laughing stock."

"But that's unbearable," I whispered. "How could you do that?"

"I admit it will be hard to take, but it will be worth it. Because at the same time, or right afterward, I'm going to buy out the Empire State. If I can't get the LIH&M from him directly, I'll get it that way."

"You'll buy the entire Empire State Railroad just to get the LIH&M along with it?"

"Yes."

"But why would he sell you the Empire State?"

"He wouldn't. He won't know I'm doing it. But I know exactly where and from whom I can buy the controlling shares. He'll be off his guard because, having just stolen the LIH&M from me, he'll think I'm in dire financial straits. He won't be watching what I'm doing."

"But can you be sure of success? It seems like a monstrous risk to me."

"It is—and no one is ever sure of success. But there is no success in this world without risk. The bigger the risk, the bigger the possible gain. Otherwise, you're just sitting on your money watching the interest accrue. That kind of life may appeal to some. Bertie Archer, for instance, is content that way. He has other interests. But for me, that's stagnation; it's death. I have to take risks to live."

"Like your grandfather."

"Yes and no. It's true, Grandfather thrived on risk, on manipulation, on making money for the fun of making money. But there's more in this for me than just the sheer joy of beating Gus Flammon at his own game."

"And what's that?"

"Well—" he paused. "Do you really want to know all this, Miss Lorimer?"

"Oh, yes!" I was terrified that he would break off and not tell me the rest. My eyes must have been burning.

"Well, then, here it is. The dream of my life is to run a railroad. A real railroad. The LIH&M is too small by itself. It's really a family toy. But the Empire State—now there's a railroad! And it's being run badly. It's being run for profit alone. Flammon milks every last cent he can out of it. No pride. Passenger service is dreadful; freight service isn't much better. Flammon operates on the principle that he gets maximum business and maximum profit by offering the lowest rates and the cheapest service. There's nothing Gus loves more than a rate war. The trouble is, he doesn't maintain the roadbed and the rolling stock. He's wearing it out. The Empire Sate is over thirty years old now, and it's going to be in very bad shape before long.

"To me, a railroad isn't just a source of unlimited profit for one man or a group of men; it's an integral part of the American economy. Railroads need to be managed, not milked. What if we ever get into a major foreign war? A strong intercontinental railroad system will be a must.

And meanwhile, the American people need and deserve decent passenger and freight service at fair, honest rates. It can be done—I know it. There's at least one railroad in this country that's been properly managed. And the man who managed it is my ideal—J. Edgar Thomson."

"Of the Pennsylvania," I said.

He gave me an admiring look. "You not only read, you learn," he said. "Thomson didn't own the Pennsy, of course; he ran it for the owners. He ran it so well he became almost more powerful than they were, because they needed him. He knew everything there was to know about railroads. He never indulged in a rate war, and he proved that good, reliable service was easily the match of cheap, shoddy service. The Pennsy was one of the few railroads that survived the Panic of '73 without a serious loss. Dividends were thin for a few years, but it was strong enough to survive. Why some other American railroads didn't learn more from Thomson, I don't know."

"Perhaps railroads shouldn't be run by bankers," I said.

"That's right!" His eyes lit up. "You've got it exactly, Miss Lorimer. Railroads should be run by railroaders. And I intend to be one. I think that by pushing Gus Flammon out of the Empire State Railroad, I can not only avenge my father and please my grandfather, I can do the country a service. Now do you believe it's worth the risk?"

"Yes."

"Good. Because I intend to take that risk. And I intend to succeed."

The magnitude of his dream left me breathless. Imagine having the sheer nerve to undertake it! And imagine his telling me about it! I felt sure he had told no one else, that he was voicing his loftiest dreams and most secret desires for the first time. It was a lot to trust me with and he must have realized it, for he added, "I know I can rely on you not to tell anyone about this."

"Certainly, Mr. Caldwell."

He had felt safe in confiding in me partly because of my unimportance, I thought, rather as one may tell one's life story to a stranger on a ship or a train, knowing they have no power to hurt you. Yet I was glad to have served as his sounding board. I fervently hoped that he would tell me from time to time how it was going, this magnificent plan of his; but of course I didn't dare ask him to.

Suddenly he looked up and about. "Now where have they all gone?" he said. "If I know those children, they'll play until we come looking for them." He stood up and reached down to me. I offered my hands and he took them in his and pulled me to my feet. My face came near his chest, and I caught a breath of the starched freshness of his shirt. I stepped back a pace.

He led the way down a narrow path between the tall oaks. Sunlight filtered hotly through the tender green leaves, and a soft breeze cooled our faces. Low ferns brushed our shoetops. Bird calls and insect hums livened the air. I wanted to walk along this path with him forever. I had never felt so content, and the meaning of my contentment had not yet penetrated to trouble my conscience.

From a small clearing a few feet off the path we heard a rustling, whispering, and giggling. He stopped and raised a finger to his lips, then whispered into my ear, "Let's surprise them."

We eased off the path toward the clearing, stepping silently over the springy humus floor of the woods, he holding intruding branches out of my way. As he reached the edge of the little clearing—and just at the moment when I expected him to bound forward and cry "Surprise!" to the children—he came to such an abrupt halt that I bumped into his back. He put out his arm as if to stop me from coming forward, but I ducked under and came up beside him.

There in the midst of the glade lay Nancy Vance and Geoffrey Hand. They were nude, their eyes wide with shock and fright. I stifled a scream and turned away, and at that very moment I saw the three children tiptoeing up on us from the path. They must have seen us passing by and followed us silently to surprise us as we had planned to surprise them. I don't know how I got hold of myself, but I did.

"Oh, there you are!" I cried gaily, reaching behind me to pull on Jay Caldwell's shirt sleeve. "Sneaking up on us, were you? Well, last one back to the log is a rotten egg!" And I began to run back toward the path.

"Last one back has to carry the pack," cried their father, his voice matching mine for unconcerned cheer, and he took off after me. We ran down the path with the three children pounding after us, shrieking joyfully. I allowed Leo to win. His father gallantly came in last. He slipped the knapsack on over his shoulders, and we started back to Soundcliff, letting the children chatter away, unable to speak ourselves. I walked ahead with Marta, and he followed with Leo and Bonnie.

When we reached the piazza, looking somewhere in the direction of his toes, I thanked him for coming with us. I made some excuse about needing to rest—I knew that my face was as red as fire and I hoped the children would attribute it to the quick pace of our return walk—and I rushed inside and upstairs. At the second-floor landing, I ran right into Eli Caldwell.

"Come with me, young lady," he said.

"Oh, but I—" Useless to protest. He was already moving off down the hall toward his sitting room. I followed and went in. He motioned me to the chair by the window and positioned himself in the chair opposite. His look told me that today's chat was going to be about something more serious than the model railroad that wound silently about us.

"Do you recall what I said to you the first day I met you at 577?"

"Yes."

"What?"

"You said if you were me you'd run for your life."

"What did you think I meant by that?"

"I didn't know."

"Well, I'll tell you what I meant. I meant that you are a very attractive young woman, and there is someone in this family, namely the mistress of the house, who is a very jealous person, very jealous of her husband."

"Mrs. Caldwell? But she hired me herself! And I have never given her any cause for jealousy—nor would I ever!" My face, still flaming from the encounter in the woods, must have darkened even more.

"Why, Eleanor is jealous of her own children," he returned, "jealous of the love and attention Jay gives them. And everyone knows that she accuses Jay of having affairs for no more reason than that he stays late at his office. Now you are here, in their very home. That was fine while he was in New York, but now he's living here, too. I know Eleanor too well not to know that she would imagine something was happening with no cause at all; but just now I saw you coming up the path from the woods with Jay and the children. You can imagine what she will make of that!"

"But he was just with us for a nature walk because the children asked him to come."

He gave me a look that said "Don't be naive" and went on. "And besides, she didn't hire you. Jay gives her no say over the children and never has. He saw you at 577 waiting to be interviewed. Bonnie had been crying and you were comforting her. He decided you were the kind of person he wanted as the children's teacher. I know how his mind works. Eleanor gives them no love, so he wants people around them who will. He saw that loving quality in you as you talked to Bonnie, and he went right upstairs and told Eleanor to hire you on the spot. Then he came and told me."

"Oh." Several mysteries about that morning I had been hired were suddenly solved. Information did not travel through the walls of 577 as I had imagined. Now I knew how Eleanor Caldwell knew I had already met Bonnie and how Eli Caldwell knew I had been hired. Now, too, I knew why Mrs. Caldwell had seemed angry when I was introduced to her and why she had hired me in spite of my lack of references.

"Now you see," Eli Caldwell went on. "She had cause to be jealous of you even before she laid eyes on you, from the moment Jay demanded you be hired. And she doesn't dare to fire you, because the one thing she'll never do is anything that might cause Jay to leave her permanently, and that includes doing anything he thinks would be harmful to the children."

"In that event, even though she might be angry about the nature walk, there's nothing she can do about it," I said rather smugly.

"Do you believe in communicating with the spirits of the dead?"

"Why?"

"Because if you do, I recommend trying to contact Charlotte. Then you'll find out how much harm Eleanor can do when she's jealous."

"What do you mean?" I said in alarm.

"I'll leave that to your imagination," he said slyly. "But if I were you, nice a person as you are and sorry as I'd be to see you go, I think you ought to get out of here."

It occurred to me at that moment that even if no

one else told Eleanor Caldwell that her husband had been alone with me in the woods, Nancy Vance most probably would—to protect herself from any tales Jay Caldwell or I might tell about her and Geoffrey by telling one about us first. Was I, then, in real danger here? Might Eleanor Caldwell mean to do me harm? Even Bertie had warned me to watch my step.

But I said quietly, "I can't. I can't go." I had promised Jay Caldwell that I would not leave, and so I could not, even if I wanted to—which I didn't.

EIGHT

I slept badly that night and dreamed heavily, the kind of dream that seems like hard work. I believe I was struggling to make sense of things; to fit together what I had seen, experienced, felt; to weave a whole fabric and to find my place in it.

I awakened in the middle of the night feeling terribly unsettled, a feeling I knew was the residue of the dream. Already, as I sat up in bed, I could feel the details of it slipping away, sliding down below consciousness. I seemed to see the dream images disappearing in a foaming tide as I stood on shore, watching helplessly. I had to rescue the dream, to see it with waking eyes, to know it and to understand it.

Moonlight was streaming in brightly. I got up, pulled on my wrapper, then drew the drapes across the window embrasure and lit the lamp on the writing table. I took out pen and paper and wrote down the pieces of the dream as I remembered them.

I had been walking through a large house. There were many rooms, and the rooms were connected by strange, twisting passageways and short, narrow flights of stairs. I knew that the house was not Soundcliff or any house I had ever seen or imagined. Rather, the rooms represented parts of my life, and the passageways and stairways represented paths between past and future, choices.

Daddy and Uncle Frank had been in one room. Another room was small and dark and contained a cot on which lay the body of a young woman. She seemed to be both me and the young worker found dead on her bed, the one Mrs. Fein's daughter had told me about. This room and the room with Daddy and Uncle Frank, I understood, represented my fear of being alone in the world and unable to care for myself.

I had climbed a flight of stairs that passed a window, and looking out over a wide, moonlit lawn I saw two figures walking rapidly away from the house, a woman and a man. I had not known who they were in the dream. Now I knew that the woman was Eleanor Caldwell, but I could not decide if the man was Jay Caldwell or August Flammon. Somehow, both ideas were disturbing.

I went on up the stairs to another room where Bertie Archer was sitting in a deep, softly-cushioned chair. He said something to me—I couldn't remember the words, but the feeling was very loving. He held out his arms to me, and I went to him and sat on his knees and put my arms around his neck. He began rubbing my back in slow circles, and I recognized it was the comforting caress I had given Bonnie the day she cried. The caressing hand moved up and across my shoulders to the back of my neck, stroking lightly and sweetly. I was trembling. And then he began talking softly—crooning, almost—into my ear. Again the words were irretrievable, but tender, so tender—and suddenly I realized that it was not Bertie Archer who held and petted me but Jay Caldwell.

I dropped the pen and crumpled the paper I had been writing on. I put my face into my hands. I was an innocent young woman; I had never known a man's love; I was without experience. But some feelings need no precedent to be understood. I might have told myself the dream meant something else. I might have told myself that it represented my search for another person to care for me, a replacement for Daddy and Uncle Frank. I might have told myself that resting in a man's lap and being thus comforted meant merely that I had found a safe haven. I might have interpreted the dream in this innocent way: but I knew better. I was in a highly agitated state, both mentally and physically, and I required no one to tell me that what I felt—what the dream really stood for—was desire, intense desire.

The knowledge struck me to the heart. How could I have wandered so far astray? Everything was wrong with it. He was married. He was my employer. I had responsibility for his children—

not only for their education, but for their moral environment. It was beyond the bounds, this feeling I had found inside myself, far beyond the bounds. I must leave Soundcliff at once.

But how could I go? How could I? I had promised him I would stay. And even if I were inclined to break such a promise, it would be unfair to the children to disrupt their young lives once again, just when they and I had come to love each other so.

I paced up and down the room and changed my mind a dozen times. I would go. I would stay. I clutched my head in despair. Exhausted but too enervated to get back into bed, I sat in the armchair. Contradictory thoughts chased each other round my brain until I fell into a miserable doze from which I awakened, stiff and wretched, at dawn. I dressed and went down to breakfast no nearer a decision than before.

The day was cooler than the preceding few had been, and the children were more subdued than usual, so we were able to pass a quiet and studious morning in the schoolroom. Even Ginger slept peacefully on her window cushion throughout our lessons. The dear, familiar routine calmed my troubled spirit.

In the afternoon, I took a long walk about the Soundcliff grounds. My mind was numb, but the air and the exercise relaxed my body and gave back the strength the sleepless night had taken. When I came back to the house, neither Jay nor Eleanor Caldwell was anywhere to be seen. I took a biography from the library and brought it to the piazza where I passed the rest of the afternoon reading. My solitude was broken only when Marta waved as she rode by with her riding master and when Leo and Bonnie ran across the piazza in a game of tag. Ginger, who had been following them about, abandoned them for my lap and stayed there until I deposited her on the piazza floor at supper time.

I went straight to bed after supper. I tried to pick up the biography again but was so tired I dropped off into a sleep undisturbed by stressful dreams.

There was dreadful news the next morning. Colonel Roosevelt's Rough Riders—Jack Van Dyne among them—had landed in Cuba. Marta was distraught, and I spent much of the morning trying to soothe her. Now I had a new reason to stay at Soundcliff: Marta needed me, at least for awhile.

As the days went by, I saw very little of Jay Caldwell, and then mainly at a distance as he accompanied his wife on a social engagement, rode or sailed or played tennis with the children, taught little Bonnie to swim, or worked with the household staff on plans for the Fourth of July party. On two occasions, he commuted to New York early in the morning and didn't return until late. When we did meet by chance in the corridors, he spoke pleasantly, cordially, but impersonally, and I replied in kind.

"Why, it's easy," I began to think. "I can keep this up forever." No one need ever know of the feelings that had surfaced in my dream. I began to believe that I could hide them even from myself.

* * *

On the third of July, several other guests arrived from New York—some aboard the private train, some by yacht—and were shown to rooms in the guest cottages. They were entertained that evening at a small formal dinner, and Leo and Bonnie watched from the second-floor landing as their parents went downstairs, Eleanor striking in amethyst silk organza, Jay dashing in white tie and tails. Marta stayed in her room, devastated by the most recent news, received only that morning: the Rough Riders had participated in two battles, one at Las Guasimas, the other a bloody charge up San Juan Hill on the first of July. There had been casualties of about one man in five. Lieutenent Colonel Roosevelt had been made a colonel. There was no word of Jack.

The Fourth dawned hot and bright. The party was not supposed to begin until the afternoon, but a number of old and special friends began arriving in the morning and, joining those who had come the day before, formed quite a crowd for the cold lunch that was served on the piazza.

Then began a parade of turnouts winding up the long drive, and a flock of yachts roosting in about the docks, as the cream of North Shore society came to Soundcliff to celebrate Independence Day. Many would return home again in late afternoon or early evening to dress for the dance. Others who had come from greater distances had brought changes of clothing which their maids and valets laid out in the guest rooms. For now the party throng, arrayed in airy cottons and beribboned straw hats or blazers and boaters, scattered across the grounds to enjoy the games and activities Soundcliff afforded.

Some had brought riding clothes and headed for the stables to try out Caldwell mounts on the bridle paths that laced the cool acres of oak and pine. On the grass courts, ladies and gentlemen at tennis performed a decorous minuet of graceful running steps and gentle racket strokes while spectators in white wicker chairs under broad red-and-blue-striped umbrellas sipped lemonade and waited their turns.

A leisurely and not very serious game of croquet occupied a velvety spread of lawn near the porte-cochere. Lovely ladies leaned gently on banded mallets to admire the ostentatious strategy of the men; but it was all frequently interrupted as one or another player left the field to greet a new arrival alighting from a carriage.

A number of guests selected bicycles from white racks by the drive, and the wheels, their spokes woven with red-and-white-and-blue bunting, spun along the pathways like so many bright pinwheels. Some of the guests, of course, were not inclined to sportive pursuits and simply strolled about the grounds or joined groups of friends on the piazza or in the huge living room whose French doors were open wide. In one corner of the great room, Eli Caldwell held court, regaling a crowd with slightly blasphemous tales of the old days.

I shall never forget the happiness of that day—the dazzling blue sky and sail-dotted waters, the dark green of the woods and the vivid green of the lawns, a salt breeze making bearable the sun's drilling heat, polished rigs and immaculately groomed horses, fashionable ladies and gentlemen spilling laughter into the air, carefree as children, cradled in the security of money and position. For that day, at least, they were innocents in Eden.

Marta had been allowed to invite some friends, and she bravely put on a pretty outfit and a cheerful face to fulfill her duties as hostess. In addition, one of her guests was to be Colonel Roosevelt's daughter, from whom she hoped to gain more news of the battle-torn regiment. No children Bonnie or Leo's age were present, and it was my duty to mind them and keep them out of the grown-ups' way, and I succeeded except for one moment when a tall woman with an extraordinarily long face came over and leaned down toward the two little ones, peering at them through a pair of spectacles she had retrieved from the end of a ribbon pinned to her shirtwaist and now held to the bridge of her nose.

"Well, well, Leo and Bonnie. Do you remember me?"

Bonnie shrank back shyly, but Leo said politely, "Yes. How are you, Aunt Nella?" A stocky man with sandy mustaches came up beside the long-faced woman and gave the children a jovial grin. "Hello, Uncle Archie," Leo piped. He pinched Bonnie's arm to make her speak up, but instead Bonnie squealed and slapped at Leo.

"Well!" said the woman, looking at me. "Their behavior might be improved, don't you think, Miss?"

Fortunately, Margaret Dobbs appeared just at that moment to take Bonnie and Leo inside. They were to have afternoon naps so they wouldn't be sleepy and cranky at supper time when they were to be allowed to eat with the guests. The long-faced woman and the sandy-mustached man drifted away, and I was free.

I felt ill at ease after Margaret had shepherded the children indoors. A governess is in an anomalous social position, not a servant, yet not a family member. I had no place in the cooking and serving the staff were doing, but neither did I feel comfortable about mingling with the guests. For a long time, I simply stayed where I had been with the children, on a bench near the croquet field. Then I spotted a familiar figure striding across the grass in my direction, and I breathed a sigh of relief. It was Bertie Archer, grinning at me as if I were exactly the person he most wished to see in the world.

"There you are! I wondered where they'd tucked you away. I just got here or I'd have rescued you sooner."

"Oh, Bertie, you can tell me. Who are they?" I asked, nodding toward the couple who had spoken to Bonnie and Leo.

"Oh, that's Archie and Nella MacDougall. She's my cousin. Why?"

"They spoke to the children. I wondered who they were."

"Nella loves to fuss over children. Usually succeeds in scaring them. But come on, now. Enjoy the party! What do you want to do? Tennis?

Bicycling? Swimming? Do you have a bathing dress?" He had taken my hand and pulled me up from the bench.

"Oh, I don't want to do anything conspicuous," I said.

"Ah, yes," he laughed. "The invisible retainer. However," he added kindly, "I can see that you mean it, and I wouldn't want to embarrass you. Or annoy Eleanor. So let's just walk about and have some refreshments and watch the society fauna in their natural habitat. Do you think that will be discreet enough?"

"Yes," I smiled. "That sounds just right."

We strolled along the path, then under the porte-cochere and round the side of the piazza where I spotted Marta among a group of young people who had recently arrived. How slender and pretty she looked in her sailor blouse and navy linen skirt. When she saw me, she broke away from the group and ran to me. Her eyes were full of tears, yet her face glowed with happiness.

"Oh, Miss Lorimer." She squeezed my arm tightly. "The most wonderful news. Jack is safe. Colonel Roosevelt's daughter just told me. There's been a wire. He was in the battle, but he's all right. Not even wounded."

"Oh, darling, that's marvelous news!" I hugged her. She gave me a quick kiss, then ran back to the group and hung on Miss Roosevelt's every word.

"Jack is her young man," I explained to Bertie.

"I know. But isn't she rather a child for that kind of devotion? And isn't Van Dyne a bit old for her?"

"A source of worry," I agreed. "Especially now

that the regiment may be home soon."

"And he'll be a war hero. Hard to resist."

"I suppose we'll cross that bridge when we come to it."

Bertie and I shared the afternoon and he stayed by my side for the supper that was spread upon long tables at six o'clock. Never had I seen such a feast, and never had I enjoyed so many delicacies I had never tasted before. There were Little Neck clams, raw, steamed, and baked. There were Saddle Rock oysters and tender Manhasset Bay scallops and huge, succulent lobsters from Montauk. Beef and ham had been barbecued in open pits, and there were corn and potatoes wrapped in seaweed and steamed among the coals. There was a Roman punch. There were tarts and cakes and trifles and ices. There was enough food, it seemed, to feed twice the number of guests, yet it was nearly all eaten.

And then, everyone dispersed to dress for the dance, and the staff quickly transformed the grounds into a fairyland. As twilight softened the sky, festoons of Japanese lanterns blazed out over the piazza, the pathways, and inside the party pavilion which had been closed and locked all afternoon but now swung open its doors. An orchestra started to tune up inside, and couples began to gather. The men were in summer formal wear. The women in their colorful, low-necked, full-skirted gowns looked like an array of hollyhock dolls.

I, too, was to attend the dance. I had not been certain of it until Susan Sayre had mentioned it to me at lunch one day. I expressed my doubts that I would be invited, and the others assured me that the governess always attended; but then I worried because I had nothing to wear. Susan came to my rescue and helped me convert a blue silk afternoon dress into an evening dress, the conversion consisting mostly of the removal of the sleeves and a rather radical lowering of the neckline. I thought Susan had gone too far until I tried it on in front of a mirror and was pleased enough with my image to leave it alone. Still I had felt uncertain that I would be included—after all, the previous governess had taken her meals with the family, a privilege Eleanor Caldwell had not extended to me, so I might well be excluded from the Fourth of July dance as well. But then I had received a note from Jay Caldwell saying, "I do look forward to your being among the guests at the party and dance." I was ecstatic.

But now that the dance was about to begin, I was still shy enough about my place in the proceedings to come down the back stairs and out onto the grounds through the kitchen door. Bertie had said he would escort me, and when I walked around to the piazza I found him with his back to me, waiting by the living room door.

"Here I am," I said.

He whirled about. "My goodness, you are reserved, coming from the back door. The last governess used to flounce around all over the front of the house and thought nothing of it." Then his eyes warmed. "But, oh dear, you do look lovely!" He moved close to me and held out his arm. I slipped my hand through the crook of his elbow, and he closed his other hand over mine. "What do you suppose the society rags would say if I were to fall in love with you?" He said it half jokingly—but only half.

He led me to the front of the piazza and down the steps to the driveway. We would walk under the porte-cochere and along the drive to the pavilion, but we had not taken half a dozen steps when we had to back up out of the way of a large landau that was just pulling up. I saw Geoffrey Hand start down the steps to open the carriage door. At the same moment, I saw Eleanor Caldwell emerge from the house, nearly treading on Ginger who had been lurking nearby in the dark. Ginger squawked and arched her back, the fur standing up along her spine, then slunk away. Eleanor had not even noticed her.

"Funny how that cat reacts to Eleanor," Bertie remarked.

"I think it's because Mrs. Caldwell chased her one day," I said.

"Cats always know when someone dislikes them," Bertie said, and then, as Ginger came purring and rubbing around my skirt, "or when someone likes them."

I had just reached down to give Ginger a quick scratch between the ears when I heard Bertie suck in his breath and give a low whistle. "Good lord," he said, and I looked up to see August Flammon getting out of the landau and striding up the steps toward Eleanor Caldwell.

"Now, who do you suppose invited Flammon?"

Bertie mused. "I'll lay odds it wasn't Jay."

"Who then?"

"Eleanor—trying to make Jay jealous. Even when she has him, she's not sure of him. Never sure enough. It'll be her downfall some day."

"And why would Mr. Flammon accept the invitation?"

"Gus Flammon would do anything to irritate Jay. It's his favorite form of recreation."

Rather more than recreation, I thought, remembering the day I had seen Eleanor Caldwell in August Flammon's arms. And rather more dangerous than even Bertie could guess. But we were moving toward the pavilion, aglow with lantern light, alive with music and laughter, and once again I put the thought aside.

I thoroughly enjoyed most of that evening, for I loved to dance, and Bertie made sure I did not sit out a single one, although a number of other young men invited me to dance as well. There was an outdoor flagstone periphery to the pavilion, and I had been fascinated by the pattern couples wove as they waltzed out one pair of doors and in another, in and out, around and around the room. Bertie and I joined them, and it was intoxicating, dancing one moment under the gay streamers and lanterns of the pavilion, the next moment under the starlit sky.

"When the fireworks start, that's the most romantic moment of all," Bertie whispered into my ear.

The Caldwells danced most of the time with various guests but frequently with each other.

August Flammon danced with a variety of ladies but did not dance with Eleanor Caldwell. Still, there was an uneasiness in the room. I had the impression that others, too, were watching for trouble because of August Flammon's presence. Everyone knew of the bitterness between the two men.

But no one, I realized with a sudden shock—not Jay Caldwell nor August Flammon nor Eleanor Caldwell—knew everything that I knew. I alone knew of the embrace between August Flammon and Eleanor Caldwell, of Jay Caldwell's spurned offer to buy August Flammon out of the LIH&M, and of Jay Caldwell's extraordinary plans for revenge. I alone unless Jay and Eleanor Caldwell had confided all of these details to each other, and I felt certain that such confidences were not a part of their marriage. It made me feel very strange to think that I knew things about a husband and wife that they did not know about each other.

And then it happened: the denouement everyone had been anticipating. Bertie had gone to get me a glass of punch, and I was standing only a few paces from Eleanor Caldwell. There was a pause in the music, then an excited buzzing from the guests, for the pause signaled that the fireworks were about to begin, and that the next dances would take place under their splendid, sparkling canopy. Husbands, wives, and sweethearts began seeking each other out among the throng.

Then, just as the orchestra struck the first chords of the waltz, just as a brilliant red rocket arched low across the sky beyond the pavilion doors, I saw three men approaching the area where Eleanor Caldwell and I stood. Bertie Archer was coming toward me, smiling eagerly. Jay Caldwell was walking solemnly toward his wife—but so was August Flammon, and August Flammon was two or three paces nearer. Indecision clouded Eleanor Caldwell's face. Then, driven by inner demons of jealousy and spite, she turned away from her husband and went to August Flammon.

Jay Caldwell did not break his stride. He merely veered ever so slightly to one side and came toward me.

I don't think I have ever had such mixed feelings in my life. I saw the smile fade from Bertie's face, and my heart went out to him; but I could no more have resisted Jay Caldwell at that moment than the planets can resist the sun. To have embarrassed the host, the master of Soundcliff, would have been unthinkable in any case. But it was no such rational thought that propelled me into Jay Caldwell's arms. He looked into my eyes, and I felt that I was melting. I had to reach for him to keep from disintegrating.

His arm circling my back and his hand touching mine drove electric reverberations through my body. I could not swallow, could not speak. He waltzed me across the floor and out onto the terrace. Rockets and pinwheels blazed and twisted overhead. He began to turn me around and around in dipping, swaying circles. My eyes closed. I was achingly aware of the smell of his cologne, his skin, him.

"I'm sorry," I heard myself saying, and I was

surprised that speech had issued from my knotted throat. What did I mean?—I'm sorry Eleanor turned away from you? I'm sorry I love you?—I wasn't sure which I meant, if not both. My voice seemed to affect him sharply. In one fast spin he pulled me close, tightening his arm around me, tightening his hold on my hand. I could feel the hardness of his body along all the length of mine. I was so weak, it was only his strong arm pressing me against him that kept me from falling.

"Don't be sorry, Lillie," he breathed as his lips touched my ear.

He danced the next dance and all the others with Eleanor. I danced only with Bertie. It was anguish, and there was no way to hide it, but dear Bertie said nothing. Before the dance was quite over, I told Bertie that I was tired. He kindly walked me back to the house and bade me goodnight, concern and sympathy in his eyes.

I went straight to bed, and after a period of nervous tossing, I fell asleep. Some time much later—it must have been well after midnight—I was awakened by voices. Incredibly, they seemed to be coming through the wall behind my bed. That was surely impossible, I thought. The room behind mine was a maid's room, and I had never heard any sound through the thick wall that divided the family wing from the servants' wing, much less the voices of a man and woman in heated argument.

"What are you doing here? How did you—" The man's voice.

"It's silly to lock your doors, dear." The woman's voice.

"Do you mean to tell me you came through the passages? Are you out of your mind?"

"Yes—out of my mind for you."

It was Eleanor and Jay Caldwell, and their voices were plainer now, as if they had moved closer to me. I realized almost at once that they must be in Jay's room below mine, but it took a moment to grasp why I could hear them so clearly. Then I understood the references to locked doors and passages: Jay had locked the door between his room and Eleanor's and his hall door as well. Eleanor, determined to get into his room, had gone through the network of hidden passageways and opened a sliding panel into his room. These, I realized, could not be locked.

There must be a passageway in the space between the family wing and the servants' wing, hence the apparent thickness of the wall which was actually hollow. I formed a mental image of the space. It must extend upward behind the wall of my room. With the panel into Jay's room open, their voices were rising through the wall space as if through a chimney. The closer they stood to the open panel, the more plainly I could hear them.

"Eleanor, what you're doing—it's the wrong way." His voice was tired, patient.

"Well, I guess it's the only way, if you're going to lock me out." Her voice was brittle and gay, as if to cajole him into regarding her uninvited visit as an exasperating but endearing antic. There was no such response from Jay.

"Oh, Eleanor. What do you hope to gain? We have so many things to work out, to settle, before we can be—together. Can't you see that?"

"I can see that you'd rather dance with that little English slut than your own wife." The gaiety had fallen away. Her tone was cold and hard, and I was horrified to realize that she was referring to me.

Now, for the first time, Jay was angry, and his level tone was even more chilling than hers: "You are never again to make a slurring reference to Miss Lorimer. She is a fine, gentle lady who is and will remain completely innocent of the ugliness between you and me. Do you understand that, Eleanor?"

"Oh, yes. I understand more than you think I do, Jay. I understand about your being alone with her in the schoolroom, holding her hand. And I understand about your cozy little walk in the woods with her." Her voice had gone shrill.

"If you must use the word *slut*," Jay returned coldly, "I advise applying it to that nasty piece of business Nancy Vance, your so-called lady's maid. If Miss Lorimer's honor were not involved in these disgusting innuendos, I would not bother to answer them. But for the record, what Nancy saw was a handshake and a nature walk with the children, which the children—not Miss Lorimer—invited me to join. Did Nancy tell you, by the way, that if it had not been for Miss Lorimer's quick thinking, the children would have seen her and Geoffrey nude together in the woods, and that our stumbling upon them in that condition is how Nancy happened to see us? Soundcliff would be far better off without both of them."

Eleanor cried out hysterically. "No! No! She's *my* maid, and Geoffrey is *her* fiance and you leave them alone!" I could not understand the vehemence of her defense of Nancy and Geoffrey, nor, it seemed, could Jay who replied in a puzzled and resigned tone, "If you insist, Eleanor. I won't interfere as long as they do no harm to the children with their indiscretions. But kindly spare me Nancy's gossip."

"I don't need Nancy to tell me how you feel about that woman. Don't forget, Jay dear, you're the one who told me to hire her. And don't—" her voice rose as if to forestall a reply—"don't tell me it was for the children's sake. I've seen the way you look at her!"

I shivered. Was there a "way" Jay looked at me? A way so obvious to others?

"You know, Eleanor," he replied, "it occurs to me that you have considerable gall coming in here in the middle of the night to play the injured wife. It was you, was it not, who invited Gus Flammon to the party?—a man I despise, a man whose presence I tolerated tonight only for the sake of decorum. And let's get this straight while we're on the subject. It was you who started the fireworks dance with Flammon. Nothing would have pleased you more than to see me standing foolishly on the sidelines, humiliated in front of our guests. It was lucky for me that Miss Lorimer was there and agreed to dance with me."

"She'd like to do more than dance with you, Jay dear. Don't think I haven't seen the moonstruck look on her face when you're around."

I gasped. Did I, too, have a "way" of looking at Jay? Was I so transparent, who thought I had so carefully hidden my feelings?

"Oh, Jay," Eleanor's voice had turned wheedling, seductive. "Let's forget all this silly jealousy. Let's make it up."

His reply was abrupt. I imagined that he might even have pushed her away. "No, Eleanor. Not—not now. This is not the way to solve things between us. I'm not jealous of you. Just disgusted."

"Disgusted?" The word seemed to have inflamed her. "Disgusted? You find me disgusting?" She had begun to scream so loudly I was sure that not only I but everyone else at Soundcliff could hear her. "Well, I'll show you, Jay! I'll fix you *and* that English whore!"

Jay's voice, cutting through hers, was quiet and cruel. He spoke very slowly, with spaces between the words. "Eleanor, if you ever harm Lillie Lorimer, I just may kill you."

Eleanor cried, "Are you threatening me? Are you actually threatening me, Jay?"

"Were *you*, Eleanor? Were you threatening me? Were you threatening Lillie?" I heard no response from Eleanor before Jay spoke again. "Now, I am going to unlock my doors—both of them. You are never to slip in here by the passageways again. If you must come in, come in through the door like a lady."

"And what's the use of coming in if you don't want me here?" she said bitterly.

"Exactly," he replied, and a swishing sound was followed by silence. He had closed the panel.

I got out of bed and lit my lamp. Then I began slowly feeling along the wall. I stepped around the armoire and continued along the wall until at last I pressed my hand up and down the length of the corner molding. At about shoulder height, it gave and the segment of wall between the molding and the armoire slid aside. I peered into the opening. A narrow flight of stairs ran downward to the side. By the landing at the bottom I could just make out a lever on the wall. It must be the lever that would release the secret-panel entrance into Jay's room, the way Eleanor had gotten in, the panel Jay had just now closed. From the landing by his room, the stairs ran on down into a darkness that the dim light from my room could not penetrate. I pressed the molding to close my panel and got back into bed, leaving the light on.

A slow shiver ran the length of my body. If a person could enter Jay Caldwell's room from the secret passageways, they could also enter mine. I got back out of bed and stood by the armoire: If I could only move it over in front of the sliding panel. I put my hands against it and pushed with all my might, but it was too big, and it didn't budge. I got back into bed.

I was afraid of Eleanor, of course. Perhaps I had been all along, even before the threat I had just heard her utter to Jay. I had reason enough to fear her. Of course I felt sorry for her—a woman who loved her husband as fiercely and hopelessly as she apparently did. But why, if she loved Jay so, had she embraced August Flammon? In some strange way, she had become sick, her love soured by her uncontrollable jealousy.

Tomorrow, I would ask one of the footmen to bring up my trunk from the storage rooms and place it in front of the panel. I would fill it with heavy objects. It might not stop an intruder, but it would be an impediment and create a warning noise.

One thing I would no longer consider, no matter what: I would not leave Soundcliff. I wouldn't run because I was afraid. For good or for ill, my life had become inextricably entwined with this house and the lives of those in it.

I sank back onto my pillows, and in spite of my jangled nerves I was exhausted enough to begin drifting into sleep. As I did, random pieces of Jay and Eleanor's argument began to float through my mind.

"If you harm Lillie Lorimer, I just may kill you," he had said in a terrifying voice. His marriage to Charlotte had been unhappy; his marriage to Eleanor was unhappy. He was suspected of killing his first wife; I had just heard him threaten his second wife, even as she had threatened him and me. Nor was Eleanor the only person who knew how to get about Soundcliff unseen. All the children who grew up at Soundcliff knew the passageways, Nellie Morgan had said. So, certainly, did Jay. Was I terribly wrong, after all? *Had* Jay killed Charlotte? *Might* his threat to Eleanor have been more than mere words?

My eyes, which had been closed in half-sleep, flew open again. No, I thought. No. Jay was not a killer; I would never believe that. Never.

I closed my eyes again, and this time sleep overwhelmed me. As I slid into unconsciousness, my mind attached itself to one more part of the dreadful argument I had overheard. "Were you threatening Lillie?" He had called me Lillie again, as he had when we were dancing. And he had not replied to Eleanor, had made no denial, when she had said, "I've seen the way you look at her."

I dreamed about the passageway. Someone was coming up the secret stairs and opening the panel to my room. But I was not frightened; I was happy. For it was Jay.

NINE

I did have my trunk placed in front of the sliding panel of my bedroom the next day. I weighted it with books and other heavy objects and placed a bell on top of it. With that, I decided to forget as best I could the whole ugly episode of the previous night.

I even gave myself a stern lecture: That Jay and Eleanor were quarreling was no reason to indulge my romantic feelings about him. The less, in fact. It was like willing the marriage to fail, a very great moral wrong. The threats they had spoken probably meant nothing. Many people say "I'll kill you" in anger without meaning it. I made up my mind to hope they would reconcile. I would have to get a grip on myself and stay away from Jay Caldwell or else leave Soundcliff after all.

Fortunately, Jay seemed to have reached a

similar resolve. I saw little of him for many weeks thereafter. Nor did I overhear any further conversations, quarrelsome or otherwise, from the room below mine. Eleanor was icy on the rare occasions when I crossed her path, but not threatening. When I chanced to encounter Jay, he displayed the same pleasant but impersonal reserve he had shown me before the Fourth of July dance. Had there been something special in his voice, his look, his touch on that magical evening? I could no longer tell what had been real about it and what imagined. I even wondered once if I had dreamed the quarrel between Jay and Eleanor and had to open the panel in my room and peer down the secret stairway to prove to myself that that, at least, was a fact.

The summer days passed by. The children's lessons were suspended until autumn, and most of my time was my own. Bertie came often. He taught me tennis and riding and sailing. He took me for long walks and drives. Often, we sat reading together on the piazza. He liked especially to come when I gave Marta her organ lessons, which she and I enjoyed too much to give up, even for summer holidays. Several times, Bertie talked me into playing for him at the end of Marta's lesson, and I was glad for the opportunity to play the lovely instrument, for I had not had the courage to ask Eleanor's permission to play it at other times.

One afternoon, I turned around after playing and saw Jay standing in the doorway. "That was very nice," he said formally. "Hello, Bertie." Bertie replied, "Hello, Jay," but Jay was already gone. I was embarrassed for Bertie. After all, they were childhood friends. Jay's behavior was almost as cold and remote as it had been the first time I had seen him.

In a flash of anger, I said, "He seemed rather rude just then. I can't imagine why."

Bertie smiled. "Oh, it's nothing to do with me. He can't afford to be in your vicinity, that's all."

My face flamed. "I don't know what you mean, Bertie."

"Oh, yes you do."

"Well, that's silly."

"Is it? Why didn't Jay just come on in here and pass the time of day, then? He's not mad at me as far as I know, and never used to be afraid of the governess."

"Oh, Bertie, do drop it," I snapped.

Except for that one incident, the days were placid and slipped by as swiftly and easily as minnows—until one never-to-be-forgotten August morning when Bertie and I were playing tennis, and I saw Marta running toward us from the house. Immediately, I dropped my racket and went to her, with Bertie close behind.

"Miss Lorimer," she gasped, out of breath, "I don't know what to make of it." Bright tears rimmed her eyes.

"Of what?"

"The Rough Riders—Jack—they're coming home, but—" She paused to catch her breath.

"But what?" Bertie couldn't resist putting in.

"But he—they—a lot of them have malaria and yellow fever that they caught in Cuba, and they're setting up a hospital camp at Montauk Point for them, and Jack's going there—he has yellow fever—"

"I see," I said, interrupting the tumble of words. "He'll be here on Long Island, but ill."

"And I won't be able to visit him. He'll be quarantined, and he might die! Oh, I don't know what to do!"

"Just wait and hope for the best, darling. You can write him there, I imagine."

"Yes, yes." She gave me a strange look, then turned and dashed back to the house.

"Trouble's back," said Bertie.

"Oh, it will be all right," I said. Marta had agreed so readily to my suggestion about writing to Jack that I was lulled into nonvigilance. But Bertie was right, and afterwards I berated myself for my insensitivity. My glib response had put Marta off. She had sensed my adult lack of understanding and had immediately withdrawn from me. I should have recognized her reaction for what it was and gone after her, if not straight to her father to sound a warning. Instead, I forgot it and was as amazed as everyone else a few days later when Marta disappeared.

She could not have chosen a worse time to run away. Jay had taken Bertie off on a fishing trip, and they would be out on the open water on a tender off the *North Star*. They were not expected back for two days, and there was no way to reach them. I swallowed my nervousness at the prospect of talking to Eleanor, then went to her and told her that I thought Marta might have gone to Jack Van

Dyne at Montauk Point. She looked at me contemptuously.

"That's ridiculous, Miss Lorimer. As you know, I have forbidden Marta to see Jack. Besides, she is only fourteen. She would hardly attempt such a trip by herself."

I stood my ground. "I know it may seem farfetched, but if you had seen her face when she told me he would be at Montauk and ill. I didn't realize it then, but she was terribly upset. I really think she must have gone there."

Eleanor gave me a patronizing smile. "I think, Miss Lorimer, that we need to explore the reasonable possibilities first. I understand that you think you know the children very well, but forgive me, I'm their mother, and I believe a mother knows better, don't you?"

"It's not a question of that, Mrs. Caldwell. I just—"

"Please. Will you leave me now?" she interrupted with a razor look. "If I find I need your advice, I'll send for you."

I was dizzy with disbelief. She hated me so much that she could not even accept information from me about her step-daughter. But what a risk she was taking, I thought. Surely she knew that if Marta were not found before Jay returned—and worse, if she had not even explored my suggestion as to Marta's possible whereabouts—Jay would be furious. Yet she rejected what I had said because it was I who had said it. I was almost mad with frustration, and I was more and more certain as the hours passed that Marta was at Montauk. I wanted to ask one of the male staff members to go there, but I dared not do so in contradiction of Eleanor's wishes.

There was only one thing to be done, and I quickly realized it: I would have to go myself. My heart quaked; but the very idea of fourteen-year-old Marta—as pretty and innocent a young girl as could be imagined—lingering about an army camp was enough to freeze my soul. I had to go—but how to arrange the journey? If I could get to a public railroad station, I could buy a ticket on the LIH&M to Montauk. But I didn't know the schedules, and I feared to ask anyone lest someone let slip to Eleanor where I planned to go.

And suppose I could accomplish the trip—how could I let Jay know where I had gone and why? I had decided that he must know for Marta's sake as well as mine, for I was not at all sure of success, and I hoped that he would come to my aid should I fail to find her or to persuade her to come home. I wanted to leave him a note, but I could hardly give a staff member a note for Jay Caldwell. The wrong interpretation could too easily be made. I thought of leaving a note propped against the telephone in his office where he would be sure to see it. Eleanor had her own telephone in her sitting room, so she would not be using Jay's and would be unlikely, I thought, to find the note. But then I recalled having seen Eleanor come out of Jay's office on the evening when she had chased little Ginger, and I was suddenly not so sure she would not discover my note before Jay did.

I was sitting in my room, head in hands, trying

to solve all the problems of the journey to Montauk, when I heard the creaking of the elevator. It was Eli Caldwell coming up for his afternoon rest. Of course! Jay's grandfather was the one person at Soundcliff who would understand and help. I rushed down the stairs to the second floor and tapped at his door.

He listened to my story, and his eyes blazed with anger. "I'd go myself if I could," he declared. "That Eleanor—pah!" He rang for Hans Arnold. "He's one we can trust. Arnold never opens his mouth," he told me.

In less than an hour, I had packed a small bag and was being driven to the private station where the family train had been ordered to pick me up. In my reticule, I carried a letter from Eli Caldwell. It would assure a place for me at the home of a family that kept a respectable boarding house not far from Montauk Point. I also carried enough money to hire a driver to aid me in my search for Marta and a letter of introduction to an officer at Camp Wikoff, the army encampment at Montauk. Eli Caldwell had promised to tell Jay where I had gone as soon as he arrived, and he had promised as well that no one but Jay would learn of my whereabouts. I told Nellie Morgan that I was going to New York to visit friends.

I was too upset to enjoy the luxury of the private train. I occupied as beautiful a sitting room as might be found at Soundcliff itself, but with the low ceiling, double row of windows, and long, narrow shape of the railroad car that contained it. And, of course, it was moving; rolling along at a brisk clip; the flat, sandy, scrubby Long Island landscape flowing past the windows. The interior was all thick carpets, velvet draperies, and brocaded chairs. A steward brought me a pot of tea and a tray of sandwiches which I nibbled at nervously.

I was in a daze of anxiety, and the two-hour trip passed so quickly that I felt as if I had jumped through time. When the train arrived at the little village of Amagansett, one stop short of Montauk, I got off, for the boarding house recommended by Eli Caldwell was located here, Montauk itself being almost entirely given over to the army encampment. I hired a livery at the station, and in no time it had delivered me to a white clapboard two-story house, its wide front porch lined with wicker chairs. I asked the livery to wait as the proprietress, a Mrs. Lester, showed me to a plain but clean and airy room. An ocean breeze billowed the white curtains at the open window by the bed, and as I placed my bag upon the patchwork quilt, I thought what a lovely spot this would be for a holiday if only I were not engaged in such a serious quest. Then I went back downstairs and climbed back into the livery. "Camp Wickoff," I said.

No look of surprise crossed the driver's face, but he said in the flat eastern-Long-Island accent, "You sure you know what you're about, ma'am?"

"Not at all."

He said nothing further, and we drove along for several miles across a flat, narrow stretch of sand. Low dunes hid the ocean on our right; more dunes hid bays and inlets on our left. The sand, topped by grasses, low brush, and stunted pines, had a wild beauty of its own; but the seemingly endless extent of it was appalling to one as anxious to reach her destination as I was. Only the tracks of the LIH&M, running along at our left toward their terminus at Montauk, kept me company on the long ride.

Then, low hills appeared in the distance. Suddenly, the land seemed to broaden out, and the LIH&M tracks vanished off to the left while the road wound up and over the hills, parallel to the ocean that now flashed below between breaks in the clifflike shoreline that had replaced the gentle dunes on our right.

"Where's Montauk?" I asked the driver just then, and he replied, "This is Montauk, but the camp's some ahead." Then, as we wound down and around a long hill, I began to see patches of white scattered over another low hill ahead and to the left. At first, I thought they were some sort of cottony vegetation. Then I realized that they were tents.

"There must be hundreds of them," I said to the driver.

"Thousands," he replied. "They've got thirty thousand men here."

"Thirty thousand," I said helplessly. I had pictured a camp like a children's camp or a summer camp for families, rather small. This was a whole canvas city. My courage nearly failed me.

"I'll take you to the headquarters, and you can make inquiries," the driver said, and I nodded dumbly.

We drew up to a group of tents and shacks, marked as the headquarters area by their larger size and by various flags and emblems. The driver handed my letter from Eli Caldwell to a young officer who had stepped up to the carriage, and he took it into the largest tent. Soon, an officer came out and walked toward me.

"Good afternoon, ma'am. I'm Major Welles. Can I help you?"

"I don't know quite where to begin," I said. He stood smiling politely, and I went on. "A young lady who is in my charge has probably come here looking for—a friend—a young man who's just returned with Colonel Roosevelt's regiment. I understand he is ill. His name is Jack Van Dyne."

"Wait here, please, ma'am." He ducked back into the tent and came back some long moments later saying, "Private Van Dyne is here, all right, and he has yellow fever. He's in the quarantine section, so there is no way your young lady could visit him if she came here."

"Is there any way I could get a message to him, just to be sure she didn't get to him somehow, to see if he might have received a message from her—anything?"

"I can try to get your message to Van Dyne," Major Welles replied. "He might not be well enough to read it or reply, but I can send a messenger to your stopping place to let you know what we learn, if anything. It may take awhile, but it's the best I can do. Will that be all right?"

I had to agree and was grateful for even this slim thread. I wrote out a message on a paper Major

Welles offered me, and then I asked the driver to take me back to Amagansett.

I joined the other boarders for Mrs. Lester's supper chowder. They were an incongruous mixture of carefree vacationers and anxious relatives come to be near loved ones at Camp Wikoff. Two of the latter, Mr. and Mrs. Donovan, were parents of a young man who, like Jack Van Dyne, was suffering from yellow fever and confined to one of the hospital tents. They had not been able to visit him in the quarantined area, but the Donovans said they had heard terrible stories of filth, neglect, and hunger among the sick.

The enormous and sudden influx of the veterans of the Cuban campaign had overwhelmed those in charge of the camp. They had been unable to build facilities fast enough, provide enough medicine or care, or acquire enough food despite the generosity of the local people. Mr. and Mrs. Donovan were afraid their son would die unless they could secure his release to a civilian hospital, but they had no way to accomplish it. Upon hearing their story, I became even more concerned for Jack.

I was at a loss the following morning whether to stay at Mrs. Lester's and wait for a message from Major Welles, or to visit the boarding houses in the area to look for Marta. In the end, I chose a third alternative. I sent a message to the livery stable, and soon I had the same driver as the day before to take me back to Camp Wikoff. I thought I might locate Major Welles again, and also I thought I might catch sight of Marta or find someone who had seen her. She was more likely to be at the camp, I felt, than sitting about a boarding house.

But when I arrived at the headquarters, I could not find Major Welles and was eventually told rather brusquely by a young officer that the major had left camp for the day in search of additional suppliers.

"Did he leave a message for Miss Lorimer?" I asked.

"I wouldn't know about that, ma'am," he replied and hurried off.

I turned to the driver. "Where is the yellow fever area? Do you know?"

"I think so. But you wouldn't be allowed to go in there."

"How close can we get?"

"Don't know."

"Well, let's start in that direction."

We drove off along the main road, past street after muddy makeshift street of tents and cook shacks, on and on until I was quite lost. At last the driver stopped at the head of a narrow track that ran down the side of a dune. Below, along the shore, were rows of tents flying yellow "pest" flags. Beyond, the deep blue water was dotted with white pleasure-boat sails, making it hard to realize that the occupants of the tents were gravely ill war veterans and not families enjoying a happy seaside holiday.

"We'll be stopped in a minute," the driver warned me and then started down the track. As he had predicted, a soldier promptly stepped out from a guard shack and halted us.

"Quarantine," he said. "You can't go on. You'll

have to turn around."

"Do you know the men here?" I asked, leaning from the carriage. "Jack Van Dyne?"

"I'm afraid not, ma'am. There's too many to know, and anyhow I just got here yesterday."

I struck my lap with my fists in sheer frustration, and my driver shrugged. Then another soldier poked his head out from the shack. "Van Dyne?" he said. "That's the fellow that young lady's been askin' about."

My heart leaped. "What young lady? Do you know her name? What does she look like?"

"I don't know her name," he said, emerging from the shack and walking to the carriage. "She's a red-head. Pretty young. She's been comin' the last couple of days with food. Tried to volunteer as a nurse, but they won't let any women in here."

"When does she come?" I asked.

He looked past me up toward the top of the dune and said, so casually I almost didn't grasp it, "Here she is now."

I blinked at him, then spun around, and there behind us was another livery and Marta was inside it. She saw me and started to cry. I got down from my carriage and went to her, and she nearly fell into my arms.

Marta's story was quickly told—indeed the guard had told us most of it. She had bought a ticket on the LIH&M, engaged a room near Camp Wikoff, tried to volunteer as a nurse, was rebuffed, and had been spending all of her money on food and tips to the civilian male nurses to take the food to Jack and his tent mates. She was not sure if it had reached him. She was out of money and very frightened. She couldn't help Jack, couldn't stay at Montauk, couldn't afford to get home to Soundcliff, and couldn't bear to face Eleanor if she did.

We left the basket of food for which she had just spent the very last of her money, then dismissed her driver and started back toward Amagansett in my livery. We had gone about halfway when we passed another carriage headed toward Camp Wikoff which immediately turned around and sped after us. We pulled off the road and the other carriage pulled up behind.

"Daddy!" Marta cried, and there was Jay Caldwell striding toward us, then holding Marta and kissing her as she sobbed against his chest. He paid my driver and put Marta and me into his own carriage.

He had arrived at Soundcliff the night before, having cut short the fishing trip because of a premonition that all was not well at home. He had immediately heard from Eleanor about Marta's disappearance and from Eli about my journey to Montauk. Before dawn, he had set out aboard the LIH&M, arrived in Amagansett, learned from Mrs. Lester that I had left for Camp Wikoff, and started off after me.

After I told Jay what I had heard from the Donovans about the inadequate care afforded the yellow fever victims and Marta begged him not to leave Montauk without finding out about Jack and seeing to his welfare, Jay ordered the driver to take us back to Camp Wikoff.

I felt that an enormous burden had been lifted

from me. As we started off, I sank back against the seat cushions, exhausted but content. Marta was safe, and Jay would take care of everything else. He would surely best all the obstacles that had conquered Marta and me. I longed for just one thing more—to be Marta, leaning against his shoulder.

As I had anticipated, things were different now that Jay had taken charge. When we arrived at camp headquarters, men moved. The young soldier at the gate ushered Jay inside, and when he came out, an escort led us back to the quarantine area. Jay, wearing a face mask, was taken inside. He returned, reporting that he had seen Jack but found him in a delirium.

"It's a disgrace," he said. "I'm sure the Van Dynes would be here themselves if they had any idea things were this bad. But never mind," he told us. "I'll take care of it."

Back we went to the headquarters, and this time Jay asked Marta and me to come with him. "I'd like you to meet Colonel Roosevelt," he said.

I couldn't believe my ears. I had not even known that the Colonel himself was at Montauk, and I was much taken aback at the prospect of meeting the hero of the Cuban campaign whose name and fame had been front-page copy for the newspapers all summer long. One glance at Marta told me that she was as thrilled as I.

Jay ducked under a tent flap, motioning us to follow. Inside, a surprisingly young man with a droopy mustache got up from the plain pine table at which he had been working. He was stocky, energetic, eccentric-looking with his broad, toothy grin and round spectacles glinting in the canvas-yellowed light. He was fully and nattily uniformed in khaki with a blue polka-dotted scarf at his neck, highly-polished gaiters, gauntlet gloves and a jaunty campaign hat which he swept off in a gallant gesture when he saw Marta and me. Jay introduced us to him, then took him aside for a short conversation. Then, orders were given and handshakes exchanged, and before I could realize what had happened, we were on our way. When we boarded the family train at Montauk later that afternoon, the Donovans were with us. In a special car, two clean and comfortable beds had been made up for Jack Van Dyne and the Donovans' son who were brought aboard on stretchers.

I don't know which young man looked sicker. Their emaciated faces were yellow, their eyes glassy. The Donovan boy was drooling and semiconscious. Jack was awake and trying to smile but incapable of coherent speech. Both had on the filthy, tattered uniforms they had worn when they debarked at Montauk from Cuba. They had not been issued pajamas or, if so, had been too weak to put them on. We were not permitted to get close to them but we tried to look encouraging from a distance as attendants carried them onto the train. Marta smiled tremulously at Jack although her face was wet with tears.

A civilian nurse Jay had hired would care for the two young soldiers en route. They would be met by an ambulance in New York and taken straight to Bellevue Hospital where Jay would see to it that they had the very best care.

Mr. and Mrs. Donovan, Marta, Jay, and I settled into the comfortable chairs of the private sitting-room car. The Donovans thanked Jay over and over for helping their son. Jay told us that he had arranged to contribute substantial sums to Camp Wikoff for food and medical care and had learned that other wealthy persons such as Helen Gould whose yacht had been anchored off Montauk when the troops arrived, were also contributing so that conditions at the camp would soon improve.

"And we must all thank Miss Lorimer," Jay said, gazing at me warmly. "If it had not been for her, I wouldn't have come to Montauk. I wish I could express my gratitude adequately, Miss Lorimer. If anything had happened to Marta—I just can't tell you what it means to me that you took this journey to find her." He did not turn away from me after his brief speech, but continued to gaze into my face. With the Donovans looking on, I was embarrassed, and so it was I who broke the moment by looking away and murmuring something to Marta. When I looked back at Jay, he had turned to talk to the Donovans, and he did not give me such a look again.

We rode all the way into Long Island City and saw the Donovans and the two young invalids safely aboard the ferry to New York before returning to the train which would take us over the private spur to Soundcliff.

Jay spent most of the short trip talking to Marta, but just before we arrived at Soundcliff he said to me, "Do you remember our conversation the day we had the nature walk?"

"Of course," I said.

"Do you remember what I told you about my plans for Gus Flammon? About the LIH&M and his Empire State Railroad?"

"Indeed yes."

"Do you read the newspapers?"

"Every morning."

"Well, I just wanted you to know that the first part of the plan is in motion. Watch the financial pages. You'll be able to see how I'm doing." He smiled, and his eyes were full of mischief.

I smiled back. "Oh, I shall read every line. Good luck."

He grinned. "You don't know how much it pleases me to know I have you as a sympathetic audience. It's no fun to show off without someone to show off for."

Then we had arrived. We stepped down onto the platform and passed through the pretty little station house. It made me sad to realize that if Jay's plan succeeded, the station and the private train would no longer be ours to use, at least temporarily. I made a small, silent prayer that the daring plan would work well enough to let us gain it all back very soon.

We were quiet during the short ride to the house. Jay sat with his arm protectively about Marta. She was pale and somber, worried about Jack and also, no doubt, about the reception she would get from Eleanor. Her father would intercede, but there were still many ways that Eleanor could make

Marta miserable, and Marta knew it.

Jay broke the silence just once as the carriage approached Soundcliff. "Thank you again, Miss Lorimer," he said.

TEN

The mid-September days were still hot and summery when the children and I resumed lessons. But soon autumn chilled the air, and we settled into our schoolroom routine in earnest.

Marta was more distracted than ever. She continued to worry about Jack Van Dyne, who had been in the hospital for over a month and was still far from well. Eleanor had been applying her own brand of mental torture to Marta, mostly as heavy sarcasm when Jay wasn't within hearing. Usually Marta was sullenly silent under these attacks, but occasionally she would ignite into screaming fury. If the relationship between them had not been hopeless before, it was now. How long could it go on before something or someone snapped?

Eleaner had begun to use the same tactic on me. Whenever Jay was out of earshot—and this was usual, as he had seemed to be deliberately staying out of my way—she would find fault with my appearance, my words, my teaching, or simply my being in some room she chanced to enter. Although no one of her unpleasantnesses was unbearable, the cumulative effect was racking. I began to feel that she was biding her time, barely controlling her hatred, waiting for an opportunity to triumph over me in some awful way. I began to have trouble getting to sleep and would sometimes wake in the middle of the night thinking that I heard sounds from the secret passageway behind my bed.

At about this time, Ginger took to coming into my room, occasionally sleeping the night through at the end of my bed. One night, I awoke again from a sound sleep with the sensation of having heard sounds in the passageway. There was a splash of bright moonlight across the foot of the bed, and silhouetted in the eerie light was Ginger—back arched, fur standing out—emitting a low, whining growl. I sat bolt upright, listening with every nerve. Did I hear footsteps fading away down the stairs behind the wall? I leaped from the bed, lit my lamp, and pressed an ear to the panel behind the trunk. But now there was nothing to be heard, if there ever had been at all, and Ginger was sitting calmly on the bed licking her paws. After a while I put out the light and crept back into bed, feeling foolish but still glad for Ginger's company.

Although Jay and I were in the same house, I seldom saw and never spoke to him. My only way of feeling close to him was to follow the articles that began to appear, as he had predicted, in the daily newspapers. Jay Caldwell's business empire was reported to be shaky, especially the railroad. The price of LIH&M stock slipped, then plunged and seemed unable to recover. One morning in late October, as the household was involved in packing up for the autumn return to New York, the story was on the front page. August Flammon had bought up the majority of shares. Now owning the LIH&M outright, he had, of course, dismissed Jay Caldwell as president. At breakfast, the staff was chewing over this dreadful news when Jay came striding into the kitchen.

"I just want to tell you all that we'll be returning to New York on the *North Star*. The LIH&M isn't ours any more. I see you've been reading about that." He nodded toward the newspaper spread out on the breakfast table. "But you're not to worry about it. Just trust me." And he flashed a big smile, a smile I thought was directed at me. Then he was gone.

"Now, what do you make of that?" said Ada Wirth, scooping a panful of scrambled eggs onto a hot platter.

"I don't know, but if Mr. Jay says not to worry, then I know we don't need to worry," said Nellie Morgan.

"Well, he's got to say that, doesn't he?" Nancy Vance put in. "He's got to keep up our spirits, else we'd all be out looking for other jobs."

"That's a disgraceful thing to say!" Mrs. Morgan cried, outraged.

"Just practical," retorted Nancy.

"Then I suggest you start looking now," Hans Arnold snapped.

"Hold on, Hans," Geoffrey snarled. "You got nothing to say about it."

"Excuse me, I've had enough," I murmured and left, unnoticed, as angry words peppered the air. I walked into the front hallway and encountered Jay.

"Is it really all right?" I asked.

"According to plan," he smiled, then hurried toward the front door where Eleanor was waiting for him. They were going out together, and I started on up the stairs. Partway up, something compelled me to turn around. Eleanor was watching me from the doorway, her eyes narrowed with hatred. She had seen my brief exchange with Jay and, insignificant as it had been, it had apparently enraged her. I decided to stay away from the front of the house altogether from then on, to try never to run into Jay at all. I started to feel that I was in a prison, the invisible bars constructed of Eleanor's jealousy and loathing. I started to wonder if she was quite balanced mentally.

On the thirtieth of October, Soundcliff was closed, the furniture under dust sheets, the chandeliers in bags. Leaving a caretaker staff behind, we descended the cliffside steps in a great procession of trunks, boxes, bundles, bags, and staff. We boarded the *North Star* which was quite large enough to transport all of us, family and servants alike, to New York.

The yacht was almost as big, it seemed to me, as an ocean liner. We didn't see the family staterooms but were ushered across the teak deck, past gleaming mahogany rails and highly polished brass fittings, to a set of stairs leading down to the great saloon where there was plenty of seating for all of us.

It was a very cold day for October, but I decided to go back up on deck for awhile to watch Soundcliff recede into a perspective I had not had of her before. We were well offshore now, and she was just one of a number of great estates ranged along the cliffs above the shore like castles on the Rhine. To imagine the life that had gone on there that summer—to remember the dazzling Fourth-of-July party, the bitter family quarrels, the pleasant hours with Bertie, the few precious moments with Jay—it all seemed unreal, something from a book. My eyes filled with tears, and I realized that I was already missing Soundcliff. Would I ever return? Or would Eleanor find a way to be rid of me before the next Soundcliff season?

We passed close by Execution Rock, and I shuddered as I glanced at the little craggy island almost swallowed by the lapping tide. When I turned back toward Soundcliff, the great granite house was out of view, hidden by the curved, wooded shoreline. Suddenly I realized that I was quite numb with cold, and I went down to the saloon to join the others.

Some time later, as the *North Star* passed through the Hellgate and began to sail down the East River, we all went back up on deck and crowded along the rails to enjoy the passing skyline of Manhattan. Before long, we had docked at Thirty-fourth Street, got into the waiting carriages, and shortly, we pulled up before the marble edifice at 577 Fifth Avenue. Nellie Morgan told me I was to have the same room I had had last April if I wished it, and I said I did. I went straight up and fell asleep on the little bed, missing supper altogether.

The next day, we started lessons in the small schoolroom at 577, and as one November day succeeded another, life began to seem much as it had at Soundcliff. True, we hadn't the Soundcliff grounds and waters to enjoy, but the weather had turned bitterly cold, and I was content to remain indoors most of the time anyway, enjoying only an occasional short walk on sunny afternoons to Central Park or down Fifth Avenue.

Christmas was fast approaching, and I began to browse in the Fifth Avenue shops and to purchase small gifts for the other staff members. My earliest and favorite discovery was a small white pin cushion shaped like a goose with yellow felt feet and black felt eyes. It had an elastic band to secure it to the wrist. I knew Susan would love it. I bought it, took it home, and tucked it away at the back of a dresser drawer, feeling very pleased with my small secret.

The daily newspapers had become the focus of staff gossip. We pored over the financial pages for word of Jay Caldwell's fortunes. The news was all gloomy. Jay had lost the railroad to August Flammon, and there was no hint of the magnificent counteroffensive he had planned against Flammon's Empire State Railroad. I knew that he had to keep his stock acquisitions an absolute secret, so I didn't expect to see anything about them in the papers. Indeed, a news item would have been a bad sign, an unwelcome leak. Yet somehow, I was increasingly nervous about his gamble: What if it failed? The entire Caldwell fortune rested in the balance. I resolutely put these thoughts aside.

Another news topic of interest was the candidacy of Colonel Roosevelt for Governor of New York State. The political boom for Roosevelt had begun at Camp Wikoff where the hero of the Rough Riders had been much in the public eye, and shortly after our return to 577, he was elected. Jubilation engulfed the household. After all, the new governor was a longtime Long Island neighbor and friend of the Caldwell family.

Joy approached hysteria when Jay announced to the staff that Governor-elect and Mrs. Roosevelt had accepted his and Eleanor's invitation to be guests of honor at a Christmas Eve ball, a celebration of Colonel Roosevelt's election and a send-off to Albany, the state capital. Some of the staff thought the ball an expensive bit of bravado in the face of Jay's apparently declining fortunes. I thought it a good sign, an indication that perhaps things were going well in his secret war against August Flammon. But whatever we thought of the extravagance, everyone was delighted at the prospect of the ball. "Much too long since the ballroom was used!" exclaimed Hans Arnold, rubbing his hands with relish.

Before the ball, a dinner was to be held for Colonel and Mrs. Roosevelt and twenty other select guests. Hans disappeared into the silver vault where he directed a polishing orgy that lasted for days. Ada went into a similar seclusion in the pantry to assemble the serving pieces and the ingredients that would be required for the menu Eleanor had ordered.

Meanwhile, Hans had sent the invitations. Ordinarily, for such a dinner, he would also have had responsibility for suggesting and telephoning last-minute fill-ins for guests who declined. But this time, no refusals were expected.

Now the ballroom—just beyond the parlor that Nellie Morgan had ushered me into the day I first came to 577—was invaded by a small battalion of servants stripping and rewaxing the woodwork and the floor. Then the great chandelier was dismantled, and each crystal droplet was washed, polished, and rehung by footmen wearing white cotton gloves in order not to dull the sparkle with fingerprints. New red plush carpeting was laid upon a raised platform that would be occupied on Christmas Eve by the very best orchestra in New York.

I caught only glimpses of all this activity. I had kept my private vow to stay away from the front of the house, and my daily round encompassed primarily my own bedroom, the kitchen, and the schoolroom. But the excitement crept even into my small realm. From my bedroom window, I could see delivery wagons, one after the other, pulling up to the service door. In the schoolroom, the children could not stop chattering about Colonel Roosevelt and the Christmas-Eve ball, especially since Marta was to be allowed to attend, her first grown-up party. And of course, in the kitchen no one talked of anything else.

One morning, I found a small envelope addressed to me upon my schoolroom desk. Inside was an invitation to the ball. Nancy Vance and Susan Sayre had been addressing the ball invitations, but the handwriting on my invitation was Jay's. Now, the iron restraint with which I had held my emotions disintegrated. Wild fantasies filled my head, along with sweet memories of the Fourth of July waltz. I pictured myself on Christmas Eve, whirling round and round in Jay's arms, the air full of music and crystal light.

I would have to wear something very special, but what? Lowering the neckline of an afternoon dress would not produce a gown appropriate for a Christmas Eve ball, it seemed to me. Yet, I could certainly not afford to purchase anything as beautiful as the dresses I dreamed of.

My dress for the ball became the topic of conversation at the breakfast table one morning, and I confessed my despair. "Surely you must have something we can alter," Susan offered sweetly. Reality pierced my dreams. After all, I really had no choice. Late in the afternoon, Susan came to my room, and we selected a black bombazine silk Susan thought she could enhance with some jet beads and black ostrich feathers she had in her trunk of sewing scraps. "I shan't be able to work on it for a few days," Susan said, "but I'll take it with me and start on it as soon as I can." I thanked her and tried to resign myself to the idea of wearing a made-over dress instead of the new one I longed for.

Imagine my amazement the following afternoon when I went to my room after lessons and found an enormous box in the middle of my bed. For a moment, I was afraid even to approach it. In fact, I sat in my chair and looked at it for a few moments before getting up and laying my fingertips on it. It was wrapped in pink tissue and tied with an enormous green bow. It was so pretty I hated to disturb it.

At last I carefully untied the bow and laid back the pink paper. Inside was a shiny gray box bearing the name "Arnold Constable and Company." I had passed the store on the Broadway cable car the day I had come to 577. It seemed a good omen.

Gently, I lifted the lid—and then I drew a sharp breath. I knew at once, of course, that it was a dress. I couldn't see the details, but the sheer beauty of the fabric stunned me. It was an emerald-green silk velvet, so lush I wanted to bury my face in its soft, rich folds. I stretched out my hand and stroked it tenderly.

After a few moments, I lifted the dress from the pink tissue and laid it out on the bed. It was simply cut, having a deep neckline and little capped sleeves gathered up at the shoulders, a smooth bodice, narrow waistline, and softly-draped full skirt. Quickly, I slipped out of my skirt and shirtwaist, raised the heavy velvet gown, and let it drop over my head. With some effort I partially buttoned it up the back and stepped in front of the tall pier glass in the corner. I could scarcely believe my eyes.

I had always felt myself to be plain, even mousy, with my pale complexion and hair and slight figure. The dress transformed me. My eyes sparkled green to match it. My skin looked like ivory, and there was a blush of excitement on my cheeks. The cut of the dress made my figure look dainty rather than just small. I was not given to flattering myself, but even to my self-critical eyes I looked pretty. I would purchase green ribbons to twine in my hair, I decided.

I glanced at the hemline drooping on the floor, and for a moment my heart sank. I needed some pretty high-heeled dancing shoes and didn't know if I could afford or even find just the right pair. But when I turned back to the bed, I saw a small bundle of pink tissue tucked into a corner of the dress box, and when I folded back the paper I discovered a pair of green satin slippers with pink satin roses at the instep. The green matched the green of the dress exactly. I slipped them on and, like the dress, they were a perfect fit.

Someone had gone to a great deal of trouble to ascertain my shoe and dress size and to select clothes that suited me exquisitely. I hugged myself and twirled around the room in tight, happy circles. Someone—someone, indeed. The darling! The dear! He had sent my invitation to the ball, then realized I would not be able to afford the proper dress. He had taken the time to buy me one, and his caring was written in the selection. Only a man in love could choose so perfectly.

How happy I was—happier than I had ever been before. A few days later, I was able to find satin hair ribbons that exactly matched the dress and shoes, and buying them gave me an almost idiotic sense of delight. In addition to the ribbons, I bought a shamefully expensive packet of scented bath salts, and on the evening of the ball, I filled the tub, poured in the entire packet of scented salts, and had the most heavenly soak of my life. I dressed slowly and took a great deal of time twisting my hair into smooth coils at the back of my head, winding the emerald ribbons in and out. Two soft curls wanted to escape in front of my ears, and I let them.

Susan tapped on my door and oohed and ahed over the dress as she buttoned it up the back for me. Just as I stepped into the satin slippers, Mrs. Morgan and Ada Wirth came in to see how I looked and expressed their approval. I had told no one about where I had gotten the dress, merely murmuring something about a gift from a friend. Since no one knew where I had come from or whether or not I had family or friends, they could not question my story. But I'm sure the suddenness of such a lavish gift from a "friend" of the little governess caused much gossip. Now, as I took a last glance at myself in the pier glass, I saw that Susan, Nellie, and Ada were giving each other meaningful glances behind me.

"Well, here I go," was all I said, however, and

with a quick kiss on the cheek from Susan and with Nellie and Ada giving my skirt a last-minute smoothing, I walked down the stairs.

I confess that my heart was pounding in spite of the confidence I had gained from the dress. The guests would all be New York society, and the very fact of the Governor-elect's presence was enough to terrify me.

As I rounded the marble staircase and the main hallway blazed into view below, I gasped. I had never imagined that such brilliant light could be achieved. The great chandelier was fully lit, and there were banks and banks of candelabra about the entrance hall. They perfectly enhanced the rich, fragrant festoons made of dark green fir boughs with red holly berries and great red-velvet bows. A deep red carpet extended across the marble floor, through the great double doors, and down the steps to the curb where guests were alighting from carriages under a deep green canopy.

A group of newly-arrived ladies passed me on the stairs. They swept upward in their velvet, satin, and brocade cloaks, chattering gaily among themselves as they mounted to a dressing area that had been set aside on the second floor. It was from there that Susan had slipped away to help me dress, for it was her duty and that of several other young maids to take and hang the ladies' wraps and to assist them in the last-minute repairs to hair arrangements that had been ruffled by the winter winds. The gentlemen were disappearing toward a cloakroom that had been arranged at the rear of the hallway under the stairs. As I stood on the stairs, alone and bewildered, another group of ladies passed me coming down, joined their escorts, and drifted into the parlor that served as anteroom to the ballroom. Just inside, Jay and Eleanor would be greeting them.

The idea of passing by Jay and Eleanor on my way into the ballroom made me so self-conscious that I actually considered going back upstairs. Yet the strains of waltz music floating into the hallway, the lights, the warm odor of the fir boughs, and the gaiety of the crowd held me fast. I could go neither down nor up. For an instant, I thought I might never move at all, but remain rooted to the spot like a statue, midway up the great staircase, forever.

It was Bertie, as usual, who rescued me. He emerged from the cloakroom, spied me on the staircase, and came to me.

"Lillie, you're a picture," he beamed, taking my arm and leading me, weak-kneed, down the stairs. "You are absolutely the most beautiful woman here. The most beautiful woman in New York." His hyperbole made me laugh, and at once I felt better—almost relaxed, almost as if I belonged.

We swept by Jay and Eleanor. "Good evening, good evening, Merry Christmas," Bertie called out as we passed, covering charmingly my own bashful silence; and then we were in the ballroom.

The very first person I saw was Colonel Roosevelt, surrounded by admirers, laughing loudly and talking with his characteristic energy. He was captivating, and Bertie wanted to take me over to talk to him, but I demurred. My courage was much too tenuous for the overwhelming experience of conversing with the Governor-elect of New York.

The orchestra struck up another waltz, and Bertie danced me out onto the floor. Even crowded with people as it was, the room seemed huge. We waltzed around and around in great, swinging loops and made only one complete tour of the perimeter before the music stopped. By now, I was breathless and flushed and very nearly intoxicated by the light, the music, and the excitement. I was not alone. Everyone seemed in the same high, good spirits. Everywhere, smiles became grins and dissolved into laughter. The party was already a splendid success.

I tried to give Bertie my complete attention, but my eyes were continually drawn to the doorway where, at long last, Jay appeared. Eleanor was with him, of course, but I saw only him. He danced with Mrs. Roosevelt, so elegant and so pretty. Then he danced with Eleanor. Then he began to dance with the other ladies, one after another. I waited calmly, happily, dancing alternately with Bertie and with a variety of other gentlemen, none of whom I remember at all. I exchanged the usual pleasantries with each one, but I was scarcely aware of what I said, even to Bertie who took as many dances as he could with me.

I knew that Jay had to act the host, to dance with as many female guests as he could. But surely he must be aware of me, aware of how I looked in the lovely dress he had bought for me. Some time, perhaps late in the evening, he would find the opportunity to have one dance with me—one dance I could live on for many weeks to come. It would look as if he were merely doing a kindness to the little governess; but he and I would know better. I anticipated his arm about my waist, his hand holding mine. There would be a subtle pressure, invisible to others but significant to us. For this, I would happily wait all night.

Marta came in. She danced with her father, and then with a string of eligible young men. She was wearing her first grown-up ball gown, a lovely powder blue silk, and her auburn hair was piled high. How pretty she was, just one week shy of her fifteenth birthday.

Marta had invited Jack Van Dyne, unbeknownst to her mother but with her father's approval. That he would come was far from certain as he was just out of the hospital and still rather weak; but he did arrive at last. Marta went directly to him, gave him two dances in a row, then sat by him on the gilded chairs at the edge of the floor, turning down all other invitations to dance, clearly disappointing greatly the young men who asked.

Eleanor glared at Marta and Jack from a distance; then she moved forward as if to go to them. I couldn't imagine what she would say, but I was sure it would be contrived to spoil Marta's evening. Just in time, Jay stepped to Eleanor's side, laid a restraining hand on her arm, and spoke into her ear. She turned away with an angry shrug. Not long after, Jack left, looking exhausted, and Marta was once again surrounded by other young admirers.

Old Eli Caldwell had come, dressed in a well-worn tuxedo. He could not join in the dancing, of course, but sat on the sidelines chatting with a succession of guests who came to sit beside him. I could see that the experience was tiring for him, however, and shortly after Jack Van Dyne's departure, Eli went upstairs.

The hours slipped by, and my anticipation intensified. At last, near midnight, Colonel and Mrs. Roosevelt left. They had stayed far longer than anyone had hoped, seeming to enjoy the party more than anyone. The Governor-elect's uninhibited, irresistible laugh rang out again and again, and Mrs. Roosevelt's shy reserve had seemed to melt away as the gay evening went on. Everyone was disappointed when they had gone, and yet, instead of winding down, the party moved into a higher key. At two o'clock, almost no one had gone home. It seemed as if the party would spin itself on and on, right into Christmas morning.

But a heaviness began to steal over me. The hour was very late, and soon the party tide would break and ebb upon the shore of morning. Now, surely now, Jay would dance with me, I thought. But he did not. In fact, I realized, he had not so much as looked in my direction all evening long. If he was aware of my presence, he was hiding it well. If he intended to dance with me, he had missed a number of opportunities.

On I went, dipping and gliding around the floor with one gentleman after another, smiling and chatting. But now my smile felt made of glass. Each time the music stopped and my partner led me back to the gilt chairs, I looked for Jay to see if he might be coming my way. I had stopped being subtle about it, and finally Bertie said to me, "Don't look at him so often. It will be noticed." I blushed deeply and ducked my head. I had thought I was keeping Bertie unaware of my feelings about Jay, but now I understood that I had hidden nothing at all. Bertie patted my hand.

At three o'clock, one or two couples left, then several more. At three-thirty, Jay and Eleanor stopped dancing and drifted toward the parlor to bid their guests good night. The orchestra continued to play, but now only a few couples were still dancing, and one or two of the musicians had begun to pack up their instruments.

The party was over. As I sat there on my little gilt chair with Bertie beside me, my Christmas-Eve dream dissolved. In spite of myself, my eyes filled with tears. I looked down at my hands, folded stiffly in my lap, and tried to keep the tears from spilling over. Bertie talked along as if he hadn't noticed—"It's been a glorious evening, hasn't it? The newspapers will be full of it. The grand success of the season"—and on and on until I got control of myself.

"I believe I shall go up now, Bertie," I said. "Do you mind?"

"Of course not, beautiful Lillie," he said sweetly, nearly causing the tears to spill over after all. He led me from the ballroom, past Jay and Eleanor who were busy with a little knot of departing guests, and into the grand hallway. The double doors were open, and Hans was seeing the guests out the door. On the sidewalk beyond, Geoffrey was helping them into the carriages that pulled up one behind the other along the curb.

I looked at Bertie. "Thank you." My voice came out as a whisper. "It was a wonderful evening. Truly it was."

He squeezed my hand. "Sleep well, dear."

I went up to my room, undressed, and hung the beautiful green velvet dress in the armoire. I stared at it bitterly. Why had Jay given it to me if he intended to ignore me? Surely he had known how the dress would raise my hopes. Surely he knew how cruelly his indifference would wound me. It was monstrous.

I crept between the sheets and slept miserably.

ELEVEN

Christmas Day was to be a divided celebration in the Caldwell house. The staff would have an early breakfast featuring Ada's famous hot cinnamon buns; then they would serve Christmas breakfast to the family. Afterwards, the family would exchange Christmas gifts in the parlor that had been the anteroom to the ball the night before. A tree was to be hastily erected and decorated before dawn to surprise and delight Bonnie, Leo, and even Marta, who was not yet too old to be excited about Christmas. While the family exchange was taking place, the staff would gather and exchange gifts around a somewhat smaller tree in the oriental parlor across the hall, and at a later moment, Eli, Jay, Eleanor, and the children would come in to give their gifts to the staff. Still later, Bertie Archer was to join the family for Christmas lunch. This was the way it had always been.

The day began according to tradition. Susan knocked on my door very early. I dragged myself unwillingly from bed, dressed in a plain black skirt and white shirtwaist, and joined the others in the kitchen for breakfast. I could have gone back to my room while the family breakfast was being served, but I had already brought down my little bundle of gifts, and I craved company to keep my mind from the misery of the Christmas Eve ball, so I stayed in the kitchen until time to gather in the parlor.

The gifts we had for each other were simple and all the more touching for that, I thought—handkerchiefs, pomanders, knitted mufflers, and so on. Everyone exclaimed happily over each little gift and showed it about. It was a very pleasant hour.

The running topic of conversation, of course, was the ball—who had been there, what they had worn, what bits of society gossip had been overheard in the cloakrooms, how one of the waiters had nearly dropped baked Alaska into the lap of an important dinner guest. The cheery talk relieved my gloom, and I began to realize, after the fact, just how marvelous the ball had been. What an extraordinary experience for a young woman of my humble background, I lectured myself. I had spoiled my own good time with fantasies, fantasies I had sworn to abandon. I had been nothing but a silly goose.

"Goose!" I exclaimed half out loud. I had completely forgotten about the little pin-cushion goose for Susan, tucked away in my bureau drawer these many weeks. I ran up the stairs to fetch it. I had regained a happy frame of mind and was looking forward to giving Susan the little gift. I knew she would find it charming. I flung open my bedroom door and then stopped, puzzled. The green velvet dress, which had been in the armoire, was laid upon the bed. Had someone taken it down to brush it? But surely not. Who would have had the time on Christmas morning, and who would have failed to hang it back on the armoire?

These were but fleeting thoughts, and I hadn't even time to complete them before I saw that there was something wrong, something on the dress—something black. I went to the bed, and then, I'm afraid, I screamed.

Someone had poured ink on the beautiful green dress. The empty bottle was on my bedside table. It was one of the little inkwells from the schoolroom. The ink had been poured carefully. A big stain spread across the bodice and long rivers ran down the skirt, yet none of it had splashed onto the bedspread or floor. The dress, of course, was ruined. It was another instant before I saw the note pinned to it, written on schoolroom paper in the same ink. In big, printed letters it read simply, "Go away."

I was at once crushed with grief and stricken with fear at the crudely vicious act. I turned, fled down the stairs, and burst into the oriental parlor, sobbing. I tried to tell the others what was wrong, but all I could manage was, "My dress, my dress." They all got up and gathered about me, and everyone began talking at once, all trying to find out what was wrong. It must have been quite a commotion, for in a moment Jay came striding through the door.

"What's going on?" he demanded.

"It's something about her dress, sir," said Ada, "but we don't know what."

I was still weeping into my handkerchief but gained control enough to blurt, "Someone has spilled ink on my dress—upstairs in my room."

"Come on. Let's have a look," Jay said, and taking me by the elbow, he led me back across the hall and up the stairs with everyone else following right behind. I was now almost as embarrassed as I was upset, but I was glad for his presence, for I had not recovered from my fright.

Jay took a look at the dress and his face turned beet red. "By thunder," he muttered, then whirled about and started back downstairs. I followed closely behind, not knowing what he was going to do but unwilling to be parted from his strength. The others came straggling along after us.

Down we came into the great hallway, and Jay stormed directly into the parlor where Eleanor, Eli, and the children were gathered. I stopped short in the doorway, but Jay turned and pulled me in by the wrist. The others hung back in the hallway, out of sight but within hearing, I was sure.

"Eleanor—" Jay's voice was choked and the veins stood out in his neck—"Eleanor, what do you know about the ink on Miss Lorimer's dress?"

As the words left his mouth, I knew as surely as I

had ever known anything that Jay's instinct was correct, that Eleanor indeed had done it. The look in her eyes was unbearable, the look of a child who has done something terrible and knows it will be punished. Instantly, however, it was as if a film had dropped over the lenses, blanking out emotion.

"Ink? What ink? What on earth are you talking about?"

"Ink," he said through his teeth, "has been spilled on Miss Lorimer's dress, and a threatening note was pinned to it."

"Might a child have done it?" she asked smoothly. I remembered the block printing on the note, but I felt sure that a child's hand had not formed those letters—no child in this house, at any rate. Bonnie's letters were not so correctly formed yet, and Leo had long stopped printing in favor of script. Nor had the careful spilling of the ink been the work of a child. So I was utterly stunned to hear Eleanor continue, "I think Leo may have done it."

Leo's head shot up and his jaw dropped. He was obviously too surprised to speak.

"Leo!" Jay snorted. "Why in the world would Leo do something like that?"

"Because Leo loves his mother, don't you darling?" She slid over along the sofa until she was next to Leo who sat on the floor playing with a toy train. She leaned forward and put her arm around his shoulders. "And I won't hear of you punishing him for it."

Jay crossed the floor in three strides and pulled Eleanor's arm away from Leo. "Say what you have to say and say it fast, Eleanor."

She jerked her arm from Jay's rough grasp but didn't put it around Leo again. "Everyone in the house knows you bought that dress for her! A little boy would be jealous for his mother, wouldn't he? To know his father prefers a servant to his mother. To think that his father would buy a beautiful velvet ball dress for a servant to flaunt in front of their guests!"

For an instant I thought she was going to cry, but she didn't. She stuck out her jaw and assumed an indignant look that would have been convincing if one had not known that the story about Leo was a lie.

"Eleanor, what the devil are you talking about? I didn't buy that dress for Miss Lorimer!" My heart stopped.

"Don't say that, Jay!" Rage now began to color Eleanor's face and roughen her voice. "She could never have afforded a dress like that for herself. She even told the servants it was a gift from a friend, Nancy told me. What other 'friend' does she have? If you didn't buy it for her, my dear husband, pray tell who did?"

"I did, I'm afraid." We all turned to see Bertie standing in the doorway. He had arrived just in time to hear Eleanor's tirade.

I felt faint with chagrin. How could I have been so stupid? Would Jay, who had been conscientiously avoiding me all these weeks, make a gesture as blatant and foolhardy as buying me a ball gown? Of course not. Yet it was exactly the sort of wonderfully extravagant thing Bertie would do. My desire to believe Jay cared had led me to distort, to ignore what common sense should have told me. But apparently the servants, or some of them, had reached the same wrong conclusion, for Eleanor had heard it from Nancy Vance.

I felt my face glow scarlet, but no one was paying much attention to me. As one, the group in the parlor had turned to Bertie. Now they turned back to Eleanor. Surely she must have felt as abashed as I, if not more. She had not only made the same mistake in believing Jay had bought me the dress, but she had made an open scene about it. I, at least, had kept my thought to myself. But if I had expected to find shame written on Eleanor's face, I was mistaken. Emotionless calm was hers once more.

"That's right. Cover for him, Bertie," she said frostily. "You always did stick up for Jay over me."

Bertie came into the room and sat by Eleanor. "Eleanor, I'm your cousin, and I love you. Do you think I would lie about this? Do you want me to show you the sales receipts?" He tried to take her hand but she snatched it away.

"Oh, I'm sure you arranged all the details between you. Jay would have given you the receipts, the 'evidence.' Maybe he even had you make the purchase for him so the salespeople wouldn't recognize him. I don't doubt that it was all done very cleverly."

Bertie was exasperated. "Eleanor, why do you persist in this?"

"Don't you see, Bertie? He insisted on hiring

her. He won't fire her, even though she displeases me. He insisted on inviting her to the Fourth of July party and dancing with her during the fireworks. He insisted on inviting her to the ball last night. And did you know about their little 'nature walk' together last spring? And did you know about their little jaunt to Montauk together? He cares for her! He can't hide it! Everyone has noticed it!"

She turned back to Leo who had grown as pale and as silent as a little mushroom. "You see? You see how he looks? The children have eyes and ears. They are aware of what's going on. But Leo loves his mother too much. He couldn't stand it. He wanted that woman to go away. So he emptied his little inkwell on the dress and wrote her a note to go away. It was very naughty, of course, but it proves how much he loves me, doesn't it? Even if the father doesn't love, the son loves. So there's some comfort. You're a comfort to your mother, aren't you, Leo?"

Tears slipped from Leo's eyes and down his cheeks as his mother moved toward him again. Jay intervened and gathered Leo into his arms.

It was a hideous moment. Eleanor had given herself away, of course, by mentioning the inkwell and the wording of the note which, according to her charade, she had not seen and which Jay had not described to her. Yet the fever of conviction lit her eyes. Through some mental transmogrification, she had come to believe what she was saying.

"Hush, Leo," Jay was crooning to the now-weeping little boy. "I know you didn't do it. We all know. Mama is just very upset, you see. She doesn't mean to hurt you."

A scream issued from Eleanor's throat, so sudden and so piercing that everyone jumped. "Now you're trying to steal him from me!" she cried. "My son! My little son! The only one who loves me!" She lunged as if to grab Leo. Jay pulled him away from her, and at the same time Bertie seized her in his arms.

"Eleanor! We *all* love you! Stop it! Stop it!"

Eleanor began to thrash wildly about. Bertie tried to restrain her. Jay motioned to Marta to take Leo and Bonnie away. I went to the doorway, then stopped. I dared not follow the children for fear Eleanor would think I was conspiring over them, but Eli Caldwell went out and beckoned to Nellie Morgan and the two of them went upstairs. The children, I knew, would be in good hands for the moment.

When they had gone, Eleanor's wildness vanished and she collapsed onto the sofa. Jay and Bertie sat down on either side of her, and then I slipped out the door. Most of the staff were still standing in the hall. I gave them a wretched look, then started for the stairs; but Ada and Susan stopped me.

"Don't go up there," Susan pleaded. "The dress is still in your room, and it will upset you."

"Come into the kitchen," Ada advised. I followed her meekly, and she fixed me some hot broth which I gratefully drank.

"He didn't buy me the dress," I said.

"We know," Susan declared.

"Perhaps I should leave, find another position," I said dismally. "I'm causing trouble just by being here."

"No, no. It's not to do with you," said Ada. "It's Miss Eleanor. She would pick on someone else if not you. She can't help it."

I didn't dare to tell them what I really felt: "But don't you see, I care for Jay. I care for him, even if he doesn't care for me." Whatever Eleanor's mental state, whatever her penchant for unfounded jealousy, this time her feelings were based on a truth. I was no threat to her—Jay would never be untrue—but in my deepest heart, I wished I were.

After some time, Bertie appeared in the kitchen doorway, and Ada and Susan discreetly retired. He sat next to me at the table.

"It's clear Eleanor is in a very bad state of mind. She's still insisting that Leo spilled the ink. She needs a rest, and Jay wants her away from the children for awhile. She's agreed to go to Soundcliff, and I'm going to go with her to look after her. Everyone else is to stay here, including you, of course."

"Oh, Bertie," I moaned. "I honestly don't know what to do."

"Nothing hasty, please," he smiled.

I smiled back. "Bertie, thank you for the dress. I didn't know it was from you." I didn't say that I, too, had thought it was from Jay, but I suppose he knew. "I'm so sorry it was ruined, but I did love wearing it."

"And I loved seeing you in it. So it served its

purpose, after all. Don't worry about it now. Get some rest for the next few days, and don't leave us, if that's what you're thinking."

I looked into his eyes. "I was thinking it."

"Don't. Think of the children. They need you."

I put my head down on my arms, and Bertie laid a gentle hand on my shoulder.

"Rest, rest. Don't think for awhile. I'll see you soon." And he was gone.

While Bertie was talking with me, Susan had gone up and removed the dress from my room. And now Ada sent me upstairs with a tray of sandwiches which I ate, looking mournfully out the dormer window over the rooftops. I lay on the bed for awhile, trying to nap, but found that I was only becoming more depressed and farther from sleep. I looked at my watch and saw that it was three o'clock.

"What I need is a long walk," I decided. I put on warm boots, heavy coat, woolen mittens, and a scarf. Then I went down the back stairs, through the kitchen, and out into the alleyway. I had met no one. I turned out onto Fifth Avenue and began to walk downtown.

It was cold. The late afternoon sky was gray and low, and there was a dampness in the air. Perhaps it would snow. I walked along at a steady pace and found the rhythm of walking to be a tonic. The cold air cleared my brain, and my thoughts ran steadily and calmly. I almost seemed to be assessing someone else's situation, so free of emotion did I feel as I covered the long blocks.

I did not, could not, know if Jay cared for me at all. What evidence did I have? Only a dance half a year ago when he had pressed my body against his. But he had been angry with his wife then, and reacting to her dancing with Gus Flammon, so there may have been nothing personal in the strength with which he had held me. He had fought with Eleanor about me that night, but she had been the one who said he cared for me. She had accused him of it, but he had not confirmed her suspicions. He had not denied them, it was true, but perhaps he was just too angry to answer her. He had defended me from her attack, had said he would kill her if she harmed me. But might these words not have been prompted more by her excesses than by his affection for me?

I had thought that he cared for me, had believed it. But then, I had also believed that he bought me the green velvet dress, and he had not. Nor had he danced with me on Christmas Eve as I had thought he would. So perhaps his caring for me had all along been only the product of my imagination.

But whether or not he cared for me, he had done nothing to violate Eleanor's trust, and I was sure he never would. Indeed, he had gone far out of his way to avoid me, to avoid giving her the smallest reason to suspect him of favoring me. He had catered to her jealousy as much as any man could.

But it had been for naught. She believed that he cared for me and would continue to think so no matter how he behaved, no matter how I behaved. I might have been able to stand it if I had felt pure at heart. But I loved him. I knew it was wrong to remain in his household feeling as I did, though nothing, nothing would ever come of it.

And what of the children? What of my belief that they needed me? Was this not just one more example of my own pride? Could it possibly help them to be exposed to scenes such as the one my presence had caused that very afternoon? Would they not, after all, be better off with another governess?

The thought of leaving was terrifying. Of course I could not go back to Orchard Street; I was no more able to support myself there by sewing or other such work than I ever had been. But now, at least, I had eight months' experience as a governess. Jay would give me a recommendation; perhaps even Eleanor would give me one in order to be rid of me. At the least, Bertie would recommend me among his friends. I would be able to find suitable employment, I thought. I would miss the children terribly—but there are times when one's feelings no longer matter.

I didn't realize how far I had gone until a park opened out at my left. It was Madison Square, empty now of the nursemaids and perambulators that had crowded the walkways last April. In the frigid twilight that now fell over the barren trees and icy benches, only one person was in the park, a derelict hunched miserably in his rags. As I stood against the low iron railing, peering into the gathering gloom, something cold tingled on my nose, then my cheek. I held out my dark mittens and watched the snowflakes nestling onto the wool, resting a moment, then melting away.

The snow began to fall rather thickly, and I was now almost twenty-five blocks south of the Caldwell mansion. I would have to turn around and go back as quickly as possible. It would be dark and the snow might be deepening before I got there. I was sure to catch a chill for, I suddenly realized, my very bones were already leaden with the cold. Even so, I wasn't ready to go back. Perhaps there was a tea room in which I could warm myself before going home. I turned and looked out over the complex of avenues and streets—Fifth Avenue, Broadway, Twenty-third Street. Everything was dark. I supposed that on Christmas night even shops that might ordinarily be open were closed, their owners at home with family and friends.

Suddenly, I felt terribly lonely, as if I were the only person on the planet, twirling through space amid the snowflakes and clouds while out beyond, the silver stars glimmered, so beautiful, so far away.

A lone brougham, its driver swaddled in woolen scarves, the horse breathing cold steam, came rattling up the avenue. I watched it approach, then pass me. I had turned away when I heard the driver calling "Whoa" to the horse and heard the carriage clattering to a stop. I looked around to see the carriage door open and a man step down and begin walking toward me. I felt very much unprotected and unprepared to meet a strange man on a dark street with no one else about, but there was no getting away. I stood still and waited.

"Can I offer you a ride?"

I pressed my mittens to my face in relief. It was Jay. "Oh, yes," I called and hurried to meet him. "I'm freezing."

He helped me into the carriage and climbed in beside me. It was warm inside, and warmer still when he spread a deerskin laprobe over our knees.

"Well, Lillie, fancy meeting you here," he smiled. "Where are you going?"

"I don't know," I said. "I was about to go home, I guess, because of the cold. But I didn't really want to go there just yet. Where are you going?"

"The same as you. Home, but reluctantly. Shall we drive about instead?"

"Yes."

"Where to?"

"I don't really care."

He opened the little sliding door and called to the driver, "Turn around, Bob, and take us down Broadway." He turned to me. "Have you ever been down this way before?"

"Yes. I lived down here for a short time." A short time indeed. Two nights.

We rode along in silence for awhile, and I gazed out the window, looking for landmarks I might recognize from the cable-car ride I had taken up Broadway on that day so many months before. Shortly, we passed Arnold Constable and Company, and unaccountably I said, "That's the store the green dress came from." It was stupid to have broached the painful subject, but Jay took it up, almost as if he had been waiting for the opening.

"Lillie, I'm so sorry all this happened. You're so

innocent. You've been so good for the children. It's unbearable that you, of all people, should suffer for our problems."

"You may as well know. I've decided to leave," I said.

"Oh, no. No. I know I haven't protected you enough from Eleanor, but I'll see that she doesn't do this to you again."

"It's not that. I wouldn't leave because she is unpleasant to me. That doesn't matter. Everyone else has been so kind—the staff, and you, and the dear children. I love them so much."

"Then why?"

"Because I'm like salt in a wound. As long as I'm there, she will believe you care for me—and I for you. The truth doesn't matter, only what she thinks: She's your wife, and so it's up to me to leave. I would have gone much earlier if I weren't such a coward."

"Coward! You?"

"I'm a very fearful person."

"What makes you think so?"

I sighed. "It's an awfully long story."

"Well, you know, everyone is frightened sometimes. The most frightening thing that ever happened to me happened right here on Broadway, down near my office, on Liberty Street."

"When the horse ran away with Marta?" Immediately I wished that I had swallowed my tongue.

"How do you know about that?" he asked. I could have said Marta had told me about it, but there had been quite enough deception in my life already this year. And besides, what difference could it make now, I thought. I was going; Jay might as well know how I had come. From my reticule I drew Jay's business card and handed it to him. "I've been carrying this with me for luck."

He examined the card, then looked at me, puzzled. "Where did you get it?"

"From my Uncle Frank. You gave it to him the day he stopped Marta's runaway horse."

His eyes searched mine, then he sat back against the seat. "Well, you have me stumped. Of course I remember the man who caught the horse. So he's your uncle, is he? But how do you come to have the card? Has it something to do with your coming to us?"

"May I have it back?" I asked. "I'd like to keep it." He handed me the card, and I went on. "I arrived in America just two days before I came to you. My father had died, and Uncle Frank was my only living relative. Instead of seeking employment in England, I came here hoping Uncle Frank would take care of me as my father had done. I had to have father's friends help me sell his shop and book passage for me. You see, Daddy had educated me extremely well, but I had not learned the most important lesson of all: how to take care of myself. I thought Uncle Frank would be my salvation. But the most dreadful thing happened. He was killed the day after I arrived."

"How ghastly," Jay said.

"I only knew Uncle Frank for a few hours, but he was the dearest man. I loved him very much. He was the sort of person anyone would like at once—

so kind, so cheerful. He seemed able to enjoy the very simplest things in life. He was a street paver—a wretched way to make a living, one would think, but he took pleasure in it. He told me that working in the streets of New York was an adventure, and then he told me about saving Marta and showed me the card. He cherished it as a souvenir."

"Who would have thought—"

"He was very impressed with you. He said he thought a man who loved his little daughter so much couldn't have—" I almost said "killed his wife," but finished, "couldn't be a bad person."

"I hope you think he was right."

I looked up at him. "Of course I do." I lowered my eyes again, embarrassed to tell him the next part of my story, but too deeply into it now to stop. "When Frank was killed and we had dressed him for the funeral, I found your card in his suit pocket. Well, you see, I was terrified. I had no experience in any kind of work, no skills—"

It was too difficult. I couldn't go on. I glanced out the carriage window, and by chance, we were just then approaching the intersection of Broadway and Grand. Impulsively, I said, "Wait. Can we go down Grand Street?" I indicated the direction. Surprised, but without questioning me, Jay ordered Bob to make the turn. "I'll show you where I lived." We rode along in silence, and I watched anxiously out the window. It was dark now, and street signs were hard to make out by the dim, snow-blurred glow of the street lights.

"What street is it?" Jay asked me.

"Orchard," I said, and Jay instructed Bob to

turn when we got there.

"Here," I said at last, and we stopped partway down Orchard Street. "This is the building."

Only a few people were walking in the streets. I looked at the doorway to Mrs. Fein's building through the veil of snow. It looked inexpressably dreary.

"Do you want to go in? Is there anyone you'd like to see?" Jay inquired.

"No. Some day I'd like to come back, to say hello to Mrs. Fein. She was Uncle Frank's landlady and awfully kind to me. But not tonight." Jay signaled Bob to move on.

"This is a very poor neighborhood," he said. "How did you plan to earn a livelihood here?"

I laughed dryly. "I had no plan at all. I was really afraid that I would die here."

"Die?"

"Not long before, a young woman who worked in a sewing shop with Mrs. Fein's daughter was found dead of starvation—and *she* had known how to sew. I didn't know sewing or any other trade. What was I to do? I had no idea."

"Poor Lillie." He shuddered. "What led you to us?"

"Sheer desperation. Believe it or not, you were the only person in the world I could think to turn to. I had lost my father. I had lost Uncle Frank. All I had was this." I nodded at the card in my hand as I tucked it back into my reticule.

"I don't understand. You say you had no skills, that you knew of me only by the card. Yet you came to us as a governess."

I swallowed deeply, afraid to tell him the truth, yet determined now that he should know it. "No. I came to throw myself on your mercy. Frank had said that you told him to come to you if he ever needed anything. I planned to find you and to invoke your promise of help to Uncle Frank, to beg you to give your help to me as his surrogate," I sighed. "At least I believe that was my intention. I was too much in a daze to understand what I was doing. It was terribly presumptuous."

"Not at all. I would have helped you, even if I had never met your uncle."

I smiled gratefully. "I couldn't have known then what sort of person you are."

Jay slapped a hand to his forehead. "Wait! Oh!" He shook his head. "Now I understand: You came to see me; I saw you waiting in the parlor, talking to Bonnie. I assumed you had come to apply as a governess and insisted that Eleanor hire you. How embarrassing! Why, you weren't there for the job at all!"

"That's true. But the fault was mine. I knew a mistake had been made when Nellie Morgan took my name and went to give it to Mrs. Caldwell. But I didn't set anyone straight. I was far too terrified to have told you the truth about why I was there." I hesitated, then added, "The fact is, you looked so forbidding when I saw you standing in the doorway, I could not have spoken to you at all."

"Dear Lillie," he said softly. "I was overwhelmed by shyness. I thought an angel had come, the magical way you held little Bonnie and soothed her. I was afraid to speak to you, to break the spell. But I knew I had to have you with the children. They'd been through such hell because of the stress between Eleanor and me, and because of her moods, her temper. I had prayed for a way to save the children, and when I saw you, I thought you were the answer to my prayers."

The carriage had rounded the block, and now we were driving back up Broadway. The wheels rolled quietly over the thickening quilt of snow.

"But now you see," I concluded, "I'm no angel. I'm every bit the coward I said I was, and a deceitful coward at that."

"Lillie, the story you've just told is the story of a brave woman, not a cowardly one." I shook my head. "Why do you insist on seeing yourself in a negative light?" he went on. "Why can't you see it as I do: A young woman is orphaned. She sails to another country, alone, and when her only relative dies, faced with almost certain destitution, she seizes the one remote chance of salvation. She crosses the great city to the home of a person she doesn't even know, and takes her courage in both hands, prepared to ask for help. Instead, the opportunity of employment presents itself. In spite of inexperience, she takes the position and succeeds at it brilliantly.... Now where in that story do you see a coward?"

I looked at him in a kind of amazement. I had never thought of myself as he had just described me. "You make me sound almost a heroine," I said.

"You are, Lillie. Don't you know it?"

"I know you're a terribly kind and generous

man. You've done some sort of magic, twisting my story about to make it seem the very opposite of what it is."

"You have real courage, Lillie. You need only to believe it. Why, when I think of that stormy lecture you gave me about neglecting the children the day I came to Soundcliff to see Gus Flammon! Wasn't that courageous?"

"Hysterical, really," I said.

"And just think of your going to Montauk to rescue Marta," he persisted. "Weren't you afraid then, and wasn't it a brave thing to do?"

"Oh, but I had to do that. I love Marta. I couldn't have let her wander about an army camp alone."

"But that's what courage is—doing what you have to do even though you're afraid."

Although the carriage was warmer than the street had been, I had now become somewhat chilled. I gave an involuntary shiver, and Jay moved closer to me. I could feel his knee against mine beneath the laprobe. I felt myself blushing, and to cover it I said, "Do you know what I wish I could do?"

"No, what?"

"I'll never be able to forget the story of that poor girl, working as hard as she could, yet starving to death. If only there could be a center, a foundation, to help working girls. I'd so like to find a way to do that."

"There is a way."

"What?"

"Marry a rich man."

"Whatever do you mean?"

Startled, I looked at him, and to my astonishment, I found that Jay Caldwell was gazing at me with longing. Without disguising the look, he said, "If you were to marry a rich man, you could probably do what you like—endow a museum, start a foundation—"

"What rich man would want to marry me?" I was challenging him, I think. I wanted to probe beneath the look, hoping he would put into words the feeling I saw in his eyes. But his reply took me aback.

"Bertie Archer. Bertie wants to marry you."

The look of longing had vanished, and I could not have sworn that it had really been there. Only his startling statement still vibrated in the air between us.

"I'm very fond of Bertie," I replied. "But I would hardly marry him, or anyone, to acquire money."

"Perhaps not. But acquiring money isn't a sin. I acquired mine, you know. That is, I inherited it; it was grandfather who earned it. But how you get money isn't as important as what you do with it, I believe. That's why I want to build something of value, a railroad, the kind of railroad America is going to need. I want to earn the place in society that I inherited. Can you see why that's so important to me?"

"Yes, of course," I said. And then my curiosity got the better of me. "May I ask how it's going—your August Flammon plan?"

I was unprepared for his reaction. He put his

head in his hands and spoke in a muffled voice, "It's not going well at all."

Frightened, I laid my mittened hand on his sleeve. "What is it?" I begged. "What's happened?"

He took his hands away from his face and shrugged, like a small boy denying that his bloody nose hurts. "The stock has dried up. I haven't been able to buy more than ten shares to Empire State stock in a month. It's as if Gus knows what I'm trying to do. At any rate, somebody has put a clamp on Empire State stock."

"What does it mean?"

"It means I've lost the LIH&M—maybe forever, if I can't get the Empire State, now that he's absorbed the LIH&M into it."

"Is it hopeless?"

"I don't know. I'd come very close to wrapping it all up before it started going bad. I had acquired quite a bit of Empire State stock through various agents of mine, almost enough to take it. And then it dried up. I don't know what will happen next. It depends on what Flammon knows and how he fights back. If he's cornered what's left of Empire State stock and can hold onto it, maybe I'm finished."

"But how could he have found out? Can you trust your agents?"

"I always thought so."

"And now?"

"Well, of course I can't be sure. Someone seems to have tipped Gus off, and if I can't find out who, then I can't win."

"You'll do it somehow. I know you will."

He smiled a little. "Do you mean it, Lillie? Do you have faith in me?"

"Absolutely," I said.

"Then I'll win out."

The carriage stopped, and I was surprised to see that we had pulled up at 577. I had wanted to go on forever, sitting close to Jay, riding along together through the snowy night. I felt as if I were waking from a dream. An impulse to delay the end of it made me speak again.

"I want to tell you something about the green dress," I said, staring into my lap. "Mrs. Caldwell was not the only one who thought it was from you. I'm afraid I thought so, too."

"I wish it had been," he answered. "You were very beautiful in it."

"I didn't think you saw me."

"I did."

What emboldened me to pursue such a conversation with him, I do not know. Perhaps it was knowing I would probably never see him again after tonight; for I had made up my mind to leave at once.

"Why didn't you dance with me?" I asked. "Didn't you want to?"

"Yes, of course. Every man there wanted to dance with you."

His words were gratifying, but I wanted more, something to remember when I was gone, something to warm my heart on long, lonely nights in whatever strange, new house I would now go to. "Were you afraid Mrs. Caldwell would be angry if you danced with me?" I persisted.

"Eleanor had nothing to do with it, Lillie," he answered quietly. "I didn't dance with you because—" suddenly, his voice broke—"because I didn't dare to. You were so lovely, like a Dresden doll. If I had taken you in my arms, I might have lost all the control I've worked so hard to achieve. Do you understand?"

I looked up at him. He bathed me in a tender gaze. Then he leaned forward.

"Give me your hand." He took one of my hands from my lap. Gently, he stripped away the woolen mitten. He tucked my hand under his arm for an instant as he pulled off his own two gloves. Then he took my hand between his. Lightly, he caressed my palm with his fingertips. A deep thrill spread through my body. I felt on the edge of danger. I thought I should pull my hand away, but I didn't want to. He bent his head close to mine, then, and whispered into my ear.

"Lillie, Lillie, don't leave me."

TWELVE

What led to the ultimate tragedy? It is difficult now to recall the sequence of events, so rapid, complex, and dreadful were they. I blame myself for starting it all. What I did seemed innocent enough at the time, but without meaning to, I tipped the domino that sent all the others tumbling down.

After our carriage ride that Christmas night, of course I changed my mind about leaving. Jay needed me, and so I would stay.

But we were in an unbearable state. I had long known that I was in love with Jay. Not knowing if he, in return, cared for me had been hard, yet comforting, too. As long as there was no outlet for my love, no possibility of its fulfillment, I had felt safe.

Now, although no declaration of love had

passed between us, we knew, both of us, that he loved me as fervidly, as passionately as I loved him. And with the wondrous joy of it came a new kind of anxiety. We were trapped in an inferno of unfulfilled desire. For of course, even if Jay or I had been tempted to violate his sacred vows of marriage, neither of us would have done so in even the smallest way because of the children. They above all had to be protected—from wrongdoing, from scandal, from loss of faith and trust in us. Yet for each of us, knowledge of the other's love and longing intensified our own, day by day.

We developed a strange and provoking way of living in the same house together. We had been equally frightened by the electric thrill of our touching hands in the carriage that night, so we eschewed all further physical contact, however mild. Nor did we exchange any more passion-motivated words such as my "Why didn't you dance with me?" or his "Lillie, don't leave me."

But in a subtle way, things had changed between us. For many preceding months we had assiduously avoided each other. Now we felt free of those cruel restraints. We were not indiscreet, for the children and servants were about us all the time; but we did speak naturally to each other whenever our paths crossed, and we took to having short conversations together in his den behind the oriental parlor, always leaving the door open so as not to arouse gossip. When we did talk in the quasi privacy of the den, our conversations were warm but platonic. The staff must have noticed that our association had become closer, and what they thought of it I do not know, but we gave them no occasion for criticism of our behavior. It was a maddeningly frustrating relationship, but it was all we dared, all we could permit ourselves.

In less than a week, however, I had destroyed the delicate web we had begun to weave.

It all started because of Marta's love of music. Since we had left Soundcliff, she had been missing her organ lessons terribly. At the same time, I noticed that she had started an album of rotogravure pictures of opera stars. I asked her if she had been to the opera, and she said, "Only once at a matinee with Uncle Bertie when I was ten."

I had read that Emma Eames was to sing *Tosca* at the Metropolitan Opera on New Year's Eve. When I saw that Marta had devoted an entire segment of her album to the famous soprano, I hurried down to the den where Jay was poring over a set of ledgers. I knew that he had been searching for an idea about how to celebrate Marta's fifteenth birthday on January first, and as Jay looked up from his desk, I said eagerly, "I know just the thing for Marta."

The Caldwell box at the Metropolitan Opera House had been little-used of late, and then most often by Bertie Archer and his friends. Jay's eyes reflected his enthusiasm for my idea.

"Wonderful! I wish I had thought of it myself. It's absolutely perfect for Marta. It will be her first night out in New York. She can wear that pretty blue gown she wore Christmas Eve. She'll look smashing. Everyone will gape at her."

"She'll love it," I said.

"And then dinner at Delmonico's afterwards! She'll be thrilled." He got up from the desk and came around to me. "You're a wonder, Lillie. And you must come with us."

"Oh, surely not," I protested.

"Yes, why not? As chaperone. It's perfectly proper."

Ignoring the alarms going off in my head, I agreed to the plan. Susan had half completed her work in converting my black bombazine for the Christmas-Eve ball before the green dress had arrived. Now I asked her to finish it. I had to admit to myself that the jet beads and black ostrich feathers, the shortened sleeves and lowered neckline had made it into a very chic dress. I tried it on and couldn't resist showing it to Jay, complete with black ostrich feathers in my hair. He heartily approved, and the next morning he called me into his den where he handed me a tissue-wrapped box.

"This time, you'll *know* it's from me," he grinned. He made me open it then and there. Inside was a simply gorgeous black-brocade cloak lined in the softest white satin.

To compound the situation, young Jack Van Dyne had called to see Marta on the afternoon of December thirtieth, and Jay invited him to accompany us to the opera and dinner the following evening. We were all four idiotically happy and ignorant of the certain storm we were about to precipitate. Jay and I had already rationalized my presence as chaperone, and now he told me, "I think the worst thing to do about Jack and Marta is to oppose them flatly. We stand a better chance of heading off anything serious between them if we play along with it a bit and let it work itself out. And what harm can there be in Jack's accompanying her to the opera with her father and governess?"

What harm indeed? Off we went together on New Year's Eve in Jay's brougham for the ride to the opera house at Thirty-ninth Street. The performance was heavenly—it was my first opera and I was enthralled—and Jay had been right: Marta caused a minor sensation. The young auburn-haired beauty in blue with her handsome escort drew all eyes to our box. At least I thought that it was Marta and Jack who were the cause of the head-turnings and buzzing as we took our seats in the family box.

Afterwards, Marta's cheeks were rosy and her eyes shiny, and so, I imagined, were mine. We floated back into the carriage, and it was another short ride uptown and across Forty-fourth Street to the legendary society restaurant, Delmonico's. It was exciting to enter with Jay who, as a famous millionaire, was greeted swiftly and obsequiously by the Maitre d'Hotel. Immediately, we were seated at the best corner table where we dined by the warm, soft light of a little pink-shaded table lamp. We had oysters and caviar, and even Marta was permitted a half-goblet of champagne.

It was well past midnight when we arrived home. Jack said goodnight in the carriage, and Bob drove him on home as Jay, Marta, and I entered the great double doors of 577. We were a gay, giddy, glamorous trio—I in my black beads and feathers and satin-lined cloak, Marta in her blue gown and little fur cape, Jay in his tuxedo. No one was up, and we were too euphoric to go to bed. We trooped into the kitchen, and I made coffee for all of us while we chattered on and on about Emma Eames's wonderful voice, the exquisite staging of *Tosca,* the delicacy of the food at Delmonico's, and the general perfection of the evening.

It was fortunate that we enjoyed it so that night, for the next day our happy bubble burst.

We had made the society pages of the *New York Journal.* On the first day of January, 1899, there I was as sketched by the newspaper artist, seated next to Jay in the opera box with Marta and Jack behind us. Jay and I were the featured item: Why was the notorious, the wealthy, and handsome Jay Caldwell seen at the opera and Delmonico's last night with the glamorous young woman reputed to be the family "governess?" Yes, *governess* was in quotation marks. And, it was noted, the scion of the Van Dyne family was part of the party as young—*very* young—Marta Caldwell's escort. Were Mr. Van Dyne and Miss Caldwell the latest romantic couple in New York society? There was more, the further implication being that Jay had, by appearing in public with me, compromised not only himself but also his daughter by making her a party to the sordid escapade. And where, it was asked, was Mrs. Caldwell while all this was taking place?

It was dreadful, and Jay was utterly abashed.

"I didn't expect it," he said, pacing about the

den. "I should have, of course, I've seen often enough what the newspapers can do to people's private lives. But I married so young, I was never much written-up as a bachelor, and I've never been out with anyone other than my wife before." I blushed profoundly, and Jay rushed to my side. "I'm sorry. I didn't mean it that way, of course. If I had thought there was anything indiscreet about it, I wouldn't have thought of doing it. It's the papers. They've been lying in wait for me, I think. The last time they got any news out of me was when Charlotte died, and they printed all those horrid rumors about my murdering her." He looked at me sharply, as if afraid he had let something slip that I wasn't prepared for. "Were you aware of that?" I nodded. "Anyway, they haven't had a good go at me since then. I suppose this was just too good to pass up."

"Will—will Eleanor see it?" It felt strange to call her by her first name, but I could no longer bear to call her "Mrs. Caldwell."

"You can count on it," he replied. "Just as soon as the papers get to Long Island."

"How do you think she'll react?"

"From the time we were children, I have never had the slightest idea how Eleanor would react to anything. Somehow, she always manages to catch me off guard. But we can be sure of one thing—she will react."

We hadn't long to wait: Within the hour, the telephone rang.

"Shall I step out?" I asked.

"No, no. Stay if you can bear it," Jay said.

He picked up the phone. I could hear Eleanor's distorted voice coming over the wire, although I could not make out her words. Jay said next to nothing. I kept waiting for him to break into her tirade, to make her listen as he explained how innocent it had all been. Instead, his several attempts to speak were aborted by her unflagging flow of words. Jay's face was ashen, and all he said at the end was, "All right, Eleanor. As you wish. But Miss Lorimer will be coming, too."

He said this latter with some power, and evidently she stopped short of challenging him about it, for when he had hung up he said in a quiet, strained voice, "We're going back to Soundcliff."

"We?"

"All of us. You, too. She won't cross me on that, it appears. I thought she would resist the idea of your coming, but she didn't—fortunately. She seems to hold most of the cards this time."

"What did she say?"

"That if I didn't come to her at once, she would sue for divorce and custody of the children. It's a rather difficult position to argue with under the circumstances. If she does it, I'm afraid she will win."

"I see," I said. "Then perhaps I should *not* go with you—no matter that she didn't argue about my coming."

"No, no. Maybe I should have let you leave when you wanted to last week. It was so selfish of me not to. But you wouldn't be accepted in another household. Not now. Not in New York.

You really have to stay with us, at least until this scandal quiets down."

"If you think it's all right." In truth, I could only have left the Caldwells then if Jay had ordered me to. I was far past being able to leave on my own.

"It's all right," he said, "but we shall have to be very, very careful at Soundcliff."

I nodded.

"Oh, Lillie," he said softly, "this is so unfair to you."

"The opera was my idea," I said.

"And mine that you should go with us."

It was pointless to assign blame. What had happened had happened. We had no choice but to press on blindly into the future.

Arrival at Soundcliff couldn't have been gloomier. A cold, soaking rain had fallen all day. Even Bertie's warm greeting and the tea Ada prepared failed to warm my spirits or my body. Everyone knew about the newspaper article and the telephone call from Eleanor, knew that our being here was born of unhappiness and boded unhappiness. Only Nancy and Geoffrey seemed impervious to the glum atmosphere, nattering away to each other as usual at tea. Once Nancy whispered something into Geoffrey's ear and gave me a sly glance. Then both of them sniggered. Ada slammed a pot hard on the stove, but it affected them not at all.

We were at Soundcliff just a bit over two months before the tragedy occurred. It was a peculiar span of time. I remember it as a seemingly interminable interval of boredom, anxiety, and depression. It seemed to me that the very climate was poisoned, for freezing rain and heavy, wet snow fell day after day and invaded the house with a damp chill that no number of fires laid in the various rooms could banish. We huddled under layers of woolen clothing and shawls that seemed only to absorb the damp.

I was once again unsure of my position in relation to both Jay and Eleanor, and again Jay and I avoided each other. As for Eleanor, she did not speak to me, and when I crossed her path, her facial expression never changed. Yet, unexplainably, menace seemed to radiate from her person. More than once, I caught myself testing the weight of my trunk against the sliding panel in my room. She said nothing, did nothing to make me fear her, but fear her I did, and I wondered more than once why she had let Jay bring me back to Soundcliff.

The children were even more miserable than I was. Leo had not recovered from his mother's Christmas-day treachery and was sad and withdrawn. Marta had received a tongue-lashing from Eleanor about allowing Jack to escort her to the opera, even though Jay had explained that it was he who had invited Jack. Bonnie was too young to understand what was the matter with everyone, but not too young to be upset by their mood. Her cheery little face turned sober, her exuberant personality subdued. She took to sitting quietly in a corner, stroking Ginger for longer periods of time than she had ever before been known to sit still.

Jay and Eleanor's relationship was a mystery.

They had dropped the pretense of marital closeness that had characterized much of the previous summer and fall. They took meals together with the children as before, but the meals passed in somber silence. The only evidence of communication between them was an occasional burst of angry voices muffled behind closed doors. They went nowhere together socially, but they were often seen, separately and at different times, driving away from the mansion. I assumed that each needed relief from the unbearable tension, and Nancy said that Eleanor had begun to immerse herself in the planning of a charity function. I envied her her ability to get away from the gloom of Soundcliff. I, for one, had begun to feel like an inmate.

The sad situation was severely exacerbated when Jack Van Dyne turned up one afternoon for a social visit. Both Jay and Eleanor were out, and I happened to be with Marta at the organ when Hans ushered Jack into the living room. Hans shrugged at me slightly as Marta, glowing, led Jack to one of the enormous sofas. Apparently, Hans had had no orders to turn Jack away, but he well knew that the visit was potentially troublesome.

I followed Jack and Marta across the room, desperately framing a little speech of caution that might send Jack quickly on his way without insulting him, which, as an employee of the house, I felt I must not do. I had barely drawn breath to suggest that Marta might wish to consult her parents before entertaining a visitor in their absence when the grating sound of carriage wheels on the gravel drive stopped me. Marta's white face told me that her thoughts were the same as mine: Please let it be Jay and not Eleanor.

It was Jay. In a few moments he strode into the room and offered his hand cordially to Jack. I started to leave the room, but Jay called me back.

"No, please stay, Miss Lorimer. We'll have tea sent in." He walked over to the bell pull, and as he passed me he said, too softly to be heard by Marta and Jack, "He's welcome here as far as I'm concerned, and so are you. I am the master of this house, and I refuse to begin behaving like a bounder to our guests." Susan came in and Jay asked her to bring in tea for the four of us. She gave me a nervous glance, but I tried to keep my face expressionless.

Marta and Jay had been deep in conversation, and as we joined them, Marta spoke breathlessly and tearfully.

"Oh, Daddy, Jack's going away."

"That's right, sir," Jack confirmed. "I've come to say goodbye."

"Goodbye!" Jay exclaimed. "But it seems to me we just got you back after all those months in Cuba and the hospital."

"Well, Cuba's partly it, sir," Jack explained. "Long Island just seems a bit too tame after that."

"Where are you going, then?"

"Alaska, sir."

"Alaska! What for?"

"Gold. A lot of men are going since the gold strike in the Klondike."

"There's more gold in your father's vault than you're likely to find in the Klondike, Jack."

"The gold in my father's vault is my father's, if you know what I mean, sir. I need to live my own life. I want to see if I can survive in a place where no one's ever heard of my father or would care if they had. Governor Roosevelt is something of an idol to me in that way, sir, spending all that time as a cowboy out west. There was gold in *his* father's vault, too."

"I can appreciate how you feel about that," Jay said, then added as he glanced at Marta's pale, tear-streaked face, "I'm not the only one who'll miss you."

Eleanor startled all of us when she appeared in the doorway. We had not heard her carriage, and only later did I learn from staff gossip that she had seen Jack's carriage as she approached the house and ordered her own driver to let her out then and there so she could walk up the drive without being heard. I presumed that she had expected to catch Marta and Jack alone together, perhaps even catch them in an embrace. Now she shrilled with false heartiness, "Well, well, Jack! Here you are, like a bad penny, always turning up."

"Jack's come to say goodbye," Jay said as he and Jack rose.

"I'm off to Alaska, Mrs. Caldwell," Jack added, "to prospect gold."

"I see!" Eleanor sallied sharply. "Your maladies have an interesting progression: first yellow fever, then gold fever!" She came across the room to the grouping of sofas where Marta and I were both trying to vanish into the cushions. "So, then, we won't be seeing you again for a *very* long time. My that is a pity."

"You're being rude, Eleanor," Jay snapped.

"Not at all," she replied. "Jack knows exactly how sorry I'll be to see him go to the other side of the continent."

Jack, ordinarily imperturbable, had colored under Eleanor's attack of sarcasm. "Well, then, I'd better be off at once. Thank you, sir." He shook Jay's hand.

Marta sprang to her feet. "But when? When are you going, Jack?"

"Not for a few weeks,' he replied, already moving toward the door. "As soon as I get my gear together. I'll let you know when. Goodbye, all." And he was gone.

"Take Marta upstairs, please," Jay said to me, and I gratefully sped her from the room, feeling as if we were running to escape a hurricane. It was an apt notion, for just as I closed the seldom-used sliding doors a storm of vitriol could be heard erupting behind them.

"I'm all right, Miss Lorimer," Marta blurted. "You needn't come with me." And she ran up the stairs without me. I turned to take the kitchen route to the back stairs and ran into Susan wheeling the tea cart toward the living room.

"I think you'd better take that back to the kitchen," I said. She nodded and turned about, for the angry voices of Jay and Eleanor could be heard even in the back hall.

* * *

I believe that Eleanor had reached a state of almost total irrationality. If she had been genuinely concerned about Marta's involvement with Jack, then his intention to go to Alaska should have relieved it, removed the source of tension, and improved her relationship with Marta. Instead, she began to taunt Marta about Jack.

"So you thought you had him on the string," she would jibe, or "You're not quite the temptress you thought you were, are you?" She aimed these remarks at Marta like poisoned darts, not just once but again and again over the ensuing days and weeks. The servants often overheard and reported the stinging remarks. Even Leo was painfully aware of the situation. "Why does Mother always pick on Marta?" he asked me one day.

Jay would have stopped it if he could. Indeed, I went to him one day and told him what I had heard. I was upset at having to interfere but too concerned for Marta not to. Jay said that he would speak to Eleanor about it, and I'm sure he did; but he could not prevent Eleanor from picking at Marta when he was absent. In fact, she never had done it when he was present.

What frightened me most was that Marta had stopped fighting back. Instead of the outbursts of temper with which she had once reacted to Eleanor's attacks, she was now wrapped in a sullen silence that bespoke an emotional state blacker and more desperate than before.

At last, poor Bonnie was overwhelmed by the anguish around her. One day, when she blotted the copy book in which she was practicing her letters, she tore out the page and threw her pen across the room. When I tried to comfort her, she pushed me away, then started to cry. Later, she became cross when Leo tried to correct her painting of Ginger and slapped paint onto his shirt. When I sent her to her room as punishment, she cried so long and so loudly that Margaret Dobbs finally went in to her and sat with Bonnie cuddled on her lap until the child's sobs ebbed. Then Bonnie came back to the schoolroom and sat on my lap sucking her thumb while I read stories to her and Leo the rest of the afternoon. Marta spent the time staring blindly out the window. Schooling had become a shambles, but that was merely a symptom of the sickness that now seemed to infect the entire household.

That night, Bonnie professed to be too frightened to go to sleep. She proclaimed loudly that if she went to sleep "that goblin" would come and eat her. Margaret told me that Bonnie had been subject to nightmares about a goblin lately, but this was the first time she had become hysterical at bed time. She wouldn't let Margaret turn out the light or leave the room, and Margaret sat by her bed, thinking to put out the light and tiptoe away once Bonnie was asleep.

But nearly an hour passed, and Bonnie was still wide awake and upset. At last she said she might go to sleep if Ginger slept with her, and Margaret crossed the hall to my room to ask for the loan of the little calico cat who had accustomed herself to sleeping at the foot of my bed. I gladly handed

Ginger to Margaret, and a short while later she stopped back to say that Bonnie was sleeping with Ginger clasped in her chubby arms. In a few moments, I was in bed myself, and I dropped off to sleep rather quickly, too exhausted to miss the warmth of Ginger's chin on my ankles.

I don't know how to describe the terror of my awakening. I briefly dreamed that I had been standing at the foot of the cliff below the mansion, and that the face of the cliff had suddenly loosened and fallen on me, forcing me backwards, supine upon the sand. A great weight of earth and rock seemed pressed against my face, blinding me, blocking my mouth and my nostrils. Unable to see, unable to breathe, I started awake to find that the horror of the dream was real. I was suffocating. It was another instant before I realized that the pressure on my face was the pressure of a pillow being held forcibly down over me. I was being murdered.

Already, I was blacking into unconsciousness. Desperately, I flung out my arms and with one hand grasped the heavy fabric of a gown or robe. I groped my other hand upward over the pillow and seized hold of a hand. With the strength begotten of fear, I took hold of a finger and bent it sharply back. There was a little grunt of pain and the pressure of the injured hand lessened. I pushed harder, the hand came away, and I sat up.

I lunged for my assailant, but as I did so, my head reeled, and I fell sideways on one elbow. My senses cleared almost at once, but the delay gave him or her the chance to get clear. The secret panel was open—my trunk moved to one side—and the flickering light of a lantern was quickly fading away in the passage.

I rushed to the panel and peered down the stairway. My attacker had already passed the landing by Jay's room, and I just saw the trailing end of a dark robe disappearing around the bend into the unknown lower depths of the system of passageways. I was now plunged into darkness, and I quickly lit my bedside lamp, closed the panel and put back the trunk. The little bell, which had been set carefully upon the floor, I placed back on top of the trunk. So much for my home-made alarm system, I thought grimly. And I could certainly have used Ginger's protection, little Ginger who once before had warned me by growling and arching her back that someone was in the passageway. I must keep her with me after this, I thought.

I gathered my blankets and carried them to the chair, stopping at the writing table to pick up the sharp-bladed letter opener from its drawer. I spent the rest of the night wrapped in blankets in the chair with the letter opener at hand, staring at the secret panel.

At dawn, I dressed and went down to the kitchen where I made myself a cup of strong black coffee and waited for the others to begin appearing for breakfast. I was silent during the meal, but I gathered strength from the presence of my friends.

Then I went to Jay's office. He was often to be found working there early in the morning, and he was there now, bent over some papers on his desk.

"Excuse me. Sorry to disturb you," I said.

He looked up, then stood and strode across the carpet to me. "Good lord, Lillie, you're white as a sheet. Sit down."

I sat down very calmly, for I had decided exactly what I would tell him.

THIRTEEN

"I've made a discovery," I told Jay.

"Oh?" He arched an eyebrow at me.

"There's an entrance from the secret passageways into my room."

"Yes, I've known about that," he said. "How did you find it?"

"Just curiosity, I suppose. Last night I struck the wall by accident and there was a hollow sound. I had always noticed that the wall between my room and the rear wing was unusually thick. I put two and two together. I thought that the passageway system must extend behind my room. I examined the wall and found the latch and opened the panel."

"I see."

"Well, the truth is, it makes me feel a little strange to know that someone could come into my room from the passageway. Not that anyone would, of course. But I was just wondering if it might be secured somehow so that it couldn't be opened from the passageway."

Jay looked at me intently. "Has something happened?" he said sharply.

"No, no," I dissembled. "It's only that somehow it makes me feel, well—vulnerable."

He continued to look at me searchingly, and then he said, "Lillie, is it I? Am I the one you're afraid of?"

"You?"

"If you've seen the passage, you must know that it connects my room with yours."

"Yes, I did notice it, but of course I didn't think that. But the stairway goes on downward—of course I didn't think it would be you who—" I broke off in confusion.

"Well, perhaps it is a good idea to nail it up, for I'll confess that there are nights when I can think of nothing but the stairway that connects my room with yours. I would never take advantage of it, of course. But perhaps it's just as well to seal it off. I'll send someone up this morning to nail it shut. Would that make you feel better?"

"Yes it would," I said. "Thank you."

Why had I not told Jay what had happened? It was Eleanor who had attacked me, I thought. (No wonder she had made no objection to Jay's bringing me back to Soundcliff. What could be better than to have her enemy, her intended victim, delivered to her doorstep.) But how could I be certain? I hadn't seen her. The robe I grasped could have been a man's or a woman's. I had no proof that it was Eleanor. And if I were to tell Jay what I thought, how could he confront her about it? She would only deny it. What could he do? What would I want him to do?

Worst of all, I feared that, suspecting Eleanor but unable to do anything about it, Jay would send me away for my own protection. That would be the one thing I could no longer bear. They say that one can survive in the desert on next to nothing, and that was how I felt. My own existence was an emotional desert now. My only sustenance was knowing that Jay was near me, under the same roof. To be separated from him now would be a fate far worse than the worst I might face by remaining in the house.

That morning, two handymen hammered three strong nails through the wooden molding in the corner of my room and into the panel. Now that the room was secured so that I could feel safe at night, I could defend myself against Eleanor the rest of the time—or so I hoped—and I had no intention of ever telling Jay what had really happened.

Gloomy as those early weeks of 1899 were, there were one or two brighter moments, or so I thought at the time. One day Jay stopped by the schoolroom, ostensibly to check on the children's progress; but as he left he said to me, "If you have time later, stop by the office. I have something to tell you."

When I came into his office at noon, he stood up

with his hands behind his back, grinning like a small boy who is about to ask a friend to guess which hand has the pebble.

"What is it?" I asked, and I started to laugh. His good spirits, so rare of late, were infectious. "What do you have there?"

Jay took a letter from behind his back and handed it to me. "Read this," he said. "What do you think it means?"

I read it twice and looked at Jay, greatly puzzled. The words meant nothing to me. It was a handwritten note, just a few lines, quickly scrawled: "Caldwell—Radford and F have had a falling out. I think he's ripe for picking. Will contact you for instructions. T."

"Who's T?" I asked.

"An agent of mine. Tom."

"And Radford? F? Who are they? What does it mean?"

"Radford is an old associate of Gus Flammon's. According to what Tom says in this note, they've had a disagreement, and Radford might be ready to sell his Empire State shares. If I move now, I think I can sew it up."

"The controlling interest in the Empire State?"

"The controlling interest." He gave a triumphant laugh and reached for my hand. I wanted so badly to throw my arms around him, and I know that he wanted to hold me, too; but instead he just squeezed my hand. "This is it, Lillie," he said. "This is it."

"Is there any chance it might not work?" I asked.

"I don't think so," he said. "The easiest

pickings of all are disgruntled associates."

"When will you know?"

"It won't be long. I've got to move quickly in a situation like this. For all I know, they may make it up tomorrow, and then I'm back where I started from."

I glanced at the telephone. "Will you call Tom now?"

"I can't call him," Jay said. "He's a man who moves around. He'll call me some time today, I'm sure."

"This is excruciating," I moaned. "I can't wait."

"Neither can I," he grinned. "But wait we must."

"Will you let me know?"

"As soon as I know."

That very afternoon, my spirits were raised even more by an item of gossip I heard from Susan. Nancy Vance and Geoffrey Hand were to leave Soundcliff. Geoffrey had obtained a position as second valet to Gus Flammon, and Susan whispered to me that Nancy was with child. Considering the compromising position in which Jay and I had discovered them in the woods the previous summer, I wondered that it hadn't happened sooner. In any event, departure for the Flammon estate and a quiet civil marriage ceremony were planned for the eighteenth of March. None of the staff were invited to the wedding. Nancy's condition was already somewhat obvious, and so it would have been out of the question to make it a public event.

In spite of Nancy's disagreeable nature, I felt rather sorry for her, having to enter marriage in disgrace, and I decided to find an opportunity to visit some village shops to look for a wedding present for her. My kindlier feelings, however, did not extend to regretting her and Geoffrey's departure.

The prospect of their leaving and the news of Jay's chance to triumph over August Flammon and gain control at last of the Empire State Railroad had combined to make me feel almost gay. I had just one day to bask in the feeling.

The next afternoon when I dismissed the children for lunch, my curiosity about Jay's Empire State adventure overcame me. Had he forgotten his promise to let me know what happened? If so, I would remind him. I went downstairs and was surprised to find his office door closed. Disappointed, I assumed that he had gone out, and I was turning to leave when I heard the faint sound of rustling papers from behind the door. I hesitated, then knocked.

"Who is it?" His voice was abrupt, even angry, but it was too late to retreat.

"It's Lillie."

I heard footsteps. Then the door opened. I was taken aback at Jay's drawn face. He looked ill.

"What's wrong?"

"Come in here," was his reply. I went in and he closed the door behind me. He walked over to his desk chair and indicated that I should take the chair opposite. When I had seated myself, Jay sat down, planted his elbows on the arms of his chair, and began tapping his fingertips together. He folded his lips into a grim line and stared at me.

"Aren't you going to tell me anything?" I asked.

"It's all over. The deal fell through."

"Fell through? The Empire State shares?"

"That's right."

"What happened?"

"Tom called just after I talked to you yesterday. I told him to go ahead and buy Radford out."

"And?"

"He called back this morning. Radford wouldn't sell."

"Why not?"

"Tom says he thinks Flammon was tipped off and got to Radford with some kind of spectacular peace offer. Anyway, Radford is back in Flammon's fold."

"Oh—this is awful. What can you do?" My heart went out to him.

His eyes betrayed the devastation his monotone disguised. "Nothing, I think. There aren't any more Radfords lurking about. It looks as if Flammon's beaten me on this one."

"It's uncanny," I said. "How could Mr. Flammon have known what you were doing? Or do you think it was coincidence?"

"It was no coincidence. It's as I told you before. For several months now, he's seemed to know every move I've intended to make. No matter where I've turned, he's been there first. This is only the latest incident. Or should I say the last, since I have no moves left."

"Could it have been Tom? Do you trust him?"

"It wasn't Tom." He pressed his hand nervously over his mouth, then leaned toward me. "It's someone right here at Soundcliff."

I was stunned into momentary silence. At last I gathered breath enough for one syllable: "Who?"

"I don't know; but I have an idea."

"What makes you think it's someone here at Soundcliff?"

"The letter is gone. The one from Tom that you read yesterday."

"Gone?"

"Gone. I had left it in the drawer of the desk after I talked to Tom yesterday. When I came back later it wasn't there."

I stopped myself from inquiring reflexively, "Are you sure?" Jay was not the sort to forget where he had put an important letter. "Who could have taken it, then?" I asked instead.

"Reason it out. Who in this household has suddenly developed a connection with Gus Flammon?"

"Oh." I took a deep breath. "Do you mean Geoffrey?"

"Yes, Geoffrey. Geoffrey's no valet. What's Flammon doing hiring him for a job like that, unless—"

"Unless it's a reward," I finished.

"Unless it's a reward," he confirmed.

"And all these months—?"

"I've always left my business papers pretty casually lying about. All the notes and correspondence about the Empire State acquisitions have been in my office at 577 or here—wherever I was at the time. And wherever I was, Geoffrey was. I often lock the office when I'm not working, but the staff has keys to all the rooms."

"What are you going to do?"

"Probably nothing. He's leaving in a few days. Let Flammon have him. There's nothing to be gained by confronting him about it. I don't want Flammon to know what I know and what I don't."

An uncomfortable notion had occurred to me: "I'm glad you don't think it was I."

"You?" he exclaimed in genuine surprise.

"After all, you confided in me about the plan as long ago as last summer. And you had showed me the letter from Tom."

"That's the very last thought I would ever have had." His voice deepened with emotion and his eyes grew large and bright. My heart turned over, but I could only think to say the simplest thing.

"Thank you."

"You're welcome." He smiled. Then he stood and suddenly began to pace about as if gathering energy. "Well, it's not so bad. The railroad has always been a minor investment for me. The rest of the Caldwell empire is in good shape. And the Empire State stock I've already bought is solid. It wasn't a bad investment. I can always dump it on the market and knock the price down, just to annoy Gus. As for losing the LIH&M—it's a blow to the family pride, not much more." His smile was bright, but forced.

"But it was your dream—owning the Empire State, running it."

"Oh, well. Dreams aren't everything."

I had to leave him rather suddenly, then, for I felt too much like crying. I knew that Jay must feel far worse than I did; yet I had become so involved with him, his hopes and dreams, his joys and sorrows that I was filled with bitter disappointment. And how especially awful Jay must feel not to have regained the LIH&M; how much I knew he really wanted it back for the avengement of his father.

For a few days, I put aside the notion of buying a wedding present for Nancy and Geoffrey. His possible treachery had soured the idea. But the day before they were to leave, I softened. Perhaps Nancy had known nothing about it; and anyway, I decided, any woman who was about to become a wife and a mother deserved a gift and the good wishes it represented.

After breakfast, I persuaded Bob to drive me into the village where I purchased a small silver tray and had it prettily wrapped. In the afternoon, I gave it to Nancy and offered her my best wishes for her future. She looked at me with surprise. It was the first time I had ever caught her with an unguarded look. She was awkward, apparently unaccustomed to friendly gestures, and obviously pleased. Her "thank you" was gruff but almost sincere. Perhaps Nancy had been ill-treated in her life. Perhaps her unpleasantness had been a defense. Whatever the case, I would never know, I thought. I never expected to see her again.

It was nine o'clock, and I was reading in my room. The mid-March weather had turned unexpectedly mild that day, and I had pushed one of the long windows outward a bit to let in some of the fresh air. I knew that there was more frigid weather to come before true spring, but the brief respite of that day had made me feel that we just might survive the wretched winter with our sanity and our lives intact after all.

I had just drawn in a long breath of tentative contentment when a loud shriek pierced the quiet night, followed by a crossfire of angry voices. The sounds were coming from outdoors toward the front of the house. By opening my window wide and leaning out, I could see, past the bridge and just by the piazza, a lamp jerking up and down and two shadowy figures, one in something green, the other in what appeared to be a dark coat. They quickly disappeared into the darkness of the piazza, and the fading voices indicated that they had gone into the house. The voices, I decided were those of Marta and Eleanor. It was only a moment before they could be heard again, and I could tell that the two had started up the stairs, but only as far as the second floor. They seemed to be moving toward Eleanor's room.

I now became extremely alarmed, for Marta had begun to scream, and her words could be heard plainly when I poked my head into the corridor: "No! Mother! Eleanor! You witch! No, let me go! Daddy! Daddy!" Her voice was full of terror and pain, and I could still hear her even when the closing of Eleanor's door intervened. There was no response from Jay, and I knew that he must be out. Quickly, I threw on a robe and hurried into the corridor where I ran straight into Margaret Dobbs and Nellie Morgan who had also been aroused by the furor below. We exchanged desperate glances, and then the three of us rushed toward the stairs. Marta's screams sounded for all the world like the screams of a person in peril of her life.

I didn't know what I would do, but I planned at the very least to burst into Eleanor's room and force my own body between Eleanor and Marta. But as we reached the second floor landing, we met Jay coming up the stairs two at a time. He passed us without a word and flung himself at Eleanor's door. We followed close behind.

Inside Eleanor's room, Marta was half crouched against the Chinese screen, trying to protect her head with her arms as Eleanor struck her with brutal fury. Jay grabbed Eleanor and threw her backwards into a chair, at the same time seizing Marta in his arms. Great hoarse sobs wracked Marta's slender body. An angry gash and bruises were already visible on the arm that protruded through her torn coat sleeve. There was blood in the corner of her mouth.

"What are you doing?" Jay's anguished voice assaulted Eleanor.

"Are you going to defend her again? Without even knowing what she's done?" Eleanor cried. Her face was a bilious green, almost as if it had absorbed some of the color of her dress. "It's always Marta with you, isn't it? Marta, Marta, Marta! My God, Jay—you love her more than me!"

Jay led Marta to the door. "Miss Lorimer, are

you a good nurse?" He forced the words through barely-restrained rage. "Will you take Marta into my room, please? There are ointments and bandages in the bathroom cupboards. I'll be there in a moment."

Nellie Morgan and Margaret went back upstairs, and I walked Marta down the hall and into Jay's room. She was hysterical, sobbing so hard she could scarcely breathe. My own heart was pounding and my head spun. At last, I believed, Eleanor had gone completely mad.

I sat Marta down at the end of Jay's great carved-oak bed. "Wait here just a second, darling," I breathed, and I rushed into his private bath to fetch her a tumbler of water. Once, a drink of water had helped to calm little Bonnie's sobs. I thought the same remedy might help Marta. Her hands were shaking violently and her teeth were chattering, but I held the glass to her lips. Slowly, she began to take sips from it and slowly her sobs decreased in violence and she gained some control of her breathing.

Jay stormed in and gave the door a hard shove but caught it before it slammed and closed it more gently. His face was deeply flushed and there was perspiration on his brow.

"How is she?" he asked me. "How are you, Marta sweetheart?" He sat by her and cuddled her in his arms. Her weeping continued, but now the sobs were more natural, less labored. I went back into the bathroom and faced a wall of varnished oak cabinets. Which one held the medicines? I opened several doors and drawers of towels and linens and toilet articles before locating the bandages and salves. A shallow basin occupied the same cupboard, and I filled it with tepid water and brought it back into the bedroom, along with a square of flannel, some of the medicines, and a gauze bandage for Marta's arm. I knelt by Jay and Marta and began to wash her arm and her face as gently as I could.

"Have things been so terrible, then?" he was asking her. "Did you want to run away?"

"I didn't want to leave *you*, Daddy," she hiccoughed. "It's her I have to get away from. She's wicked. And I *hate* her!" She began to sob again.

I raised my eyebrows inquiringly and Jay said, "Our little Marta was eloping tonight. She was intending to go to Alaska with Jack."

"Oh, Marta, my dear." I patted her hand.

"Eleanor discovered her. My dear wife was pacing around the living room in the dark waiting for me, I think—that's what I get from her now—waiting to catch me coming in, to find out where I had been. She was standing there in the dark and saw Marta crossing the piazza with her little bag.

"And Jack?" I asked. "Where was he?"

"He was at home," Marta wailed. "He told me I couldn't come because I'm too young. But I was going to go anyway. I had to get *out* of here!"

"But if he told you no—" I began.

"I didn't care. I thought if I could just get to his house and talk to him, he'd see. Well, he's leaving tomorrow, and I thought if I came over with my bag he'd see I meant it." She began to cry hard again, and Jay petted her soothingly.

"Instead," Jay explained, "Jack called me. I've been in New York all day talking to Tom. Jack reached me at my office. He told me he thought Marta was extremely upset and likely to do something rash. So I hurried back and came in to find this going on." He shook his head. "I can't understand how Eleanor's gotten into this state. Did you hear her accuse me of loving Marta more than her? Grandfather always said she was jealous of everyone, even the children, but I never thought she'd become so twisted—" His voice began to shake with anger and he pulled a paper from his pocket. "That's not all, by the way. Look what I found on Eleanor's table just now." I took the paper from him and unfolded it.

"Caldwell—" I read. "Radford and F have had a falling out. . . ." I gasped and looked up at Jay. It was the missing letter.

"I was wrong. It wasn't Geoffrey after all," he said bitterly.

Two memories sprang sharply into my mind: Eleanor embracing August Flammon under the stairs; Eleanor emerging from Jay's office flapping a handful of papers at Ginger. Eleanor, I realized—Eleanor in league with August Flammon, spying on her own husband. And this was a woman whose jealous "love" for Jay was so well known.

Could it ever have been true love—once, long ago? Can real love twist and pervert itself into hatred and betrayal? I thought not, for true love is selfless, and Eleanor's love for Jay had never been that. From the very beginning, in childhood, hers had been a sick love, a greedy love. Now she had become a kind of monster.

I had finished washing and treating Marta's wounds, and Jay rose. "Take her upstairs, now, please, Lillie. I'm going out." He went to the door and had opened it when Marta cried out: "Daddy! Don't go away. Don't leave me here alone with Eleanor. Take me away. Take me to New York. Please. I can't live with her. I can't!"

Her face was contorted with fear, and Jay gazed at her in anguish. He came back across the room and kissed her. "You won't have to darling. Daddy will fix it." And then he was gone.

I took Marta out into the hallway and saw Nellie Morgan just edging into Eleanor's room with a tray. I took Marta up the back stairs.

The commotion had wakened Leo and Bonnie, and Margaret was having a time getting them settled. I took Marta to her room and saw to it that she put on night clothes and got into bed. Eleanor had beaten her more brutally than had at first been apparent. Now, her small face was pitifully red and swollen against the white pillows, and a very large and ugly bruise was already darkening along one cheekbone.

I was glad when Nellie, having finished serving Eleanor, brought a tray of warm milk and crackers in for Marta. We sat with her a long time, and she stopped crying and lapsed into a kind of angry silence which upset me more than her crying had. Nellie and I were left to chat along by ourselves, for Marta would not speak. Over and over again, we told her that everything would be all right, which we none of us believed for a moment.

Finally, Nellie suggested that we were probably keeping Marta awake, and Marta assured us that she would be all right and would be able to sleep before long. We put out the light and tiptoed out. We listened at the nursery door and noted that all was quiet there; Leo and Bonnie must be asleep. It seemed that no one in the servants' wing had heard anything, separated as they were from the front of the house by the thick, hollow wall containing the secret passageways. The whole house was silent.

I went back to my room and sat shivering in the chair, my nerves so taut that I jumped at the smallest sound. Ginger came and curled up in my lap, and I stroked her fur absently. She went to sleep, and I envied her her blissful ignorance.

I had no idea what would happen next and didn't know how even to begin thinking about it. Jay's one concern now would surely be to get the children away from Eleanor. But how? Suppose she refused a separation? A divorce was only possible if one partner admitted or was proven to have committed adultery. The problems this presented were incomprehensible. Eleanor would not admit to an affair with August Flammon, and gaining evidence against her would be a nasty business. Jay would probably not attempt it, and it might prove impossible even if he did. Jay was in the worse position, his evening at the opera with me having made the newspapers.

And then, if a divorce were achieved, custody of the children would almost certainly be awarded to the mother, even if those of us who witnessed her abuse of Marta were to testify to it. Custody by even a bad mother would be considered preferable to custody by a father. It was unfair, but the precedents were overwhelming. I doubted that Jay would dare risk challenging the age-old system in a court of law.

To my tormented mind, there seemed to be no solution, none at all. Yet Jay had told Marta that he would "fix it." As drowsiness at last came over me, I concluded that, like Marta, I would simply have to rely on Jay to find the way.

There was a terrible scream, and a crashing sound. For an instant I thought I had fallen asleep and dreamed the scene between Marta and Eleanor all over again. But this scream had been closer and louder than the earlier sounds, and after a few moments of silence, I heard stirrings from the servants' wing. Nellie, looking incredibly weary after the stressful events that had already taken place, came in to tell me that Hans Arnold was going to investigate. I opened my window wide, and Nellie and I, soon joined by Ada and Susan, huddled in our robes and watched as Hans's lantern appeared at the kitchen door and bobbed slowly along the side of the house. He passed under my window and started across the little bridge, then stopped.

"Oh!" cried Nellie. "Look at the railing!"

Even from where we stood, we could see that the outer rail of the bridge had been broken. Hans had seen it too and was peering down over it toward the rocks below the cliff. Then he straightened and came back toward the kitchen.

"What is it, Hans?" Ada called. "Can you see anything?"

He looked up at our window. "Something. I'm not sure what. I want someone to go down the cliff with me."

Just then, another lantern appeared near the kitchen, and Bob came toward Hans. The two men conferred for a moment, then headed back toward the bridge. They paused on the span while Bob looked over the edge, and then Hans came back and stood below the window again, looking up at us.

"It looks—it looks like a body at the bottom of the cliff. Wearing something green."

Nellie and I both gasped. Each of us had seen Eleanor that evening in her green dress.

"Oh, my land," Nellie was the one brave enough to say, to Hans, "Mrs. Caldwell was wearing a green dress tonight."

As one, we turned our eyes to Eleanor's window which was directly above the little bridge and the notch in the cliff.

"It's open," Hans said. "It's swung all the way out, and a couple of the panes are broken."

We watched in horror as Hans rejoined Bob and the two lanterns disappeared over the edge of the cliff in the direction of the wooden steps. Some minutes later, they reappeared and moved back toward us over the bridge. Hans called up from below.

"Where's Mr. Caldwell?"

"He went out. We don't know where," Nellie replied, looking at the rest of us for confirmation. "Why? Is it her?"

"Yes. It's Mrs. Caldwell."

"Is she dead?"

"She's all smashed up." He shook his head. "She's dead all right."

FOURTEEN

The open window, the broken bridge rail—it was apparent that Eleanor had jumped or had been pushed, knocked, or thrown to her death.

The four of us—Nellie, Ada, Susan, and I—did the natural thing. We rushed toward the second floor with the idea of storming Eleanor's room to find—what? We didn't know. In the hallway, we met Margaret Dobbs who had slept through most of the uproar and only just roused to the increasing chaos. Hastily, we told her what had happened, and she assured us that Bonnie and Leo were still sound asleep.

At her words, we all stopped abruptly and stared at one another. "Oh," Ada moaned. "The poor babies." The children would have to be told about their mother's horrible death, but that was something to face later.

We hurried on down the stairs, and we saw Bob and Hans already in the second-floor corridor. At the threshold of Eleanor's room, we halted as abruptly as if the open doorway were a solid barrier. There was little to see from where we stood. The window with its broken panes was banging gently back and forth in a light wind. That was all.

"Well, let's go in and have a look." Bob started forward.

"No, wait." Hans laid a hand on his arm. "We'd best stay out of there. The police won't want anything disturbed, any clues."

"Clues?" Susan murmured nervously.

"Something that was dropped, a bit of torn cloth—who knows? If we mess about in there, we might destroy evidence."

"Maybe that's not such a bad idea," Nellie said. I thought I understood her strange remark. Deep in her heart, despite her loyalty and love for Jay, she was afraid that he had done it. Don't be afraid, Nellie, I thought—not of that. Jay is not a killer.

"This isn't for us to interfere with, so no one had better go in,' Hans was saying. "I'll go downstairs to Mr. Caldwell's office and telephone the police."

Nellie spoke sharply. "Don't you think Mr. Caldwell should be the one to do that?"

"Does anyone know where Mr. Caldwell is?" Hans challenged. We shook our heads. "For all we know he's gone to New York and won't be back until tomorrow. Do you propose to leave poor Mrs. Caldwell lying at the bottom of the cliff until he gets here?"

Our horrified silence was answer enough. He started down the stairs, and we stood in a miserable knot by the doorway. Suddenly, a figure in a long gown appeared at the end of the hall. Susan noticed first and emitted a small, startled scream. It was Marta.

"Oh, my stars," groaned Ada. "What do you suppose that child has heard?"

Margaret and I hurried toward Marta, our minds racing to frame answers to the questions she would surely ask.

"Now, now, darling. You oughtn't to be down here," Margaret said helplessly, taking hold of Marta's arm.

"Is it Christmas yet?" Marta mumbled. "Is it time to get up?"

Margaret and I exchanged glances.

"Can we open our presents? I hemmed handkerchiefs for Daddy," Marta rambled on.

Handkerchiefs had been Marta's Christmas gift for Jay just the December past. "She's sleepwalking," I whispered to Margaret. "She doesn't even know where she is. She thinks it's Christmas."

"Thank heaven," Margaret breathed. "Time enough for her to know about all this in the morning. I'll take her back to bed." And she led Marta away, talking to her softly. "Better come to bed, dear. It's not morning yet."

"That's an awful coincidence," Nellie said when I reported that Marta was somnambulant. "She hasn't done that since her mother died—her own mother. And that's just what she used always to say when we'd find her wandering the halls. 'Is it Christmas?' She always seemed to think it was Christmas Eve."

"Trying to go back to a happier time," I speculated.

"I expect it was the fight with Miss Eleanor that set her off this time," Ada said. "Let her think it's Christmas for another few hours."

The local police arrived, and the night dissolved into an endless sequence of trampling feet and bobbing lanterns. Men moved down the face of the cliff to bring up the shattered body of Eleanor Caldwell. Then they were treading methodically back and forth over the bridge and among the shrubs under her window, through the corridors, up and down the stairs, and in and out of her room.

The police had been followed by newspaper reporters, one or two at first, then a small crowd, asking endless questions, writing in their notebooks, sketching on their sketch pads, attempting to take photographs—even making free use of Jay's telephone, in spite of Hans Arnold's protests.

In the midst of it all, Jay arrived, and it was the reporters who broke the news to him, their crude questions telling him all he needed to know about what had happened and why his house had been so invaded in the middle of the night.

I happened to be standing on the grand stairway, and over the heads of the milling crowd I saw him come in, saw the stricken look on his face, the pain, the bewilderment. He raised his head and looked about. Somehow I knew that he was looking for me. He found me, and for the merest instant, we embraced each other with our eyes. Then he looked away. Heaven help him if his feelings for me should be detected now with Eleanor lying dead in the black wagon outside the door. How I wanted to go to him! But I turned and went upstairs. It was the most difficult thing I had ever done.

Miraculously, the children were still asleep. The massive old house with its thick walls and deep, carpeted corridors absorbed sound, and the third floor was quiet. The voices below seemed just a murmur in the hallway, the kind of sound that might once have carried upstairs from a party.

I stopped at Marta's room, listening at the door before opening it a crack. A shaft of light from the hallway fell across the bed, and I could see that Marta was sleeping quietly, peacefully. I closed her door and went on to the nursery.

For a few moments I stood beside Margaret between the little beds where Bonnie and Leo slept, rosy in the dim glow of the night light and more innocent than they would ever be again. She raised her eyebrows at me as if to ask, "What's happening downstairs?" but I just shrugged and shook my head. I tiptoed out and went into my own room.

My window was still wide open, but the weather had turned colder. I pulled the window to. Suddenly, I was overwhelmed by exhaustion. I shivered in the frigid air as I undressed and slipped into my nightdress. I pulled an extra quilt onto my bed and crept between the chilled sheets, shaking as much from nerves as from the cold. Ginger gave me a start when she jumped up onto the bed, but I welcomed the familiar warm weight of her chin on my feet.

"Eleanor is dead," I told myself as drowsiness overcame me. "There's nothing to fear from her any more." Yet fear was the feeling that accompanied me into sleep.

Early in the morning, Jay called the children to his room, gently closed the door, and told them Eleanor was dead. Then he sent for me. I knocked hesitantly at his door, then went in when I heard his firm "Come in."

Jay was in an armchair. Leo was between his father's knees, half sitting on one of them, with Jay's arm around his shoulders. His chin was quavering, but his eyes were dry.

Marta sat on the edge of the bed and looked at me with wide, solemn eyes. Her hands were limp in her lap. Her skin was as pale and transparent as alabaster beneath the bruises and cuts, the cruel reminders of her last encounter with Eleanor.

Marta and Leo were silent, but Bonnie's grief erupted as free and untainted as a woodland spring. She ran to me, threw her arms around my neck as I stooped to her, and sobbed, "Miss Lorimer, my mommy's dead. She fell on the rocks."

"I know, darling, I know." I lifted her up and held her in my arms, feeling her chubby legs about my waist and her hot tears on my neck.

"There are arrangements I have to make for the

funeral," Jay said to the children as I listened. "I think the village church is the best place to have it, even though most of our friends are in New York. They can come to Long Island. I don't want to go through the turmoil of moving all of us and—and your mother—back to New York for the service. Do you all agree?"

Bonnie had turned her teary face toward her father to take in his uncharacteristically sober words. All three nodded their heads.

"So I shall drive to the church to arrange things there. I won't be gone very long, and when I get back, I'll come directly up to the third floor and stay with you all the rest of the day. While I'm gone, Miss Lorimer will be with you, and probably Miss Dobbs and Mrs. Morgan. And if I'm not back before lunch, Mrs. Wirth will fix one for you to have in the nursery. But I promise to be back no later than one o'clock. Is that all right?"

I was moved very deeply by the care Jay was taking that the children, while knowing the worst, should feel his presence and his strength, should know where he was going, when he would be back, and what would take place in the interim. He knew that Leo and Bonnie especially, having just had their mother snatched away from them, could fear that their father might disappear just as suddenly and capriciously. He was taking infinite pains to be certain that they did not feel abandoned by him even for an instant.

Jay went out, and I led the children up to the nursery. Nellie Morgan was nowhere to be found, and at last Hans told me that she had undertaken to give the secret passageways a thorough cleaning. "It's her way," he said. "When she's upset, she always does some kind of hard work." So Margaret and I shared the care of the children that morning.

Margaret read a story to Bonnie and Leo while I talked with Marta. She was quiet, bewildered. She evinced no memory of the sleepwalking incident; she recalled only the fight with Eleanor and then waking up and being told that Eleanor was dead. It occurred to me that she must be feeling guilty, for she had hated Eleanor; perhaps she had even wished her stepmother dead, especially after the terrible scene of the night before. Then to have Eleanor die so directly afterward . . .

"You mustn't feel responsible, you know," I told her. "You were angry with her, and that's perfectly normal. Anger doesn't cause death. It was a coincidence, a terrible coincidence, that's all. It's not your fault."

Marta nodded abstractedly. I didn't know if my words had helped her or if she had even really heard them. She seemed almost as dazed as she had while sleepwalking. I was afraid for her. Would she recover from this?

We had our lunches brought up on a tray. Marta ate nothing, but Leo had part of a sandwich, and Bonnie finished everything on her plate. I noticed that Marta and Leo were both glancing nervously at the clock, and I was grateful when, at five minutes before one o'clock, Jay came in.

"I've just had some air, and I think you children need some, too. Let's have a ride," he said and bundled them off to the stables.

In mid afternoon, Bertie arrived. Finding Jay not in, he sent Susan to ask me to join him in the living room.

I had scarcely thought of Bertie since January, and when I heard that he was here, I was ashamed of my indifference. I had seen him, of course, when we all returned to Soundcliff after the opera fiasco. Then, with Jay in residence and there being no more need of his services as companion to Eleanor, Bertie had gone back to New York. He had come by on five or six occasions since then. "Come by" now struck me as an inadequate phrase, for of course one did not simply "come by" Long Island from New York City. I realized suddenly that Bertie had made those long trips as much to see me as to check on Eleanor's welfare. Yet I had been so preoccupied by my dealings with Eleanor and my feelings for Jay that I had hardly noticed Bertie's visits.

I went down to the living room and found him looking pale and drawn. "Bertie, I'm so sorry," I said.

"It's a dreadful shame, this." He shrugged helplessly as if to convey how inadequate he knew his words to be. "Jay telephoned me this morning. He didn't seem to know how it happened. He thinks she jumped." His look was questioning.

"I don't know, Bertie. Anything seems possible."

"Jay wasn't here?"

"He was out."

"Was there any—warning? Any disturbance?"

"There was a terrible scene earlier. Marta tried

to run off—"

"Jay told me all about that. But while he was gone—?"

"I heard her scream when she fell. That's all."

Bertie passed his hand over his eyes but maintained his composure. "Poor Eleanor, *however* it happened."

"Yes."

"Eleanor and Charlotte were like sisters to me. It's hard to believe they're both gone."

"Oh, Bertie." I went to him and touched his arm. "If only there were something I could do."

"I'll be all right, I suppose. I am worried about Jay. How is he taking it?"

"Seemingly well. He's been making quite an effort for the children."

"Look, Lillie. I'm going to head for the stables and find a mount. I'll see if I can catch up with them. But I'll stick around for awhile, as long as I'm needed." He took my two hands in his. "Now, listen. It may not occur to anyone else, but I know this whole thing is going to be awfully hard on you." He gave me a deep look, a look that told me he knew everything about Jay's and my feelings for each other. "Anything I can do, any help I can be—I hope you'll think of me as your best friend, Lillie dear." He kissed my cheek and then went out.

I was terribly touched. In the midst of his own pain, he had considered mine. Had I underestimated Bertie? Had I taken him for granted? I had.

It was tea time, I noted gratefully, for I craved companionship now. In the kitchen, Ada was setting out bread and butter and jam. The staff were gathered about the table, talking edgily, rehashing the same grizzly details they had doubtlessly been discussing all day. But now there was even more to ponder: The afternoon papers had come out, and they were full of the story of Eleanor's death.

I picked up one paper that was lying in the middle of the table and read the front-page article. Its tone took me aback. Jay was described as "handsome millionaire Jay Caldwell" and Eleanor as "his beautiful wife, the former Eleanor Archer, a leader of New York and Long Island society."

"Police were summoned to the opulent Caldwell estate Soundcliff late at night to discover Mrs. Caldwell's body smashed upon the rocks beneath her open, broken window," the article related. "Mr. Caldwell was not on the premises but turned up somewhat later and expressed surprise and shock at his wife's death.... Mr. Caldwell had previously been married to the former Charlotte Archer, a first cousin of Eleanor Archer Caldwell. The first Mrs. Caldwell died under mysterious circumstances in 1888. Mr. Caldwell was married to Eleanor Archer in 1889. The only surviving heirs to the Archer fortune are Pemberton Archer of New York City and Long Island and Nella Noble MacDougall of Rhinebeck, New York, first cousins of Charlotte and Eleanor Archer...."

Susan blurted, "It almost sounds like they're saying Mr. Jay might have—well, killed Miss Eleanor."

Stern looks from Nellie, Ada, Bob, and Hans sent Susan into a deep blush and silence. "You just put that nonsense out of your head," Nellie snapped.

At Nellie's words, I automatically looked toward the end of the table where Nancy Vance and Geoffrey Hand had always sat, steeling myself for Nancy's usual sarcastic rejoinder. It was then that I first realized they were gone.

"Oh!" I exclaimed. "When did Nancy and Geoffrey leave? I didn't say goodbye."

"Don't worry," Ada replied. "No one did. They drove off at the crack of dawn with scarce a word. Didn't want to get mixed up in all this, I expect. I stepped out the kitchen door at daybreak, and there they was, big as you please, all loaded up in the wagon and about to pull out. 'Well, good luck,' I says, and they give a wave and a 'so long' and off they went."

Off to Gus Flammon, I thought and wondered once again why he had hired Geoffrey. Had Eleanor arranged it? After all, hers was the Flammon connection. Perhaps Geoffrey and Nancy had left so early in order to arrive at the Flammon estate and establish themselves there quickly before Gus Flammon—released from any obligation to Eleanor now that she was dead—could change his mind.

I shook my head. Eleanor seemed to have created as many complications in death as in life. I wondered if her hold over us would ever end.

After tea, I felt a need to be alone with my thoughts; yet I couldn't bear to sit in my room by the window from which I had witnessed the ghastly scenes of the night before. I shrugged into a heavy coat, for the weather was cold, and went out by the piazza door.

The little bridge with its rail hanging forlornly in jagged segments compelled my reluctant curiosity, and I walked to it and looked down at the rocks below. Of course there was nothing to be seen, but I could all too well picture the broken body in the blood-stained green dress that had lain there.

I would have to pass near the place where Eleanor had fallen in order to walk on the beach; nevertheless, I descended the wooden steps over the face of the cliff and soon was striding across the cold, hard sand. Several hundred yards along there was a large rock, and I sat on it and stared out at the white-gray water so near the color of the sky that the demarcation was hard to detect. A pair of gulls dipped and dove overhead, taking long, gliding rides on the wind. They landed awkwardly on an upturned derelict boat and turned their beaks, exactly parallel, into the breeze.

Ordinarily, I would have thought the desolate winter beach beautiful. Today it seemed just desolate.

I tried to sort through my feelings. What was most distressing, of course, was not knowing how Eleanor had died, whether she had killed herself or had been killed by someone else. Given her deteriorating mental condition and her complex and strained relationships with so many people, both conjectures had merit.

Worse was Nellie Morgan's oblique suggestion last night, echoed in the newspapers today, that Jay might have done it. All of my instincts told me that he had not killed Eleanor, but if Nellie had seemed worried about it, and if the newspapers began to play on it, then surely it would be believed by others as well. Was he in danger?

And what would now become of Jay and me? I realized—there was no denying it—that Eleanor's death had seemed to remove the barriers to our love. After a decent interval, propriety would permit us to be together. But of course it was not as simple as that. Propriety was not my chief concern, nor would it be Jay's. He would mourn Eleanor, no matter how unhappy their marriage had become. Their lives had been intertwined since childhood, and one does not recover easily from such a loss. Besides, the idea of profiting from another's death is repugnant to any decent person.

In sum, I was deeply afraid that guilt and grief would taint our love, perhaps forever.

I examined my heart and my mind and I confronted my feelings, the noble and the ignoble alike. I thought about all of the problems that awaited us. In the end, I knew that I could face it all if . . . if Jay truly loved me.

But did he? My courage would surely fail without confirmation of it; yet now, especially, Jay could not give it to me. Almost an entire day had passed, a day he must know was dreadful for me as well as for him and the children. He had gathered them to him; they would see one another through the nightmare. But he had not included me. He had asked me to stay with the children while he went out to make funeral arrangements, but he would have asked that of any governess. Except for the one moment last night when his eyes had met mine, the moment when he had first returned to Soundcliff to find Eleanor dead, he had given me no sign of caring. Now he was off riding with the children, and I, alone and disheartened on that cold, rocky beach, felt more an orphan than ever I had felt since Daddy and Uncle Frank had died.

"Jay. Oh, Jay," I breathed into the cold wind. "I know the children need you. But I need you, too."

The two gulls started up and reeled off into the wind. Something had disturbed them, but I had not moved. I looked about and saw a distant figure coming toward me over the beach. Was it Bertie, or was it—? My heart leaped. It was Jay.

Was he looking for me? And if so—to say what? that he loved me? or that Eleanor's death made our love impossible? I sat still—numb with cold and pain, hope and fear—and watched him come nearer.

He wore tan jodphurs, boots, and a thick black turtle-necked sweater under his tweed riding jacket. His muscular body in full stride was lithe and powerful. Suddenly, in spite of my anguish, I was thoroughly aroused. The blood coursed hotly in my veins. "Please, please," I thought in silent agony, "don't abandon me now. I need you so. I want you so."

He stopped in front of me, and I looked up into

his glistening eyes. The cold wind had ruddied his cheeks and ruffled his dark hair. He stood with his legs apart and his hands on his hips. I waited for his words, words I feared would change my life. But he said only, "It's getting pretty cold out here. The sun will be setting soon." And he sat beside me on the rock.

The two gulls dove back toward the upturned boat, spread their wings, extended their feet, and did a silly little hoppity-hop landing. Then once again, they paralleled their beaks, like weather vanes into the wind.

"Funny, aren't they?" Jay said absently.

"Yes. I've been watching them."

We sat in silence for some moments, and then Jay began to talk to me about his marriage to Eleanor.

"I hated what happened to us," he concluded at last. "We should never have married. She was— she became ill, mentally ill." He paused, then, not looking at me, and he said, "Do you think I really killed her?"

"Whatever do you mean?" I asked, astonished.

"Do you think I drove her mad? Do you think I destroyed her? that I drove her to kill herself?"

He had turned slightly away from me so that when I saw his shoulders heave and heard the rasping intake of breath, I did not understand until he raised the hand nearest me to shield his face that he was crying.

Oh. Oh. My heart turned over. My dearest, my love, oh don't, don't. My thoughts were wild with anguish for him, my body strained to shelter his, my arms ached to hold him. But I sat still and silent. In spite of all that had passed between us, I was in awe of this man and dared not reach out to him.

Then love conquered restraint. I turned and put my arms around him. I tugged away the hand that shielded his face and kissed the tears on his cheeks. I pressed the palm of my hand against the back of his neck and moved my fingers upward through his hair.

"Darling, darling," I murmured and pulled his dear head to my breast. He wrapped his arms tightly around me and buried his face against me. I kissed his hair again and again.

Suddenly, I felt his body surge and tighten. He raised his head and met my lips in a hard, kneading kiss that left me weak with desire. I clung to him, bleating and moaning.

After a long moment he pulled away from me with a sobbing groan. "This isn't right, Lillie. We have to wait."

Now it was I who began to sob in sheer frustration and he who kissed the tears and cradled me, tenderness now tempering his rough passion. Slowly, we comforted and calmed each other, our kisses growing gentler and sweeter, and at last we rose and walked back along the beach together, arms about each other, stealing one more kiss and then one more until we drew near enough the house to worry about being seen.

Then Jay said, "I'll go another way," and we parted. I walked toward the wooden steps that tacked up the cliff; he veered off toward the jagged spit of rocks that extended into the Sound by the dock. What "way" was there to reach the house by that strange route, I wondered? Then I climbed the steps, entered the house, and went to my room.

I picked Ginger up and sat in my chair, too agitated by far to join the others for supper, too engrossed in the memory of the afternoon to notice the gathering gloom. I stroked and stroked the little cat—and longed instead to be stroking Jay's body.

Two days later, the funeral was held at the village church. Friends and acquaintances of the Caldwell family filled the small sanctuary to overflowing. From the pew where I sat between Nellie Morgan and Hans Arnold, I could not even see Jay and the children.

After the service, Eleanor's casket was carried up the aisle, and the congregation filed out into the cold, bright March sunlight. A throng of reporters and the curious pressed against police barricades as the mourners got into the carriages that rolled up, one behind the other, and formed a procession behind the wreath-laden hearse. There was, then, a very long, slow ride to Greenwood Cemetery in Brooklyn, Jay's carriage at the head of the line, ours at the rear.

It was the first day of spring. Only the sparsest hint of new green showed among the dead grasses, and the trees were bare of all but the earliest-swelling buds. Yet Greenwood was lovely and would surely be breathtaking in full summer. Naked branches arched thickly over the handsome markers that lined the broad avenues. The number of massive, ornate monuments and magnificent mausoleums was truly astonishing. Through the trees to our right, beyond the sloping grounds, the island of Manhattan glimmered like an enchanted kingdom across the sapphire waters of Upper New York Bay. As the procession wound its way along to the Caldwell plot, I gazed from the carriage windows and drew in a breath of wonder. If the dead could see, I thought, they would surely be happy at Greenwood. "The best families in New York are buried here," Ada told me solemnly.

Only a few carriages had made the journey all the way to Greenwood. The congregation at the graveside was small—just the minister, Jay, Eli, the children, Bertie, the servants, a few close family friends, and one police sergeant who had accompanied the cortege all the way from the church.

It was not until the sacred words had been spoken and the casket lowered, not until Jay and each of the children had thrown a handful of earth into the open grave, not until Jay had bidden farewell to each mourner and turned to join the family in their carriage that I realized why the sergeant had come along. I was standing nearby when he approached Jay and spoke to him politely, almost obsequiously:

"Excuse me, Mr. Caldwell. I'm sorry to bother you, but I have orders to place you under arrest for the murder of your wife."

FIFTEEN

Bertie and Eli posted bail before Jay had spent half an hour in custody, and the three men arrived at Soundcliff almost before I could realize what had happened.

Jay stood charged with murder.

He had pled innocent, of course. In due time, a date would be set for commencement of Grand Jury proceedings, and if the Grand Jury should indict him for murder, a trial would ensue. The prospects were horrifying—almost the more so because for now, he was in limbo.

Jay retired to his office as soon as he came in. I was in anguish. I had to speak to him, to hear what had happened, to know how he felt, and to know what he thought lay ahead. Yet I was terrified to knock at that closed door. I paced up and down the short corridor outside the office, my heart pounding; and then I thought, "What if someone sees me lurking about here?" and chagrin propelled me to the door. I knocked rather more loudly than I had meant to.

Jay opened the door, but instead of stepping back to let me in, he stood square in the doorway, forcing me to remain standing awkwardly in the hallway.

"I had to—well, know how you are—" I stammered.

"I'm all right. I expected it."

"But how could they?" I demanded. "You weren't even in the house when it happened."

"I suppose that even Jay Caldwell is allowed to have only *one* wife die mysteriously with impunity."

"Oh, don't joke," I moaned.

"I'm not joking. When Charlotte died, they took my word that it was suicide. There was no investigation. But the papers have gotten hold of this now, and the District Attorney is under pressure not to let the rich man off so easily this time."

"Oh, Jay. It's unbearable." I moved toward him, longing for a moment of privacy with him, longing to take him into my arms. But his reply stopped me.

"I have work to do, Lillie." He said it abruptly and without warmth. I could not have been more hurt if he had slapped me.

"I see," I managed to reply. "Then I shall leave you alone." I turned and walked quickly away, and when I glanced back over my shoulder, I saw that he had closed the door.

The hurt welled up and spilled over. Tears streamed down my cheeks. I dashed for the elevator, slid shut the little doors, and set the controls for the third floor. I had but one overwhelming desire: to reach the privacy of my room before someone saw me.

To my horror, the elevator stopped at the second floor, the doors opened, and I confronted Eli Caldwell. I buried my face in my hands, and he reached into the elevator and gently drew me into the hallway.

"I was about to go down and talk to Jay, but yours looks like a more urgent case," he said kindly. "Come along."

He led me through the west wing to his rooms and sat me down by the windows. "Now stay there. I'll be right back," he told me and disappeared into his bedchamber to return at once with an enormous red and white handkerchief. I dabbed at my eyes with it obediently.

"And now tell me what's got you so upset," he said.

"Oh—" I faltered. "It's just that I'm so worried about J—uh—Mr. Caldwell—the murder charge." I couldn't have explained how Jay had treated me just now and how his sudden coolness had hurt me. It would have revealed too much about how close our relationship had become.

Yet, Eli seemed to know something about it anyway, for he said, "No need to call him 'Mr. Caldwell' in front of me. And try not to worry about the murder charge," he continued. "The

District Attorney will mollify the snapping dogs by bringing Jay before the Grand Jury. They won't indict him."

"How can you be sure?"

"There's no evidence. And they won't find any, either. Jay's no killer. You ought to know that."

"I do, I do. I just don't know your American system of justice, I suppose. The whole idea of a murder charge is so terrifying."

"Well, take my word for it. They won't push very hard for an indictment. The District Attorney is an elected official, and no politician wants to get permanently on the bad side of a family as rich as the Caldwells. The Grand Jury proceedings will make the D.A. look good. That's all he wants."

"I wish I felt as sure of the future as you," I sighed and wiped another tear from my eye.

"Well, now, it's my turn to confide in you, Lillie," Eli said, and a shadow of worry fell across his face. "I'm not at all sure of the future. Not at all."

"But you said—"

"I only said that Jay won't be indicted."

"I don't understand. What else could happen?"

"Do you believe in premonitions, Lillie?" he asked and leaned toward me, almost as if afraid that his words would be overheard.

"I can't really say. Do you?"

He shook his head. "I have a feeling of dread, and I can't get rid of it."

"Dread? of what?"

"I don't know. But it's not for myself. It's for Jay."

"Dear heaven."

"The odd thing is that I thought Jay was in danger years ago when he married Eleanor. I felt it all the time he was married to her. When I heard she was dead, I thought, 'Well, now I can breathe a sigh of relief.' But do you know, I can't. There's an evil presence here still. I don't know—maybe I misjudged Eleanor and maybe it's someone else that's the source of the evil in the house—someone still among us. Or maybe—"

"What?"

"Maybe there really is such a thing as a haunting." He sighed and patted my hand. "But don't pay any attention to me. The mind can play tricks on an old man."

I went to my room, more deeply disturbed than ever—for I had been experiencing the very same feeling of dread Eli had described.

When Bertie came that afternoon, I asked him to walk with me in the woods. The early spring day was almost warm. A clear, white-gold light filtered through the bare branches and dressed the tender green grasses that poked up among the roots. We had walked quite some way before, on an impulse, I told him of my conversation with Eli.

"I believe Jay's grandfather thinks that Eleanor is haunting us," I said at last.

Bertie said, "Perhaps the dead do survive in some sphere tangential to ours. And where the two spheres touch, perhaps the dead can sometimes penetrate the living world." I had anticipated a smile or a joke to break the baleful spell Eli had cast over me. Bertie's response had been unexpectedly somber, and I said so.

"I've always thought it an interesting speculation," he said. "I've gone to a few seances, just out of curiosity. Some were obviously faked, others—oddly convincing."

"Oh, Bertie. I thought you'd laugh at the idea. Mr. Caldwell said himself that his mind might be playing tricks on him. And yet I can't dismiss the idea that there *is* some evil influence at Soundcliff. I feel it myself. Whether it's Eleanor or not, there is something or someone that wants to harm Jay. I'm afraid for him and—" I hesitated, for I did not wish to seem egocentric when it was Jay who was in so much trouble. But Bertie was the sort of friend from whom no secrets needed to be kept, and I confided, "I'm even afraid for myself. Whatever is menacing Jay may be menacing me as well. At least—well—it's what I feel. Do you think I'm just giving in to hysterics?"

"Hysterics? Not you, dear Lillie. Your grasp on reality is far too firm. But if you want me to dispel the supernatural air Eli has given all this, why I can explain your feelings in very ordinary terms. After all, Jay is in a dreadful situation, and if you care for Jay—" I blushed, but Bertie went right on, "if you care for Jay, a threat to him is indirectly a threat to you and to your happiness."

"I suppose so."

"I will say, though," Bertie continued, "that if anyone is capable of reaching from beyond the grave, it would be Eleanor. I've never known a soul as fierce as hers. She could pierce the veil if anyone could."

"A rage more powerful than death," I murmured.

"I once overheard a conversation between Charlotte and Eleanor," Bertie said after a moment's pause. "I've never told it to anyone before. It was when Charlotte and Jay had been married for a few years, and Marta was a very little girl. Her birth had been difficult for Charlotte, and it was well known that afterward Charlotte and Jay had rooms at opposite ends of the hallway and that he was never seen to enter or leave her room at night. Even before Marta was born, Charlotte was a very shy and private, even a fearful woman. She can't have given Jay the—well, the satisfaction he must have wanted and needed.

"One afternoon, Charlotte and Eleanor were having tea in the library. I came to the door—they didn't see me—and they were in the midst of a furious argument. Eleanor was so angry her face was scarlet, and she was fairly hissing at Charlotte. 'How can you be so cold? I would give my soul for just one night in his arms.'

"And Charlotte said in a small, intense voice, 'All our lives, you've had everything you wanted, Eleanor. But Jay is mine, and he'll never be yours.'"

"And then?"

"And then I stepped into the library with a cheery hello and acted as if I hadn't heard them. Charlotte poured me a cup of tea and Eleanor cut me a sandwich."

I shivered as Bertie and I turned our steps back toward Soundcliff. Were the two dead cousins,

Jay's dead wives, alive somewhere in the universe? Whether they were or not, I knew that the residue of their tormented lives would not soon fade from the fabric of ours.

Strangely, it was from Jay that I soon learned more about Charlotte and Eleanor.

I had gone back to my room after walking with Bertie and seated myself in the chair by the window. My heart was torn with fear of the evil that seemed to pervade Soundcliff and even more sorely rent with misery because of Jay's coldness. Ginger hopped into my lap and settled herself into a comfortable ball, purring in anticipation of the leisurely scratching she so often received from me when I was in a pensive mood.

I was almost as startled as poor Ginger was when I suddenly stood up, dumping her unceremoniously from my knees.

"Ginger! What on earth am I doing?" I exclaimed. Apologetically, I picked her up and held her in front of me. She gazed into my face with wide, round eyes. "All my life I've been afraid of my own shadow," I told her. "Sitting passively by, waiting for fate to knock me about." I set her rather more gently on the bed, and she continued to stare at me as I went on. "Just look at me! Biding my time in this wretched chair in my solitary room, the good little governess, waiting upon Master Jay's whim, moping and hoping and doing nothing. Well, no more!" I declared. "It's wrong for Jay to treat me that way. He owes me an explanation!"

Ginger got up and yawned, fanning her snow-white whiskers and then settling them neatly back against her cheeks. She turned, flipped up her tail, and jumped off the bed. "Stop talking and do something, then," she seemed to be telling me, and she sauntered to the door and meowed to be let out. I opened the door and followed her into the hallway.

I had to laugh at the comic picture we must have presented, walking along the corridor side by side and on down the stairs to the second-floor landing. But there Ginger took her leave of me and headed toward the nursery to find Bonnie while I continued on down to the great entrance hall. Without Ginger's friendly presence, my determination to confront Jay had begun to falter, but the alternative—the meek and helpless waiting—now seemed intolerable. For the second time that day I knocked at the office door and Jay opened it.

"I came to see what you're doing." My voice rang out with the excessive force of untested resolve.

Jay frowned, then half-smiled in spite of himself. "You did, did you?" he said. "Well, then, come in and I'll show you." He led me to his desk, sorted through some papers, and handed me a sheet of undecipherable figures headed "Bronx-Battery Elevated Railroad, Inc."

"I'm trying to set the family finances on a firmer footing. I have to make up for the loss of the LIH&M, you see. It depleted our capital and diminished our credit more significantly than I realized at first. I don't—I may not have as much time now to make it up as I had thought I would. That is, if anything should happen to me as a result of this murder charge, I've got to know that the children are provided for and that everything will be there for Leo to control when he's old enough."

I swallowed the panic his words evoked and spoke calmly. "And this Bronx-Battery Elevated Railroad—it's part of your plan?"

"Yes. Fortunately, the principal stockholders of the Bronx-Battery Elevated are having troubles on other fronts, and they've approached me about buying it up. I think it's just the opportunity I want. It won't quite compensate for the LIH&M yet. But it will grow as New York City grows, and by the time Leo is ready to take over, it should be worth a great deal."

"And until Leo is old enough?"

"I'll run it myself, of course. And if I—if I can't, I'm arranging a trust with Grandfather and Bertie as co-trustees, and Marta as well when she's twenty-one."

"It seems a very sound plan." I responded as serenely as I could, but I felt as if we were discussing Jay's impending death, and my voice quavered slightly.

Jay came to me and took my hand. "I know this is terribly difficult for you, Lillie. Come. Let's have a talk."

A fire had been laid against the chill of the evening, and heavy curtains were drawn across the windows. Jay led me to a low sofa by the fire and drew me down beside him. He kept hold of my hand as he said, "I owe you an explanation for my behavior. I've been reluctant to offer it, for it has to do with Charlotte and Eleanor, and I've been afraid to talk about them for fear of upsetting you. If you'd rather not hear it, please tell me and I'll understand."

"No," I said firmly. "I'd like to know."

He leaned back as if to begin a long tale, and his voice grew lower and more thoughtful. "Eleanor was always strange. Even as a child, her personality was fervid, over-heated. She would try so hard at games—harder than anybody. And she couldn't abide failure. She would weep bitterly if she lost to anyone but me. But if I won, she was happy, happier than if she had won herself.

"I was flattered by her attachment to me, but it made me uncomfortable. I would have preferred her to be more independent. It upset me to feel so reponsible for someone else's happiness. I was young and selfish.

"Charlotte was Eleanor's opposite—quiet, sweet, and undemanding—a pale little elf, not a beauty like Eleanor. We were very close, all of us— Eleanor and Bertie and Charlotte and I. I suppose I took it as much for granted as anyone else that I would marry one of the Archer girls, but everyone was surprised when I chose Charlotte.

"As much as Eleanor's forwardness drove me away, Charlotte's shyness and passivity attracted and intrigued me. Eleanor wanted everything and so I wanted to give her nothing. Charlotte wanted nothing, and so I wanted to give her things and gain her gratitude. My attitude toward Charlotte was as perverse as my attitude toward Eleanor.

"I wanted to bring Charlotte little presents and hold her in my arms as she unwrapped them and have her look up at me with surprise and pleasure, and she did. Unfortunately, the gift I most wanted to give her was the gift she wanted least—my body, the physical union of man and wife. Even her pregnancy made her unhappy. She was ill most of the time and suffered terribly when our dear little Marta was born.

"She did love Marta. But she informed me sadly and sweetly and quite firmly that we would never again share a bed. And so things remained for four and a half years until she died.

"I tried as gently as I could to change her mind. And when it became evident that she would not change, I tried to accept it and to make her happy in other ways. It was no use. She became more and more withdrawn, sadder and sadder.

"She was killed by a blow to the head. It seemed unlikely to most people, but I still believe that she killed herself somehow. I was not charged with her murder, but my reputation was nearly destroyed, for the society gossip circuit had not only accused but convicted me.

"Eleanor stood by me. So did Bertie, of course. But Eleanor was quite a force in the New York social world, and as Charlotte's closest female relative—almost a sister—her insistence on my innocence eventually gave me back a kind of respectability. And she was really wonderful for me. She kept me company and cheered me up and made me believe life could be worth living again.

"The one off-note was her jealousy of Marta. I had been trying to spend a great deal of time with Marta after her mother died, and Eleanor seemed to resent it. She resented Marta until she died. I could never persuade her that Marta was not her rival, that a child can never be a woman's true rival. She grudged every ounce of affection I gave to anyone else, even to Leo and Bonnie, her own babies, later on.

"Anyway, after Charlotte died I soon realized that Eleanor wanted to marry me. Grateful as I was to her, I was as nervous of her as I had ever been. I tried to extricate myself from the situation tactfully. I told her that after a normal period of mourning I hoped to be able to see other women and to remarry one day. The not-so-subtle message was that I would probably not marry her.

"We were alone that afternoon, and I was glad of it. She became hysterical. She said that we were meant for each other, that she had always known it. She said she would make me happy. And she said that she would kill herself if I didn't marry her.

"I had not killed Charlotte, but I wondered if she would have died if I had been able to make her happy, if I had been less clumsy with her. I felt responsible for Charlotte's death, and I simply could not chance being responsible for Eleanor's, too. Besides, Eleanor had been loyal to me when almost no one else was. And little Marta needed a mother.

"We were married, and at first we were content. Eleanor was very gay, and she enlivened our home with dinners and balls and parties of all sorts. And when she gave birth to Leo and then to Bonnie, I was very happy.

"At first I was not concerned about the things that began to go wrong. Marriage had not cured her jealousy of Marta as I had hoped it would, and I thought she treated Marta unkindly. And then there was her growing belief that I was seeing other women. But then—well, you know the rest. There was no reassuring her that I cared for her and was faithful to her. All of her actions stemmed from her belief that the opposite was the case. I can only suppose that that is why she betrayed me to Gus Flammon.

"The point is," Jay swallowed hard and had to pause a moment before going on. "The point is that I've had two wives who were so unhappy that they killed themselves."

He was holding my hand on his knee, and my fingertips were slightly pressed against his inner leg. I could feel his trembling. Jay believed, and with obvious sincerity, that both his wives had committed suicide. Yet I knew that many people believed Charlotte had been murdered. And as yet, of course, the exact cause of Eleanor's death had not been established.

I could see all too clearly where Jay's morbid conclusions were leading him, and my heart raced as I protested, "But how can you be so certain that they were suicides?"

"Ah," he sighed. "If you had known Charlotte. There never was a gentler woman. No one could have wished her harm. And as for Eleanor—well, you know how unhappy she was. Besides, who could have murdered her? I didn't, and who else could have wanted to? It would have to have been someone in the house, wouldn't it? But who? There's no one anyone could even begin to suspect."

I gazed wordlessly into Jay's anguished eyes. I had no reply. I already knew what his next words would be, and I was helpless to prevent his saying them.

"What I'm trying to tell you, Lillie, is that I can't—we can't make plans to be together. Do you understand?"

"No! No I don't!" I said vehemently.

"You've got to see it, Lillie. I'm simply not going to do to you whatever I did to Charlotte and Eleanor."

"Jay, how can you say such a thing? How can you think it? Whatever is wrong in this house, it isn't you."

"I'm determined not to take the risk. That's why I had to pull away from you at the beach. That's why I was so rude this morning. I'm sorry for that. But we just cannot be as close as we were becoming. I'm putting a stop to it now." He released my hand, and I felt as if a part of myself had been severed. "It's not because I don't care for you, Lillie. It's because I do."

"Then you must know that I care for you, too," I said. "I don't want to be shut out, Jay. You need me now, and I need you. I don't care about the risks. There are no risks as far as I'm concerned." With difficulty, I restrained myself from reaching for the hand he had withdrawn.

"Lillie," he moaned. "I do need you. But I can't—" He couldn't continue.

"Let me just be your friend," I said desperately. "Let me be near you and talk with you and help you."

"It wouldn't be fair, Lillie. There would be no future to it."

"Then what am I to do?" I spoke with a flash of anger. "Am I to stay here with the children, yet have nothing to do with you? Or am I to leave Soundcliff and only read about you in the papers?"

Jay passed a hand wearily over his eyes, but he didn't answer.

"Let us just be friends," I pressed. "If it can't be more than that, then it can't. But at least we'll be near each other."

He raised his head and his eyes brimmed with tragic longing. "If ever I kiss you again, Lillie, a fire will start that I'll not be able to put out."

"I know," I said quietly.

He stood up. "I'm in torment. You must bear with me—or go."

"I'll stay on as a friend, just a friend," I said firmly.

"If you understand that it can be only that between us—a friendship. No more."

"I do."

"I'm going to New York tonight," he said as he led me to the door. "Tomorrow morning, I'll conclude the Bronx-Battery Elevated purchase. Please reassure the children that I'll be back in the afternoon."

"I will."

"Good night, Lillie." And he closed the door behind me.

Jay had sent me away again, but this time I was not so miserable, for it was plain to me now that he loved me, even though he had never yet said that magical word to me. He had resolved to renounce me because he did not want to bring me harm as he believed he had Charlotte and Eleanor. But I knew he was wrong. Whatever the cause of their deaths, it was not Jay Caldwell; and I was filled with a new resolve of my own. Somehow, I did not know how, I would prove Jay blameless— to himself as well as to the world—and free him to love me fully at last.

How would I begin? Where would my quest lead me? I felt a thrill of fear, for I knew instinctively that I would have to confront the evil force that Eli and I and even Bertie had seemed to feel. But there was no turning back. I might fail, or even die; but if I were not to try, I felt that Jay would be lost . . . and I no longer cared to face life without him.

"The most awful thing has happened!" Susan spoke urgently as she woke me with a violent shake early the following morning. I sat bolt upright in bed.

"Tell me!" I demanded, fearing that harm had befallen Jay.

"Mrs. Morgan went into Miss Eleanor's room to

dust just now, and her safe has been opened," Susan blurted, her eyes wide with fright.

"Her safe has been opened?" I repeated uncomprehendingly.

"Yes, her little wall safe. And it wasn't open yesterday, because Mr. Jay asked me to begin packing up Miss Eleanor's dresses for charity, and I was in there all last afternoon. No one knew the combination but Miss Eleanor."

I got up, slipped into a robe, and hurried down to the second floor. In a scene all too reminiscent of the night Eleanor died, Nellie Morgan, Hans Arnold, and a gathering of other servants were at Eleanor's room. My eyes followed theirs to the open wall safe.

It was quite empty.

SIXTEEN

Soundcliff was incredibly beautiful in April. The blue waters of Long Island Sound sparkled and shone. Soft rains soaked deep into soil warmed day by day as the northern hemisphere tilted toward the sun, and the earth gently greened itself from the ground up. Fragrant blossoms burst upon tree and shrub. Over an old stone wall near the stables, forsythia hung like a veil of yellow stars. Birdsong filled the air from morning till night.

But I could not enjoy the beauty of spring. The Grand Jury was to consider the murder charge against Jay in July, and time seemed cruelly telescoped. However unlikely an indictment might seem to the men at Soundcliff—Jay, Eli, and Bertie all professed to be unconcerned—I felt daily more afraid. I knew that Jay was in danger, and my vow to save him had begun to seem like so much empty bravado, for I had discovered not one clue, not one shred of evidence, not one item of information that might exonerate him. In the beginning, I had thought that love as fierce as mine could overcome any obstacle. Now I merely felt foolish. I had looked all around Eleanor's room for evidence of her real killer and had found nothing. If there had ever been anything to find, I decided, it was the police who had found it.

For I firmly believed now that Eleanor's death had been a murder, not a suicide. There was no more proof of it than before, but I had developed an idea about the robbery of her safe that seemed so plausible I could not give it up. All of her jewelry had been taken, but perhaps the theft of the jewels had been an afterthought or a blind. Perhaps, I thought, the murderer had known that there was something locked in Eleanor's safe that would incriminate him or her, something there had been no time to snatch up on the night of the murder. Hidden as the little safe had been behind a small painting, it had been overlooked by the police on the night of the murder—luckily for the killer who had come back to empty it, to take not only the jewels but the incriminating evidence. So ran my reasoning, and I could find no fault with it.

But who could the killer be? I agreed with Jay that no member of the household could have murdered Eleanor. Old Eli had hated her but was hardly strong enough to kill a tall, robust woman in the prime of life even if he had so suddenly developed an incentive after eleven years of living in the same house with her.

The servants were all loyal and good people who could never be suspected of killing one of their employers. Nellie Morgan, Ada Wirth, Margaret Dobbs, Bob, Hans, Susan—I ran down the list of names and included all of the household and grounds staff. All were longtime employees above reproach. The only servants I had disliked had been Geoffrey Hand and Nancy Vance. These two strange and unpleasant characters alone of all the persons I had met at the Caldwells' seemed capable of wrongdoing. In addition, their abrupt departure the morning after Eleanor's murder was disturbing. Could one or both have been involved in Eleanor's death? After all, Nancy as Eleanor's personal maid would have had easy access to her room. The night of the murder had been the night before Nancy and Geoffrey's marriage. Nancy might have gone to Eleanor's room to say goodbye, and then—

My imaginary scenario dissolved. What motive would either Nancy or Geoffrey have had? After all, Geoffrey was on his way to begin a new position with August Flammon, a position Eleanor might well have arranged for him. What reason would they have had for killing her? I could imagine none.

And so I had firmly concluded that it was not a household member who had killed Eleanor and then robbed her safe. In that case, the killer, whoever it was, had come into the house from outside. But how had the killer been able to get into Soundcliff and into Eleanor's room without being seen? There was only one way, I decided, and that was to have come in through the network of secret passageways.

Yet I had been warned often that the uninitiated could not negotiate the dark labyrinth with its blind turns and secret rooms hidden behind false panels. The double bends and cul-de-sacs and escapeways built to foil the wiliest hunter of runaway slaves would surely foil any intruder but one who knew the passageways well. This, too, tended to eliminate Geoffrey and Nancy, for Nellie Morgan was the only staff member who cleaned and thus knew the elaborate maze that old Eli Caldwell had designed and built.

Both Eli Caldwell and Nellie Morgan were, as I had already concluded, unlikely suspects. But who else was there who knew or had ever known the passageways? Nellie had once told me that only the children who grew up at Soundcliff—Jay, Eleanor, Charlotte, and Bertie who had taken their studies together in the Soundcliff schoolroom and had played together in the passageways—really knew the secret maze.

Four little children who knew the labyrinth, and two of them—Charlotte and Eleanor—were dead now. Bertie still knew the passageways well. He had demonstrated that by emerging from the panel by the organ on the day we met. But would Bertie have killed Eleanor? I almost laughed. Bertie actually avoided killing flies, waving them away instead with his hand or a hat or trapping them alive in a half-closed fist and carrying them outside. Besides, Bertie had loved Eleanor. Bertie it was who had brought Eleanor to Soundcliff and cared for her after the horrid scene about my green velvet dress on Christmas morning. If he had wanted to kill her, he could have done it then while they were alone together. In any event, I had seen Bertie with Eleanor and heard him speak of her often enough to recognize the genuineness of his love for her despite, perhaps even because of his having no illusions about her character.

That left Jay. Jay had been gone the night Eleanor died. I did not know where. I knew from newspaper reports that he had told the police he had simply been "riding around after a quarrel with his wife." Reluctantly, my mind drifted back to the previous summer when I had picnicked with Bertie. I remembered his words clearly. Jay had also been gone from Soundcliff the night Charlotte died, he said. But, he had added, Jay could easily have returned unseen through the passageways to kill her. Of course, Bertie did not believe that Jay had killed Charlotte. But his pointing out that Jay could have done it by using the passageways and my own conclusion that this was what Eleanor's killer had done now struck me as a particularly chilling coincidence. I hoped fervently that the District Attorney would not think of it.

I was in despair. All of my searching in Eleanor's room had gleaned nothing. All of my thinking led me back to Jay as the most obvious suspect. What was wrong? Why couldn't I solve the puzzle? Why couldn't I help Jay?

Day in and day out the same thoughts pursued

each other in an endless cycle, often keeping me awake until late at night. Thus sleepless, more than once I thought I heard noises in the passageways, faint echoes from far parts of the house. And more than once I got up to check the security of the secret panel in my room. "It's my imagination," I told myself each time I heard the sounds. "Old houses make noises, and my mind is magnifying them."

Imagination or not, my insomnia continued, and I began to suffer from the lack of proper sleep.

My relationship with Jay remained exactly as he had said it must. We spoke frequently about household matters, the children, the impending Grand Jury procedure. We talked together a great deal about his business affairs, for I was as fascinated as ever by stocks and bonds and corporations, the manipulation of railroads and banks and mercantile ventures, the game of big business. And Jay never seemed to get over his surprise and pleasure at my interest in what he was doing nor seemed to tire of telling me about it. He was wonderful to be with at such times. His eyes would sparkle and he would give off an almost electric energy as he recounted his successes and setbacks and strategies day by day, pacing back and forth across the office, gesturing broadly, laughing, his words tumbling over each other. I would sit quietly, nearly swallowed up in his great wingback chair, following him with my eyes and listening, his own special audience.

And so we were together often and often lost in

conversation for hours at a time. But true to his resolve and to my promise, we did not kiss, did not exchange endearments, did not even touch.

In some ways it was a pleasant time during which we became closer and truer friends. In the beginning, when I was optimistic about finding a way to prove Jay innocent to his own satisfaction and the world's, the platonic arrangement was bearable as a temporary necessity. As the days passed and I found no way to help him, it became more and more difficult to support. Still, I had promised Jay that I would stay on at Soundcliff as a friend only, and I intended to keep my promise until he released me from it.

One early May morning, I tapped at his office door and opened it without his bidding me to, as I had begun to do in recent weeks. It had become such a joy to see his face light up when I came in. But this time, when he looked up from his desk, his eyes held a dull and hopeless look that shocked me. With all the anguish we had been through, I had never seen quite so wretched an expression on his face. I thought at once that he had received bad news regarding the murder charge or the Grand Jury. Instead, I was surprised to hear him say, "Well, Lillie, I think Gus Flammon has his fingers around my throat again. I've just heard from the State Attorney General."

"About what?" I had no idea who the State Attorney General was or what August Flammon might have to do with him. The title "Attorney General" sounded to me like someone who might be connected with the murder charge, so it took me a moment to grasp that Jay was not referring to the murder charge at all but to his business.

"The Bronx-Battery Elevated. Do you remember when I bought it?"

"Of course. About two months ago."

"Well, I've just been notified by the Attorney General of the State of New York that the Elevated is being investigated as a fraudulent corporation."

"What does that mean? Is it fraudulent?"

"Of course not."

"Then how can they—?"

"The charge is insolvency. There'll be an official probe. While it drags on, the stock will drop."

"But won't they find that the corporation is solvent?"

"Eventually. But they may be in no hurry to reach that conclusion."

"But why? I don't understand why the Attorney General would make such a charge if it's without merit."

"Neither did I. So I thought about it, and a peculiar fact brought itself to my attention. August Flammon was the biggest contributor to the Attorney General's last election campaign. Isn't that a coincidence?" He spoke bitterly.

"But—" I thought a moment. "How could Mr. Flammon know you've bought the Elevated?"

"An excellent question. I've made an effort to keep it quiet for this very reason. I didn't want Flammon getting his fingers into it."

"Then maybe he has nothing to do with it after all. Maybe the Attorney General is acting on his own. Maybe there were irregularities you didn't know about when you bought it."

"No," he said gently. "I don't buy corporations I don't know about in minute detail. As for Gus Flammon, we'll just have to wait and see. If he's behind this, we'll know soon enough."

Jay had spoken the truth. The Attorney General's investigation made daily headlines, and the value of Bronx-Battery Elevated stock plunged so steeply that by late May it had lost over ninety per cent of its value. With ease, August Flammon bought up the majority of shares, and the Attorney General promptly dropped the charges of fraudulence. Mystery seemed compounded upon mystery. Eleanor was dead, Geoffrey gone. How had information about Jay's ownership of the Elevated leaked to August Flammon?

It was cruel and inexplicable and it seemed to sap Jay's strength as none of his earlier troubles had done. The game of business and high finance that he had so reveled in had become a nightmare. The fortune he had sought to secure for Marta and Leo and Bonnie seemed to be slipping away. And Jay seemed now to be paralyzed by depression and without the energy to fight back.

I must help him, I must, I must. The anguished imperative burned in my heart, but still I could not answer the terrible question—how?

The children and I ended our school year's work on the last day of May. In spite of the circumstances, I had tried to maintain a regular routine for them and even proposed a school-end beach party for the first day of June.

The day dawned hot. Jay was too preoccupied to join us, and so it was just the children and I who set off to the beach at noon with our picnic basket and blanket. Because of the heat, all three of them wore bathing costumes, and after we had eaten, they ventured knee-deep into the Sound. But the water still retained its winter frigidity, and my three would-be water sprites gasped and shrieked and ran back to the blanket where they fell in a giggling heap over my lap.

They contented themselves with a big red-white-and-blue beach ball then, and I was as absorbed in watching them as they were in playing, so that none of us noticed the sudden piling-up of thunderheads until their gloom obscured the sun. In a few minutes a handful of fat raindrops peppered the hot sand, and we quickly gathered our things and hurried back to the house.

Rain threatened all the rest of the afternoon, but except for two or three short spatterings that quickly steamed dry in the heat, the storm held off. Black clouds would heap themselves up, then thin and scatter to let uncertain sunshine dart through. It was going to rain hard and we all knew it, but when? The unsettled atmosphere invaded the house and touched off quarrels among the children and the staff, quarrels that meant nothing except that everyone was on edge.

At bedtime, incredibly, the weather had still not broken. I debated whether to close my bedroom window against the coming storm or to leave it ajar. I chose the latter, for the humid heat was stifling. I donned a sheer white lawn nightdress, the lightest garment I owned, and did not even draw the sheet over myself. "I'll not sleep," I thought, but sleep I did at last with Ginger pressed in a hot little ball against my knee.

I woke to a flash of lightning, a terrific clap of thunder, and raindrops pelleting the windowsill like bullets. I sprang from the bed and rushed to pull the window to, but not before another bolt of lightning lit the world with silvery fire. I slid quickly back into bed and pulled the sheet up as if to shield myself from the bombardment of electrical energy the heavens had finally loosed upon Soundcliff.

I have never witnessed a storm like it. One stroke of lightning followed another in such rapid succession that it almost seemed to be daylight. Peal upon peal of thunder ripped across the sky. I felt safe inside the great stone mansion, yet in awe of nature's violent power. Ginger slept on, oblivious to it all.

With a sudden staccato sputter, the storm abated. Curious, I got up and opened the window again. Clouds in tattered shreds slid across the full moon, its bright light now falling over the midnight-blue Sound, now caught up in the net of clouds, the choppy swells clearly limned in silver, then obscured. The pulsating light atop Execution Rock beamed its steady rhythm in counterpoint to the capricious moonlight. Black clouds boiled on the far horizon, harbingers of another storm to come. The scene was so mysterious, so dramatic that I could not tear myself away.

I don't know how much time had passed before a glimmering light caught my eye. Far out upon the sound, it was less regular than the Execution Light, yellower than the quicksilver moonbeams. I glimpsed it, then lost it, glimpsed it and lost it again. I could think of only one thing—someone was out on the storm-churned waters in a small boat. With the bank of black clouds now seething rapidly up the dome of the sky, I wondered who might have undertaken such a foolhardy venture and where they might be trying to go. I found myself watching for the light. At first it was hard to gauge its distance or direction of movement. Then it seemed to be approaching the shore near Soundcliff. And then it vanished as if the craft had suddenly been swamped—or as if someone had doused a lantern.

Staring so long into the blackness was hypnotic, and I became drowsy. I closed the window against the next storm and crept into bed. This time, however, sleep eluded me, for I began thinking about Jay again and about how far I was from finding a solution to any of his problems—the problems that were keeping us apart, the problems I had begun to fear would keep us apart forever.

I knew that I would be no good to Jay at all if I were too tired to think clearly, and so I closed my eyes and tried to summon sleep but only succeeded in driving it away. My pillow had begun to feel hot and lumpy under my neck, and the sound of thunder rumbling again from across the Sound and the flashes of lightning gleaming whitely through my closed eyelids riveted me to consciousness. In disgust, I sat up and punched the pillow. I turned it over and laid my cheek against the cool side, but it grew hot and damp again in a moment. I resigned myself to discomfort, and after I lay still for some time, drowsiness began to blur the edges of awareness once more. Perhaps I would drift off now, I thought.

Then, abruptly, Ginger emitted a peculiar whining growl, and my eyes flew open. I watched as she drew herself up to a standing position and arched her back. Her fur stood out like porcupine quills.

"What on earth—?" I said softly. And then I was aware of a movement across the room. It was the panel beside the armoire. It slid open a crack, but the brace Jay had ordered affixed held and prevented it from opening further. The dull gleam of a lantern—evidently set well away from the panel—sent a narrow shaft of barely perceptible light through the breach. Ginger flew off the bed and sidled stiff-legged toward the panel with a loud howl. I heard a muffled tattoo of retreating footsteps, and I leaped from the bed and brushed my long, loose hair away from my eyes. The intruder was here, inside Soundcliff. It was, it must be, the person who robbed Eleanor's safe, the person who killed her, the person who was now evidently determined to assault or kill me as well. Whoever it was must not be permitted to get away.

I raced to the panel and pulled at it. So intense was my compulsion to get through the barrier that I ripped the brace entirely away from the wall and the panel slid aside.

Lantern light shone dimly up the steep stone stairs, and the descending footsteps echoed faintly. I thought fleetingly of Eli's conjecture that Eleanor was haunting us. "But this is no ghost," I thought.

Recklessly, I pulled shut the panel so Ginger couldn't follow me and plunged down the secret stairway, running as fast as I could in my bare feet, glad that my own footfalls were silent and that my quarry could not hear me following.

Once having begun my pursuit, there was no turning back I knew at once, for the only light in the stairwell was the lantern light rapidly receding before me, and I was now its prisoner as well as its pursuer, forced to keep pace with the fleeing intruder lest I lost the light.

Down and down, around and around the old stone steps spiraled, past tiny landings, past levers marking sliding panels, past dark passageways branching off at different levels and in different directions. I became disoriented. Surely by now I had descended well below the level of the first floor, I thought. The passages must burrow deep into the cliff itself.

The flight of steps ended abruptly, and three passageways extended outward from it. I chose the center passage without hesitation, for the light was fading away down its length and the other two were dark. But the passage I now followed was neither straight nor consistently narrow. It widened in spots with side passages and peculiar cul-de-sacs and alcoves. Then, still taking my direction from the leading light, I passed through tapering corridors so confining it seemed as if their walls would meet and squeeze me between them, although wider and more inviting ways opened nearby.

My heart had begun to pound and not only from exertion. I was hopelessly lost now, and I knew it. I should have stopped at the bottom of the stairs, I told myself despairingly. After all, my room was at the very top of the flight, and I could have found my way back even in the dark. But no longer.

Then unexpectedly, as I rounded a sharp bend, a metal pail stood in my path. I saw it too late, and I struck it with my foot. It toppled over and rolled against the granite wall with a loud clatter. Ahead, the light went out. In the sudden darkness I stood frozen with terror.

Silence. There was only the sound of my breathing and of the blood pounding in my ears. I listened into the blackness, trying to make my ears do the work my eyes could not. Moments passed, whether long or short I could not tell. Then I heard a step. And another. I had been the pursuer, but now? Was my quarry about to slip away and leave me alone in the dark? Or was I to become the quarry? Which way were the footsteps moving?

The next step was almost imperceptibly louder, I thought, and the one after that just slightly louder still. I took a step backwards, then another and stubbed my heel against the pail again. The noise wrenched a thin scream from my throat. I turned and began to run in the dark, half clinging to the passage walls, and the footsteps behind me now rapped out sharply in pursuit. Whoever it was knew the passageways well, I realized, and could move more quickly than I. My advantage still was my bare feet. I might be able to elude my stalker by slipping silently into a side passage. Unless the lantern were lit again—and whoever it was obviously did not want to be seen—there would be no way to know which way I had gone.

But now that I wanted to find one, my groping hands could detect no break in the wall. The narrow passage I was running through seemed to go on and on. And now the pursuing feet were just paces behind me. I ran and ran, my breathing so loud it gave me away as clearly as shoes would have, and then I half felt, half heard a lunge and a grunt from behind. A hand grasped at my elbow, and at that precise moment the wall to my left gave way as I dodged against it and I fell through into a still blacker void.

I had fallen on my knees and a panel had snapped to behind me. On the other side, I could hear my pursuer moving back and forth, feeling along the wall. I scrambled forward away from the panel and there was much space in front of me. I must have stumbled into a hidden room, I concluded, and in a moment I touched a piece of furniture, a bed, its springs bare, and then a small table and a chest of drawers.

This, I realized, must be the secret room where the escaped slaves Joe and Effie and their children had hidden so long ago, perhaps hearing as I did the sound of someone scratching along the passageway just beyond, looking for them. But the men who had long ago searched for escaped slaves had not known about the secret rooms, and it was possible, even probable, that my pursuer did. In a moment, surely, the panel I had fallen through would open again and I would be trapped, perhaps killed and left here where no one would find me for a long time. I held myself rigid against the wall between the chest and the bed and did not breathe.

The sounds in the passageway stopped. Then, incredibly, I thought I heard the footsteps moving away. I remained stone-still until I felt sure they were gone. Should I try now to find my way out of the secret room? Had the attacker really gone? Or was the quietness a trick? Would I open the panel and emerge only to be seized by someone waiting outside?

I waited a seeming eternity, but fear of staying in the room, fear of not being able to find my way out of it, overcame at last my fear of what might be outside. I walked unsteadily across the pitch dark room in the direction I thought I had come and when I reached the wall opposite I began feeling about for the lever. To my vast relief, I found it at once, pulled it, and stepped out into the passageway. Strangely, although the passage was quite as dark as the room had been, I felt better, as if I were back on relatively familiar ground. There was no movement near me. There were no sounds. I had no sense of another human presence.

Now I had to get out of the passageways. But which way should I go? If I went foreward, I might overtake the intruder again which I had no further desire to do. But if I tried to find the way back to my room, I felt sure I would become hopelessly lost.

My instincts told me that the maze of passageways must be at its most complex and difficult inside or very near Soundcliff itself and that if I went forward, eventually I would emerge outdoors somewhere. I began to move forward, no less terrified than before but knowing that I had to act on my choice, whether rightly or wrongly, or never get out at all.

I had been stepping carefully along, hands pressed to the wall, for what seemed a very long time when, to my disgust, I tripped over the pail again. It didn't make such a clatter this time, and there was no responding sound of another's footsteps. All was still. But I was furious to know that I had come no farther than the spot I had reached in the first place. If it had taken me this long to retrace just that short distance, how long would it take to reach the end of the maze?

I tried to picture my location in relation to Soundcliff. There was no way to know, of course, but whatever addled sense of direction I still had told me that I must now be moving out and away from the mansion and toward the Sound. I tried to gauge the distance from memory. There must not be so very far to go, I told myself, for the rocky strand below Soundcliff was rather narrow, and the tunnel would simply have to end soon or be beneath the waters of the Sound.

But even when I had gone the distance, I wondered, could I be sure of finding egress? Or would the passageway simply turn back on itself and involve me even more hopelessly in the labyrinth? I tried to maintain my sense of direction, but it was no use. I might even now be going around and around in the puzzle of passageways, retracing the same pattern again and again. I felt as if I had been stumbling along in the dark for hours already.

Suddenly, a puff of air brushed my face and stirred my hair. It was neither cooler nor warmer than the air in the passageway, but it was different. Its very movement distinguished it from the stagnant air I had been pulling into my lungs in panicky gulps. With a giddy rush of relief, I realized that it was fresh air, outdoor air, the same rain-cleansed air I had breathed from my window in the moonlight.

Heedless of the danger of stumbling in the dark, impelled by terror of entrapment and drawn by the hope of deliverance, I began to run again. And then—oh, thank heaven—a patch of black less black than before, of nighttime in the open world rather than the nighttime of burial. I didn't care that I was barefoot and clad only in a thin cotton gown. It was the end of the tunnel, and I rushed through and was standing on the jagged rocks at the edge of the Sound.

The moonlight had been blotted up by the accumulating storm clouds, but a vicious fork of lightning revealed the dock to my right and a small boat tied to it. Then, a deafening blast of thunder shook the air, and at the same instant I was seized violently from behind.

An arm like a band of steel garroted my throat. I could neither draw nor expel breath. I struggled, and my spasms increased my desperate need for air but failed to loosen the vise. I felt the shoulder of my gown tearing as I thrashed about, but the grip of my attacker did not give. "I shall die now," I thought, "but I'll not give up my life. It will have to be taken from me." And I continued to fight and to pray soundlessly, "Oh, help me, help me."

Consciousness dimmed like a guttering candle, but I was faintly aware that great globular raindrops had begun to fall. The second storm, the one I had seen from my bedroom window building on the far horizon, now swept across the shoreline and drenched my assailant and me, as oblivious of us and of our mortal contest as if we had been insects.

But was it impersonal nature merely, or was it personal God answering my anguished prayers? For the downpour slickened the rocks, and while my bare feet gripped and held the stone, my attacker's shoes lost their traction. The stranglehold loosened and the arm flew outward. I had the peripheral impression of a body stumbling backwards a bit, arms flailing for balance. In seconds I would have been seized once more, but seconds were all I needed. I ran for the dock, cutting my feet on the jagged rocks but not slowing down. Across the dock I sped and up the wooden steps that scaled the cliff face, then across the grass at the top. I gained the piazza and only then looked back. I had not been followed, or at least I saw no one. But panic had devoured reason. Whimpering, I pulled at the piazza door and found it locked, and then I screamed.

"Jay! Jay!" I ran back over the little bridge, scooped up a handful of gravel, and threw it with all my might at his window. "Jay! Help me!"

The window flew open and Jay's dear face appeared. What a sight I must have presented— bare feet muddy and bleeding, my long hair streaming, my gown torn and soaked. "I'll be right there, darling!" he called. I ran back to the piazza and in a moment he wrenched open the doors and was holding me in his arms.

I was sobbing now, too hysterical to answer questions, and so he asked none. He just held me and petted me, and the rain came in torrents beyond the piazza walls and lightning shredded the sky and thunder roared, but I was safe.

I had wakened Jay from a sound sleep. He, too, was barefoot and his upper torso was nude. I had never before touched a man's unclothed body, but now I clung to him, need overmastering shame, and I found my lips upon his throat and then his chest. His hands burned through my thin, wet gown. He pressed my body to his, and I felt his thighs, hard as tree trunks against mine. He stroked me as if I were naked. My shoulder and the curve of my breast were exposed by the torn gown, and he lowered his head and kissed and nuzzled the bareness. My body began to ache and then to throb with desire. The gown that had seemed so thin and inadequate a covering now seemed an intolerable barrier between us. I raised my fingers to my breast and began to pull away the torn bodice. But at once, Jay cupped his hand over mine to stop it. He raised his head and stood silently a moment, still clasping me against him. I could hear his heart pounding as if to tear itself from his chest. Then he bent his head and began to kiss my lips, but this time his kisses were gentle and so sweet they nearly shattered my heart. He held my body, but softly now, and his lips brushed my forehead and my eyelids and the tops of my ears until my sobs subsided and I told him brokenly what had happened.

"Whoever it was may still be somewhere on the beach," he said. "I don't see how a person could walk very far or launch a boat in this storm. But it sounds as if your attacker knows Soundcliff very well, and there are so many hiding places among the rocks. I'm afraid there's no use my trying to make a search tonight."

"Oh, no, no, I wouldn't want you to." I hugged him fiercely as if to squelch the very thought.

"I'm sure there'll be no more trouble tonight. It would be insanity to attempt to come through the passages again. But just to be sure—and until we can secure them better—I'll leave the panel to my room open for the rest of the night and set a lamp on the landing. I won't sleep. I'll keep watch. Will you feel safe?"

"Safe enough," I sighed. I wanted to beg him to take me to bed with him where I would feel totally safe and utterly happy. I dared not. But I was unable to restrain myself from murmuring,

"There'll be no more talk of being just friends, will there, Jay?"

He folded me into his arms again and kissed me so deeply that our very souls entwined.

It was all the answer I needed.

SEVENTEEN

I woke the next morning to find bright sunlight drenching the room, and my joy was such that I wondered if the light was radiating inward from the sun or outward from me. Ginger woke and yawned and stretched, and the movement struck me as so sensual and satisfying that I too stretched and writhed slowly, limb by limb, and luxuriated in the ripeness of my love-filled body.

Then I lay still for a long, happy time, remembering how it had been with Jay the night before, remembering how we had come in from the piazza together, crossing the darkened living room so slowly, our arms about each other, stealing small caresses, then stopping partway across the room. I leaned back against his supporting arm and raised my face, and then— Was there ever in the history of the world a kiss so thrilling, so memorable?

He touched his mouth lightly to mine, and then, slowly, as if releasing passion by degrees, he brushed the hot tip of his tongue across my lips, and I pressed eagerly upward as he explored more deeply, each movement of his lips and his tongue setting off new spasms of desire that ran the length of my body. We stood slightly apart. Touching me only with the arm that supported my back and with his mouth now hard with need, he set me afire from head to toe and kissed me and kissed me until the room spun and my knees gave way and he had to hold me with both strong arms. I leaned helplessly against him, and his kiss went on and on until at last he tore himself away with a low moan.

"Oh, Lillie. I love you so much, I can't bear it. Please, please marry me when this trouble is all over. I'll make you happy, I swear it." And I told him that I would marry him whenever he liked, that I loved him and needed him more than he could know. And he held me tenderly and whispered, "Sweet Lillie. Sweet, sweet Lillie. You are the dearest and purest girl there ever was. I want to take you to my bed—so, so very much. . . . But I want to take you there as my wife."

And then we walked on toward the entry hall, and in a cabinet by the grand staircase Jay found a candle to light. He held it high for us, and as we climbed the stairs to the third floor, I was burningly aware that, bathed in candlelight and with my thin white gown still damp from the rain, every curve and outline of my body must be revealed and presented fully to Jay's eyes. When we reached the door of my room, he didn't touch me or kiss me. He just stood for a long moment, gazing at me helplessly. "You're so beautiful," he said in a low and tremulous voice. And then he walked away down the long corridor.

The secret panel was still open when I went into my room, and fear returned for a moment until I saw a light appear and knew that Jay had placed a lamp on the landing by his room as he had promised. Recklessly, I left my panel open to be comforted by his light, and when I had changed into a dry gown and crept into bed, I slept very soundly.

Now I was wide awake and eager to greet the new day. Jay loved me—He had said it at last!—and wanted to marry me. He was mine and I was his and we would be together forever! For the moment, my joy crowded out the dire problems we faced. I even resisted thinking about the two attempts on my life that had taken place since first I had come to Soundcliff—the pillow-suffocation I had believed Eleanor responsible for, and now, after her death, the horrid experience with last night's intruder. I had told Bertie not long ago that I felt menaced. How right I had been. But all I wanted to think of now, all I *could* think of was Jay. All I could feel was happiness.

I sat up and hugged my knees. And then, unexpectedly, I thought of my mother and father. I got up and went to my trunk and opened it. Under some lengths of fabric was a heavy cardboard folder. From it I took the old photograph of

Mother and Daddy on their wedding day. There was Mother smiling at the camera and Daddy holding her hand and gazing at her with much the same look that Jay had given me last night.

As I knelt by the trunk staring at the picture, I thought, too, of Uncle Frank and how he had taken me in, of the happenstance of his saving Marta's life and carrying Jay's card in his pocket and showing it to me. If only Mother and Daddy and Frank had lived to know Jay, to know of my happiness. But then, of course, I wouldn't have met Jay if they had lived. I would never have left England or come to the Caldwell mansion. How strange and bittersweet life was. I slipped the old photograph into its folder and put it back into the trunk.

As I stepped back from the trunk, I caught a look at myself in the dressing table mirror. I was smiling as if I had the happiest secret in the world—which I did. Well, I would have to put on a sober appearance for the household today, I thought as I stepped to the armoire to select a dress. Jay would not want our love known until after the Grand Jury when he would be free of the murder charge. So I dressed deliberately in a plain dark blue dress. I brushed my hair until it gleamed, then parted it severely down the center, pulled it back, and wrapped it into a bun. Then I held up a hand mirror to see the back of my head. My bun looked like a small, shining, round, blonde donut perfectly centered above the demure white collar of my dress. Very governess-like, I thought, pleased.

I went down the front stairs—on purpose, I

think, to run into Jay. He was in the entrance hall, as I came down the grand staircase, and he, too, was dressed conservatively in a gray suit, waistcoat, and dark necktie. Although he had often dressed that way in New York, he usually wore riding or sailing or tennis costume at Soundcliff. I wondered if he had dressed so formally today for the same reason as I—the better to hide the wildness inside. Hans Arnold was with him.

"Good morning, Mr. Caldwell," I said as I passed them by, and I'm certain that I didn't betray my feelings by so much as the flicker of an eyelash. Jay did rather less well. His face lighted with happiness when he saw me, and his voice was a shade too warm when he returned, "Good morning, Miss Lorimer." I could feel his eyes fastened upon my little governess' bun as I walked down the hallway toward the back of the house and breakfast with the rest of the staff. How odd it will seem, I thought, to breakfast with Jay in the dining room when we're married.

This thought began to bother me. I had often wondered idly how I, a shopkeeper's daughter, might fare as Jay Caldwell's wife. But until last night, the dream had been too remote for the idea to disturb me much.

After all, I now tried to reassure myself, my father had educated me beyond my class. I knew all the requisite punctilios. I could set a fine table and sew a fine stitch. I dressed well. I knew etiquette. I spoke correctly and wrote correct letters. I could draw and sing acceptably, and I played the piano and the organ. I was well-versed in the classics of music, painting, and literature. And I was intelligent enough to understand a man's business affairs if he should care to tell me about them. I was quite adequately prepared to be the wife of an English gentleman. Surely, then, I would not embarrass Jay.

In England, of course, a move upward from one class to another was nigh impossible. Few English gentlemen would have had me for a wife, no matter my education and demeanor, for class was inborn and ineradicable in England, and mine was definitely the low end of middle.

But America was different—or was it? I was not so certain after all. For a man, yes. In America, a man could move up in class by getting rich and wielding power. But a woman? Even in America, that was a different case. A woman had no power and no money save what her husband or her father gave her. I had no money and no position. I was only a governess after all. And once I summoned the courage to face it, I realized that Jay might marry a governess if he pleased, but she—I— would never be accepted by society.

From the heights to the depths. As quickly as that, my joy turned to depression.

Late in the afternoon, still wearing the modest blue dress, I took a long walk to think things through. I was wandering aimlessly along a path in the woods, lost in glum reverie, when I became aware of the sound of a rider coming up behind me. I turned, and in a moment Jay appeared astride his favorite bay gelding. His boots gleamed in the filtered forest light as he dismounted. His white shirt was open at the throat and the sleeves were rolled back. I watched the tanned, muscular arms moving expertly as he knotted the reins about a tree.

Without a word, he came and put an arm around my waist and guided me off the path and into a tiny hidden copse. He turned me to face him, and his hands bracketed my shoulders, then moved across my back until the fingertips met at the center of my white collar. Slowly, he slid both hands downward, the fingertips caressing my spine, until his palms rested at the small of my back, and then he pressed me hard against him. I twined my arms about his neck and gave myself to his kiss.

"I love you so," he murmured. "I'm so sorry about what happened to you last night. I won't let anyone harm you again. I'll protect you. Do you believe me?" I nodded, and he kissed me again.

We were more restrained in our caresses than the night before; but it was the happy restraint of people who know that satisfaction is not far off. We were content to delay fulfillment for a little while and to relish our lingering on its threshold.

Jay pulled me down beside him onto a bed of moss, half-reclined against a tree, and nestled me closely into the crook of his arm. "Beautiful Lillie," he said softly.

"I'm not beautiful," I said.

"You are to me."

With his free hand, he stroked the smooth bands of hair on either side of my head and lightly kissed my exposed ears. "I love your hair this way," he said. "It's so neat and pretty. But it does make me long to remove the pins. Seeing it loose about your face last night excited me terribly."

I smiled. "But my hair was all wet last night. It can't have looked pretty at all."

"It made you look vulnerable," he said. "Tell me how it will be on our wedding night. What does it look like when it's loose, when you brush it before bed?"

"Oh, it's quite full and rather curly. It falls in my eyes a good deal."

"When you bend over me, it will fall across my face," he said. "Or my body."

I blushed and pressed my hand to his lips. "Don't draw such clear pictures," I said. "I'm having trouble enough waiting as it is."

Suddenly he sat forward and, keeping me cradled in his arm, he looked down at me. "Is that true?" he asked wonderingly. "You want it as much as I do?"

"Of course."

"How much? Tell me how much."

"How can I say how much?" I smiled. "Very much. Too much."

He sighed deeply and leaned back again. "To love and be loved in return. I really never thought it was possible for me." Then, almost roughly, "Look at me, Lillie. What do you see?"

"A dear man. A sweet man."

He laughed. "I wonder what Gus Flammon would say to that! Or the newspapers! You know what I am to the world: a railroad builder—an empire builder. It's been said that I'm the richest man in America. I didn't get to be those things by being dear and sweet. You know that, don't you?"

"I hadn't thought of it."

"I'm a hard man, Lillie—and not a very nice one most of the time."

"You're a wonderful father and a thrilling lover. You're tender and kind to me and the children."

"But not to Charlotte and Eleanor. Don't you see what I'm telling you, Lillie? You've seen only one side of me. Until now, I've been capable of love and tenderness only with my children."

"It's not my place to say this. But Jay, Charlotte and Eleanor can't have been without blame. They had problems, each of them, that made it very hard for them to give you real love."

"No. A man should be able to make his wife happy. I believe that. I failed them wretchedly. And I'm still so afraid of doing it to you. Last night didn't change that."

"You won't. I won't let you," I said hotly.

"How? What will you do?" He had begun to smile at my determined face. But he couldn't make me smile back. I was serious.

"When you come home at night, I'll be there to listen to you and encourage you, to share your triumphs and ease your pain. I won't be indifferent to your life like Charlotte, or jealous of it like Eleanor. You'll go on building your empires, but you won't be doing it alone. And after we've dined together and talked and we go to our room, I'll give you love enough to warm you all through the next day and last you till you come home again. And that will be my happiness—just your coming home to me each night."

His face had grown solemn again. "That's the ideal, isn't it, Lillie? Total needing and total giving between a man and a woman." I nodded. "You make me believe it's possible after all."

I could feel his body trembling, and not with desire now but with fear and hope. He wanted so to believe that our marriage would be different. But he was still convinced that his two marriages had failed so miserably that they had caused the suicides of Charlotte and Eleanor, and that conviction would not be easily erased.

He had expressed his misgivings to me, and I decided to tell him mine. "Jay, I am afraid of one thing. Charlotte and Eleanor were Archers. They were woman of money and breeding. In society's eyes, you'll be marrying far below yourself if you marry me. Suppose you're not invited anywhere because of me? Suppose people refuse our invitations and snub us at the opera?"

His eyes flashed fiercely, and a hard arrogance toughened his voice. "Lillie, you must understand this once and for all. I don't give a damn about 'society' and I never have. They bow to me because I'm Jay Caldwell and I can buy them and sell them, and the only one who doesn't know it yet is Gus Flammon. And if any so-called leaders of society turn up their noses at you, I'll rub those noses in who I am until they bleed. I'll make them crawl to you."

"Oh, Jay—" I gasped, taken aback, yet thrilled by the power of his defense of me.

He bent down over me then and said softly,

"Don't worry. They'll love you." And then his mouth was on mine and his tongue parted my lips, and I no longer cared about society.

They indicted Jay.

The District Attorney had pieced together testimony as to the frequency of Jay and Eleanor's quarrels and had even introduced the newspaper accounts of our ill-fated New Year's Eve evening at the opera in New York when Eleanor was at Soundcliff. There was a passing reference to my still being in residence at Soundcliff as if there was something sinister about a governess living in. And on the seventh of July, the Grand Jury had handed up its indictment.

My feelings may be imagined. When Bertie telephoned to tell me the news, I felt as if I had been shot: a great, raw wound had opened somewhere in the middle of my body. Was Jay to be snatched away from me just when our happiness seemed within reach?

It was just over a year since Jay and I had touched for the first time during the Fourth-of-July dance. I could scarcely believe that so much had happened in the year since that warm, beautiful night when I first began to realize that I loved Jay, when it had seemed so impossible that anything would ever come of it. In quick succession I thought of our journey to Montauk to rescue Marta and Jack, the loss of the LIH&M, the return to New York, the Christmas-Eve ball and Eleanor's mad destruction of my gown, the carriage ride with Jay that snowy Christmas night, our evening at the opera, the sad return to Soundcliff, the growing bitterness between Marta and Eleanor, their quarrel, Eleanor's death, the murder charge against Jay, and at last, at last, the love between me and Jay and our marriage plans. To think that we could go through all that love and all that agony to have it result in this.

I had been so happy in my love for Jay, had wanted to marry him so much, that I had believed, had had to believe, that they would not indict him. Eli had told me they wouldn't, and I had had faith in his faith; but he had been wrong. Thus, the very day when I had expected the nightmare to end, the day when I had thought the murder charge would be dropped, the day when I had believed that Jay and I could really start to plan our wedding—this was the day my hopes were shattered.

When Jay and Bertie drove up to the house, I met them in the entry hall. Jay was ashen. Oblivious to the presence of Hans Arnold and Nellie Morgan, careless of what they might think, he took me by the elbow and said roughly, "Let's go into the office."

Inside, Jay sank into the wing chair. He let his feet sprawl out in front of him and dangled his hands over the arms of the chair. I knelt beside him and kissed his cheek. He lifted his arm over my head and circled me with it.

"I'm sorry, darling." His voice came almost as a sob. "I didn't think they would do it."

"Oh, Jay." I had to struggle to hold back the tears. "I thought the District Attorney wasn't going to press very hard for the indictment."

"So did I."

"Then why did he?"

"Who knows? Maybe he got a good offer from Flammon. Or maybe—"

"What?"

"Maybe he really just thinks I did it."

My disappointment, I realized, was infecting Jay and making him feel all the worse. I blinked away my tears and said, with all the courage and firmness I could muster, "Well, the why isn't so important. We just have to think about winning the trial."

Jay leaned forward and looked deeply into my eyes. "All the way home, all I could think of was you—having to face you with this, having to put off all our plans."

"Oh, sweetheart," I murmured, wrapping my arms tightly around his neck. "We must just think about getting it over with now, so we can get on with our lives."

"Do you mean it, Lillie?" And when he saw that I did, "How I love you." He kissed me hard, and when he spoke again, he seemed charged with new vigor. "I'm going to call my lawyer and get him out here today. We'll start working on this right away. And don't worry, darling. I didn't kill Eleanor, and they're not going to be able to make this stick."

"Of course not," I agreed.

"You'll help me see the children through this, won't you? I think of you as their mother now—almost."

He didn't wait for my reply, nor did he see the

tears spring to my eyes again. He bent to my lips and gave me a long, sweet kiss, and then he got up and strode to the door. He held it for me, and we walked together to the doorway of the living room where Bertie was waiting.

"Bertie, I'm going to find the children and talk to them about what's happened. But let's get Frank Morris out here right away. No point in letting him get stale before we start planning my defense. I have a dozen ideas for him already."

With an almost cheerful wave, Jay left.

Bertie looked puzzled. "I thought he'd be depressed. He was awfully quiet on the way home."

"He didn't kill Eleanor, and he's determined to win, that's all," I said. "It's just as he is when he makes up his mind to succeed in some business venture. It's like an electrical charge. It energizes him."

"Rather higher stakes this time," Bertie said dryly.

His remark deflated me. "Be honest, Bertie. Can they convict him?"

Bertie gave me a long, sober, appraising look, and seeming to find the strength he sought, he replied simply, "Yes."

"Without evidence?"

"If they can establish motive and make the jury accept it. They'll drag in Charlotte's death. They'll drag you in. And they'll be talking to twelve average citizens who may well resent Jay's wealth and privilege. Yes. They can convict him."

"They might subpoena the staff to testify about

the quarrel Jay had with her the night she died, mightn't they?"

"I suppose so."

"They might subpoena me."

"They could."

"Oh." I sat down, and Bertie sat next to me. "Bertie, listen." I gripped his arm. "I've been trying to find some clue to Eleanor's real murderer. Some evidence that someone else did it. That's what we really need, isn't it?"

"It would certainly help."

I told him about my encounter with the intruder, the blind pursuit through the secret passageways, the attacker seizing me on the rocks, my escape through the rainy night. I did not, of course, tell him about the wonderful moments with Jay afterward. I could hardly bear to think of it myself now that our ultimate fulfillment seemed so far off and so uncertain. Instead, I said, "I'm sure it was Eleanor's killer. I don't know why the same person would want to kill us both, but doesn't it make sense? Her killer must have come in through the passages. And when her safe was robbed, it must have been the same person. And then—trying to get into my room and escaping out onto the rocks—mustn't it have been the same person every time, someone coming into Soundcliff from outside, always coming in and escaping through the passageways?"

"It does seem that way. But what has it to do with Jay's trial?"

"We've got to find a clue. I've looked in Eleanor's room again and again and there's nothing. But maybe in the passageways—well, we've got to try, haven't we?"

"What do you mean 'we'?" Bertie said with a half smile.

"You'll help me, won't you, Bertie? You told me once you'd go through the passageways with me."

"Do you really expect to find something there?"

"Oh, I don't know," I said despairingly. "But I have to explore the possibility. If you won't help me, I'll go by myself."

"Of course I'll go with you," he said. "You couldn't do it by yourself."

"Oh, thank you, Bertie." I hugged him fiercely. "But please, don't tell Jay. He would worry."

"I won't tell," Bertie smiled. "When do you want to do it?"

"Whenever you say."

"I expect Jay's lawyer will come out here tonight. They'll probably spend most of tomorrow together. Let's do it then, in the afternoon after lunch."

I was awake nearly all night worrying about Jay, wondering about the passageways, fearing them. But when the sun came up, I was full of hope and energy and eager to begin. The minutes crept by with exasperating slowness. Lunch had never taken so long, and the family had never lingered so interminably in the large dining room. I passed the doorway more than once to glimpse Bertie still deep in conversation with Jay and the lawyer Frank Morris. I began heartily to wish that Jay and I had not agreed that I should continue taking meals with the servants and not with the family in order to keep our romance a secret. I longed to hear what they were saying now, longed to be able to tug at Bertie's sleeve to get him to come with me to the passages now. I thought I was being subtle, but after passing the dining room door unnoticed a time or two, I caught Bertie's eye and he winked at me. I fled, embarrassed, to the living room, and soon Bertie joined me.

Jay and Frank Morris were closeted in Jay's office, Bertie reported. "Are you ready?"

"Yes."

Bertie took a scroll of paper from a table and brought it to the sofa. He began to unroll it, bidding me to take an end. I knew at once what it was.

"A map of the passageways."

"Yes. I drew it myself when I was about fifteen. Old Eli would never let anyone see the plans, but after all those years of coming to Soundcliff and playing in the passageways, I had a very good map of them in my head. So I put it to paper, finally. As you can see, it's a very elaborate layout. It took me a surprisingly long time to draw it."

"One really could get lost in them, couldn't one? I believe I was quite lucky to get out onto the rocks that night."

"If you call being nearly strangled lucky," he said. "Do you still want the tour?"

"Oh, yes," I said grimly.

"I'll show you how to locate the main passageways—the ones that will always lead you to a room of the house or to the outside. Once you understand the pattern—and if you can retain a mental image of where you are in relation to the house—you won't get lost." He traced a broad finger across the map. "You see, here is a central passageway through the house at the ground-floor level. And here is a passage that circles the house. All the other passageways and the secret stairways to the rooms on the upper floors branch off these."

"Oh, yes, I see. It's not quite regular, but—"

"But basically it's one big ring around the house and one corridor straight through it. Then there are the passages that lead to the outside. Here's one from the west wing to an old wall by the stable. It's a narrow exit that looks like a break in the wall. In the spring, the forsythia almost covers it."

"Yes. I've seen it. I'd never have known what it was."

"Here's one that runs almost directly from Jay's office out under the driveway. You can get out of it by a ladder and through a trap door into a little gazebo by the woods."

"I've noticed the gazebo, of course."

"And here's the one you found in the dark, behind and below the house, between it and the Sound. You *were* rather lucky. Eli built an intricate system of baffle passages down there. That was the way he took the slaves down onto the rocks and loaded them into small boats. Out on the Sound, they'd be transferred to a bigger ship and taken on to Canada. Eli was determined that no pursuing bounty hunter would track them down in that last passageway to freedom, so he outdid himself in planning that part of the maze. You see, the passageways are fairly simple elsewhere. It's there by the rocks that they become so confusing and frustrating.

"But even there you can find your way about once I show you how to do it. When I come over here by boat, I often come in through the very passage you escaped from. Do you remember the day I met you? I had tied up my boat down by the rocks, came up through the passageways—" he traced it for me on the map—"and came out just over there by the organ. Imagine my amazement at finding you there."

"Imagine mine!" I exclaimed.

Bertie rolled up the map, tucked it under his arm, and picked up a lantern he had left next to the table. "Well, let's get started," he said.

We climbed the stairs to the second floor as Bertie explained, "We might as well start from Eleanor's room. The killer probably did come into her room from the passageways and certainly must have left that way, for she screamed when she fell, and the killer must have known everyone would come running. The passageways were the only sure way to escape without being seen."

I nodded my agreement, but a shiver was running along my spine to think of going into Eleanor's room and following the killer's steps into the passageways. I had managed almost to forget the sound of Eleanor's dying scream, to push the imagined details of the death scene out of my consciousness. Now it would come all too vividly back again. I would feel Eleanor's desperation and terror. I would feel sorry for her—terribly sorry and terribly guilty to be taking her place, benefiting from her awful death.

Nevertheless, I followed Bertie to her room without voicing my misgivings. Jay had to be saved now, and squeamishness could have no place. Bertie opened the door to Eleanor's room and we stepped inside. The stillness rang in my ears. No one lived here now. The very air seemed dead. The room needed to be opened up, needed a fresh breeze to scour away the staleness.

Bertie walked across the room rather briskly. He disliked it too, I thought—being here where it had happened, thinking how it had been for her.

Beside the door to Eleanor's bath, Bertie pressed a segment of carved paneling. A narrow panel slid aside revealing a dark hollow space. "It runs behind the cupboards in her bath," he explained, "so it's hard to detect. Come." He had lighted the lantern and was holding it into the opening. I stepped up close behind him and peered over his shoulder. There was a narrow flight of stone steps running steeply downward, then angling out of sight around a corner. Bertie handed me the map, and I opened it and located our position. We stepped onto the tiny landing and Bertie pulled an inner lever to close the panel. The space was so confined that he had to step onto the stair below to make room for me. I had the sensation of entering a crypt.

"Are you all right?" Bertie asked.

"Yes. I'm fine."

We descended the stairs and reached a level passageway at the bottom. It was in the central secret passageway that paralleled the "real" hallway that ran from the great entrance hall to the kitchen.

"The hallways and stairways of the house are so broad and these secret passageways are so narrow that it's almost impossible to detect them, even when you know they're here inside the walls," Bertie said. And indeed, as I thought of the entrance hall and the great staircase and the hallways to Jay's office and the rear of the house, I could not picture how the secret corridor we were now in could exist.

We proceeded a few steps to an intersection where another corridor led off toward the living room, then dropped out of sight. "That way leads between the living room and the library. The little stairway dips under the doorway between the two. If you went that way, you could circle under the living room and the piazza door, go up another short flight, and come out by the organ. That's how I came the day I met you."

We passed on toward the rear of the house, and soon we had turned a corner into another short corridor and saw a flight of stairs descending from above and continuing on past us, downward and out of sight. "Do you know where you are?" Bertie asked me. I looked up and drew in a sharp breath. The panel at the top of the stairs must lead to Jay's room, I realized. And above, beyond the turn in the stairway, was my room.

"This must be the way she came—" I mused, half aloud.

"Who? When?" Bertie asked.

"Oh," I flushed. "Once Eleanor came to Jay's

room through the passageways when his doors were locked. They argued, and I heard the argument."

"Poor Eleanor," Bertie said to my chagrin. I was glad not to have to reply as Bertie had already started down the spiraling stone staircase and I made haste to follow him.

"I was right," I remarked in a moment. "I felt that night of the storm that I was going down far below the first floor. These steps must core right through the rock of the cliff under the house."

"They do," Bertie responded. He came to a stop, finally. We had reached the bottom, and before us were the three passages I had seen in the dim receding light of the intruder's lantern.

"How did you decide which of the three passages to take that night?" he asked, and I explained that I had followed the light. "Well, if you ever get lost in here again, here's the trick you should know." He took my hand and guided it to a strip of vertical molding mitred over the corner where two of the passageways intersected. I had seen similar moldings at every corner and had wondered vaguely why so ornate an item of decoration had been placed in these dark, secret corridors.

"What do you feel?" Bertie asked as I ran my hand over the molding.

"I don't know. Just some carving."

"Yes, but look." He pointed to the molding that I had touched. "It's carved on this face, but not on this face."

He was right. The molding extended about the

breadth of an inch on either side of the corner. The half that extended into the central corridor was deeply carved. The half that extended into the corridor to the right was perfectly smooth.

"Eli designed the moldings as signposts for those who knew about them. Even in the dark, you can find your way. The carved moldings mark the main passages. The plain moldings mark the cul-de-sacs. By merely touching the moldings at the corners, you can keep to the main passageways and find your way out even in the dark."

"I wish I'd known that before," I said ruefully, thinking of my panicky groping through the corridors that terrible night.

We started along the central passageway, and I scoured the floor with my eyes, searching, searching for any small thing that might have been dropped on any of the occasions when the intruder, the attacker, the killer had come into Soundcliff.

"Aha!" Bertie said suddenly, and my eyes flew to where he was standing, his hand cupped against the wall.

"What is it?" I asked.

He took his hand away and revealed a dark area about two inches square on the wall. I stepped closer and saw that it was the remnant of a lever broken off nearly flush. "There it is," Bertie said, kicking at a length of wood by the wall. "You must have broken it off when you fell against it."

"What are you talking about?"

"This is the room, the secret room. You can just see the outline of the panel here." He marked it with a finger, but even so I had to peer closely to see it. "As you fell into the room, you must have snapped off the lever. And no wonder—it's been half-rotted for years. I know because we used to play in there as children. You said you heard your attacker feeling along the wall, and I wondered why someone who seemed to know the passages so well wasn't able to open the panel and come in after you. Now we know."

I shuddered deeply.

"Has Eli ever told you any of the stories about the escaped slaves that were hidden down here?" Bertie asked.

I nodded. "Yes. He told me about one family, Joe and Effie and their children."

"You remember the part about how Eli was leading them to the boat when the boat boy ran into the passage from the rocks and told them there were bounty hunters at the dock?"

"Yes."

"They were just here." Bertie dug into a pocket and pulled out a penknife. He pried at the broken lever and the panel slid aside revealing the little room whose dimensions and furnishings I had vaguely discerned when I had stumbled into it in the pitch dark of that terrible night. Now illumined by Bertie's lantern, the room appeared very much as I had imagined it would.

"Eli pulled this lever and the four of them slipped inside, and they stayed there till the bounty hunters left the next morning."

"Well, I certainly know just how they felt, hiding in there."

"I guess you do," Bertie said, giving me a comforting little hug. "I'll tell Nellie about the broken lever and she'll get someone down here to fix it," he said, and we moved on.

Bertie led me through the system of passageways that ran out below Soundcliff, the main passages and the cul-de-sacs as well. And at last we came out, just as I had on that stormy night, into the open on the rocks. We had searched carefully all along the way but had found nothing except the broken-off lever and the pail that I had kicked over that night in the dark.

"Oh, Bertie," I moaned in disappointment as we picked our way over the rocks to the dock. "I really thought we would find something."

"Thought or hoped?"

"Hoped, I suppose. But maybe there is something somewhere else in the passageways, a way we didn't explore today. We know the intruder left this way, but we can't be sure that whoever it was came in this way."

"You said there was a boat tied up at the dock. You saw it by the lightning."

"Yes. A small boat."

"The boat wasn't Jay's. Jay wouldn't leave a boat out in a storm like that. He'd have put it in the boathouse. It must have been the intruder's boat. So whoever it was came in this way, all right. It's the only way in from the rocks."

I remembered, then, that I had seen a yellow light moving across the water that night as I watched the gathering storm from my window. Who would be out in a boat on such a night, I had wondered then, and where were they going?

The "where," apparently, had been Soundcliff, I mused as Bertie and I climbed the wooden steps to the house. The "who" was still to be answered.

EIGHTEEN

Jay's trial was not to take place until autumn. Frank Morris had obtained a postponement and hoped to obtain others, believing that additional time would dim the memories of hostile witnesses and soften the impact on a jury of the sensational press about Eleanor's death.

I found the long delay upsetting. To have to wait so long for a resolution of the matter seemed insupportable. The only comfort was in knowing that there was still time to find evidence of Eleanor's real killer. I refused to entertain the possibility that there might be no such evidence.

I began to hope that the intruder would return. If we could only lay hands on that person, I believed we would have the real killer, could somehow force a confession or somehow, in some other way, prove Jay's innocence. I even began to sit up in the tower at night, having from there a much broader view of the Sound than from my own window. I watched for a reappearance of the little yellow light that had marked the approaching boat on the night of the storm. But I saw nothing, heard nothing in the house at night, and again my thoughts turned to finding a clue in the passageways.

Bertie had concluded, and I had agreed, that the intruder had probably come and gone by the route we explored, the route leading from the rocky shore to Eleanor's room. But a person who knew the passageways so well might have gone, for reasons unknown, into other parts of the house. If I had found nothing in the obvious places, then oughtn't I to look in the less obvious places?

I decided to go into the secret passageways again. But this time I would tell no one, not even Bertie, for I was afraid that Bertie might ask the one question I didn't want to answer: Was I not deluding myself that I could still help Jay, pretending there was hope when there was no hope? No, no. I would not entertain the question. I had to keep trying, for I loved Jay so, and my love was so strong that it could not countenance defeat.

I procured a small lantern, and one morning when Jay had gone to New York to take care of some business matters and Bertie had gone with him, I opened the panel in my room and, carrying my lantern, stepped onto the stone staircase. I slid the panel shut behind me and only then noticed that Ginger had slipped into the passageway with me. "Well, come on," I said. "You may as well keep me company. I guess I can count on you not to tell anyone." I had all but memorized Bertie's map, and I felt no qualms as I started down the steps.

I paused outside the panel to Jay's room, and I couldn't resist pressing the lever and watching the panel glide to one side. I snatched Ginger up in my arms to keep her from going into Jay's room. Nor did I go in myself, but I did gaze about for several moments. The room smelled of him, the scent pervasive and intimate. I rested my eyes on the big, masculine bed. "This will be our room. No separate bedrooms," I thought. And then, "No wonder Eleanor came to him through the passageways that night. How terrible it must have been to be locked out. She wanted him as much as I do."

There I went, feeling sorry for Eleanor again. I pushed the thought away, closed the panel, and put Ginger down. "Don't lose me, now," I told her.

At the ground floor, I took a few steps and turned into the long central passageway that ran through Soundcliff's heart, then I took another turn into the secret corridor that led to the living room. Down the little steps I went, Ginger pacing happily along next to me, then followed the curving corridor, up another short flight, and there before me was the panel that must open beside the organ. I was tempted to try it, but I could not be sure that there was no one in the living room, and I did not want to be seen. Another corridor had branched off at the bottom of the last small flight of steps. It seemed to circle on along the front perimeter of the house, and I decided to follow it. Before long, it intersected with the long central corridor again. Looking down it, I could see the opening where I had turned off moments before to follow my detour around the living room. I passed on toward the west wing.

The passageway I was now following seemed very long, and I imagined that it must be the one that ran under the west wing and all the way out to the break in the old wall by the stables. I decided to follow it as far as it led, but before I had taken another half dozen steps I came to a kind of crossroads with a short corridor branching off toward the interior of the house and another very long one leading away in the opposite direction. The long one must lead under the front driveway to the gazebo, I decided. And, according to Bertie's description, the shorter one must lead to Jay's office.

How long ago it seemed, that day when I had seen August Flammon kissing Eleanor under the stairs, and I had ducked back into Jay's office and pushed accidentally through the panel when I heard Jay and Gus Flammon coming in. This, then, must be the little corridor I had hidden in then, I thought. And just as I thought it, Ginger darted that direction and I followed her. "Ginger, come here," I demanded, but she was busy playing with something at the end of the corridor next to the panel that led into the office. As I approached, she batted a small object from one side to the other, then pounced on it, fell onto her side, and worried it between her paws.

"What have you got there, Ginger?" I bent down and retrieved a small jet button. It had a steel loop on the back, and it was delicately carved on top to resemble tiny, coal-black rose petals. Some blue threads were wound through the loop.

A woman had been here, a woman other than myself. But who? When? And why? I would ask Nellie if the button were hers without saying where I had found it, I decided. She might have lost it while cleaning the passageways. But already I knew it didn't belong to Nellie. It was too fancy a button to have come from one of her housedresses. I put it in my pocket and clucked to Ginger to follow me. There were many passageways still to explore, and I had no desire to linger in them.

I followed the long corridor out to the old stone wall, and there Ginger took her leave of me, gliding out through the narrow break into the sunlight, trotting away briskly in the direction of the stables. "Deserter," I murmured and turned to retrace my steps to the intersection with the office corridor. Then I followed the long passageway opposite it to its end. I looked up at the daylight filtering through the cracks in the gazebo trap door. Then back I went to the intersection.

On and on I went, following the other passageways that wound through the house and the stairways that led to various rooms on the upper floors—Eli's room, I surmised in one case, Marta's room in another. But when I had completed my tour of the passages inside the house, the only "clue" I had to show for my efforts was the small black button.

"This can't be it," I said to myself. "This just can't be all there is." And so I didn't go directly back to my room but, when I had reached the secret stairway that led to Jay's room and to mine, I turned downward instead toward the maze of passageways below the cliff. I explored them as thoroughly as I could. And in spite of Bertie's assurance that I wouldn't get lost, knowing now how to use the moldings as guideposts to the main passages, I was relieved when I came upon the old pail again and knew that I was in the passageway that would lead me out onto the rocks.

It was a shock to emerge into the bright July sunlight. I doused my lantern, opened my pendant watch, and noted that it was after eleven o'clock. Jay would be home in the late afternoon or early evening. It would be hard to pass the time until he came. How I wished that I had found something to show him, some piece of evidence so convincing that it would prove his innocence and end our ordeal once and for all.

I had gained the dock and was heading for the wooden steps that scaled the cliff face. Just to one side was the bed of sharp rocks where Eleanor had fallen. I always avoided looking at it as I passed. But now I thought, "Maybe here where she fell there's a clue," and wondered why I hadn't thought of it before.

It was difficult to negotiate the long step from the edge of the dock, and I had to set down my lantern and lift my skirt well above my ankles. And once down upon the rocks, it was hard to make progress because they were bigger and sharper here than nearer the shore where the action of the waves and tides had worn them down. I wished I had worn sturdier shoes, but having undertaken the exploit, I was loath to abandon it.

I tried to climb to the top of one great boulder, gaining purchase by placing my foot sideways into a crevice and clutching at a sharp projection near the top. I pulled myself up and could climb no farther for there was no other foothold, but I could just peer over the top and was intrigued to see—wedged into a sandy crevice behind the boulder—a long, flat, mottled gray-and-black object, apparently of tarnished metal. It might have been a piece of the underchassis of a carriage, or part of an old bed frame, or some sort of crowbar or other long tool. I couldn't identify it, partly obscured as it was in the crevice.

But whatever it was, what was it doing there? The grounds at Soundcliff were immaculately kept. No one would have discarded a large and apparently heavy piece of metal such as this by tossing it over the cliff.

I saw that the big boulder I was clinging to sloped off to the right and that, although it was braced tightly against another large rock, the sloping part was probably low enough to climb over. I let myself down, maneuvered my way over and around some smaller rocks, and found the low end of the big boulder. I sat on it, swung my feet over, and found myself half standing, half leaning against the boulder but within reach of the long metal object.

I bent forward and picked up the end of it. With

a gentle tug, I pulled it free of the sand-filled crevice and the handle that had been buried in the sand came into view. It was a sword, and I was pulling on its badly tarnished silver scabbard. I took a fresh grip toward the middle so I could lift it balanced in my hand. I brought it up onto my lap and looked at it closely. It was an old sword, and both scabbard and handle were beautifully etched. The tarnish was thick, but it was impossible to guess how long it had been here. Exposed to the salt air, it could have tarnished in a very short time. Indeed the handle, which had been buried in the sand, was a good deal less tarnished than the rest except for one area that seemed almost black. I wondered why just that one spot on the handle had tarnished and, somehow, had tarnished even more deeply than the scabbard.

As I gazed at it, a sickening idea occurred to me: What if the blackness on the handle were not tarnish but dried blood?

The longer I looked at it the more I believed I had hit upon the truth. Yes, yes—I recoiled in horror—it could be blood. Blood that the rains of four months had not washed away because the handle had been wedged in the sand. Eleanor's blood.

If only we could discover who the sword belonged to. I couldn't believe that it had been Eleanor's. It was not the sort of thing she would have kept in her elegant bedroom. But it was equally hard to imagine why her killer would have brought such a weapon to her room. Someone planning a murder would surely have chosen an instrument other than this heavy, old-fashioned sword.

It was a mystery indeed. But I felt somehow certain that I had found, at last, the evidence I had been looking for, certain that the sword I held across my lap was the murder weapon, the object with which someone had struck Eleanor and struck her so hard as to hurtle her from her window to the rocks below, the sword either falling with her or being thrown after.

With great difficulty, but being very careful not to knock the blood-stained handle against the rocks, I made my way back to the dock, slipped one arm through the lantern bail, and continued up the steps over the face of the cliff carrying the sword with me. I encountered no one, and I took it directly to my room.

"Now, hurry home, Jay," I thought urgently. "I have something to show you."

I was in a fever of excitement all that afternoon. I kept looking at the sword and almost breaking into smiles, very much as if it were a surprise birthday gift for Jay. I was becoming so overwrought that I knew I would have to get away from my room and the sword and find something else to occupy the time until Jay got home.

I went down onto the lawn and watched Marta trying to teach Leo and Bonnie tennis. Leo was beginning to play well for his age; Bonnie could hardly lift the racket. It was amusing to watch them, but not enough to keep my thoughts from straying to the sword lying in wait on a towel on my bed, not enough to keep me from consulting my watch again and again. It occurred to me that I might pass the time more absorbingly in conversation with Jay's grandfather.

I found him seated in a large wicker chair on the piazza, and I asked if I might join him. "Please don't get up," I protested, but he struggled to his feet and pulled up another chair for me.

"Well, I owe you an apology," Eli said when he was seated again. "I told you they wouldn't indict Jay."

"You're not the only one who was mistaken about that," I said.

"I only hope he's up to this."

"Why wouldn't he be?"

"Something's happened to him since Eleanor died. He's been letting things slide, letting Gus Flammon rook him."

"What do you mean?"

"He lost the LIH&M to Flammon, then he couldn't bring off the big coup—to get the majority of Empire State stock away from Flammon. Ordinarily, that would have been just a temporary setback, something he'd try to overcome again right away. But when's the last time you heard him mention the Empire State?"

"A long time ago, I guess."

"That's right. Has he given up on it? Who knows? He won't discuss it with me. Gets up and leaves the room if I mention it. And then he let Flammon engineer the Attorney General into that attack on the Bronx-Battery Elevated."

"How could he help that?"

"Pah! The day a Caldwell can't pull his own political strings is a pretty sorry day. He could have forced the Attorney General to back off if he'd put his mind to it."

"Do you really mean that?"

"I get the picture that Flammon is throwing rocks expecting Jay to throw them back, and Jay's slinking off with his tail between his legs. He sure isn't the Jay I know, the Jay I brought up, the Jay that was more like me than me."

"It's Eleanor's death. He's mourning. And this being under suspicion. The arrest. The indictment. I'm sure he's worried about what will happen if he's convicted, what will become of the children. I suppose he isn't himself, but it's hardly surprising."

"I know. I don't blame him. I'm just pointing it out. Everyone says he's taking it so well, working so hard on his defense, and I guess he is. I just know he isn't the Jay Caldwell he used to be. I guess he's got to get out of this before he can be his old fighting self again."

"Well, I'll certainly help if I can," I said.

"You do help," Eli said. "I believe you're all that's keeping Jay together." I looked at him in astonishment, and he chuckled. "I suppose you think everyone here is blind. Oh, *you're* being very discreet, although I can see you care for him. But Jay has love written all over his face when he looks at you. So don't let him down."

"I won't," I said, blushing hotly.

"Well, it's time for the old gent's afternoon nap," Eli said and got stiffly to his feet. "Please excuse me."

Far from calming me, my talk with Jay's grandfather had made me more impatient than ever for Jay's return. I had not realized that Jay had changed so much, but as soon as Eli Caldwell had mentioned it, I knew it was true. Never would Jay Caldwell have allowed Gus Flammon to get the better of him—never until now. His talks with me about business affairs, his apparent interest in them, masked the plain fact that his daring, his cunning, his ability to fight back were at a very low ebb indeed. He was still planning, working, doing—but perhaps more from habit than from zeal. If this was true, and if Eli had been right that I was all that was keeping Jay together, then how much greater was my responsibility to free him from the web that had entangled him, how much more must he need my help with his defense, how much more crucial might be the evidence I had found.

I went up to my room and gazed at the sword. Yes, yes, I told myself, it must be blood on the handle. I went back down to the piazza and tried to sit quietly, then found myself on my feet and pacing. I stepped down into the flower garden and walked along its paths but saw the brilliant blooms and luxuriant foliage as a blur. I went back to my room, could find nothing to occupy myself, and came back to the piazza. I had given up all effort or pretense of behaving rationally and prowled about the house and grounds uncaring of who might see me or wonder what I was doing.

At supper time, Jay had not returned, and I sat at

the long kitchen table with the rest of the staff but could hardly eat, and afterward I went up to the tower and sat in the south window, watching for the first appearance of Jay's carriage emerging from the woods at the far end of the driveway.

At last he came. He was alone; Bertie had apparently gone on to the Archer estate. I breathed an enormous sigh of relief, for if I had had to wait until Bertie and Jay finished a brandy and a talk before having Jay to myself, I would have expired from sheer exasperation.

I ran down the tower stairs and into my room. Quickly I wrapped the towel over the sword, and then I all but flew down the two flights of stairs to the entrance hall. The lamps were lit in Jay's office and his door was open. I paused to gather what reserves of self-possession were still at my command, and I approached the doorway. Jay looked up and beamed at me.

"Hello," he said. "I was hoping you'd still be up and about."

"Yes . . . look. I have something to show you." I extended the towel-wrapped bundle. "May we close your door?"

"Of course. Come in." He closed the door behind me. "What do you have there?"

"I found this on the rocks where Eleanor fell." I held the sword out before me, cradled across both hands, and let the wrapping fall away. "There's blood on the handle, I think." Excitement was pushing the words out rapidly. "Don't you see—it must be the murder weapon. Someone hit Eleanor with it and knocked her through the window. If we can just find out who it belongs to—"

"Give that to me!" Jay's voice was gutteral with an emotion I didn't recognize. His face was white. He came at me with an awkward, stumbling gait and seized the sword from my hands. He carried it to his desk and examined the handle in the lamp light. He scratched at the dried blood with his thumbnail, then looked up at me sharply. "Have you told anyone about this?"

"No. Just you."

"You mustn't. No one must know about it."

"But why?" I cried. "What are you afraid of if you didn't kill her?"

A pause. Then, "I did. I did kill her."

"But you didn't! I know you didn't! You weren't even here!"

"Yes. I came back through the passageways. I did it and no one saw me."

"Jay, what are you saying?" I cried hysterically. I ran to the desk and started to grasp at the sword. Jay clapped his hand over it, pinning it to the desk. He, too, seemed on the edge of hysteria. "Don't touch it," he snapped. "And promise me you won't tell anyone about it."

"I'll promise no such thing! This is the evidence that you didn't do it! It's got to be!"

Jay gave me a look like a dagger. "You must drop this. Forget about it."

"No! I won't!"

A wild look came into his eye, the desperate look of a cornered animal. "Then I'm going to put a stop to it right now."

Still holding the sword with one hand, he

reached for the telephone with the other. He took the receiver from its hook, and to the operator he said, "Get me the police."

"What are you doing?" I gasped.

"What I have to," he said grimly and would say no more until someone at the police headquarters came on the line. Then urgently, as if rushing the words out before I—or he—could stop them he said, "This is Jay Caldwell. I want to confess to the murder of my wife."

I stayed long enough to hear Jay ask to speak with the Chief of Police—a family friend, I gathered when Jay addressed the chief by his first name—and arrange to be taken into custody in the morning.

Then I fled to my room. My confusion and terror were such that I can scarcely recall the next hours that I spent alone. I cried, of course, and paced about, and a series of contradictory thoughts ran through my mind in jumbled sequence. Jay had never had an alibi for the time of Eleanor's death, and when I had tried to imagine who might have killed her, had thought of the small number of people—Jay, Eleanor, Charlotte, Bertie, Eli, Nellie—who had ever known the passages well, Jay had seemed the only one who might be suspected, who had both the motive and the knowledge of the passageways. And hadn't I once heard him tell Eleanor "I'll kill you"? And just before Eleanor died, when Marta said she couldn't live with Eleanor any more, hadn't Jay said, "I'll fix it?" What had he meant by that? Had it never crossed my mind then that Jay might have done it?

No. No. Never.

It grew very late, and at last I undressed for bed and put on my white cotton gown, the one I had worn in the storm the night Jay had come to me on the piazza and kissed me so thoroughly. The gown had been badly torn, but I had laundered and mended it and tucked it into a drawer, for it had become a precious token to me. Now I took it out and wore it again, forlornly trying to derive comfort from it.

Sleep was impossible. I went to the dressing table and brushed my hair for a long time. Then I went to my bed and sat on its edge but couldn't bear to lie down.

I don't know how long I had sat there, but a shaft of ghostly moonlight that had earlier shone through the open window against the far wall had crept around the room and now lay across the bed. My back was to the light, and I was staring at the long shadow my body cast across the floor. Both fists grasped the edge of the mattress and my arms were stiffly braced. My hair had fallen forward about my face and it shone like silver in the moonbeams.

The room was perfectly still, and when I heard cautious footsteps beyond the secret panel, my heart seemed to stop beating. I raised my eyes. The shaft of moonlight was on the panel like a spotlight. I knew it was securely latched—Jay had seen to that after the night of the storm and the intruder when I had torn open the nailed panel. Now the panel did not move, but I knew that someone was out there on the stairway. I jumped when I heard a tapping sound.

I slid off the edge of the bed and tiptoed across the room. The tapping came again, and now I could hear a husky whisper from the other side.

"Lillie. It's Jay. Can you hear me?"

I undid the latches, my fingers shaking and fumbling. The panel slid open. Jay stood on the landing. He was in pajamas and a light silk robe. He had the sword in one hand, a candle in the other. He blew out the candle, stepped into the room, and closed the panel.

"You look like an angel in this moonlight," he said, his voice choking with emotion. "Your hair is shining. Your gown is like gossamer."

I started to weep. Jay leaned the sword against the wall, set the smoking candle on the trunk, and took me in his arms. He led me to the bed and sat holding me as I sobbed.

"Lillie," he said. "If you love me, you've got to help me."

"You know I love you, but I don't understand what you're doing." My voice was distorted by my sobs and I gripped the lapels of his robe to prevent myself from beating on his chest. I was filled with anger and grief.

"I know. And I'm sorrier than I can tell you. But please listen. I've brought the sword. I want you to keep it here and don't let anyone see it or know about it ever. I know you're angry with me, but you're the only one I can trust, and you've got to trust me. This is the only way."

"Why? Just tell me why!"

"I can't. But I have a reason, an urgent reason."

"That you can't tell me?"

"That I can't tell anyone. Do you believe me?"

"Yes," I groaned and leaned my head against his shoulder, defeated. I loved him so terribly, I had no choice. I had to believe him. I had to do what he asked.

"Will you keep the sword for me?"

"Yes."

"Now, this is the most important thing of all. I want the children to be with you. You're the best thing that's happened to them. They love you. You must take charge of them. You mustn't leave them."

"I won't."

"Promise me."

"I promise. I won't leave them." I began to sob again. I couldn't put my thoughts into words: that he was going to prison, that I might never be in his arms again. But there was no need to say it. He knew. And he held me for a long time and kissed my trembling lips. Passion flamed between us. I tried to draw him down on the bed with me, begging him with my arms and my lips and my tears to make me his just this once, to give me one memory for my lifetime.

But Jay said, almost cruelly, "It's too late, Lillie. You'll be wanting to marry someone else." I shook my head vehemently, but he went on. "Eventually, yes. You will. You should. And I'll not spoil you for that. I wouldn't want that on my conscience, too." He kissed me again, a kiss so deep and sweet that I prayed it would never end. Then he whispered, "Goodbye, darling." And he was gone.

I sat still for a long time, and then I went to the corner where he had left the sword. The moonlight had moved almost all the way around the room now. I carried the sword over to the window and examined it by the last of the light.

There were almost no traces of tarnish on the scabbard. The dark substance on the handle that I had decided was blood was completely gone. The sword had been scrubbed with a stiff brush and polished.

Jay had trusted me to keep it and not to talk about it. And he had taken an extra measure of insurance by cleaning it thoroughly. He had confessed the murder but destroyed the evidence.

It made no sense at all.

NINETEEN

Chief of Police Lenahan came to Soundcliff at ten o'clock the following morning. Out of consideration for everyone's feelings, he wore a business suit instead of a uniform. Jay had breakfasted privately with the children and, I supposed, had told them that he would go to prison for Eleanor's murder. How can such a message be framed for the ears of children? And can any words prepare them for the reality?

Obviously not. As he got ready to leave with Chief Lenahan, all three were in tears and clinging to him. Marta and Leo sobbed wordlessly, but little Bonnie wailed at the top of her lungs.

"Don't take my daddy. Don't take my daddy."

Eli and Bertie waited near Chief Lenahan. Hans stood by the door holding a small case he had packed for Jay. Nellie and Margaret and I hovered about, each ready to take a child to hold and comfort when Jay at last would break away. His eyes were dry but red-rimmed, whether from sleeplessness or his own private weeping I could not tell. He gave each child a last hug and at the same time gave me a desperate look over their heads.

"Remember, you promised," he said to me almost inaudibly.

I nodded. I would never have left the children, promise or none.

"It's time, Mr. Caldwell," Chief Lenahan said, and Jay stepped away from the children. Margaret took Bonnie by the hand, and Leo wrapped his arms around my waist and pressed his face against my dress. Nellie had stepped forward to put a protective arm around Marta, but suddenly Jay turned back and took Marta in his arms again. He held her very close, stroked her long auburn hair, then kissed her cheek.

"Remember how much Daddy loves you," he said.

Then he was at the door taking the small case from Hans. He hugged his grandfather and walked out the door followed by Chief Lenahan and Bertie.

I held Leo tight and looked at Marta who was now weeping against Nellie's shoulder. Jay's extra farewell to her lingered in my mind.

Sorrow was so compounded in that house that day that no one of us could truly comfort another. The servants had lost the employer they admired and loved, the man many had known as a small boy in this very house. Eli had lost the heir to his fortune and his ambitions, the grandson he loved more than a son.

The children had suffered so many brutal shocks and losses it was almost too painful to catalog them. Marta's mother had died when she was tiny and her stepmother had disliked and mistreated her. All of the children had witnessed years of unhappiness between Jay and Eleanor and had witnessed Eleanor's mental deterioration. Then had come the terrible night when Eleanor had so badly beaten Marta. And the following morning their father had had to tell them of Eleanor's death. More shocks followed: Jay's arrest, his indictment, and now his confession and imprisonment.

Jay's grief must be worst of all, for he had borne it all, the death of two wives, the unhappiness of his children, the suspicion and accusations that he had murdered first Charlotte and then Eleanor, and now incarceration. He had had to explain each fresh disaster to Bonnie and Leo and Marta, buoying them up at every turn with his strength, his optimism, his love. He had all along been the one trustworthy person in their young lives, the one person they could depend on, the one who would always protect them and take care of them, the unchanging, calm center to every storm. To leave them thus must have hurt him profoundly, knowing as he must that his departure might well shatter the three tender spirits whose only security he had been. He had had a reason, he had said, but it must remain secret. What could it be?—a secret so compelling it had forced him to abandon the children he loved more than life.

Margaret and Nellie and I stayed with the children all day. Eli took Leo and Bonnie down to play with his trains for an hour, and when Bertie came back he took Marta for a long walk.

Finally, rather late at night, when the children were asleep, I went to my room. It was the first time I had been alone all day, and I was terrified. With the children to think of and the others nearby, I had been able to push aside my own feelings. Now they came rushing at me.

Alone, alone, alone. Of all the sad people in that sad house, at that single moment I felt myself to be the saddest.

Our love had always been beyond the bounds. I had fallen in love with a married man. Moreover, he was a man far above my class and station. And just when these problems seemed to have been overcome and our happiness together within reach, it had all slipped away again. Yes, our love was beyond the bounds: beyond the bounds of propriety, beyond the bounds of society, and now very simply beyond our grasp, possibly forever.

One lives. Somehow one lives, even without joy.

Jay had received a life sentence. I wanted to stop living, but I had the children to look after, and that precious mission was my link to Jay and my purpose for getting up each day and talking and eating and moving until time to go to bed again to try to sleep and try not to dream.

It was a demanding job. One morning in

August, Leo and Bonnie came to fetch me from the piazza. Marta was in her room crying, Bonnie informed me, and Leo confirmed it. I went upstairs and tapped at Marta's door. She opened it for me. Just as Bonnie and Leo had said, she was crying.

"What's wrong?" I asked.

"Oh, Miss Lorimer," Marta wailed. She threw herself face down across the bed and pulled a pillow over her head. Muffled sobs issued forth.

I sat on the bed. "If you don't tell me what's wrong, I can't help."

She threw the pillow aside and sat up. Her blue-and-white-striped cambric dress was rumpled and the blue ribbon about her hair was askew, the bow hanging comically over one ear. Her teary eyes glittered like emeralds under water. She made a wry face, reached for her handkerchief, and blew her nose. Then she pointed to an envelope on her bedside table. I took it and, at her nod, withdrew a letter.

"Read it," she said. "It's from Jack."

Quickly I glanced at the envelope and saw that it was postmarked Grand Forks, Yukon Territory. I unfolded the letter and read, "Dear Marta." Jack thanked her for writing to him and expressed his shock and sympathy about Jay's imprisonment, his disbelief that Jay could have done murder. Then he told her that he would be home in a few months and that he looked forward very much to seeing her again and hoped that she felt the same. Then, "Ever your devoted friend, Jack Van Dyne." That was all.

I looked at Marta inquiringly. "But this is a very nice letter."

"I know," she said, and the tears began to flow anew. "That's the trouble."

"You'll have to explain that," I said, exasperated.

She sniffed into the handkerchief again and then said, "Well, I hadn't heard from Jack in a long while. I wrote him about Daddy, and then a few weeks went by and I didn't get his answer until today."

"And you're unhappy because he hadn't written for so long?"

"No. Not that. What happened is that I met this other boy. Well, Jack isn't a boy, so this isn't another boy, just a boy. Anyway, I went to a birthday party at my friend Ella Fairfax's house last week—you remember—and I met this boy Andy Southwell. And he asked me to go to the Sunday School picnic his church is having next week, and I said I would tell him yes or no tomorrow. He's going to telephone."

I raised my eyebrows.

"Oh," she said quickly, "I know. I have to ask Great Grandfather's permission. But I know he'll say it's all right. It's a chaperoned picnic. And Great Grandfather knows the Southwells. So does Daddy. Anyway, that's the point. I was just going to ask Great Grandfather when Jack's letter came."

"I don't see the connection."

"I promised Jack I'd wait for him till he came back and not see anyone else."

"When did you promise that?"

"When he left."

"Did he ask you not to see anyone else?"

A pause. Then, "No."

"In fact, didn't he perhaps tell you you should see other young men?—Not that you're quite old enough to 'see' anyone."

"Yes. He told me that. He said I shouldn't even think about him while he was gone because I was too young and he had already embarrassed me—you know, the night at the opera and Eleanor not liking him."

"Then you have no obligation to keep that promise. Indeed you shouldn't. Jack was quite right about that."

"But I feel so disloyal. And now here's this nice letter, and he's coming back and he says he's looking forward to seeing me again and hopes I feel the same. And he signed it 'devoted.'"

"Oh, Marta," I said, hugging her. "Go to the picnic with Andy Southwell and enjoy yourself. I believe Jack has better sense than you do."

"Maybe you're right," she sniffed. She was quiet for a moment, and then she said, "Now I have another problem."

"What?"

"I don't have anything to wear."

Once having decided to attend the picnic, her spirits soared, and she began to describe the dress she wanted for the occasion. At first I was of a mind to insist that she wear one of the dozen or so perfectly suitable frocks she already had. But her delight and anticipation were infectious. Oh, to be fifteen when sorrow can be dissipated like a summer mist by natural sunny spirits. Her green eyes sparkled and danced as she described the dress of her dreams. She quite carried me away with her vision.

"Seafoam-green lawn," she said, bouncing slightly on the edge of her bed, "with a sailor collar that's open down the front to a tie at the waist and an inset of white embroidered organdy. I saw the fabric in the village. Susan could make it for me."

The notion of Marta in seafoam-green lawn was irresistible. I found myself hurrying down three flights of stairs to the basement laundry where Susan was instructing a new laundress in the use of the iron tubs and copper boilers that lined two sides of the tiled room. I explained Marta's dream dress and asked if Susan could sew it for her in a week.

"Oh!" she beamed. "I'd love to make something for Miss Marta. She's so pretty, it would be such fun to dress her. To tell you the truth," she confided, "I'd really like to be a seamstress. I'm good at designing dresses as well as sewing them. Now that Miss Marta is growing up, maybe she'll want me to make a lot of things for her. Especially if I can please her with this one. I'll ask Mrs. Morgan if I can go to the village and buy the material today."

I went to the kitchen with Susan and found Nellie Morgan working over the household account books. Susan posed her request, and Nellie looked at me sharply.

"Has she Mr. Eli's permission to go to

the picnic?"

"Not yet, but I don't think he'll object."

"Susan, you'd better stay with Loretta in the laundry this morning. And there's the dining room to be cleaned and aired this afternoon. Let's just go about our business until Mr. Eli tells Miss Marta she can go to the picnic. Then we'll see."

"Yes, ma'am," Susan said, abashed. She threw me a look of distress and went back down to the laundry.

My face was pink as I turned to go back upstairs. I would tell Marta to speak with her great grandfather and then, if he approved, she herself would have to speak to Nellie about sparing Susan to make the dress. Nellie was not going to take direction from me, the governess. She had made that perfectly plain, and she was quite correct. Jay had asked me to take care of the children, but neither he nor I had foreseen the difficulty this charge would pose. But now I saw it clearly. I had no standing to match the responsibility he had given me. I might be "their mother—almost" to Jay, but that "almost" bespoke a chasm between wish and fact.

I was not their mother, and since Jay was no longer with us, I did not have his authority to back me up, his orders to carry out, his dear self to appeal to when Marta wanted to go to a picnic or to have a new dress. Nor could I ask Jay to send a message to the staff telling them to obey my orders regarding the children. It would be unseemly and offensive to Nellie and the others. No, it was Eli Caldwell who must oversee Marta and Leo and

Bonnie—a lonely, heartbroken gentleman of eighty-eight years, now responsible for the upbringing of three young children. It seemed unlikely to work, but what the resolution of the problem might be I could not imagine.

The immediate problem resolved itself rather easily. Eli gave his permission and himself directed that Susan make the seafoam-green dress for Marta. But first, Susan had to complete the tasks Nellie had assigned her. As I went by the dining room after lunch, I saw her moving the furniture, rolling up the rug, and scrubbing the floor. It took her all the afternoon. But the next morning, Marta and Susan and I went to the village and purchased six yards of seafoam lawn, a yard of white embroidered organdy imported from Switzerland, and assorted trimmings and notions.

"I shall have to cream my hands to keep from snagging the lawn, it's so sheer," Susan said, ruefully examining the hands reddened and roughened by the menial work she so longed to give up.

None of the buttons displayed for sale matched the delicate green of the dress fabric, and Susan decided to make covered buttons from the fabric. But the small shop had no button bases in stock.

"I have a set of covered buttons I cut from an old dress," I said. "You can remake them for Marta's dress." And so we trooped happily back to Soundcliff and up to my room where I rummaged through my trunk to retrieve my button box.

"Here's a pretty button," I heard Marta saying behind me. I turned and saw her holding up the little jet button I had found in the secret passageway by Jay's office. I had placed it on a small tray on my dressing table and nearly forgotten it.

"Why, that's Nancy's button," Susan said, taking it from Marta and examining it. "What's it doing here?"

"Oh, I found it in a—a hallway one day," I said. "Mrs. Morgan said it wasn't hers. How do you know it's Nancy's?"

"She got a dress from Mrs. Caldwell once with these buttons on it. Mrs. Caldwell used to give Nancy her dresses sometimes when she was tired of them. Only Nancy was slightly bigger than Mrs. Caldwell, so sometimes a few buttons would have to be set over to make the dress fit. I used to do it for her. I remember these buttons on a blue dress she got from Mrs. Caldwell last year. They were such pretty buttons. And such a pretty dress—an afternoon dress, a little too elegant for Nancy, I thought."

"Hm," I responded and thought, "What was Nancy doing in the passageway outside Jay's office?" Not housework. Cleaning passageways wasn't the sort of work Nancy did, especially not in an elegant afternoon dress.

But I had no chance to pursue the thought, for suddenly I glanced up from the button box to see Marta stepping up onto my trunk and reaching for a straw hat with blue-green ribbons that I had put on top of the armoire.

"Oh, Miss Lorimer. What a pretty hat! May I try it on? It would be perfect with the green dress if you'd let me borrow it."

My voice failed me. I couldn't respond, for I had put the sword on top of the armoire under the hat where it was hidden from view by a high carved-mahogany facing around the top. Marta's movements seemed slowed to half speed as if in a nightmare. I saw her eyes come level with the top of the armoire, her hand extend toward the hat. And then, as I knew she would, she saw the sword. In the attenuated nightmare tempo, it seemed to take an irritatingly long time for her to say, "Oh, look. Look at this!" She clapped the hat onto her head and lifted up the sword and brought it down. Time resumed its normal speed.

Marta was shaking her head in disbelief and looking at me very strangely. "Miss Lorimer, where did you get this sword?"

"I found it," I said truthfully and realized that it was the second time in just a few moments that I had accounted for possession of something—the button and the sword—by saying that I had found it. It sounded as if I had spent my time prowling about Soundcliff scavenging lost items, which, in recent fact, I had done. I blushed as I asked, "Why?"

I was utterly unprepared for her answer.

"It's mine."

"It's yours?"

"Yes. It's my Civil War sword. Great Grandfather gave it to me when I was little because I used to admire it. It was before Leo was born, or I suppose he would have saved it for Leo. It belonged to Great Grandfather's brother who was a cavalry officer. He was much younger than Great Grandfather, but he died not long after the war."

"I—I found it outdoors, dear," I said rather gently. A suspicion I didn't want to entertain began inexorably to form. The events of the murder night ran through my mind—rushing to Eleanor's room and then seeing Marta at the end of the corridor. She had seemed awake but dazed. "Sleepwalking," Nellie had said. But now I thought, "No—not sleepwalking. Amnesia."

"However do you suppose the sword came to be outside?" Susan asked innocently. But Marta did not seem curious, did not respond to Susan's query. It was as if she were turning aside from a path she did not want to follow, a memory she did not want to pursue.

"You know," Marta said strangely, a deep frown on her face, "perhaps it's better here in your room. Will you keep it for me?"

"Of course I will," I said quickly, ignoring Susan's look of puzzlement. I gathered up the button bases I had found and pressed them into Susan's hand. "Well, off with you now. You'd best get started on the dress."

Marta brightened then as if she had forgotten all about the sword. "Oh, yes. Do let's get started, Susan." And off she went, pulling the bewildered Susan by the arm.

I put the sword back on top of the armoire and made a mental note to think of a new hiding place for it. Then I sat on the edge of my bed and stared at my hands knotted together in my lap.

"I don't understand what you're doing—why?"

I had said to Jay before he went to prison as Eleanor's confessed killer. And he had said, "I have a reason, an urgent reason."

It was all clear now, very clear. The only thing that could possibly have forced Jay to forfeit the children and me, to forfeit his freedom—why had I not realized it—would be the need to protect one of his children.

He had turned pale when I showed him the sword; I had to admit that for one awful moment I had thought his charge of demeanor had meant that he *had* killed Eleanor and that I had unwittingly found the evidence of his guilt. Instead, he had reacted as he did because he recognized it at once as Marta's heirloom sword. Perhaps he had suspected Marta all along, knowing the hatred she and Eleanor had for each other, remembering that brutal fight and the beating Eleanor had given Marta the very night of the murder. And here was I, handing him the proof, proof that must never come to light lest it destroy the merciful veil of amnesia that kept Marta from knowing what had really happened that night.

I remembered the awful morning Jay had left us for prison, how he had turned back to Marta for one extra embrace. "Remember how much Daddy loves you," he had said. I wept now as I thought of the terrible price his love for her had exacted. But he was right: there was no other way.

"No, Jay my darling," I murmured as the tears flowed over my cheeks. "Marta must never know that she killed her stepmother."

* * *

In all the wondering I had done about who might have killed Eleanor, I had not thought of the children. It was the one possibility I had not considered. Now, it seemed certain that it was Marta who had been responsible for Eleanor's death, Marta who had once said of Eleanor, "I could *kill* her."

But there were still so many unanswered questions. What, for example, of Eli's feeling that Eleanor's evil influence still ruled our lives? Well, that was easy enough to explain. Eleanor had driven her stepdaughter to murder, her husband to prison. Thus her sinister influence continued to haunt us and always would.

But what of the intruder who had robbed Eleanor's safe after her death, who had tried to enter my room from the secret passageways and then had attacked me on the rocks in the storm? And what of the strange sounds I had heard more than once in the house at night? Marta could not be responsible for all of this. Nor could a ghost, Eleanor's or anyone else's.

Finding the sword had not solved the mysteries. It seemed to have created more mysteries than before. And it had separated me from Jay. How I rued the day I had decided to search for a clue; how much more I regretted finding it.

Perhaps it was these thoughts roiling my mind, torturing my imagination, that made me think I heard the sounds again that night—strange, soft, creeping sounds, deep within the walls of Soundcliff.

* * *

More than ever I was determined to do what Jay had asked: to look after the children—especially, now, Marta. But the incident of the new dress for the picnic had shown me how little real authority I had to make decisions about them. And my powerlessness to guide and protect them was about to become even more apparent.

It was Bertie who broke the news to me one warm September afternoon in the great living room.

"Do you remember my cousin Nella MacDougall?"

"Yes. She was at the Fourth-of-July party last year." I remembered the tall, long-faced woman Bertie had introduced as his cousin and her jovial, mustached husband. I remembered, too, that the newspapers reporting Eleanor's death had listed Bertie and Nella MacDougall as the remaining heirs of the Archer fortune.

"She's the daughter of my aunt Edna. There were the three Archer brothers—my father and Eleanor and Charlotte's fathers—who built the adjoining mansions here next to Soundcliff. Edna was their sister. She married Foster Noble and they built their estate at Rhinebeck, up on the Hudson River above New York. Edna and Foster both died rather young. Nella had no brothers or sisters, and she inherited everything. She married Archie MacDougall, and they still live on the old Noble estate. They have a lot of money but no children."

"Why are you telling me all this now?" I asked, alarm already rising in my breast.

"Nella and Archie have filed suit to gain custody

of Bonnie and Leo and Marta. They're contending that Eli is too old to bring them up and that they need a real father and mother."

I went weak all over, and I stammered my response: "C-can they win?"

"Probably."

"Would they retain me as governess?" It was an idiotic thing to say. But I felt the children being torn from my grasp, my promise to Jay about to be shattered by the sudden interference of Nella Noble MacDougall, a woman I had met only once and never imagined I would encounter again. Even in my panic and terror, I knew that she was right, that Eli was too old to be guardian to the three children, that they did need real parents, that she had probably instituted the suit out of concern for their welfare and that she could not, thus, be totally a monster. But I could not let the children go. I had to stay with them as I had promised. And so my reflexive response: If they were to be snatched away from Soundcliff and carried off to another realm, then perhaps I could go with them.

"I hardly think so," Bertie said bluntly. "Nella will want to do things her own way if I know her. She'll want a brand new governess to mold."

A terrible, gasping sob escaped from my throat.

"I know. I know," Bertie said. "Jay wouldn't want them separated from you or from Eli or from Soundcliff. Unfortunately, he'll have no say in the matter."

"Oh, Bertie, isn't there anything we can do?"

"Yes, I think there is."

"What? Tell me," I implored.

"Now, listen carefully and don't say anything until you've had time to think about it. It's this: If I were married, or at least engaged, I could file a counter suit for custody. I could make a good case. I'd promise to keep the children here at Soundcliff in familiar surroundings and with their great grandfather. I'm sure I could prevail. Besides, I can influence a judge just as easily as Nella and Archie can. More easily, in fact. I have more money, and I've financed more than one judge's campaign."

I looked at Bertie with astonishment.

He smiled grimly. "Oh, yes. I'm not above bribing a judge, or shall we say persuading one. The problem is, no judge is going to give custody to a bachelor even if he's Croesus himself and the judicial elections are next week."

He got up and walked all the way across the room and back again. Then he sat down beside me and shyly took my hand. "Lillie, I've loved you since the day I met you. I've an idea you know that. This is a horrible way to ask you to marry me."

"Oh!" I put my free hand to my cheek. "I don't—"

"No." Bertie raised a hand. "Please don't answer right now. I know it's the last thing you've considered. A shock, I'm sure. Let's talk again tomorrow." Swiftly, before I could answer, he got up and left the room.

My head spun. Everything Bertie had said made perfect sense. It seemed the only way to save the children from the MacDougalls. Not only that, but if I married Bertie and we won custody, it would make me really their mother, give me the power to protect them and guide them that Jay had wanted me to have, the power I never would have as governess. Marta especially needed my protection. What if she were to remember how Eleanor had died and be far from home, far from me? I could not, I must not let it happen. Besides, I was terribly fond of Bertie. I even loved him in a way. So marriage to Bertie was the solution to everything.

I started to cry, my heart protesting what my head told me was the only thing to do. Surely, some day, Jay would win release, parole. I had secretly believed it and resolved to be here for him. And even if Jay were never to get out of prison—unthinkable thought—I had no desire to marry anyone else.

Very simply, how could I marry Bertie or anyone when it was Jay I longed for, Jay I would always adore. I knew that Bertie would say he understood, say it didn't matter. But did he deserve half a wife?

I looked ahead to the years that would come, the nights spent lying in Bertie's arms while the memory of Jay's manly body, his burning caresses stormed in my heart. It would not be fair to Bertie or to me. And though he might bear it, I wondered if I could.

Yet, how could I refuse? Indeed, Jay had not asked me to wait for him—had suggested that I should marry another—had refused to take my body, to spoil me for marriage. He had asked only that I not leave the children. Marriage to Bertie seemed the only way to keep that one promise to Jay.

Still, I could not make up my mind to it. My whole being resisted it. I did not sleep the whole night through, did not even lie upon the bed but paced my room, then wandered up to the tower to watch the September moon playing over the Sound and the throbbing beat of the Execution Light. When the horizon lightened and dawn's purple bathed sky and water, I was still sitting at the tower window. Stiffly, and no nearer a decision than before, I got up and went to my room to dress for breakfast. Soon, Bertie would return, and I knew that I could not delay my answer, for Archie and Nella MacDougall's suit for custody had already been filed. Countermeasures, if any, must be taken at once.

Halfway through breakfast, Hans summoned me from the table. In the corridor, he handed me a letter. "I thought you would want to read this in private," he said. As I took it, I saw the prison address in the corner. I fled to my room and tore open the envelope. With shaking hands and heaving bosom, I read the message from Jay, the first and only I had had from him since he had gone.

"Dearest Lillie,—"

I read the words twice, repeating back to him across the miles, "Dearest, dearest Jay...."

"I know about the custody suit the MacDougalls have filed. I was able to get a message to Bertie yesterday, and the warden allowed me to speak to him by telephone last night. He told me about his proposal to you. Indeed, he was about to try to call me about it himself.

"Darling, if Bertie had not thought of it, I would have suggested it. Bertie loves you, just as I do, and he is free to be your husband as I shall not be for a very long time, if ever. He will care for you and protect you from whatever cruel fortune might bring to a young governess. If you marry him, you will be safe and near.

"And then, of course, it is the only way to keep the children at Soundcliff with you. They will have parents there, wonderful parents in you and Bertie, and they'll have their great grandfather, too. I cannot bear to think of them at Rhinebeck with Nella and Archie. Though they mean well, they haven't the temperament and sympathy to take care of my three babies who have been through so much.

"I am sending this by messenger and hope it reaches you in time. I love you. Never doubt it, never forget it. But please do marry Bertie.

"My heart forever, Jay"

I had regained my composure when Bertie arrived. I looked at myself in the dressing table mirror before going down to him. My eyes were red, my face very pale. But I was calm.

"I spoke with Jay last night—" he began; I raised my hand to stop him.

"I know. He's sent me a message." I wanted to complete my sentence by saying, "I'll marry you, Bertie." But the words would not come.

"Will you do it, then?" he pressed gently, seeing my difficulty in speaking. "Will you marry me?"

I nodded.

I was full of Jay at that moment, full of his feel

and his scent, my body and spirit nearly shattered by the longing that could never, now, be fulfilled. I had nodded my consent to Bertie, and it was all I could manage. I restrained my tears with the utmost effort of will. I could not look into his face. I could not touch him.

Bertie stood near me. He did not reach for my hand, though I knew he wanted to, knew that he longed for me as much as I for Jay.

At last he spoke, softly, and without moving closer. "My lawyer has told me that I can file the countersuit for custody if I am engaged to be married. So I believe that our engagement is all that is necessary just now. I'm certain society would be scandalized by too hasty a marriage. Possibly the judge himself would view it as a ploy. So if you are willing, let us merely announce our engagement. We can consider marriage perhaps in December or January. I think a winter wedding will be seemly, and it will give you time to get accustomed to the idea."

"Oh, Bertie," I said. And then I went to him. I laid my face against his collar, and he patted me gently. It was a chaste embrace, but very dear and comforting. I put my arms about his neck and kissed him on the cheek.

TWENTY

The engagement of Mr. Pemberton Archer to Miss Lillie Lorimer was announced within the week. Eli Caldwell held a tea in honor of our betrothal—"Haven't done this in over twenty years, and then my daughter-in-law, Jay's mother, was the hostess," he grumbled. But unaccustomed as he might have been to giving teas, he was a gracious host and stood more erectly than I had ever seen him stand and greeted all the guests and presented Bertie and me with an aplomb I had not imagined him capable of. I knew that I was seeing, for the first and possibly the last time, Eli Caldwell as he had been long ago.

None of Bertie's family were present, for his only living relative was Nella MacDougall. She had been invited but sent regrets by return post.

The children were all there. Bonnie and Leo

were permitted a small cake apiece and a cup of tea that was mostly milk and sugar before Margaret Dobbs led them off to the nursery. Marta stayed on with the grownups. I couldn't take my eyes off her. She wore a peach-colored voile dress with a high collar of ecru lace. Her auburn hair was piled high atop her head, soft tendrils escaping about her small ears and the nape of her neck. "She's nearly sixteen," I thought, "and already a beauty. Dear heaven, let nothing spoil the long, happy life she deserves. Let her never remember—" I stifled even the thought lest it escape my mind and fly to hers. No wonder Jay had been unable to say, even to me, what he thought she had done.

Young Andy Southwell, her Sunday School picnic escort, appeared to be attached to her by an invisible chain of short length. He had come with his parents, friends of Bertie's as were most of the guests. The guests were a strange mixture of Long Island and New York society; bohemian artists, writers, and musicians; and various politicians. The artists and political types far outnumbered the society types. For as I had expected, Bertie's engagement to me was not considered totally acceptable: Not only was I a mere governess, but because of the opera incident nearly a year earlier, I was viewed by many as a climber who had attached herself first to Jay Caldwell and then, callously, to Bertie Archer when Jay Caldwell was no longer available. Only the fond indulgence with which some members of his own class treated Bertie's "eccentricities" had persuaded some of them to appear at the tea. Enough of his non-society friends had come, however, to make it a very gay party that spilled from the enormous livingroom onto the piazza where the Sound sparkling sapphire in the perfectly clear September sunshine formed the ideal backdrop.

I carried it off, somehow, on sheer instinct and the training my father had paid for. I made my very best effort for Bertie's sake, and he was so pleased and proud of me that the effort became effortless. Each time I saw Bertie looking at me with happy propriety, I was glad that Susan had taken such pains with my dress, a gray silk with slender, elegant lines. With it I carried a peacock fan, Bertie's gift, and on my left hand I wore the ring he had given me, a large diamond circled with rubies. It had been his mother's.

When the party was over and the last guest had gone, Eli and the servants left Bertie and me alone in the living room. Dusk was gathering, and memories of Jay's kisses there in the dark night of the storm stirred uncomfortably. I lit a lamp.

"Come here," Bertie said, and he took my hand and led me over to the organ. "Please," he said, "sit here where you were the day I met you." Obligingly I stepped up to the ornately carved organ bench and sat as if I were about to play. Bertie stood leaning against the secret panel he had emerged from that long-ago morning. He laughed happily. "Can you imagine how often I picture you sitting here as you did that day—so beautiful, so sweet."

I smiled.

He came to the side of the organ. "If only I could make you as happy as you've made me, Lillie." Then he bent forward but could not quite reach me, and he took my hand and tugged at it gently. I leaned forward and met his lips. It was the first time he had really kissed me. Then he pulled away and patted my hand. "Well, I'll be off now. You must be tired."

And he was gone.

Bertie suggested that I resign as governess and that a new governess be hired for Bonnie, Leo, and Marta. I resisted the idea. I loved teaching them, and what would my position at Soundcliff be if I were not to continue as their teacher—at least until Bertie and I were married? Besides, I needed the work to keep my mind occupied.

There was a surge of excitement in our little schoolroom one day when another letter from Jack Van Dyne arrived, and Marta read it aloud to us. It was long and full of exciting stories about the Klondike and the gold camps and even more thrilling reminiscences about the Cuban campaign in which he had fought with Colonel Roosevelt's Rough Riders.

Leo was quite carried away with the war stories. He asked so many questions that at last Bonnie said, "Leo wants to study all about war." Marta and I laughed, but Leo's eyes lit up.

"That's a great idea, Bonnie," he exclaimed. Then, to me, "Can we, Miss Lorimer? We could study all the wars America's been in. We could learn a lot of history that way."

Ever since Jay's first visit to the classroom a year ago, I had tried to obey his directive that Leo learn more American history—but with limited success. Leo was bright but found history dull. I dared not discourage his new-found enthusiasm, and so we launched our "war school" as Bonnie called it.

We started with the French and Indian War and worked our way week by week through the Revolution and the War of 1812 and the Mexican War. Eli Caldwell had become involved in our studies, for he had fought in the Mexican War and quite readily gave in to Leo's pleading to come to the schoolroom one day to tell us about his war experiences and show his souvenirs.

By mid October we were ready to study the Civil War. Once again we invited Eli for, of course, he remembered the Civil War well even though he had been too old to fight in it. His own involvement had been with the abolition movement, and the fact that Soundcliff had been a major station on the underground railroad made Eli a rich source of information on the years before the war. With only a little coaxing, he agreed to give us a tour of the secret passageways and to tell us stories of the slave escapes he had supervised.

The children were all but dancing with excitement the morning Eli, lantern in hand, lead us single-file into the passageway that opened from his own room. Marta, Leo, and Bonnie had been far more strictly brought up and closely supervised than Jay had been. They had never been permitted to play in the passages as Jay and his schoolmates had done. At most, Marta and Leo had been allowed to peek into the passageways from the threshold of a sliding panel while being strictly warned never to go into them. Obedient children, they had apparently never done so, for their surprise and excitement at the tour their great grandfather now lead was genuine.

I was as enthralled as the children with the escape stories Eli told. I had already heard the one about the runaway slaves Joe and Effie and their two children, of course. But I had to pretend amazement when Eli pulled the lever to reveal the little room where they had hidden. Thank goodness the lever had been repaired, I thought. Eli would surely have wondered how it had come to be broken off, and at the very least it would have ruined his story not to be able to spring it dramatically open at the key moment.

We emerged at last onto the rocks so that Eli could show them just where the slave family had boarded the little boat that took them to the bigger boat that took them to Canada. There was a considerable fall chill in the air, however, so we did not linger but hurried back to the house for lunch.

Just as we reached the piazza, Eli said, "Now this afternoon, I'll tell you about the Civil War and my little brother Daniel who was a cavalry officer. In fact—" he turned to Marta—"you bring Dan's officer's sword with you this afternoon." And he hobbled off to the elevator for lunch and a nap in his room.

Marta stared at me and I at her. I thought of several ploys. We would call off the lesson, or I would pretend to be ill. No, it would only come up again another day. I could tell Marta to say she had lost the sword. No, it would upset Eli and Marta, too, and be even more likely to jog her memory than simply showing the sword as he had asked. "I'll get it," I told Marta. I had rehidden it among some folded linens in the bottom of a long drawer below the armoire, and I took it out and carried it to the schoolroom.

Eli gave an excellent lesson on the Civil War: its causes as he saw them, the troubled years before the war, the war itself—liberally laced with anecdotes about his brother—and the bitter aftermath. Leo was entranced, and his eyes never left Eli's face. Even little Bonnie listened eagerly to most of it. But Marta's eyes were glued to the sword; and mine, I fear, were fastened on her. Eli seemed to sense nothing amiss. Perhaps he did not expect a girl to be interested in war stories, and he appeared to be more than satisfied with Leo's rapt attention.

At last the lesson was over and Eli had gone. Bonnie and Leo ran to the nursery to put on coats. They would play outside in the chilly October sunshine until supper time. Marta took the sword and held it across her lap.

"I'll take it back upstairs if you like," I said, anxious to get it away from her, to let die the hideous memory now seeking admission to her consciousness. She gripped it the more tightly.

"No. Great Grandfather gave it to me. I'd better take care of it. I shouldn't let anyone else take it. I shouldn't have let Eleanor take it."

"Eleanor?" I said and could have bitten

my tongue.

Marta raised her eyes to my face, the wonder and fear of dawning memory plain in their depths. "Eleanor took it. There was going to be a charity function, an exhibit of historical objects—"New York State in American History," I think. All the ladies were supposed to contribute something for the display, and Eleanor wanted to let them show my sword because Great Grandfather's brother was an officer in a New York regiment." Tears welled up. "I said, 'No, it's Great Grandfather's and what if something should happen to it?' I didn't really think anything would happen to it, but I just didn't want her to take my things as if they belonged to her!"

"Of course, of course. But that's a long time ago. Why not just forget it now," I protested.

Marta ignored my words and continued her story. "But Eleanor insisted, and she just took it from my cupboard—you know, in that high-handed way she had. 'Don't be silly,' she said, or something like that, and off she went with it. I don't know why she had to take it right then. The exhibit wasn't for another week. Anyway, she never took it to the exhibit. She died before it happened. And she just had it in her room for those few days."

For a moment hope lit my heart. If Eleanor had had the sword in her room, then anyone might have picked it up and struck her with it, not necessarily Marta.

But then Marta added, "I was looking for it that night."

"The sword?"

"Yes. I wanted it back."

"Why? Why that night?"

"For Jack. Oh, it sounds so silly now, but—do you remember the fight Eleanor and I had that night?" I nodded. Could I ever forget the vicious struggle, the screams, Marta's cuts and bruises? "I was going to run off with Jack to Alaska, and Eleanor stopped me, and then Daddy talked to me and I could see how stupid it was to think of going. Jack wouldn't have let me go, anyway.

"Well, I couldn't sleep when I went to bed. I wanted to give Jack something special so he wouldn't forget me in Alaska. I was lying in bed and trying to think of something I could take him in the morning for a going-away present. All I could think of that I had that Jack might like was the sword. So I got up and started looking for it.

"I knew it was in Eleanor's room, and I guess I went to her room, but—but I don't know if I went there or not. I remember that I wanted to get the sword, and I got up out of bed, and then I was in the hall—I went down to the second floor—and then I don't remember anything!"

"That would be natural," I said hastily and in great relief. The main memory, the awful memory had not come back. "After all, you had had that terrible fight with her, and then hearing about her death the next morning— It would be natural not to remember everything that night quite clearly."

Marta looked me directly in the eye. "I know something about Eleanor's death, but I don't remember what it is."

"Maybe that's nature's way of protecting you from sorrow," I said helplessly. "Maybe you're just not meant to know. I think you should stop trying to think about it."

"Oh, Miss Lorimer, you don't really think that, do you? Daddy is in prison, and we know he didn't kill her. If I could remember who did it and help Daddy, how can you say I shouldn't?" Then she gave a small, startled cry. "You think *I* did it, don't you?"

"No, no," I protested.

"Yes, and Daddy must think so, too. That's why he took the blame!" Her eyes were wide with horror. "Oh, dear—I can't remember. Oh, Miss Lorimer, what can I do?"

"Just try not to worry, darling," I said, holding her. "Now that you've remembered this much, you may remember the rest. But don't be afraid. No one will let anything bad happen to you, no matter what. And your father will be all right. Don't worry. Don't worry."

They were meaningless words meant to comfort her. But to remember what she had remembered, to suspect but not to know that she had killed Eleanor, was a worse torture for her than knowing could possibly be. Marta said quite firmly, "I'm going to try to remember, Miss Lorimer. I've got to try."

"But don't tell anyone else about it just yet," I cautioned her. "Let's keep it between you and me."

"All right."

I held her in my arms for a very long time.

* * *

The decision was made not to close Soundcliff as early as last year but to remain there well into the winter, for we did not want to disturb the children's lives unnecessarily.

And so the weeks went by, but Marta seemed no nearer to knowing what had happened the night Eleanor died than ever. Once in a while she would look at me and just shake her head, and I would hug her silently or hold her hand. We kept our secret. She told no one, nor did I—not even Bertie, although I was sorely tempted to seek his solace.

Meanwhile, the problems at Soundcliff multiplied. The MacDougalls' suit for custody of the children had been kept quiet, but when Bertie countersued, citing his betrothal to me as proof that he would be able to provide them a suitable family upbringing, the newspapers got hold of the story and gave it wide play. Naturally, the children heard of it, for Leo and Marta, at least, were quite old enough to read the papers, and they were thrown into a state of panic. None of them had the least desire to leave Soundcliff or to live with Nella and Archie MacDougall, whom Marta and Leo disliked and Bonnie couldn't remember. The children asked Bertie again and again if he was certain he would win, and he could only assure them, helplessly, that he thought he would. Much as they missed their father, they all felt that having Bertie and me as parents was the very next best thing and were terrified at the thought of being separated from us.

Late in November, we were all vastly relieved

when the judge handed down his decision and custody was awarded to Bertie and me, custody to reside with Eli Caldwell until our marriage. "Shall we plan a Christmas wedding?" Bertie asked, and I agreed. "But please," I begged, "you make the plans. I know so little about the customs here, and you know how to make the arrangements." I really didn't have the heart to plan the wedding.

Bertie said that he would, and he did. But day by day he consulted with me, seeking my approval for every aspect. It should take place at the Grace Church on Tenth Street in New York, he suggested. It was dizzying to realize that I had first seen Grace Church from the rear platform of the Broadway cable car that sad and terrifying April morning in 1898, the morning after Uncle Frank had been buried. I remembered the fellow passenger who had pointed out the church to me and explained that it was a society church. April 1898—a mere nineteen months ago, and now I was to be married there to the wealthy Pemberton Archer. I simply could not accept it as real.

Bertie was quite rich enough to care for the children and me, and although he didn't much care for the world of business, his money was well handled by a firm of trusted financial counselors.

The Caldwell fortune was another story. Things had slipped badly in the months preceding Eleanor's death and Jay's imprisonment, as Eli had pointed out to me; since then, new disasters had seemed to follow upon the old. Early in November, a bill had passed the New York State

Assembly restricting the practices of a corporation Eli, at Jay's instruction, had just arranged to buy. It was the sort of bill, Bertie told me, that certain corrupt assemblymen regularly introduced, expecting to be paid to let it die in committee or, at worst, to vote it down on the floor. Drafting, introducing, and killing each spurious legislation was a chief source of income for many assemblymen. I shook my head, aghast at the corruption of lawmakers, judges, and district attorneys I had observed as Jay's empire had come under attack.

"I thought American democracy was so perfect," I said to Bertie, and he laughed.

"Not quite," he said. "But there are enough honest types, reformers. Governor Roosevelt is one. And somehow, all together, it does seem to work."

But it wasn't working for Jay and Eli that year, for the bill restricting the practices of the corporation they hoped to buy—the sort of bill regularly voted down for a fee—had passed the legislature, and this time the pay-off had come from Gus Flammon, according to Eli and Bertie. "How do you know?" I asked and received the reply, "We know. We have informants in Albany. But we couldn't stop it. It was too late when we found out, and Flammon had gone too far with it."

"But how did he know you intended to buy it?" I asked.

"How does he know anything?" Eli answered in disgust. "Sometimes I think he has ears in the walls of Soundcliff."

"This has happened before," I pointed out. "He

does seem to get information about Jay's business that he could only get by going through the papers in Jay's office."

The two men looked at each other. "Yes. That's exactly how it seems," Eli said grimly. "But since we don't know how he's getting the information, we don't know how to stop him."

"Jay would know how," Bertie said.

"The old Jay would have known how," Eli replied.

The three of us sat and looked at one another glumly. The old Jay would never have permitted things to get into such a state. He would have stopped Gus Flammon and given him better than he gave. But the old Jay was not here, and the fortune and the enterprises and the dreams to which Leo should be heir were eroding; and Eli was too old, Bertie too inexperienced, and I too ignorant to prevent it.

The children and I neared the end of our war studies and were able to use a stack of old newspapers from the basement as sources of information on the battles in the Philippines and Cuba and other aspects of the war with Spain of the year before. When we were finished with them, Leo offered to carry the papers back to the basement, and as they were too heavy for him to lift by himself, I divided the stack with him and helped him carry them down; and there in a corner of the basement I spied Nellie poking into a small packing barrel.

"I wish I knew what to do with these things," she sighed. "I suppose I ought to send them over to her, but if she didn't think enough of them to take them with her, why should I bother?"

"What are you talking about?" I asked, and Leo and I approached the barrel Nellie was peering into with seeming disgust.

"Why, these few things that belong to Nancy," she said. "She had them packed into this barrel and set it by the kitchen door the night before she left, but then she went off that next morning without it."

"I suppose she was upset by the—the—" I looked at Leo and just let the sentence trail off. It had been the night of Eleanor's murder.

"Anyway, they're just taking up space here. Not much that's worth anything. Most of it could just be thrown away, I expect. Just a few odds and ends of china. But this is nice," she said and pulled out the little silver tray I had given Nancy as a wedding gift.

"Why, I gave that to her," I said. "I thought she liked it. She seemed awfully pleased with it. I can't understand why she would leave it behind, even under the circumstances." I felt a little stab of hurt, for I remembered clearly the look of gratitude on Nancy's face. At least, so I had thought.

"Well, if you bought it, why don't you take it," Nellie said, handing me the tray. I took it to my room and put it on my dressing table. It was a lovely little tray. If I had been the departing bride, I would not have left it behind, I thought, nor could I really believe that Nancy had meant to. Absently, I picked up the little jet button and put it on the silver tray. Now I had two things that had belonged to Nancy. Strange, strange . . . I could not get her out of my thoughts; but what it was that troubled me so about Nancy I could not formulate.

The days passed, and I became caught up in the wedding plans. Bertie, as he had promised, was arranging everything; but his enthusiasm was contagious, and I began to feel almost excited myself. At Susan's urging, I had begun to make sketches for a wedding dress. There was just a month to go before the day of our wedding, and I became preoccupied with it.

Still, each time I returned to my room I would look at the silver tray and look at the jet button and think of Nancy. Why had she left the tray behind, indeed the whole little barrel of china things that one would think a new bride would have been anxious to have? How could she have forgotten it, even in the uproar of that night? And how had the little jet button come to be in the passageway outside Jay's office? The thought of Nancy was like a splinter in a finger, bothering me, worrying me vaguely.

And then one morning I was thinking about the dreadful day after the murder when Margaret and I had sat with the children. And suddenly I had a new thought about the button.

Nellie Morgan was a very thorough person, I knew. When she cleaned something, it shone. Never was there a particle of grime to be found in even the narrowest crack or remotest corner of the kitchen, for even though Nellie did not usually do the cleaning herself, she directed those who did, and her eye was sharp and her inspections intense. One bit of cleaning only did Nellie do herself, and that was the cleaning of the passageways. Although it was not done often—perhaps twice a year—it was surely done meticulously.

The morning after the murder, after Jay had told the children about it and had gone away and left them in our charge for several hours, I had not been able to find Nellie. Hans had told me that she was cleaning the passageways, drowning her own misery in hard work. What a cleaning she must have given them that day!

According to Ada Wirth, who had waved to Nancy and Geoffrey from the kitchen door, the bridal couple had departed at daybreak, at least an hour or two before Nellie commenced cleaning the passageways. And Nancy had not returned to Soundcliff since—or had she? For I had found the button in the passageway by Jay's office in July although Nancy had left in March and Nellie had cleaned the passageways just after her departure. Surely, if the button had been in the passageway in March, it would not have escaped Nellie's broom. And so it must have fallen there later.

Nancy must have come back.

The scenario unfolded rapidly in my mind. Eleanor had betrayed Jay to August Flammon. Nancy, her lady's maid and a woman of few scruples, had probably aided her in her skulduggery, had possibly carried messages from Eleanor to August Flammon. And Geoffrey had probably been involved, too, had probably driven Nancy to Foxfield to deliver the messages and to carry messages back to Eleanor. That was why Geoffrey had been rewarded with the job at the Flammon estate.

That much I had suspected already. But why had I not also realized that with Eleanor dead, August Flammon would need a new informant?

It all made horrible sense. Perhaps there had been information detrimental to Flammon in Eleanor's safe. Nancy, as Eleanor's former maid, might well have known about the safe's contents, might well have been the one who came back one night to rob the safe, merely taking the jewels for good measure and to cover up the real purpose of the robbery. And might Nancy not also have gone through the passages to Jay's office, stolen or copied information about the papers on his desk, information August Flammon doubtlessly paid handsomely for?

I remembered the soft sounds within the walls at night. I remembered the light bobbing across the Sound on the night of the storm. It had come from the direction of Foxfield. It was the night the intruder had tried to enter my room, had attacked me on the rocks. Had the intruder that night been Nancy? But why would she have tried to hurt me? What had I ever done to her?

And then I remembered the day in the schoolroom, the day of Jay's first visit when we were talking alone together about the children and Nancy had come in to find Jay holding my hand. I remembered the mocking look she had given us, a look I had thought of amusement and contempt. Had I misinterpreted that look? Had it, instead, covered jealousy? In spite of her affair with Geoffrey, had she, perhaps, been infatuated with Jay—so much so that she would try to kill me? And what of that night so long ago when someone had actually come into my bedroom and put a pillow over my face? I had always thought it was Eleanor. Had it been Nancy then, too?

It all seemed farfetched, and yet it all fit together so neatly. I gazed at the silver tray. No wonder she had left it behind. She wanted no gift from me.

But what could I do about it? I had no proof that Nancy had been responsible for anything, anything at all. Perhaps the best thing was simply to persuade Eli to have the passageways sealed off and especially the panel to Jay's office. Then Nancy's access would be cut off. Then, perhaps, she would stop her mischief.

I wonder now why I didn't put the last piece of the puzzle into place at once. Perhaps it was because I had always thought of Nancy and Eleanor as allies and cohorts, not enemies.

It was Marta who made the whole picture come suddenly together. I had been thinking a lot about Nancy, and one day when Marta was in my room, I showed her the silver tray and told her about Nancy leaving it behind. "Nancy was a strange person, wasn't she?" I said. Marta gave me a strange look as if I had startled her and replied in a remote voice, "I don't want to think about Nancy."

But later that afternoon, Marta came to me. She had found her own response to my mention of Nancy odd. Why had she said she didn't want to think about Nancy? Was it because Nancy was part of whatever it was she couldn't remember? Suddenly, as if a veil had been torn away, she had remembered about the night of Eleanor's murder—all about it.

"I did go down to Eleanor's room that night," she began tremulously. "I don't know what I thought I was going to say to her or how I even had the nerve to go down there after that awful fight. I just know I was determined to get that sword back. I was so mad at her for taking it from me and so on fire with the idea of getting it for Jack.

"I listened at her door, and I thought I heard water running. That was lucky. She was probably in her bath and I might be able to slip into the room and get the sword without her even seeing me. I opened the door a crack and I could hear her splashing in the tub. I went in. I knew where the sword was. I had seen it earlier, propped up against the wall by the window. The window was ajar, just a crack—it was a warm night for March, do you remember?—and the curtains were stirring in the breeze, and I saw the sword. I suppose she didn't think it looked very nice in her elegant room, so she had hidden it behind the curtains.

"I had to pass the door to the bath to get to it, and the door was open, but I thought she wouldn't be able to see me around the corner of the tub. I tiptoed across the room and got hold of the sword. I had it in my hands, and I had turned around with it, when I heard someone coming along the hallway. It frightened me so that I let go of the sword and ducked behind the big Chinese screen. I could see the sword sticking up over the arm of the chair by the window. It had fallen against the chair and was just sort of propped there.

"I was mad at myself for jumping away and hiding like that, and I was about to come out again and grab the sword and hurry off when I realized that there was someone in the room."

"Who was it?"

"I couldn't see, and I was afraid to move for fear I'd be seen myself. But I could hear someone moving around in the bedroom, and I could still hear Eleanor splashing in her bath.

"Finally, the splashing stopped and I guess Eleanor came out of the bathroom and I heard her say. 'Oh, that's not for you.' And then the other person answered, and I knew who it was—Nancy."

"Good heavens!" I gasped, and I began to anticipate the end of the story.

"Nancy said, 'Oh, I've admired this dress, and I thought you'd want me to have it. It would be so nice for my trousseau.' And Eleanor said, 'Well, you're wrong. That's a new dress, and I've already given you plenty.'

"Then Nancy laughed. It was as if she were just ignoring what Eleanor said—as if she were the mistress and Eleanor were the servant. That's the way her voice sounded, not bothered by what Eleanor said. And she said, 'And in addition. I could use a few hundred dollars for the honeymoon.'

"And Eleanor became furious, of course, and

she said, 'I don't know why I should give it to you. Jay already knows about everything. He found the letter, and he knows I've given information to Gus. He's furious with me, and it's all but ruined anyway. So I don't really need to buy your silence any more, do I? Have you thought of that, Nancy?'

"'Oh, yes, I've thought of it,' Nancy said back. She was very sneering, very sure of herself. 'But Mr. Jay doesn't know quite all, does he? He doesn't know you've been—'"

Here Marta broke off and blushed deeply.

"What is it dear?" I asked.

"Oh—" Marta gasped. "It was a terrible thing to say. I don't know if I can repeat it."

I sat quietly next to her, loath to press her, yet afire with curiosity. I held my tongue, and at last Marta continued.

"What Nancy said was, 'Mr. Jay doesn't know you've been sleeping with Mr. Flammon. Does he?' Eleanor just sort of screamed. 'You witch! You don't know that!' And Nancy said, 'Oh, yes. All those times Geoffrey drove you to Foxfield, you don't suppose he was just waiting in the carriage, do you? The windows there are very low and easy to see into.'"

So that's where Geoffrey had been taking Eleanor on those mysterious drives. I might have known! For Eleanor and Gus Flammon had not been especially discreet, I reflected grimly. I remembered all too clearly their kiss under the staircase at Soundcliff—unobserved, so they had thought, unaware of my presence. But I was not the only one who knew, after all. Nancy and

Geoffrey had known as well and had kept the information back, a trump card.

Marta went on. "Now Eleanor really wanted to scream, I could tell. But she must have been afraid of being heard, so she sort of strangled her voice back to a low pitch, but you could hear it shaking. She was furious. And she said something like, 'It's not fair! It's not fair! You've been paid—Geoffrey has the job with Gus. What more do you want from me? Are you going to hold this over my head for the rest of my life? If Jay ever found out—I think I can fix it up with him now—but if he ever found this out he'd surely kill me!'

"But Nancy wouldn't back off. She said, 'Just this, then. A few hundred for a little wedding present, that's all.' And Eleanor said, 'No! This is just too much! Geoffrey's got the job, you're leaving this house, that was to be your last payment. And I come out and find you parading around in my dress, and I can see that this is just going to go on and on forever. Well, I'm not going to have it!'

"And then there was a scuffle. I thought—well, I honestly thought Eleanor was going to kill Nancy. You know her temper."

"Yes. But what did happen?"

"All I could really see was the edge of the chair by the window. I could see the sword propped up there, and I saw someone pick it up—just an arm, a hand. But there were no rings on the hand, I remember noticing, and Eleanor always wore rings, so I knew it was Nancy. Maybe she was trying to defend herself. And I heard more scuffling, and then an awful deep groan, and I saw Eleanor stagger back toward the window and then—"

Marta began to weep. "Oh—it was so awful—no wonder I wanted to forget it. I want to forget it now. But I never shall, I never shall." She shuddered as she sobbed out the rest of the tale.

"There was blood all over the side of her face and her dress. And as she staggered back to the window—I could just see her through the little space between the screen and the wall—I saw the sword swing out toward her. Nancy was swinging it by the scabbard, and I just saw the handle come around with—oh—such force. Eleanor was off balance, and the window being slightly ajar—the sword struck her in the head and she was just knocked right through the window, and she gave that awful scream. And I remember that the sword went right out the window after her. Nancy must have thrown it to get rid of it. That's why it was outside, why you found it outside.

"I stood so still I wasn't even breathing, I was so terrified that Nancy would discover me there and know what I'd seen. I kept waiting to hear her leave, but several moments went by, and I could still hear her moving about. And finally I couldn't stand it and I peeked around the edge of the screen, and I saw Nancy by the secret panel. I saw her pushing on the molding, and I saw the panel sliding open. That must have been what she was doing in those moments when I heard her moving around, don't you see—she didn't dare go out into the hallway for fear she would be seen there. She must have known there was an entrance to the passageways from Eleanor's room, but not quite how to open it, and it had taken her a few moments to figure it out. But as I looked around the screen, the panel slid open, and I saw her step into the passageway, and the panel slid shut.

"I wandered out into the hall. It never occurred to me that if anyone saw me they would think I had done it. Anyway, no one had come yet—I don't know why."

"They were searching the cliff," I said. "Everyone was watching Bob and Hans search the cliff. No one thought of going to Eleanor's room until after she'd been found."

"Well, I don't remember anything else. I don't know where I went after that."

"Nowhere," I told her. "We found you wandering at the end of the corridor. We thought you were sleepwalking."

At last, I thought, we know the real cause of Marta's amnesia: Not that she had killed her stepmother, but that she had seen her stepmother killed. I gave her a huge hug and a kiss.

Marta raised her head. A sudden joyful thought had occurred to her, a thought I had already entertained and dismissed as she was telling her story. "Oh, Miss Lorimer, we can get Daddy out of prison now, can't we?"

"No, not yet," I said. It was better, I thought, to cut the notion short. Marta was fifteen, nearly sixteen, after all, and able to grasp a difficult truth. "You see, darling, there's only your word that it happened this way. Oh—" I patted her knee quickly as a look of hurt flickered in her eyes. "I believe you, of course. But think how it would sound in court: You're his daughter. You might well have made up the story to get him free. That's the way it would seem."

"But we have the sword to show," she insisted.

"That's the worst of it, Marta. Your father cleaned the sword and gave it to me to hide."

"Because he thought I'd done it."

"Yes. You can imagine what he thought when I showed him the sword—*your* sword—with blood on the handle and told him I'd found it near where she fell. And after the terrible fight you'd had with her, how badly she'd treated you—"

"Oh, I know, I know. I understand. He wanted to protect me. But—"

"But he destroyed the evidence. And think how that would look if we came into court to tell your story now, eight months after the murder, and we said, 'Here is the sword that Nancy killed her with, but it's been cleaned up and hidden away because Mr. Caldwell thought his daughter did it, but now she's suddenly remembered witnessing the murder, and now here we are after all these months and this is the true story.' If you were the judge, Marta, would you believe it?"

She shook her head in despair. "No, of course not."

No, a judge would not have believed it. But it all made terrible sense to me. It *had* been Nancy in the passageways, Nancy robbing the safe, Nancy stealing Jay's business secrets, Nancy who had tried to kill me, Nancy who had succeeded in killing Eleanor. I revised my opinion of why she had left the silver tray and the small barrel of china things behind. She had simply forgotten them in her haste to get away before daybreak, before the investigation of the murder could begin. And I revised my idea of why she had come back to rob Eleanor's safe, for if Eleanor had kept any evidence of Nancy and Geoffrey's blackmailing scheme, incriminating notes or letters from Nancy for example, Nancy would have had to come back and get them before they were found. She might have considered the jewels a bonus, a last payment.

But however well I had convicted Nancy in my mind, I had told Marta the truth. Her story would not free Jay. For she had now placed herself as well as Nancy in Eleanor's room on the night of the murder, and while no one else had seen Nancy, we had all seen Marta in the corridor. Not only did I not dare tell the police what Marta had told me, I scarcely even dared tell Jay; for although he would be overjoyed to know it had not been Marta, would believe her story as I did, he would see the danger in it too and feel so helpless to defend her from it. I decided to wait just a little while, to see if there would not be some way to corroborate Marta's story, to prove that Nancy had done it. Marta had the same thought.

"We have to get Nancy to confess, don't we?" she said.

"Yes. But why would Nancy confess? Can you think of a way to make her do it?"

Marta hung her head. "No."

"Nor can I," I said. "But I'll think of something.

And let's just keep this between us a little while longer until I do."

But after Marta had gone, my gaze fell upon the silver tray, and I began to wonder what would happen if I were to pay her a call, a friendly call just to return the tray. I might be able to form a friendship and go to see her a few times. And slowly I might get her to forget herself and let slip something about the murder.

"And what good would that do?" I asked myself sternly. "Even if she blurted out a full confession over her teacup—just the two of you sitting there together—what use would it be?

"I don't know," I answered myself. "Maybe I could show her how many lives are being ruined by her silence. Maybe I could persuade her to give herself up."

It sounded unlikely, even to me, that there could ever be such an outcome to my visiting Nancy. But what could it hurt at least to go and see her once? The tray was the perfect excuse. She wouldn't suspect that I knew anything. What would it hurt to try?

And what would I say once I had returned the tray? I didn't know. "But something will occur to me when I get there," I decided.

Once again I felt compelled to act, to confront, to move things along and not to wait for them to take a natural course. I had done it once before when I had looked so hard for a clue and found the sword. It had only made things worse; but I refused to take a lesson from that terrible experience. I had to try again.

I wrapped the silver tray in tissue, and I asked Bob to hitch up a small buggy for me to drive out by myself. He did as I asked, and before I had time for second thoughts I was driving along the road toward Foxfield. I had gone some distance when I realized that the drive to the Flammon estate was longer than I had anticipated, that it was already mid-afternoon of a late autumn day, that evening would come early. Well, I would use this first visit just to make "friendly" contact with Nancy. I hoped it would not take long, and that I would be home not long after nightfall.

I arrived at the gates to Foxfield—great wrought-iron gates with foxes' heads on them set into a broad stone archway. A gate keeper stepped from the gatehouse, and I said, "I've come to see Mrs. Hand. She is Mr. Flammon's valet's wife."

"Oh," he told me, "they don't live on the estate. They have a little house down the road apiece, back in the woods. But it ain't hard to find. Just drive on along here until you see a big white rock by a lane on your right. You turn there and drive, oh, about half a mile. You'll see the house. It's the only one back in there." I thanked the man and turned on down the road as he had directed me. The shadows were lengthening, but I was determined to complete my mission.

I drove and drove and still I did not see the white rock he had described. I must have passed it, I thought, and was about to turn back when I saw it just ahead and pulled up next to it. Dusk was deep upon the landscape now. The lane that wound away beyond the rock was thickly canopied by branches and seemed almost dark. Moreover it was narrow and rutted, and I would not have enjoyed driving it under any circumstances. But I had become possessed with my idea. I turned down the lane.

Night seemed all but at hand when I found the little house at last. It was very nearly nothing but a cabin with rough-hewn siding and a crude, wide-board door with an iron latch. Square windowpanes of mean dimensions peeped out from, perhaps, no more than two or three rooms. A faint light as from a single lamp shone behind the ones just by the door. I was abashed to find that Geoffrey and Nancy were living so poorly and in such a lonely place. I wondered if Nancy would be embarrassed or even angry to have me call on her. But no such notion could stop me now.

I stepped down from the buggy and wound the reins around a slender tree trunk. Then I went to the door, less frightened than before. After all, I thought, how menacing can a person be who is forced to live in such humble circumstances?

I knocked firmly at the door, and I heard slow footsteps from within. They seemed to approach, then pause. I knocked again, and at last I heard the lock scraping back. The door opened. My eyes widened and my heart all but stopped beating; for I was face to face with Eleanor Caldwell.

TWENTY-ONE

I took a step backward and passed my hand over my eyes, sure I was hallucinating. Eleanor was dead. Marta had seen her fall. Hans and Bob had identified the body as she lay at the bottom of the cliff. I had gone to her funeral, seen the casket lowered into the earth. Yet here she stood, and she was no illusion.

I was confused, but not so confused as to be oblivious of the danger I had put myself in. I took another step back and turned my head toward the horse and buggy tied about twenty feet away.

"No, you'd better come in," Eleanor said, cutting short the notion of flight. I turned back and saw that she was taking a pistol from behind her back and pointing it at me. "I imagined that someone would come eventually. I never thought it would be you." She motioned with the pistol, and I went into the cabin and sat down in the wicker chair she pointed to.

The interior was as I had imagined it from the outside. A wood-burning cookstove, a dry sink, some shelves with a few pots and pans and pieces of china, and a deal table occupied the far corner and formed a kitchen area. I sat in one of the three mis-matched chairs, two of wicker and one in elaborately carved walnut with a cracked leather seat that must have been salvaged from among Gus Flammon's Foxfield discards. A braided rug covered a patch of the rough floor between the chairs. A Franklin stove glowed with warmth, the only pleasant aspect of the room.

Not only were the furnishings sparse and shabby, they were in ill repair. Neither cookstove nor Franklin stove had been blacked in some time, and both were badly rusted about the pipes where rain water had leaked in. The woven wicker feet of one chair were broken and unraveled. The coils of the braided rug had come about half unsewn so that strips of floor showed between them. The floor was dull and grimy. There were no curtains at the windows but plain wooden shutters to close across them were now laid back against the walls, and the hinges of one were sprung so that it hung crooked. Behind me, I had seen a low doorway covered by a heavy, dark curtain not suspended from a rod but tacked across the top. Beyond it, I supposed, was a bedroom. The cabin looked its part—a hideout, not a home.

Eleanor sat down opposite me in the other wicker chair. "Who knows you've come here?" she asked. I hesitated, not knowing which response would put me in greater jeopardy: that I had left word of my destination or that no one knew where I had gone. The latter was the truth, and at last I said so. Perhaps Eleanor would be less panicked, less hasty about acting against me if she did not feel that someone would be looking for me soon.

"I suppose I'm going to have to kill you," Eleanor said dully, "but I think I'll wait for Geoffrey. I'll need his help."

The blandness of her tone was as chilling as the words. She sounded like nothing so much as a housewife admitting the necessity of getting started with spring cleaning. I didn't answer. I was afraid that any words of mine might upset her and precipitate the threatened deed.

She looked at the tissue-wrapped parcel I now held in my lap. "What's that?" I held it out and she took it from me. She tore aside the tissue and held up the silver tray. "Well, what's it for? Why did you bring it here?"

I was forced by her direct question to speak at last. "It's Nancy's. She left it behind at Soundcliff. I thought I'd bring it to her."

Eleanor began to laugh. "That's not all Nancy left behind at Soundcliff." I stared at her and it seemed to unnerve her. "Well, haven't you figured it out? Nancy's dead. That's my joke, you see. The tray isn't all she left behind at Soundcliff. She left her life behind there, too." She smiled oddly.

I suppose I had realized the truth almost as soon as I saw Eleanor, but my mind had been too benumbed to make the last connection. Now I responded as if the idea had sprung to my lips without passing through my brain. "It was Nancy who fell from your window. You killed her."

"Very good," she answered. "You're a smart girl, Lillie." She contemplated me for another moment. "Have you figured out yet why they thought it was I who died?"

I shook my head.

"Well, I couldn't understand it at first myself. But then Goeffrey told me Bob had told him the head was all smashed in on the rocks. *My* head was all smashed in. But you know, Nancy resembled me in some ways. She was about my height. Her hair was dark like mine, and she sometimes wore it in a similar fashion. And that night she had put on my dress, my green dress that I had been wearing earlier in the day. Because of the dress and the hair, and since she had obviously fallen from my window, the natural mistake was made. It seems they accepted the identification Bob and Hans made at the bottom of the cliff. They must never have asked Jay to identify the body. I'm sure he would have noticed that she wasn't wearing my rings. But of course, we don't bother a wealthy man like Jay Caldwell with nasty things like identifying bodies, do we?" She gave a short laugh.

"The dress—" I thought. "Of course." It had fooled Marta, too. She had seen Nancy stagger back, her face covered with blood. She was wearing the green dress we had all seen Eleanor in earlier. In the brief glimpse she had, she had assumed it was Eleanor.

"Of course, I didn't know they would make that

mistake," Eleanor said. "I just thought, 'I've done murder. I have to get away.' I did count on some initial confusion. Nancy had left her dress on the bed when she put mine on. I had just come out of the bath, and I took off my robe and put on Nancy's dress. I took along a scarf to throw around my hair that would partially hide my face. I almost forgot my rings—I had left them on my dressing table during my bath. In fact I almost decided not to take them for fear someone would notice me wearing them, but I put them on. I thought I could keep my hands hidden until I got away."

There had been a few moments after the murder, Marta had said, when she heard 'Nancy'—really Eleanor—moving about. When she had peeked from behind the screen and seen Eleanor, now wearing Nancy's dress, opening the secret panel, she had assumed that the time had been used by Nancy looking for the panel. In fact, those were the moments Eleanor had taken to dress in Nancy's clothes. And as for the ringless hand Marta had seen grasping the sword, it had been Eleanor's, not Nancy's, for she had taken off her rings to bathe.

"I went out through the secret passageways to the servants' wing. I reasoned that there would be at least half an hour before they discovered that it was Nancy who had fallen. I thought that once in the servants' wing I could slip through the corridor to Geoffrey's room, and if anyone should see me I could duck my head and they would think I was Nancy. By the time Nancy was identified, I hoped to have found Geoffrey in his room and persuaded him to get me away.

"I didn't meet anyone, but when I got to Geoffrey's room, he wasn't there. I waited until he came in. He'd been out with the others watching Bob and Hans search the cliff, and of course I didn't know it but he'd just heard that I was dead." She laughed again. "When he saw me, the look on his face was just the same as yours just now when I opened the door. He thought he was seeing a ghost.

"I told him what had happened, and he told me that everyone thought it was I who had died. I expected him to be furious. I'd killed his bride—his *pregnant* bride at that. But all he said was, 'I told her not to push it that far.' You see, he and Nancy had been blackmailing me for quite some time because— Well, you don't need to know about that, or why Nancy thought she could get another ounce out of me. That's none of your concern.

"As I expected, I had to offer Geoffrey a great deal of money to get me away from Soundcliff. But of course it was not so difficult since everyone thought I was dead and Nancy was not suspected of killing me. In her clothes and with a shawl over my head, I looked enough like her to drive away with Geoffrey and for anyone not looking closely—and, of course, *expecting* him to be leaving with Nancy—to think I was she.

"The grounds were thick with people almost all night—police and so on. So we waited. Geoffrey had already packed up all their things, including a trunkful of her clothes which I've been wearing. A lot of them were mine to start with. Finally, we got away at daybreak. Ada came out just as we were leaving, but she appeared to suspect nothing.

"We found this place. It's dreadful, but it's isolated. I made Geoffrey bring me the newspapers every day, thinking surely Jay would discover that the body wasn't mine; but of course he didn't. I enjoyed reading about my own funeral. It's amusing to think of Nancy buried there at Greenwood next to Charlotte, isn't it?"

I wanted to fling at her: "And is it amusing to think of Jay in prison in your place?" But I kept silent.

"The papers didn't report my safe being robbed. Just like Jay to keep a 'family' matter quiet."

"You robbed your own safe?" I couldn't help asking.

"Geoffrey has a lot of practice at blackmail. He demanded more money, and I knew I was only safe as long as I could keep paying him. I gave him my rings to sell, but the money ran out. He wanted more. So I had to go back to Soundcliff. He rowed me across one night, and I came in through the passageways and took my other jewels from the safe. Geoffrey sold them, too.

"I knew that even that money wouldn't last. Geoffrey squandered it almost at once. Then he wanted more, but I didn't have more. He threatened to go to Jay and extort money from him for information about my 'death'—and then to hand me in for a fee. I told Geoffrey Jay would send him to prison the moment he learned the truth. I proposed that we go to Gus Flammon."

I thought that my capacity for astonishment had been reached, but the notion of the "dead" Eleanor appearing before August Flammon amazed me anew.

"I thought of killing Geoffrey. He was getting to be a danger to me. But where would I be without him, after all? And besides, I didn't think I could go to Gus and tell him I'd killed Geoffrey, too. That would have been a bit too much, even for Gus. So I had Geoffrey drive me to Foxfield. He went in to see Gus while I waited in the carriage. We thought he should be prepared a bit before I came in. Finally, Geoffrey came out and told me it was all right to go in to Gus. He was in the library. I suppose that he was surprised to see me, but Gus had made a lifelong practice of hiding surprise. 'What do you want, Eleanor?' was all he said.

"I knew it was a desperate chance to take. Gus could just as well have turned me over to the police. But we'd been—close friends. And he hates Jay, you know—hates all the Caldwells. So I hoped he would agree to pay Geoffrey to stay quiet and to keep me here and protect me—in return for information I could get for him about Jay's business affairs.

"Well, the long and short of it is that he agreed. He seemed to be amused by the idea. And so I came back to Soundcliff more than once to get the information I'd promised Gus."

And so the jet button outside Jay's office. Nancy's button, I had thought. Really Eleanor's button from a dress she had once given to Nancy but was wearing again when she came to Soundcliff to spy for Gus Flammon.

"Geoffrey would row me across at night," she went on. "Once we came on the night of a terrible storm. The storm was over, but another was building up and the water was choppy. I hesitated about going, but Geoffrey insisted. He said we had to keep supplying Gus with information or the payments would stop. He said it was safe enough and that we could be over and back before the next storm broke.

"But you know about that night, don't you?" She peered intently into my face. "It was you who followed me through the passageways."

"You tried to kill me," I said. "You tried to get into my room from the secret stairway. It was your second attempt, wasn't it? What were you going to do, try to smother me again?"

"Yes," she said. "I hated you from the start, from the day Jay made me hire you. I could see that he preferred you. If only I'd succeeded the first time with the pillow . . . You never told anyone about that, did you?" I shook my head. "Teddibly brave, aren't we?" she sneered, mimicking my English accent. "I couldn't resist trying again that night of the storm. But when I got to your room, the panel wouldn't budge. I might have known you'd have had it sealed after the first time. I suppose I woke you trying to open it."

"I was already awake."

"Anyway, I thought I might have wakened you. I kept listening to hear if I was being followed. Finally, I heard you behind me. I thought, 'Now

I'll get her,' but you vanished into the hidden room, and I couldn't get in. The lever was broken. I wanted to wait in the passageway for you to come out, but Geoffrey was waiting out on the rocks, and I didn't want him to come back in looking for me. He would have made me come away anyway. 'Why make complications?' he's always saying.

"We were near the dock, and I wanted to get away. I hadn't found anything in Jay's office, and I had disturbed you—I felt I was in danger. But we could see that the next storm was about to break. We would have gotten back across in time if I hadn't made that detour to your room. But it was too late by that time. We were going to have to wait out the storm. We stood just inside the tunnel to wait and stay dry, and then I heard you coming along behind us. I nudged Geoffrey and we scrambled out onto the rocks. And then there you were, right next to me. I made a move toward you. I could feel Geoffrey clutching at me to hold me back. I got away from him and I grabbed you, but then the rain started and I slipped and you got away."

I was silent. There was no need to confirm the story. She sat quietly for a few moments. Then she said, "You'd never have satisfied Jay. You're just a little nobody." I didn't reply. "Bertie would have been happy with you," she continued. "He never had any high aspirations."

"Would have been—" I reflected on her words with a shudder, and I kept looking at the pistol in her lap. Eli's words from long ago echoed in my mind: "Run for your life." Too late now. Or was it? Had I a chance against her?

"I couldn't believe my good fortune when you turned up here just now," she went on. "I had almost given up on the idea of killing you, Jay being in prison and you engaged to Bertie. What did I care about you any more? But the idea of you as mistress of Soundcliff still galls me. I grew up there, almost. It's mine. And here you are. It must be destiny giving me another go at you."

I sat quietly, but my mind was working clearly, rapidly, assessing my chances of rushing at Eleanor, taking her by surprise, getting away. Then from outside came the sound of wagon wheels, and my heart sank. It must be Geoffrey. My chances of escaping from the two of them were almost nonexistent.

He strode through the door, stopped abruptly, and kicked the door shut behind him. "How did she get here?" he demanded.

"She came to visit Nancy," Eleanor replied, smirking.

Geoffrey sat down in the leather-seated chair and clutched at his head. "Well, what now?" he said.

"We have to kill her," Eleanor said.

"We? Not *me*," he snapped. *"I've* never killed anyone. I don't need that on my record. You've already committed murder twice. You can only go to hell once. You do it."

"Twice?" I blurted.

Geoffrey looked at me. "Yeah. She killed Nancy, I guess you know. And she killed Caldwell's first wife. I bet you didn't know that, did you?"

"Charlotte? Your cousin?" I spoke to Eleanor.

"I—I didn't mean to. I had come to see her and bring her a gift, some bronze bookends I had gotten for her. I'd ridden over on horseback and left my mount down by the stables. No one was about. I tied him up and came in through the passageways from the old wall by the stables. I don't know why. Nostalgia, I guess. Bertie and I used to do it often. Bertie still does. We used to play in there as children, the four of us.

"Anyway, Charlotte was in her room, and I came in. We talked, and then we argued. About Jay. We always argued about Jay. She was so cold to him. I couldn't stand it, knowing what I would have given him if he had married me. The quarrel became violent, and the bookends were on the table next to me. I picked one up and I came at her and she said something to me—she said, 'Jay can't stand you, Eleanor. Stop thinking he would ever want you.'

"I struck out at her. I didn't really mean to hurt her—at least, I hadn't thought about it ahead of time. But she fell backwards into a chair, stunned. I had struck her in the temple. She wasn't dead, but I knew the scandal there would be if she lived to tell what I'd done. Why, Jay would never have spoken to me again! And it occurred to me that she'd made Jay so miserable, and I knew I could make him happy no matter what she'd said. I struck her in the head again, and I knew she was dead. I slipped away through the passageways and rode back home and no one had seen me.

"Well, then Jay married me, you know."

"So you had what you wanted: Jay," I said boldly. "Why did you betray him to August Flammon?"

"I began flirting with Gus to make Jay jealous. But it didn't work. Jay spent more and more time working over his business deals, less and less time at home. I thought if I gave Gus some information so Jay would lose out on some of those infernal deals, he'd lose interest in them and spend more time with me. And then I thought I might get some information from Gus that would be useful to Jay and Jay would be grateful to me. But Gus would never tell me anything. And by then I couldn't stop seeing him because he said he'd tell Jay, and then with Jay gone so much I really needed Gus's attention—" She broke off as if deeply confused. "I don't really know how it got started or why it went so far. I just had to get even somehow for—for—for being left alone—I don't know." She looked at me defiantly. "I could have made Jay happy. I *would* have, but he never let me!"

I gazed at her in horror. Eleanor had let Jay suffer as the suspected murderer of his wife Charlotte, had let him bear the agony of feeling responsible for what he thought was Charlotte's suicide. Then she had taken advantage of his gratitude for her loyalty, her belief in his innocence, had taken advantage of his goodness and his guilt and his conscience to maneuver him into marrying her. And when he did, she had betrayed him, had almost ruined him. And she had killed Nancy to keep him from knowing the full extent of her treachery, was ready to kill me to get me out of his house, out of his life.

"Why? I still don't understand why you did it all," I said to Eleanor.

She looked at me as if surprised, as if the answer were obvious. "Because I love him," she said.

She turned to Geoffrey. "Well, you have no choice; I need your help. I've already thought this through. She can't be killed here. She must have gotten directions at Gus's gate on how to find this place—didn't you?" Helplessly I nodded my head. "So someone eventually will ask around and figure out that this is where she came. There can't be any blood or a body around here. If someone asks, you're just going to have to say Miss Lorimer never arrived here and let them look around to their hearts' content. They won't find anything."

"And when they ask where *Nancy* is?" he retorted.

"Who knows? She went to visit her mother, so the little governess here probably came and found no one at home and went away. You'll have to find another place for *me*, of course."

"So what are you planning to do with Miss Lorimer?"

A dreamy look came over Eleanor's face. "When we were children we used to play 'Execution Rock.'" My heart began to thud, for I knew what she was thinking. Bertie had told me about it long ago: "They used to tie criminals to the rock at low tide and let them slowly drown as the tide rose. . . . We used to play 'Execution Rock,'" he had told me.

Geoffrey seemed to know what she meant as

well, for he said, "What do you mean—haul her all the way out there?"

"Oh, I think it would be poetic. We'll take her down to the landing in her buggy, and then we'll row her out there. We'll row another boat with us to cut adrift. She'll never be able to swim to shore from there. They'll think she rowed out in a boat and drowned."

"Why would she be rowing out in a boat from Flammon's landing?" Geoffrey asked. "They'll recognize it as his boat."

"I don't know!" Eleanor snapped. "It doesn't matter. There'll be no way to tie us in with it. It'll be a mysterious accident, that's all."

"No way to tie *you* in with it. Everyone thinks you're dead. They'll tie me in with it all right if anyone knows she came to my place."

"No. Why would they? What reason would you have to take little Miss Lorimer out in a boat?"

"No reason, I guess."

"That's right. No one would think that. Just be sure she doesn't leave anything behind to show she was here."

For a moment I hoped that Geoffrey might decide that he was better off turning himself in as an indirect accomplice in Nancy's murder for hiding Eleanor, rather than face the possibility of being found out as a direct accomplice in my murder. I hoped that he might suddenly bolt and run for the police.

But he didn't, and I quickly realized that while such an action might have saved Geoffrey's skin, it would not have saved mine. Eleanor would only have been forced to kill me herself with the pistol. The Execution Rock scheme, at least, would take more time.

"Here." She thrust the silver tray at Geoffrey. "We'll take it along and leave it in the buggy."

Eleanor held the pistol pointed at me while Geoffrey wrapped the silver tray in its tissue again. Then he brought some ropes from the back room and bound me hand and foot as Eleanor tied a gag over my mouth. I began to pray silently and did not stop as they carried me from the little cabin to my buggy. Geoffrey climbed in next to me and drove off down the little lane. Eleanor followed in their wagon.

We took a different road than the one I had come by—it seemed to be a service road, perhaps part of Foxfield itself—but we were bearing roughly back in the direction I had come earlier. The distance that had seemed interminable as I had driven it in the falling light of late afternoon now, in the dark, seemed incredibly short. Soon, we had turned into a very narrow path along the shoreline, and we pulled up at a small dock set well back in a tree-lined cove, an ideal sheltered fishing spot for someone. Also an ideal spot for hiding a foul deed. It was not the main Flammon dock where we would probably have been seen.

I looked out over the Sound and there it was, Execution Rock, with its lens turning rhythmically, throwing shafts of light out over the water. It will earn its name tonight, I thought morbidly.

Geoffrey left me in the buggy as he and Eleanor inspected two small boats tied up at the dock.

"There's just one problem," I heard him say. "You don't want to leave her out there on the rocks too long, do you? She might attract attention of someone passing in a boat."

"How?"

"She might yell."

"A remote possibility, but a possibility, I suppose. Well, if that's the problem, how do we solve it?"

"The tide's too low. Low tide was only a couple of hours ago or a bit more. We take her out there now, she'll have three hours to wait before high tide covers the rock, at the least. We'd better wait till nearer high tide."

Eleanor stomped her foot in disgust. "And what? Sit out here with her for three hours?"

"Maybe two and a half," Geoffrey returned. "You got a better idea?"

She paced up and down the dock, then turned to face him. "You're right. We'll hold her here." She withdrew a small watch from a pocket and sprung it open. There was only a quarter moon, but the air was very clear and the light bright enough for her to read the watch by. I tried to estimate the hour, but I had lost all track of time. It might have been seven or eight o'clock. One thing I did know, the November air bore the cold snap of frost. I shivered. Eleanor and Geoffrey were cold, too, and passed the time pacing up and down the dock or stamping their feet on the hard-packed sand for warmth. Occasionally, they came to the buggy to check on my bonds. All I could think of was how cold the water would be, what a wretched death.

Eleanor had certainly been right about my not being able to swim to shore from Execution Rock. Even a strong swimmer would not have survived the cold of the water, and I could barely swim at all.

I surveyed the shoreline. It was beautiful in the moonlight. My last look at the world, I thought. Lights glimmered sparsely along the black and silver shore, fewer than in the summer, for many households were closed up for the cold weather. One cluster of lights was more brilliant than the others: Soundcliff, I thought. It's Soundcliff. I tried to send one message across the water. "Help me. Find me." But I knew it was futile. No one would find me here at this tiny, hidden dock. Certainly, no one would find me at Execution Rock.

I turned my thoughts to Jay and determined to hold him in my mind till earthly thoughts ceased. His strength would comfort me in death as it had in life.

I fell into a reverie and was startled when at last Geoffrey and Eleanor approached the buggy and lifted me down from it. They carried me onto the dock and dumped me roughly into one of the small boats. The other was tied to it, and Eleanor and Geoffrey stepped down into the boat with me.

Eleanor was carrying a small lantern, and Geoffrey said, "What do you want that thing for?—to attract attention?"

"No," she snarled. "But we'll need some kind of light out there to see what we're doing. I'll keep it shaded the rest of the time."

Eleanor pushed against the dock and we rocked sideways to clear it as Geoffrey began to row. The other boat glided silently along behind us. I lay awkwardly between the seats. I had bruised my wrists, which were tied behind me, and my shoulder as I had fallen into the boat. The pain was almost distracting.

Eleanor closed the shade over the lamp, and we slid out of the blackness of the tree-shadowed cove and onto the calm, silver surface of the Sound. Neither Eleanor nor Geoffrey spoke, and the only sounds were the splash of the oars and the steady slap of small waves against the wooden boat. I lay facing the Execution Rock, and I watched it loom steadily larger. And then we were there.

The tide had already come up quite high over the craggy rocks at the base of the light. I had no way of estimating how long it would be before they were completely covered. Geoffrey jumped out and secured the boat by throwing a line about a jutting rock. Eleanor opened the lantern shade to light his way.

"Now, you shove her toward me," he directed, and Eleanor slid her hands under my shoulders and pushed me forward. Geoffrey reached in, took me by the arms, and dragged me over the side, Eleanor lifting my legs. I fell over into the shallow water, and the cold water soaked into my clothing and left me sodden and gasping with shock. Geoffrey propped me upright, braced between two rocks. He tried to untie the ropes that bound me, but the wet knots would not give. Cursing, he reached into his pocket and took out a penknife.

"What are you doing?" Eleanor hissed anxiously from the boat.

"Do you want people to think she went out in a boat and drowned? You don't want them finding her with ropes on her, do you?"

Eleanor said nothing, and Geoffrey sawed away at the ropes. It took him some time, and his feet were soaked in the cold water. I could hear his teeth chattering. I was shivering hard myself, which didn't make his task any the easier. Finally, the last rope came free, and I scrambled up onto a higher level of rocks almost with my back against the lighthouse itself. It was as high as I could get, and the water was lapping at my toes.

"Now, you'll get your gag off in a minute, but Eleanor and me'll be sitting in the boat here, so if you scream or anything, we have the pistol and we'll shoot you. I didn't want to get into this, but now that I'm in it, I don't want it messed up."

With that he slid back down the rocks, cast loose the ropes that held the boat, and stepped in with Eleanor. I pulled the gag loose and threw it down. I could breathe better and even see better without it, for it had been pushing up against my eyes. I said nothing, but just stood with my back pressed against the lighthouse. I watched Eleanor and Geoffrey cut the empty boat adrift. Then Geoffrey began to row in a small circle, staying near enough for Eleanor to keep the pistol trained on me. Eleanor had shaded over the lantern again, but I could see them clearly in the moonlight, just as they could see me. Then the light seemed to fade away, and I wondered if I were fainting until I looked up and saw that clouds were beginning to gather, not threatening rain or snow, but just obscuring the moon and creating random patterns of light and darkness as they moved across the sky. Eleanor uncovered the lantern just enough to focus a narrow beam of light on me. Then she covered it again.

The water was rising rapidly, it seemed to me. Already my feet and ankles were plunged into the icy black. I thought fiercely of Jay, and I turned my face toward Soundcliff; I was determined to keep it in my vision as long as I could. It glimmered like a fairy castle in the distance.

My mind was almost as numb as my body, but slowly a thought formed. Soundcliff should not have been glimmering so brightly at this hour of the night with only Eli and the children in residence. It must be very late by now, an hour when all of them would ordinarily have been asleep. Indeed, I could see that some lights were moving about the periphery—lanterns, they must be—as if not one but several persons were outdoors.

"Dear heaven," I thought. "Could they be looking for me?" The thought plunged me into blackest despair: to be perched here on the brink of perdition and to be tortured with the sight of those I loved looking for me and not being able to find me even though I was nearly within their view.

The lights came and went as if people were moving in and out of the house. And then the moving lights stopped, but the lights within Soundcliff shone as brightly as ever.

The water had risen to my knees, and as the clouds broke about the moon I could see Eleanor and Geoffrey, still circling in the boat in grim silence, watching me. Every once in a while, when the clouds covered the moon, they would shine a beam of the lantern on me as if to make sure I had not moved—or perhaps to see if I had drowned yet. I wondered if they had noticed the lights at Soundcliff, but apparently they had not.

Cautiously, I turned my head to look again at the shore. Nothing more seemed to be moving there. And now, determined as I was to keep Jay in my heart and Soundcliff in my vision, it was impossible not to let the rising water take over my thoughts. It was nearly waist high. I had lost all feeling in my legs, and I was no longer sure that I would be able to keep myself erect, that my knees would not at any moment and without warning just give way and let my body slide helplessly under.

Desperately, now, I turned my eyes back toward Soundcliff and saw a single light moving along the water line. Was I hallucinating now? so close to death that I imagined someone was coming for me?

The little light bobbed along the shore and then vanished. I closed my eyes in despair, and when I opened them again, Soundcliff still shone in all its glory atop the far cliffs, but there was nothing else.

"Only a few moments more," I thought, and I tried even harder to keep my eyes toward Soundcliff, to make it the last sight my eyelids would close over.

And then I saw a movement on the water, and as a cloud edged clear of the moon a shaft of silver light darted down to the glassy surface, and I saw a small boat almost halfway out from Soundcliff, moving silently but swiftly toward Execution Rock, and someone rowing hard.

I turned quickly toward Geoffrey and Eleanor. Had they seen it? They had not, for Geoffrey was rowing in place close by the tiny island and the rocks jutted up in such a way as to hide from them the little boat I could see so clearly.

I turned back and the boat had drawn much nearer, and as the fitful moonlight illuminated the water and Execution Rock itself, I saw that the rower had turned and was looking over his shoulder toward me. I wanted to wave, but I dared not move, for Eleanor and Geoffrey's eyes were riveted on me.

Soon, soon the little boat would draw near, but just as Eleanor and Geoffrey could not see the rower, so he could not see them, nor could he know about the pistol. Nearer and nearer he came, and then suddenly he rounded the Rock, and I nearly collapsed as I saw at last that it was Jay!

Eleanor saw him too, and she screamed. Geoffrey stood up in the boat, grabbed the pistol from Eleanor, and fired it at Jay almost point blank. But he had lost his balance slightly, and the shot went wild. With a swift, powerful pull of one oar, Jay swung his boat alongside theirs and, lifting the inner oar in its lock, he swung it hard over the side of their boat and knocked Geoffrey off his feet. The pistol flew out and dropped into the water as Geoffrey fell heavily over the side with a loud splash.

Jay pulled a pistol from inside his shirt and pointed it at Eleanor. "Any more guns aboard?" She shook her head violently. "Then you fish out Geoffrey," he said. He didn't seem especially surprised to see Eleanor, but then only seconds had passed, and he was intent on getting to me. He looped a rope about the oarlock of Eleanor's boat. Then he climbed over the side and, holding the pistol high out of the water, he scrambled up the rocks to me. I raised my arms above the water and put them about Jay's neck. He seized me about the waist with his free arm and pulled me quickly back to the boat. "Here—take the pistol and hold it up out of the water," he said. I took the pistol and he lifted me up over the side of the boat, then hoisted himself over the side. From the bow, Jay pulled two blankets packed in waterproof tarpaulins. He shook one out and wrapped it around me.

Eleanor had found Geoffrey and had pulled him into her boat. "Now, I'm going to tie onto the back of your boat, and you're going to row us all back to Soundcliff," Jay said through chattering teeth. He tethered our boat to theirs as I continued to hold the pistol. Then, noticing that Geoffrey was also shaking with cold, he took the second blanket from its tarpaulin and tossed it to Eleanor. "Put this around his shoulders," he directed. "I don't want him freezing before he gets us to shore," he said grimly. Then he took the pistol and sat next to me.

I opened the blanket he had given me and folded his violently shivering body inside next to mine.

TWENTY-TWO

As we rowed in toward Soundcliff, more lights appeared at the top of the cliff and then spilled down over its face. When we drew close, I could see that, except for Leo and Bonnie, the whole family and most of the staff were gathered on the dock.

"They found me out," Jay said cryptically. "Well, that's good. They can give me a hand with Geoffrey here—and Eleanor." Hands reached down to help Geoffrey and Eleanor from their boat and Jay and I from ours. "Those two are to be placed under arrest for attempted murder," Jay called out. A man I had never seen before stepped forward and stood next to Jay. The stranger was the only calm person in the group. Everyone else seemed to be in shock.

Bertie assigned Ada and Nellie to take charge of Eleanor, Bob and Hans to guard Geoffrey. They were to be taken to secure rooms, rooms with no secret escape panels, to bathe, change into dry clothes, and wait for the police whom Bertie immediately telephoned.

When Jay and I had bathed and changed, we met outside the nursery and, while Jay's police escort waited respectfully in the corridor, we went in together to reassure Leo and Bonnie that we were home and well; but we told them nothing of Eleanor's presence in the house nor any of the other upsetting details. That would come tomorrow when everything was settled and they had had a good night's sleep under Margaret's tender eye.

Then we went to the library where Eli and Bertie and Marta were waiting for us.

"Please," I said to Jay. "Tell me what happened. How did you get here? and how did you find me?"

"I think Marta should begin," he said. "It was her quick thinking that really saved you."

Marta, she said, had realized her error shortly after I had departed with the silver tray to look for Nancy.

"One thing about that death struggle I had seen in Eleanor's room kept not making sense to me," she said. "Why would Nancy have killed Eleanor when it was Eleanor who was so angry? But I kept remembering seeing Eleanor stagger back in her green dress. Then I realized what was wrong with what I *thought* I had seen: Eleanor had been in her bath. She would not have been fully dressed when she came out and found Nancy in her room; she would have been in a dressing gown. And I had heard her say to Nancy, 'Oh, that's not for you,' and heard Nancy say, 'I've admired this dress, and I thought you'd want me to have it.' It must have been the green dress they were talking about, I realized. And suddenly I remembered that I had seen it lying across Eleanor's bed when I came in, while Eleanor was bathing. Nancy must have come in, seen the green dress, and decided to put it on. Then I knew: It was Nancy I had seen staggering under the blow—Nancy in Eleanor's green dress and with her face bloodied.

"And I recalled something else, too. The woman with her hand on the panel whom I saw fleeing the room had been wearing rings, Eleanor's rings."

"She'd had them off for her bath," I told Marta. "That's why her hand that you saw reaching for the sword had no rings. That's why you mistook it for Nancy's hand."

"Anyway," Marta went on, nodding, "I knew then it was Nancy I had seen killed and Eleanor I'd seen fleeing."

As soon as Marta understood what had really happened, she had hurried to my room to tell me but had found me gone. She had run about the house and the grounds looking for someone who knew where I had gone; but no one did, of course. Bob told her he had hitched up the buggy for me and that I had driven away at about three-thirty. That was all anyone knew.

In despair, she had gone back to my room, and then she had seen that the silver tray was gone. I had told her whose it was, and in a flash of intuition, she guessed that I had gone to find

Nancy. Alarmed, she had alerted Eli who had called Bertie. Thus, Eli and Bertie learned from Marta that it was Eleanor who had killed Nancy.

Bertie explained what had happened next. "At first no one realized the danger you were in, Lillie. All we knew was that you had gone to find Nancy and that Nancy was dead. No one thought about where Eleanor might be. But then Ada, who had seen Geoffrey and 'Nancy' drive away at dawn after the murder, said mightn't it have been Eleanor who had escaped with Geoffrey, and mightn't she be in hiding with him, and mightn't you be about to stumble onto their hiding place?"

Bertie and Eli had turned to each other and had agreed at once that they needed Jay. It was an instinct born of many years of dependence on Jay, of relying on Jay to know what course to take and to have the strength to take it. Bertie and Eli had tried hard to run things, to hold things together while Jay was in prison and had seen their efforts fall short of success again and again. Now, in a genuine emergency, both of them desperately wanted Jay.

"I had some chits outstanding," Bertie said, referring to political favors he had done, "and I thought it was time to call them in. I made some fast phone calls during which I explained the likelihood that the woman Jay Caldwell was in prison for having murdered was alive and might, at that very moment, be threatening the life of my own fiance. I strongly suggested that an immediate furlough be arranged for Jay and that he be brought back to Soundcliff at once; otherwise certain political favors would be revealed to the newspapers; otherwise certain monies for certain new political projects would not be forthcoming."

At six o'clock, Jay, escorted by a plainclothes policeman, had left the prison grounds in a special carriage—then by train into New York and by ferry to Long Island, arriving at Soundcliff at ten o'clock. I had lost track of time during my ordeal, but it seemed, in thinking back, that Jay must have arrived at Soundcliff at almost exactly the time when Geoffrey, Eleanor, and I were rowing toward Execution Rock.

Eli said that he was on the porte-cochere steps when Jay arrived. "First I hugged him, then I told him that Bertie had left at about six o'clock, as soon as he was sure he'd secured Jay's release. As far as I knew, he'd headed for Foxfield to try to trace your journey, Lillie."

"When I got to Foxfield," Bertie said, "the gate keeper told me you'd been there two hours or more earlier and that you'd driven off toward Geoffrey Hand's cabin, and he pointed me in that direction."

When Bertie found the cabin, we had been gone perhaps no more than half an hour. But he found no evidence that I had been there.

"I was frantic with worry," Bertie continued, "so frantic that I drove back to Foxfield and confronted August Flammon himself, who professed amazement when I said that Eleanor might be alive, although I had the sneaking suspicion he already knew it."

"He did," I told Bertie. "He knew all along."

"At any rate, Lillie, he had no idea where you were or where Geoffrey was. Geoffrey had left the estate at five-thirty, he told me, and was to have the next day off. I asked permission to telephone the police from Foxfield and was given it. The police came quickly and we combed the area. We drove up and down roads and poked into ditches and culverts and shone lanterns into dark barns and sheds, me shivering at every step, afraid we'd find you dead somewhere."

August Flammon must have wondered quite as much as Bertie whether we would be found, I thought—whether Eleanor would be found.

"At about nine-thirty," Bertie went on, "the police told me that a further search in the dark of night would be futile and that they would begin again in the morning if you hadn't turned up by then. I had begun to hope that you had, after all, returned home while I was looking for you, and I went back to Soundcliff.

"When I got there, I found that you had not come back, but that Jay had arrived and was somewhere upstairs with his police escort. I dismissed the searchers who were still flocking about the Soundcliff grounds with their lanterns."

The lanterns I had seen bobbing about as I had looked toward Soundcliff from the Rock, I thought.

"That's about the time Jay got away from his police escort," Eli said. The policeman, who had been listening avidly to our stories, colored in embarrassment. "Jay was missed almost at once, to give credit to the officer here; but no one could figure out where he was. I was the one that saw there was a small boat missing from the boathouse. And then I spotted Jay—I could just make him out, rowing toward Execution Rock. I wouldn't have been able to see him at all if I hadn't known where to look. I didn't tell anyone where he'd gone till I saw the two boats coming back toward shore. Then I gave a yell and everyone came running."

Then it was Jay's turn to tell his own part of the story. Arriving at Soundcliff at ten o'clock, he had found that Bertie had been gone in search of me for several hours. He telephoned Gus Flammon directly and learned that Bertie had been there and had obtained a police search group.

"What could I do? Doing nothing was unbearable. To join Bertie would be redundant. There were already searchers all over the Soundcliff grounds with lanterns. I thought maybe if I could survey the whole scene from the tower, something would occur to me. With my escort on my heels, I ran up all three flights to the tower and went around to all four walls of windows. From the north window, of course, I saw the Execution Light—and then I saw another light, a small one, dancing around the base of the Rock, disappearing, then appearing again. Was it a boat? But why a boat out there at this hour—and in November!

"In a rush, a perfectly awful idea came to me. If Eleanor were alive and planning harm to Lillie—as everyone feared—what would she do? The Rock itself gave me the answer; it reminded me of something I had not thought of in a long time: the

Execution Rock game I'd played with Charlotte and Bertie and Eleanor as children. Eleanor loved that grisly game, and she often begged the rest of us to play it. It terrified Charlotte and bored Bertie. But I was always willing to indulge Eleanor. And so we played at tying one another up on the rocks below Soundcliff; and when the tide came up it would sometimes cover the victim's toes, and if the victim was Charlotte she would scream and beg to be let loose although she was in no danger at all there; and so I eventually decreed that only Bertie or myself or Eleanor could be the victim any more, and Eleanor was angry because she loved to scare Charlotte and make her cry.

"I would never have imagined that Eleanor would—at last and after all these years—carry the game to such a hideous conclusion, with Lillie as the victim and the game no longer a game. But then I saw the little light at the base of the Rock, and I felt absolutely compelled to investigate it.

"I knew I would have to do it alone, and I knew my escort would never let me go. So I turned on him and said, 'I have some private papers I want to go over in my office, and I'd like to be alone. If you like, you can lock the office door behind me and post a guard by the window, but I would appreciate the privacy.'

"So we went down to the first floor, and I went into the office, heard the door lock behind me, and drew the drapes across the window. Then I took the pistol from my desk drawer, and I got a lantern from the cupboard, and I slipped into the secret passageway.

"I went through the passages to the rocks below Soundcliff. Bertie had called off the searchers, so no one was around. I hurried across the dock to the boathouse. I took down the oars from the rack on the wall of the boathouse, and then I thought about how cold it was, so I took two tarpaulin-covered blankets and threw them into the bow of the boat. Then I climbed in and started to row toward Execution Rock—as silently as I could, and with no lantern. When I was most of the way there, I thought I was on a wild goose chase, for I couldn't see anyone or anything out of the ordinary. But then there was a little patch of moonlight, and my blood turned cold, because I turned to give one last look over my shoulder before turning back to Soundcliff—and there was Lillie."

There was a crackling silence in the library when Jay finished telling how he had rescued me and captured Geoffrey and Eleanor, a silence broken at last by Eli's words directed at me.

"I told you Eleanor was still influencing this household, didn't I?" I nodded. Yes, but neither he nor I nor anyone else had carried his intuition to its logical conclusion: that Eleanor was still alive.

There had been more than one clue. Even Ginger had tried to tell me it was Eleanor, I mused, for she had risen up and arched her back and howled when Eleanor had approached my room from the secret passageways, and now I recalled that Eleanor was the only one Ginger had ever reacted to in this manner. Indeed, when we had come into Soundcliff from the boats just now, Ginger had been in the entry hall and had screeched and run when she spotted Eleanor.

And the robbery of the safe: It had been opened, not jimmied. And Susan had told me that only Eleanor knew the combination.

Yet, I had ignored the clues, and if I hadn't I might have made another important connection: I had reasoned that someone who knew the passages well had committed the murder—of Eleanor, I had thought, really of Nancy. Yet who besides the obviously innocent servants and Jay's helpless old grandfather knew the passageways? Only the four children who had played there long ago; and I had correctly thought Bertie incapable of murder and incorrectly thought that both Charlotte and Eleanor were dead. Thus suspicion kept focusing on the only one who remained, Jay.

Thinking Marta had done it—Marta who would not have used the passageways to escape, who had been found in a daze near Eleanor's room—had seemed to clear up the mystery for awhile. But what of the intruder who had tried to kill me on the rocks during the storm? And what of the secrets that had continued to vanish from Soundcliff even after Geoffrey's departure and Eleanor's "death"? All had to be the work of someone who knew the passageways. Why had I, even briefly, developed the idea that it was Nancy, who had never known the passageways at all? Why had I not realized it must be Eleanor, Eleanor alive and responsible for everything?

Well, it was all over now; and yet, I thought, it

would never be all over between Eleanor and me. For here she was again, Jay's *wife*, and if our love, his and mine, had not been utterly impossible before, it was now. I felt he would never divorce her, even if she spent the rest of her days in prison or an asylum. Our fates were sealed; it only remained to settle the sad details.

The others had all told me their parts of the story, and the moment came when Bertie turned to me and said, "Now, Lillie, tell us your part of it."

It was the moment I had dreaded most, for it involved revealing to Jay—Jay who had suffered more shocks and horrors than any man should ever have to—that Eleanor had confessed to killing Charlotte.

In great pain, I told the whole story, including everything Eleanor had told me. I was terrified that she would deny it all, for then it would be merely my word against hers. But when the local police arrived, Geoffrey and Eleanor were brought into the library so that Jay could tell the police what the charges were against them.

Suddenly, Eleanor moved toward Jay. She knelt by his chair and buried her face in his lap. He stiffened in horror. She lifted her face and reached for his hands.

"I know I've done terrible things, Jay," she sobbed. "But we can make it up, can't we? It's not too late."

Such anger was written upon Jay's face, such grief, such pain. I wanted to run to him, but Bertie held my hand protectively, and I remembered with a start that I was Bertie's fiance. Rage at Eleanor overwhelmed me. That monster! She had ruined our lives by seeming to be dead. And she had ruined them anew by turning up alive. She seemed incapable of beneficent influence, a living curse upon herself and all who came within her sphere!

And then, as suddenly, my rage turned to pity, for Jay had pushed her away and, fighting for control of his voice and his emotions, he said, "Eleanor, tell me. Did you kill Charlotte?"

And Eleanor's body sagged, as if her bones had turned to cartilage, as if she had literally been broken. She was on her knees next to Jay's chair, and she sat back and clasped her hands over her breast and threw back her head, and she began to keen, rocking forward and back as the high, thin wail rose over our heads. "I didn't mean to kill her! I didn't mean to!" she cried. Jay reached out to her instinctively, to comfort her, but she pulled away and screamed.

"No! Don't! You're going to send me to prison! I'd rather be dead!"

Jay's police escort had been sitting with his handgun held loosely in one hand. With the speed of a snapped spring, Eleanor spun to her feet and snatched the gun from the officer's hand. She was too near the door and all of us were too startled. She ran into the corridor and slammed the door behind her. Jay was on his feet and after her in the fraction of a moment, but Eleanor had slammed the door so hard it was jammed, and Jay had to tug at it once, twice before it opened.

She had fled—but where? Everyone started to

run in all directions but stopped, frozen, at the sound of the gun. A single shot had rang out. It seemed to come from a distance, but I, still standing in the library, heard it plainly and knew that it had come from outdoors. I rushed into the corridor and cried, "The cliff!"

Everyone rushed toward the great living room. The door to the piazza was open, and Jay was through it and across the flagstones before anyone else. When I arrived at the edge of the precipice, a small crowd had already formed. Eleanor lay dead, cradled in Jay's arms.

He wept.

Nancy was quietly reburied in the servants' plot at Greenwood, and Eleanor was interred beside Charlotte. Soundcliff was closed for the winter, its furnishings shrouded in sheets, its cold, winter-dampened corridors lending it the air of a mausoleum. It would be opened again in the spring when sun and warm air and refound laughter would bring it to life again. For now, we were glad to return to 577, to the hustle and bustle of New York.

It would be a different sort of Christmas, this Christmas of 1899: no parties, no balls, no elaborate celebration. Gifts for the children as usual, of course, and their young pleasure would warm all our hearts and help us to begin our recovery from the dreadful events of the past and from our grief—yes, even mine—over Eleanor's unhappy life and death.

No green velvet gowns this year; we all wore the

somber colors of mourning. But Marta managed to look beautiful. When Jack Van Dyne returned from Alaska on the fifteenth of December and called without warning, he found her at tea with her father and Bertie and me; and when she stood to greet him, her tall, willowy figure so dignified in black silk, her green eyes swimming with tears as she looked up at him from beneath the soft crown of unswept auburn curls, he looked as if he had been smitten a blow from which he would never recover.

"Well, I think that's the end of Andy Southwell," I said softly, and Jay smiled.

Bertie and I had agreed to postpone our marrige, of course. Christmas would have been far too early, far too unseemly a date after Eleanor's suicide in November. We had not set a new date, and I had almost ceased to think about it, although I still wore his mother's ring on my left hand.

On Christmas Eve, after we had all wrapped our gifts for the children and hidden them among the branches of the Christmas tree, Bertie motioned to me to follow him across the entrance hall to the oriental parlor. "I have something I want to discuss with you," he said, and my heart lurched alarmingly. Surely, now, he would want to set a new date for our marriage, and I knew that I was not ready to do it. But how would I say so? Why must he bring it up now and force me to ruin our Christmas?

I stepped into the parlor, and memories flooded over me as they always did when I came here, memories of little Bonnie looking for her lost cat, memories of the tall, dark, somber-looking man who had stood silently in the far doorway—and who had later stolen my heart.

"It's about our engagement," Bertie began, and I looked down at my hands. I saw Bertie's hand reaching out, and then he took my left hand in his. Slowly, he slid the diamond-and-ruby ring from my finger. Then he turned my hand palm upward, laid the ring in it, and curled my fingers over it. "You must keep it," he said simply. "It's a gift for your marriage to Jay."

I looked into his eyes, startled, tears beginning to form behind my lids. He bent forward and kissed me tenderly on the lips and slipped out of the room before I could speak. I sat on the oriental divan and gripped the beautiful ring in my hand. Great, warm tears flooded over my cheeks, releasing a mixture of joy and sorrow, of love and gratitude.

I went up to my little room and stared out of the dormer window over the snow-laden roofs, and a long while later, there was a tap at the door. I opened it, and there was Jay.

"Bertie came to me this afternoon," he said softly. "He said he had decided to release you from your promise to him. It took him a long time, he said, because he loves you so. But that's why he finally had to do it—that's what he said, at least. He had to do it because he wants you to be happy, and he says you love me."

He looked shyly into my eyes. "I know you loved me once, before all of this, before I went to prison. But then, when you decided to marry Bertie, I thought perhaps you had truly fallen in love with him. I dared not interfere. It was driving me insane, you must know. I love you to distraction."

I took his hands in mine, and pulled him inside, and pushed the door shut behind him. Then I leaned forward and sought his lips, and the icy chill of our long separation melted away.

"Let's be married right away," he said when at last he was able to speak.

"Don't you think it's too soon?" I asked, alarmed. "Won't the newspapers make a fuss about it?"

"The newspapers be damned," he said. "I want you now." And then, very seriously, "Dearest, only you know how unhappy I've been for so long—thinking I'd caused Charlotte's and Eleanor's deaths. Poor Charlotte's is no mystery any more. And as for Eleanor, well, I realize now that her sickness began in childhood. I'll always wish I could have helped her, but I don't feel responsible any more. I'll feel sad for Eleanor all the rest of my life, but I think we deserve our happiness. And *I* don't want to wait."

We kissed again, a kiss of pure joy.

"Let's be married on New Year's Day," he said, "January first, 1900. Can you be ready by then? We'll start the new century together."

"Officially, the new century doesn't begin until 1901," I teased.

"You must stop being a teacher," he smiled. "Anyway, a lot of people are celebrating 1900 as the new century, and it certainly feels new to me."

"To me, too. But my goodness! It's only a

week away!"

The week passed in a whirl of preparations. My wedding was to be at Grace Church after all, but a very quiet ceremony with only family present. Eli would give me away, and Marta would play Bach on the organ. And then, wanting all three children to be included in our wedding, wanting the feeling of security and family from the very start of our marriage, I asked Leo to be our ring bearer and Bonnie to be the flower girl, Leo to wear a little dark suit and Bonnie to be in pink velvet.

"Are you going to get Ginger a pink collar so she can be your bridesmaid?" Leo said with twinkling eyes.

"Oh, Leo! You made a joke!" I cried and smothered him in a joyful hug. Since Eleanor had accused him of ruining my dress the Christmas before, Leo had been the saddest, soberest little boy in the world. This was the first sign that he was still himself, that he would survive the horrors.

Oh, there was so much to do in that short week. There were purchases to be made, purchases of the sort every new bride understands, items of trousseau, a beautiful nightdress. And Susan insisted on working night and day to make me the loveliest gray-blue faille wedding dress with narrow tucks at the front of the bodice and a softly draped skirt.

"Jay, may I promote Susan to seamstress?" I begged him one afternoon. "She is so skillful, and she does prefer it to housework."

"You may do whatever you like, my dear," he laughed. "You're to be the lady of the house, now."

"Oh, dear. That does sound a formidable job," I laughed. "But with Nellie Morgan at the head of staff and Ada and Hans and Bob and the others—it can't be too difficult, can it?"

"No, darling," he smiled reassuringly. "You'll be fine, and they'll do their best for you."

And then, before I knew it, it was New Year's Eve, and Jay asked, "How do you want to celebrate the last day of 1899, your last New Year's Eve as Miss Lorimer?"

"Alone with you," I said.

"Do you remember that carriage ride we took last December, the day after Christmas—the day I found you wandering about on Fifth Avenue down by Madison Square?"

"Indeed yes."

"Let's take a ride again."

"Let's," I agreed.

It was dusk and snowing again as we emerged arm in arm from 577. Jay took my elbow as we walked down the wide, stone steps toward the waiting carriage. Bob, all bundled up in greatcoat and woolen scarves, held the carriage door as Jay helped me up into the interior. Then he got in beside me and settled a fur rug over our knees. I pressed close to his side as we set off down Fifth Avenue.

"Let's take exactly the same route we did before," I said. And we did.

"It's a miracle," I told him as we rode cozily along together. "Just a few weeks ago, our marriage seemed so impossible. And now, it's about to happen."

"You're the miracle, Lillie. I was a goner, you know. I had no more strength for the struggle. I couldn't fight Flammon any more. I couldn't keep the Caldwells going. I would have lost it all for Leo, for Marta and Bonnie, too. But you never gave up, never lost your courage. You saved me. And Marta, too. I *thought* I'd saved her by going to prison for her. But you *really* saved her. Leo and Bonnie would have been lost without you, as well. My darling, we owe everything to you."

"Oh, Jay," I said fervently. "You talk about my strength and my courage. Don't you know I get them from you? When I came to you for help so long ago, I was the weakest, the most frightened girl in the world. I'd always been looked after by my father and my uncle. I wasn't exercising courage, I was looking for shelter. The wonderful thing is that I found my shelter in you—yet my courage, too."

"Maybe it's just simply that we were meant for each other," he said, and he kissed me and held me tenderly as we rode along the familiar streets.

When we came to Orchard Street, I said, "I'm going to come here and see Mrs. Fein after we're married. I want to be sure she's all right. She helped Uncle Frank and she helped me, and I want to help her, if she'll accept it."

"Of course," he replied. "And I hope you're going to start working on that foundation for working girls."

"You remembered!" I exclaimed, delighted.

"Certainly I remembered. And do you remember how I told you you would accomplish it?"

I smiled. "Yes. You said I should marry a wealthy man."

"I did, and it was good advice. Of course, at the time, I had no hope that the fortunate man might be me."

"Do you mean it? about the foundation, I mean? Would you permit me to do it? Would you finance it?"

"If you organize it—absolutely. It's time the Caldwells gave something to the world instead of just taking from it."

"You've never just taken," I said. "You've built railroads and businesses that have contributed so much—"

"I hope so. But you know, I still haven't achieved my one special dream."

"Building a major railroad like the Pennsylvania," I said.

"Aha! So *you* remembered!" he grinned.

"Certainly. If you can remember my dreams, I can surely remember yours. And what are you going to do about it, your dream?"

He threw back his head and laughed happily. "Ah, you'll see."

"Don't tease me!" I warned. "I want to know."

"All right, here's my plan: When the Stock Exchange opens one of these mornings, I'm going to begin dumping my Empire State Railroad stock. It will cause a small panic. Others will sell. The price will plunge. And then I will be thoroughly prepared to buy back mine and enough more to gain control. It's called stock dumping. It's not very nice.

"But, I've been thinking it's really too bad that Gus Flammon isn't in jail right alongside Geoffrey—for sheltering Eleanor and being an accessory after the fact to Nancy's murder, and for paying for information stolen from my property. But then, as I've pointed out before, rich men *almost* never go to prison. So, I think Gus richly deserves what I'm about to do to him, don't you?"

"Yes. But isn't it dangerous?"

"Oh, yes. That's the fun of it. Besides, you once told me—in this very carriage when I was telling you how rottenly my 'Flammon plan' was going—that you believed in me, and I said that if you believed in me, I'd win out. Well, Lillie, you did—and I will!" His eyes danced. "Gus could catch me out and buy up the stock before I do and shut me out altogether. But I don't intend to let that happen. I *am* going to win this time. I'm going to *take* that railroad he's been running into the ground and squeezing the last ounce of profit from, and I'm going to build a railroad that serves the public and serves the nation. Of course," he smiled, "I plan to make a profit, too."

"And we'll have the LIH&M back, won't we?"

"Yes."

"Won't your grandfather be pleased!"

"And my father, I hope, wherever he is. This one is really for him." He squeezed my hand tightly with emotion. Then, more lightly, "Won't you be glad to see our little private station at Soundcliff again?"

"Oh, yes! I *have* missed it."

"And it will be so much easier to get to—because

I'm going to build that tunnel under the East River right away."

"I want to be on the first train under the river," I exclaimed.

"And now, darling," he said, "let's discuss our plans for next summer."

"Next summer?" I asked.

"Europe or Soundcliff?"

"Oh, Soundcliff, please! We didn't have a Fourth of July party this year. Shouldn't we be there to have one next year? to keep the tradition going?"

"If that's what you want, dearest, we'll have the gayest and most beautiful Fouth of July party Soundcliff ever had. And we'll go abroad in 1901. The little ones will be at better ages for it then. Leo will be eleven and Bonnie will be six. They'll appreciate it more. And Marta will be seventeen."

"I'm afraid, sweetheart, Marta might be married by then," I laughed. "I think Jack is getting impatient."

"Well, then, they can just travel with us! Mr. and Mrs. Caldwell and Mr. and Mrs. Van Dyne touring Europe together. It'll be marvelous!"

He held me even tighter, and I hugged him back. We were full of thrilling dreams.

We had come back up Broadway to Union Square, and here Jay slid open the little trap door and asked Bob to drive across Fourteenth Street to Sixth Avenue. "Have you seen the display there?" he asked me.

"Display? No."

"Then you've got to see this."

We pulled up before a large granite building with broad plate glass windows. Jay opened the carriage door and helped me down. There was no one on the snow-blanketed sidewalk, and Jay plunged across to the display window, unheeding of the ankle-deep whiteness, pulling me along with him. There behind the glass, perched on a carpeted platform and sparkling under electric lights, was an automobile.

"I've seen a few on Fifth Avenue," I said.

"Not one of these, I'll wager."

"Why? How is it different?"

"Well, you've seen steamers and electrics. The electrics don't go very far without recharging, and the steamers require an open flame, and people don't like that."

"And this one?"

"This one runs on gasoline, and gasoline is scarce and expensive."

"I guess automobiles will never be a threat to the railroads."

"I don't know; but someone I trust wants me to invest a great deal of money in a company that's going to manufacture gasoline-powered automobiles."

"It doesn't sound like a good investment if there are so many problems."

"Maybe. But what if someone finds a big, cheap source of gasoline?"

"Will they?"

"There are some searches being made. They *might*. It's a risk, but—"

"But you can't succeed without risk. Your

motto, I believe," I laughed.

He laughed back. "Exactly. Well? Should I do it? Should I invest in the automobile? We might get very much richer—or quite a bit poorer. *You* decide, Lillie."

"I can see you want to do it," I smiled. "It's written all over you. Well, why not? It's a bold new idea for a bold new era."

"Oh, Lillie!" He hugged me hard. "I love you so much! You actually make me believe I can conquer the twentieth century!"

Suddenly, he unbuttoned his coat, opened it wide, and folded me inside, pressing me to him, moving his body against mine. *Let Jay take care of the twentieth century*, I thought as I gave myself to his loving kiss. *I'll take care of Jay.*

SOMETHING FOR EVERYONE—
BEST SELLERS FROM ZEBRA!

CALY (624, $2.50)
By Sharon Combes

When Ian Donovan and Caly St. John arrive at the eerie Simpson House in Maine, they open a door and release a ghost woman who leads them beyond terror and toward the most gruesome, grisly experience that anyone could ever imagine.

THE ASHES OF TAMAR (412, $2.50)
by Elizabeth Wade

When the restless spirit of Tamar is released from a 400-year-old urn at an archaeological dig in a modern Israeli town, a ruthless battle ensues between the sorceress and a modern-day warlock for the body and soul of a virgin child-woman.

THE SOUL (321, $2.25)
by Ron Gorton

Possessed by an angel, a man named Rebuck suddenly appears to found the Church of Michael which threatens to destroy the foundations of organized religion and plunges the world into chaos, terror and religious war.

THE RITE (529, $2.50)
by Gregory A. Douglas

When a beautiful actress Judith Bradford accepts a leading role in a movie, she never suspects she would play the part of a virgin sacrifice to the leading man, the Baron of Darkness . . . the Devil in disguise!

REPLICA (370, $2.25)
by Lionel Saben

Scientist Alfred Eberhard knew he had to die, but he wanted his genes and intelligence to live. He devises a way to clone an exact replica of himself, and creates a perfect self-image . . . even down to the one genetic warp which makes his clone try to destroy him!